THE PHOENIX MANDATE

THE PHOENIX MANDATE

THE LIGHT THIEF, BOOK 2

DAVID WEBB

This is a work of fiction. Names, characters, places, and incidents either are the product of the author's imagination or are used fictitiously. Any resemblance to actual persons, living or dead, events, or locales is entirely coincidental.

Copyright © 2020 by Lux Publishing

All rights reserved. No part of this book may be reproduced or used in any manner without written permission of the copyright owner except for the use of quotations in a book review. For more information, address: admin@jdavidwebb.com.

First paperback edition February 2020

ISBN 978-1-7343511-2-5 (paperback)

www.jdavidwebb.com

This book is dedicated to the Robertson family.

Some of my favorite people in the world—you showed me what a family should look like.

I love you all.

It is during our darkest moments that we must focus to see the light.

— Aristotle

PART I

SHADOW AND STRANGER

1

The ground shuddered as an explosion sounded throughout Ravelta.

Aniya Lyons shook her head, attempting to focus. The battle raged on before her, lit only by muzzle flashes and torchlight.

It was strange to see her old enemies, the Silver Guard, fight side-by-side with the rebels from Refuge. The only thing that gave her solace was the green, four-fingered hand that glowed on her allies' body armor.

Because wearing the same silver armor, taking cover behind a shelter before them, was an army of Silver Guard still loyal to the Chancellor. However, their armor was clean, untouched by the glowworm juice. Their helmets offered no light, as the first thing the rebels had done upon entering Ravelta was detonate an electromagnetic pulse bomb.

And then there was Refuge's army. They wore brown moleskin armor, which was almost as effective as the Silvers' metal armor. After the demise of Refuge's leader, Salvador the Scourge, during the battle in the Hub, this army was led by Corrin, the second-in-command to the legendary warlord.

In front of the rebels' combined forces was a line of metal

barriers, a defensive blockade that Corrin had engineered to defend against the Lightbringers for as long as possible. They didn't have to completely wipe out the enemy. They just had to stall long enough to find the Chancellor and capture him. If the disgraced leader of the Lightbringers was in Ravelta, his capture would solidify the rebels' victory and signal the end of the Lightbringers.

As the battle continued, Aniya stood on the edge of the sector, watching the firefight as she resisted the voice inside that softly beckoned her.

"Aniya."

There it was again. Her heart rate quickened as her temperature spiked, and Aniya held her breath and closed her eyes until the whisper vanished into the recesses of her mind.

It was better that she separate herself from the fight. She hadn't been able to concentrate on anything for the last several weeks, not since the incident underneath the Citadel that culminated in the destruction of the Lightbringers' reactor and the end of the electricity that powered the underground civilization of the Web.

Besides, her mission here required no fighting. All she had to do was wait.

As the battle raged, she looked past the warring factions to the city of Ravelta.

The innocent civilians were surely locked in their homes, not aware that the savages trying to invade their sector were rebelling against the evil government that had held their friends, brothers, and sons hostage, enslaving them in a torturous machine.

Aniya may have destroyed that machine, and the rebels may have won the battle of the Hub, but the war for the Web had only begun. The Lightbringer leader, the Chancellor, was hiding somewhere in the underground world, still commanding an army that ruled the sectors.

It would be hard to convince the people of each sector that the mission of the rebels was a noble one, a mission that would free them from tyranny. Aniya had seen the cruelty of the Lightbringers firsthand, but in most sectors, things were as normal as they could possibly be. People were somewhat happy.

How could they ever be expected to believe that the government that gave them power and stability was only able to do so because they had found a way to suck energy from humans, using them to generate electricity?

If any of them could see the horrors that Aniya had witnessed beneath the Citadel, if any of them could see the tens of thousands of men imprisoned in tanks, spending their lives in a black nothingness, they would all of them turn against the Lightbringers in an instant.

But Kendall said that this was a secret that they would have to hold on to until the Web was ready to hear it.

Kendall.

Aniya shuddered. The man that had helped them destroy the Lightbringers seemed to have the purest of motivations. But her twin brother, Roland, had put enough doubt in her mind to make her second-guess Kendall's every move.

An explosion rang out near her, too close for comfort, and the ground shook again, this time enough that she lost her balance, toppling to the dirt and rock below, jarring her shoulder.

"You okay?"

Aniya looked up to see Tamisra, who carried a stalagmite spear in one hand and a gun in the other. She was breathing heavily, and with each exhale, blood dripped from the tip of her spear. Putting her weapons away, she helped Aniya to her feet.

"Yeah, I guess." Aniya steadied herself and looked down at her own gun, which had not been fired yet. The bulky metal weapon felt unnatural in her hands. She had held one once before, deep in the cavern below the Hub. She didn't know whether it was a fear for her life or the adrenaline of the moment that kept her from really thinking about it then, but she had used the weapon without a second thought. Now, she felt as if the gun simply didn't belong.

Tamisra gave her spear a sharp jerk, and more blood splattered to the ground. "You ready? It's almost time."

Aniya nodded. "Why didn't you hang back with me? You're wasting energy."

"And miss out on all the fun?" Tamisra flashed a grin as her eyes sparkled. "I wouldn't dream of it. I just wish Roland was here with us. Where is your brother, anyway?"

"He had a mission of his own," Aniya said, thinking of her brother, whom she had last seen leaving Refuge with Nicholas.

She grinned slightly as she thought of Nicholas, her childhood friend. After years of avoiding the issue, she had finally come to peace with his feelings for her. What surprised her more was she found herself feeling the same way.

"What are you smiling about?"

Aniya shook her head. "Nothing." She looked down at the ground and realized that the green crystal hanging around her neck had slipped out of her body armor, now dangling free. Aniya quickly tucked the trinket back inside her shirt as her smile vanished.

A grinning, dirty face flashed through her mind. Kira. The girl that had given Aniya shelter when she was utterly alone. A selfless friend that eventually gave her life while trying to help Aniya.

Kira's necklace was a painful reminder of her death, and it hung around Aniya's neck as an albatross, but she couldn't bring herself to remove it.

She shook the thought away and looked back at Tamisra. "What are *you* smiling about?"

Tamisra's smile was quite different from Aniya's. It was a

wide grin that revealed her teeth. Combined with her narrowed, twinkling eyes, it was an unsettling sight.

"Ravelta's the closest sector to the Hub and probably where the Chancellor is hiding after he escaped the Citadel. I'm about to get my hands on the man who tortured me and got my father killed. What's not to smile about?"

"Ladies, we're in position."

Another voice joined them as a figure approached from the direction of the battlefield, placing a gun in a holster at his side. He was a native of Refuge, though he was armored in the same silver armor as the Lightbringers.

"Yes, sir, Lieutenant Haskill, sir." Tamisra gave a lopsided salute as she stuck out her tongue.

The lieutenant shook his head as he smirked. "Save the sirs for General Corrin. Besides, you're Salvador's daughter. I should be calling *you* sir."

"Sir," Tamisra said, rubbing her chin as she looked up as if deep in thought. "I like the sound of that. What do you think, Aniya?"

"I think we need to get moving," Aniya said. "The Chancellor's had plenty of time to escape."

Tamisra shrugged. "It's not like he has anywhere to go. The tunnel we're standing in front of and the train station are the only two exits, and we have scouts at the trainyard. If he's here, we'll get him. Trust me, no one wants to find him more than I do."

She had a point. The exiled leader of the Web had kidnapped and tortured Tamisra. Of course, he had kidnapped and tortured tens of thousands of people over the years, squeezing the literal life out of them so that the Web could have power, but at least they were at peace now that the reactor was destroyed, putting the prisoners out of their eternal misery. Tamisra, however, still had scars from her horrific experience with the Lightbringers, and Aniya knew she would hold that grudge until the person responsible answered for it.

"Then let's get moving." Lieutenant Haskill grabbed his radio and pressed a button on the side. "Malcolm, Xander, get your squads and head into the sector. It's time for phase two. You go left, we go right."

A sharp voice came over the radio. "Negative. We're going right. We're closer to that side."

"That's not the plan, Malcolm." Haskill narrowed his eyes.

"Don't care. Over and out."

Tamisra groaned. "Does he have to come along?"

"He's one of our best fighters," Lieutenant Haskill said as he put the radio away.

"So shouldn't he stay here and, you know, fight?"

Aniya smirked. "What, you don't want your ex-boyfriend to come with us?"

"He volunteered, Tamisra." The lieutenant shrugged. "I'm not going to turn the general's son away. Besides, if the Chancellor is here, you can bet he'll be heavily guarded. Fighters would come in handy." He turned back to the army behind him and shouted, "Archers, light it up!"

An orange glow appeared behind Aniya, and she turned to see a hundred flaming arrows fly through the air, landing among the enemy and lighting a few of their barriers ablaze.

"That'll give them something to think about. Less chance they'll spot us." Haskill pointed toward the wall of the sector. "Let's move out."

The group set out along the barrier of Ravelta, quietly skirting the bottom of the skydome and bypassing the battle entirely. The massive shelter the Lightbringers hid behind stretched hundreds of feet wide, but it didn't reach the edge of the sector.

As they moved away from the battle, the small group stepped into utter darkness. They eventually made their way to downtown Ravelta, where the housing district and the marketplace met.

"All right, let's go," the lieutenant said. "Meet back here in three hours unless Corrin signals the retreat. Split up and scan."

Without a word, Aniya and Tamisra paired off and began their sweep of the sector. They traveled primarily by alleys and side roads, and Aniya found herself grateful that they hadn't tried to clear Ravelta as a group. She knew she was much faster than the rest of them, and if they slowed her down, she would only get frustrated.

Tamisra was different. It seemed that she had a limitless amount of energy, even though it was only a few weeks after her capture and torture. She was recovering quickly, not that it surprised Aniya that much.

Her ability to keep up proved to be invaluable. Ravelta was one of the Web's largest sectors, as its location next to the Hub made it an ideal region for residential and industrial purposes. The circular Ravelta was around ten miles in diameter, making the chore of sweeping the entire sector a daunting task.

On top of the sheer size of Ravelta, the lack of light made the rebels' job even harder. Not a single torch was lit throughout the sector. Not even any candles in the windows of the houses, which made sense given that the civilians would be hiding in their homes from the vicious savages they knew lived in the caves.

A green light caught Aniya's eyes, and she quickly glanced up at Tamisra. It didn't seem like the girl had noticed the soft, green glow emanating from Aniya's body.

In fact, few people had said anything about the light that seemed to cover her skin. Nicholas and Roland had both noticed, but other than that, no one had commented on the anomaly. Maybe it was because they weren't looking that closely, but more likely because the luminescence was negligible. It certainly wasn't enough to light their path.

Of course, Aniya knew that it was capable of so much more than mere light. The incident beneath the Citadel was just weeks past, but it seemed like a lifetime ago. Though it was remarkable enough that she would never forget it. The same light that tingled over her body now was the same otherworldly power that blew up the reactor, saved the lives of Nicholas and Roland, and protected them from the meltdown that destroyed the Hub.

Surely it could light their way now if it grew strong enough, but it was too dangerous in an unfamiliar sector. Besides, Aniya couldn't have controlled it even if she wanted to. It seemed that the light had a mind of its own. Aniya could only hope that it didn't choose to come to life at the wrong moment.

Several minutes later, they stopped again when Aniya spotted a soft, orange glow coming from a building in the distance.

"What do you suppose that is?" Aniya asked Tamisra.

"Depends. Could be the Chancellor. Could be bait."

"Do you want to wait for the others?"

Tamisra shook her head. "If it's a trap, I doubt a few more men would make a difference against an army. Might as well scope it out. We'll just be careful."

They neared the building, slowing their approach as they got closer. It was the town hall, standing five stories tall, high above the rest of the nearby buildings. The glow came from a room on the top floor, flickering in a way that was obviously candlelight.

"Ready?"

Aniya nodded.

They entered the town hall slowly, their guns raised in preparation. The front door was unlocked, and the building appeared to be empty. Aniya and Tamisra took their time and slowly made their way through the building before finally reaching the top floor.

There was only one room, and it was empty except for six small candles sitting on the floor next to the window.

"Doesn't seem normal," Aniya said. She approached the candles and knelt down next to them. They had obviously once been much larger, but the wicks were almost gone now, and the collective pool of wax that dripped on the floor had turned into one big mass with six small lumps protruding from the top.

"Nothing normal about this sector," Tamisra said, looking out the window. "We haven't seen anyone. Forget house arrest. I don't think there's anyone left besides the Silvers."

"You think they evacuated?"

"Or they were executed." Tamisra pulled the radio from her belt. "Lieutenant, you copy?"

Nothing but static.

"Corrin, do you copy?"

Still nothing.

Tamisra sighed and walked back toward the stairs. "I'm going outside to get better reception. Stay here. If anyone comes for us, you'll have the best view of it anyway. I'll be right back."

Aniya turned back to the candles. It didn't make any sense. It was either the least effective trap she could imagine or the most pointless endeavor by a random citizen. Or by the Lightbringers, for that matter.

Footsteps behind her caused her to turn around again.

"Did you get any—"

Aniya froze as she spotted the glint of silver armor.

One of *them* stood directly in front of her, a government soldier in full body armor, with an unpowered light built into his helmet.

Survival instincts kicked in, and she drew her gun.

"Whoa!"

The man dropped his gun and raised his arms above his head.

Aniya resisted the urge to shoot the unarmed man, but her finger twitched in anger, a lifetime of hatred against the Lightbringers fueling an itch to pull the trigger.

"It's me." The man nodded to a green smear on his chest, a stain on his otherwise flawless armor. Sure enough, it was the four-fingered emblem that Aniya had come to know as the Mark of Salvador. He stepped into the candlelight, and his face became clear.

She sighed and lowered her weapon. "I'm sorry. I saw your armor and didn't think." As Xander smiled, Aniya couldn't help but wonder at the stark differences between him and Malcolm. "Why aren't you in moleskin like the rest of Refuge?"

"Corrin wanted me and Malcolm in silver, just to be safe," he said as he fidgeted with his armor. "I'm still getting used to it myself. I don't really enjoy looking just like the rest of them."

"Where's your brother?"

"Malcolm's out with Tami. Sorry about stepping on your toes, by the way. We spotted the light from a mile away, and Malcolm said this had to be where the Chancellor was hiding." Xander looked at the candles and shifted uneasily. "I'm not sure what this is, but it's not the Chancellor. I don't think we should take too long up here anyway. If we leave Malcolm and Tami alone too long, they're going to be at each other's throats pretty soon."

Aniya nodded, but her eyes had drifted away and now looked out the window. Something was off.

"You okay?"

"Yeah." She didn't look back to see if he was satisfied with her answer, but instead studied the sector from her vantage point. Everything looked normal.

Aniya could just barely make out two faint outlines on the

dark streets below, and she could hear Tamisra talk into the radio. But she couldn't hear anything else. They had traveled so deep into Ravelta that the sounds of battle were no longer distinguishable.

The battle.

Aniya realized what was different. Not only could she not hear the firefight anymore, but the light from the flaming arrows had disappeared. Even this far into the sector, she had been able to look back before they entered the building and see the dim light of fire from the edge of Ravelta, but as she looked now from the top floor of the town hall, she couldn't make anything out.

The plan was to volley a constant barrage of fire to keep the enemy Silvers busy as the smaller squadron scouted out the rest of the sector. Even if the Silvers kept putting the fires out, there should always have been one more flaming arrow to douse.

But now there was nothing.

Aniya turned around and ran downstairs, pushing past Xander without explanation.

She burst out of the town hall and dashed to Tamisra, who was still trying to contact someone on the radio. Malcolm was standing nearby, tapping his foot impatiently.

Tamisra looked up at Aniya. "Hey. Still no word from anyone. I don't know—"

Aniya grabbed Tamisra's shoulders. "We need to get out of here."

"What's going on?"

"Not sure. The battle is over."

"Over?" Tamisra's eyes widened. "That shouldn't have happened. The only way it would be over is if—"

"We lost." Aniya finished her thought and looked around wildly. "They're coming for us. They have to be."

"If that's true, then I don't think we can leave the way we

came. They may even be inside the tunnels, if not guarding them."

"There's no other way out. If we run into trouble, then we can fight our way through."

Malcolm sneered and spoke for the first time. "Four of us versus dozens of them? That's suicide."

Aniya opened her mouth to fire back a retort, but paused as a tingling feeling raced through her body, her temperature beginning to rise as her heartbeat sped up. She set her jaw as she felt the light swelling somewhere within. It was coming again. The terror that had destroyed the reactor.

"No, it's not."

Tamisra shifted uncomfortably. "Let's get out of here."

But on the fifth floor of the town hall above them, the wick of one of the candles reached its base and lit a long fuse that traveled into a compartment in the floor, where a large package awaited.

And then, Aniya was knocked backward by a massive explosion that obliterated the town hall and lit up Ravelta in flame.

2

On the edge of the Web, in his home sector of Holendast, Roland stood in the middle of the trainyard, staring in surprise at the sight before him.

Despite Aniya's sacrifice and destruction of the reactor underneath the Hub, the only source of power throughout the Web, Holendast seemed to be fully powered.

The sky ceiling was shining in its full glory, digitally displaying a beautiful sunny day. The sun was just past its midpoint and partially hiding behind a thin, silver cloud. After spending the last few months in darkness, it was a welcome sight to Roland, albeit a foreboding one.

"That's impossible," a voice came from behind him.

Roland turned to see Nicholas staring up at the fully functioning sky ceiling.

"We destroyed the reactor," Nicholas muttered. "Aniya killed herself to take out the power and end the Lightbringers, and it was all for nothing?"

Roland frowned and tried to keep his voice even. "You mean Kendall hasn't mentioned this was possible? I thought you two were close."

But his tone apparently slipped, and Nicholas looked at him defensively.

"He hasn't said anything, no. And I get that you don't trust him, but I don't think *I've* done anything to earn your suspicion."

Roland turned away and took a deep breath. "Any thoughts on how the power is back on in the Hole, then? Surely you have some idea. You're the genius."

Nicholas stepped past him and looked around. "I guess it's possible with backup generators. But most of the sectors on the edge of the Web only have one, if that. I don't think the Hole is equipped to stay live for more than a few days. And it looks like they've had power for a lot longer than that."

Roland looked around the sector. Nicholas was right. Holendast had always featured very modest architecture, and the buildings rarely consisted of more than roughly pieced-together sheet metal and wood.

But since Roland's last time in the Hole a few months ago, several new buildings had cropped up, all of them a dazzling silver color.

A chill raced down Roland's spine as he realized what this meant.

"The Chancellor is here," he said softly. "He has to be."

Nicholas nodded as if this made perfect sense. "It's the last place anyone would think to look for him. If we didn't come here to get Gareth, we probably wouldn't have found out until Kendall made his way back through here several months from now."

Roland softly grinned at the sound of Gareth's name. He hadn't seen his lifelong mentor and friend since leaving Holendast with Aniya several months earlier, and there was a lot to catch him up on.

Gareth had no idea what horrors had awaited Aniya in the Hub. He had no idea what she had done to stop the Lightbringers. And now that he was within mere miles of the dictator that had killed his family, there was no guarantee that the gruff bartender/doctor was even still alive.

Roland took one step forward, but Nicholas placed a hand on his arm.

"Hold up. I don't think we should go any farther. Not without backup."

Roland pulled his arm away. "Gareth's down there. You want to just leave him?"

"Of course not," Nicholas said, his voice taking a sharp edge. "He trained me just as much as he trained you. He's family. But it's not safe for us to go out there alone. We need to go back and tell Kendall we've found the Chancellor."

"Knock yourself out," Roland said, gritting his teeth as he thought of Kendall. Sure, the man had helped them destroy the Lightbringers, but Nicholas's loyalty to him seemed blind, unwavering, despite Kendall's cloudy motivations. "I'm going to go get Gareth. I had to beg Kendall to let us come here, and I'm not wasting what will probably be our only opportunity."

Nicholas narrowed his eyes. "You won't be able to rescue him if you're dead, Roland."

"What, you don't have any faith in me? You forget that I've beaten you before."

"Yeah, in wrestling. The Silver Guard won't challenge you to a tussle, Roland. They'll shoot you."

Roland clenched his fists. "Yeah, you *would* know how they think. You were one of them for a few weeks, weren't you?"

Nicholas's voice turned soft. "You know I didn't have a choice, Roland. Listen, just come back with me. We'll come back with or without Kendall's permission. I promise. But there's no point in heading out there with nothing but a couple of handguns. Besides, I need you to take me back. You know I don't have the hang of riding those moles yet."

"Good, then you have no choice," Roland said as he

looked away. "I'm going to get Gareth, and if you don't have any way back to Refuge, then you're stuck with me."

Without waiting for a response, he walked out of the trainyard and onto the winding path that led to the main city.

Nicholas eventually caught up, and they walked through Holendast as outsiders, no longer feeling at home in this strange place. The Hole had completely changed. The poor, cobblestone-laden sector they had grown up in had morphed into an industrial, paved, even thriving community.

But the people had changed as well.

Just weeks ago, it seemed that the balance of the sector was evenly split between Silvers and citizens. Now, the population of the Hole seemed to be entirely Silvers. Every now and then, someone clothed in the familiar, brown Holendast garb would pass them on the road, their head down, avoiding eye contact with everyone, native or Silver.

Finally, Roland and Nicholas approached the tavern, the building in which they had met so many times in their youth for secret discussions and training.

They stepped inside and immediately found themselves in a throng of people, mostly Lightbringer personnel. And, of course, behind the bar across the room was Gareth Tigoro.

With a grin, Roland approached the bar and sat down with Nicholas, waiting to be approached by their old mentor.

After a moment, Gareth finished with a customer and turned toward them. He froze in place, and for the first time in the lifetime Roland had known him, his face read nothing but panic.

Gareth slowly approached them, leaned across the bar, and whispered below the noise of the tavern, "You shouldn't be here. I'm being watched." He looked past them, and Roland turned but saw nothing.

Nicholas gave a toothy smile, hoping that any onlookers would observe nothing but a casual conversation. "That's no way to greet your old students, Gareth."

"Cut it, boy. It's incredibly dangerous for you to be here. What are you doing here? Did you find William? Where's Aniya?"

"We have a lot to tell you, Doc," Roland said. "Is there someplace we can talk?" He looked around, and this time, he noticed a Silver sitting on the other side of the bar. As soon as Roland made eye contact, the man looked away.

"Hardly. As an instigator of the Uprising, the Lightbringers have very few reasons left to keep me alive. If they see me with you, all of us die."

Nicholas nodded. "Then we'll make this quick. We've come to get you out of here."

Gareth laughed a deep, throaty chuckle that Roland had greatly missed. "Slim chance of that, son. We wouldn't make it halfway out of Holendast."

"Please, Gareth," Roland said. "Aniya needs you. She's . . . sick." He shuddered as he recalled the horrifying incident underneath the Citadel that had left Aniya with a strange, rather terrifying condition. The Refuge medics were not very well trained and hadn't offered any answers, and it was the only reason Kendall had finally agreed to let them make the journey home.

Gareth frowned. "Where is she?"

"In the tunnels, with Salvador's men," Roland said.

"Salvador?" Gareth's eyes shot open.

Roland nodded. "He was still alive when we went into the tunnels. He helped us fight the Lightbringers and blow up the reactor."

"You blew up the reactor?" Gareth shook his head. "But we still have power here. And what do you mean *was* alive?"

Nicholas started to respond, but Gareth held up a finger.

"Take over, Hilga," he said to a woman behind him. Stepping out from behind the bar, Gareth guided them to a table in the corner and sat down across from them.

"Tell me everything."

Roland and Nicholas gave him a condensed version of events, quickly covering everything that had transpired since they left Holendast. By the end of it, Gareth was speechless, and he studied the grain of the wood table for several minutes.

Roland looked up and noticed the same officer staring at them again. "We need to get out of here, Doc. We can talk more in Refuge."

With a firm nod, Gareth glanced between the two of them. "Meet me out back."

Roland stood immediately, not wanting to risk any further delay. He walked with Nicholas straight out the door, around the building, and to the alley behind the bar.

He glanced at the trash bins, shuddering as he remembered finding William, Aniya's brother, lying there several months ago, almost dead. If he hadn't tried to destroy the reactor first and flee to Holendast just to be taken again, none of this would have ever happened. Roland bit his lip as he found himself resenting William for it.

A minute later, Gareth opened the back door and stepped outside.

Roland opened his mouth to speak but froze as Gareth raised his hands in the air.

Directly behind him was the officer that had been staring at them at the bar, his weapon drawn and jabbing into the bartender's back.

"Welcome home, Nicholas," the Silver said. "Roland." He leaned over Gareth's shoulder and hissed in his ear. "I suppose it's a good thing we kept you alive after all. We might never have found these two if it weren't for you."

"Sorry, Gareth," Nicholas grumbled, staring at the ground in shame.

But Gareth stood up tall, almost proud. He turned around and pushed his chest out. "Do it, then. Do your worst."

The officer laughed. "Do my worst? That's rich. What do

you think I am, an operative? I don't have the authority or a reason to kill you. Besides, someone's been wanting to talk to you."

As the officer smiled, several Silvers poured out from the bar behind him and surrounded Roland and Nicholas.

"Now, let's go see the Chancellor."

3

A hand pulled Aniya to her feet, then wrapped around her and braced her by the shoulder as she stumbled. She turned to see Xander, who was now supporting her weight.

Behind him, Tamisra was helping Malcolm up, who let out a sharp howl as he stood. Tamisra let him go for a second and exchanged indecipherable words with Xander.

Xander nodded and made a spinning gesture with his finger. Tamisra grabbed Malcolm again and started moving back toward the edge of the sector.

Aniya's mind finally cleared, and she pulled against Xander, stopping to look at her surroundings. Another explosion went off, this one smaller, and she looked to the left to see another building go up in flames. Almost immediately, a building to her right partially exploded, sending burning wreckage flying out into the street in front of them.

"Are you stupid? We can't stay here. Let's go!"

Aniya barely heard Malcolm's muffled command above the ringing in her ears, but it was enough to get her legs moving. Her shock was replaced by adrenaline, and she began running, first with the help of Xander, then breaking free and sprinting ahead of the others, leading the way back toward the tunnels.

The ground shook with every explosion, but Aniya managed to maintain her balance. She glanced behind her to see that the others were able to stay on their feet as well, but her heart sped as she looked behind them at a horrific sight.

The entire sector was going up in flames. Ravelta was bright as day, the fire spreading across the entire sector and advancing rapidly. The flames burned brightest where the town hall used to be and reached out in a growing circle of fire, spreading exponentially faster every second thanks to explosives planted in several buildings throughout Ravelta.

Aniya and the others managed to stay ahead of the flames, but not by much. Even now that Malcolm had separated from Tamisra and was running on his own, they still just barely edged past the advancing wall of fire.

Finally, they neared the edge of the sector and the shelter where the battle had taken place.

Lieutenant Haskill was already there, along with the rest of the scouting party that had been searching for the Chancellor. Wordlessly, they joined and continued on toward the tunnels.

Aniya looked behind her again and was relieved to see that the fire had finally stopped its advance a few hundred feet away. But when she turned back around, her relief dissipated.

From behind the shelter came dozens upon dozens of Silvers, hundreds, none of them bearing the glowing Mark of Salvador. It was more than enough to destroy the small army that had attempted to distract the Lightbringers while Aniya's group looked for the Chancellor.

But Aniya didn't see very many bodies on the battlefield, rebel or Silver. If the Refuge army was indeed wiped out, their remains were either blocked by the giant shelter or placed elsewhere. Or perhaps the Refuge army had managed to escape.

As the Silver Guard settled in place, one officer in a gray uniform stepped away from the group, holding Corrin by the collar, and Aniya's hopes fell.

The officer spoke firmly. "Annelise Lyons, please come with us. The rest of you are free to go."

Aniya froze. Even now, they were still coming for her. Even now that the Chancellor was removed, now that thousands of people in Refuge knew the secret of the Lightbringers' power and were free to tell the entire Web, they still targeted *her*.

She closed her eyes and took a breath, trying to summon the strange power she knew resided within. Whatever had manifested itself below the Citadel was still inside her somewhere. Aniya could feel it from time to time. It was close even now, judging by the way her hands tingled. If she could just harness this power, the threat that faced the rebels could be eliminated in an instant.

But no matter how hard she strained, the tingling in her hands remained just that. Whatever power that dwelled within her body refused to be controlled.

Aniya sighed as she opened her eyes, knowing what she would have to do if her new family was going to live.

"You won't hurt them?" she asked slowly.

"Aniya." Tamisra hissed behind her. "What are you doing?"

The man in gray gave a nod. "They will not be harmed if you come with me. As a sign of good faith, we will release your general."

Corrin was pushed by the officer, and he stumbled toward the group. He placed a hand on Lieutenant Haskill's shoulder and muttered, "Most of our army escaped. They're in the tunnels."

The lieutenant breathed a sigh of relief as Corrin grabbed Xander and Malcolm and embraced them.

"You know better than to trust them," Tamisra's voice whispered in her ear.

This was true, but Aniya knew what would happen if she resisted. The same thing that happened to Kira. The same thing that always happened. She couldn't take that chance again.

Corrin turned from his sons to Aniya. "It's up to you. If you don't want to give yourself up, we will fight."

"Thank you, Corrin," Aniya said with a sad smile. But she couldn't let anyone else die because of her. Never again. She stepped forward, stretching her hands out to be bound.

"Stop," Tamisra said. "They'll probably kill us even if you go with them. You know they're murderers."

Aniya shook her head. "If there's a chance that they'll let you live, I have to take it."

She kept walking and almost didn't hear Tamisra curse under her breath.

Then, the shooting began.

Tamisra must have fired first, Aniya reasoned later. She must have refused to leave her fate to chance, deciding to kill the Silvers before they could kill her.

But it didn't matter who shot first. In an instant, everyone else began shooting, and Aniya froze as the enemy fired a hail of bullets on the small group, apparently not caring anymore about keeping her alive.

"No!"

She screamed and thrust her hands out in front of her, a spark flashing at her fingertips and igniting into a massive barrier of green light. Bullets from both sides collided with the wall of light and were incinerated upon contact.

The volume and pitch of her scream escalated as the energy overwhelmed her. Her hair stood on end, her body swelled with a sense of fullness, a scorching heat covered her from head to toe, and her skin glowed green as light raced across her body, shooting out from her fingertips in a continuous stream.

As much as her natural instinct was to close her eyes and

wince in pain, she was forced to keep them open due to light that kept pushing her eyelids open and spilling out.

Then, everything vanished.

Aniya was standing in a black void. For miles in every direction, including below, there was only the dark. Green flames licked her body, but the dark void seemed to be completely unaffected by the light.

"Aniya."

She spun around as a masculine voice whispered in her ear. It was a voice that meant the world to her, one that she would give anything to hear again. But she couldn't put a name to it.

Very faintly, Aniya heard a soft voice cry out, "She needs help!"

But even as she focused on this distant cry, another voice spoke and drowned everything else out.

"Aniya."

This call came from the opposite side of the void. It was a different voice, a feminine one. An ominous one that filled Aniya with dread.

"Who's there?" She spoke for the first time in this strange world as she turned again. Her own voice was crystal clear, free of the ringing that had persisted in her ears for the last several minutes.

Several seconds passed in silence.

"Aniya."

The first voice spoke again, booming loudly from behind Aniya. Her heart racing, she turned around.

A pillar of green light faced her, roughly resembling the shape of a person. This Stranger stretched out a burning hand toward her. It was a terrifying sight, but Aniya felt a kind of peace as the hand grew nearer. Her heart longed for her to touch it, but she didn't know why. She tentatively reached to take it, but even as she did, she sensed another presence behind her.

Another hand was suddenly on her shoulder, and a cold feeling raced over her body as she shivered. She trembled in fear, all too aware of the Shadow looming behind her. With a growing terror, she looked down at her shoulder but saw nothing.

She looked back up at the Stranger and reached for its hand again, but as she did, the void collapsed around her, and then everything was gone.

Aniya was back in Ravelta, facing an army of Silvers. The light was still shooting from her hands, and the wall was still in place, but it was shrinking rapidly. She felt a presence at her side, and she turned to see Xander holding onto her left arm, his eyes wide as a pained look spread across his face.

She realized why as the smell of burnt flesh invaded her senses. Xander's hands, glued to her arm, were burning.

Then the voices came again, saying her name over and over and over.

The wall disappeared as she gasped for air.

Silence fell over Ravelta as the Silvers looked at her in terror.

Then, they seemed to all recover at the same time, and they raised their guns again.

A gunshot pierced the air. That was all it took, and as Aniya let loose an earsplitting scream, light burst forth from her once more.

This time, it didn't manifest itself in a protective barrier. Instead, it came out as twin streams of light from her hands, blasting into the silver army and washing over them in a brilliant blaze of yellow. She stared in horror as the light consumed everything in sight, incinerating all it touched.

To her left, Aniya heard a tortured cry of pain, then what sounded like Malcolm crying out in shock. She felt another hand on her right shoulder, followed by a trembling, feminine shriek.

Then, finally, it was over.

The light was gone, and there was only Aniya.

She fell to her knees and vomited.

When there was nothing left to spit up, Aniya looked up. The Silvers were gone. All of them. Nothing remained in their place, not even ash.

Through her tears, she turned to see Tamisra sprawled out on the ground, crying as she held her smoldering hands to her chest. On her other side, Malcolm sat on the ground in shock, staring at the blackened ground to Aniya's left, softly weeping.

Xander was gone.

Aniya's heart sank as she stared at where he had last stood, and tears quickly came. She turned around on her knees to see the rest of the scouting group standing behind her. Lieutenant Haskill was staring at her with an indecipherable look, and Corrin's mouth was hanging open in horror at the sight of his son melting away before his very eyes.

"I'm sorry," Aniya forced out as her chest heaved. She inched on her knees for a few feet until she realized she didn't have the strength to move anymore. "I'm so sorry."

She collapsed on the ground and wept as Corrin's agonizing cry echoed throughout Ravelta, rising above the sound of the crackling flames.

Glowing, yellow tears fell from her eyes and trickled over the ground, and Aniya wished more than anything that she was back in the void.

Instantly, her wish was granted, and she returned to the black.

The Shadow was looming before her, and as Aniya stumbled backward in fear, she blinked and was suddenly in Ravelta again.

She looked again at where Xander used to be, but even as she turned, the sector around her disappeared as the black surrounded her again. As she began to hyperventilate, she took a deep breath and closed her eyes, and when she opened them again, the void was gone.

Malcolm was staring back at her with a look of pure hatred, and the guilt of killing his brother latched onto Aniya like a vice, crushing her heart as tears sprang to her eyes.

Aniya's hands burned, and she looked down to see her fists pulsing orange. With each pulse, her vision grew darker, and she looked back at Malcolm as her head spun.

"Help me."

Then, her vision went black, and she crashed to the ground.

4

Roland, Nicholas, and Gareth approached what used to be the ragged, wooden town hall and ascended a dozen ivory steps. Escorted by Silvers, they continued into the building, which was nearly entirely white. Marble pillars supported the ceiling, which was dozens of feet above their heads. The floors were a shiny, reflective material, and with every step of the Silvers' heavy boots, a clacking sound echoed against the pristine walls.

After a moment, they arrived at two large, white doors. The Silvers opened them and motioned for their prisoners to step inside.

Roland was the last to enter the large room, and he gaped at a lavish spread of food on a massive table that stood before them. Across the table, casually reclined in an oversized armchair, was the Chancellor, eating grapes from his hand with one leg propped up on the arm of the chair. Gone was the infamous white suit, and he now wore white robes, hanging loosely around his white shirt and pants.

"Welcome," the Chancellor said jovially, spreading his arms out wide, letting a few grapes fly loose and roll across the floor carelessly. With a lick of his lips, he stood up, wincing slightly, and motioned for the group to sit down.

"Come in, come in," he said. "Forgive me. I would be a more welcoming host if not for a chest wound, courtesy of your fearless leader. How is the Scourge, by the way?"

"He's dead," Roland spat, folding his arms.

The doors closed behind Roland, Nicholas, and Gareth with a loud thud.

"Is he? I'm truly sorry to hear that," the Chancellor said as his smile faltered. "It's been many years, but we were once good friends. Please, join me."

None of the three men made any move forward, and the Chancellor frowned.

"You must be hungry," he said as he sat back down. "I'm sure it's a long and dangerous road to Holendast from Salvador's camp. Refuge, isn't it? Anyway, I certainly can't eat all of this food myself, so surely you can help me out."

Slowly, Roland stepped forward and took the chair directly across from the Chancellor, sitting down but ignoring the food. Nicholas and Gareth joined him at either side.

"Do you like what I've done with the place?" The Chancellor gestured around him and grinned. "Certainly an improvement from the dreary, old sector it was when I arrived. I must say, the nickname you gave this sector is quite appropriate. Or at least it was. I myself had never ventured out this far in the Web in my entire tenure as chancellor, and I was amazed to find such poor living conditions. A hole indeed." He motioned again to the food on the table. "Please, eat. It's quite good."

Finally, Roland could hold it in no longer. "How do you have power for the entire sector?" he blurted out. "Backup generators can only last for so long."

"Surely you didn't think I would leave myself without a contingency plan? I rerouted power here with time to spare."

Roland's brow furrowed. "Rerouted from where?"

The Chancellor waved his hand. "Don't worry about that. Tell me," he said, leaning forward. "Where is Annelise?"

"Aniya. And don't worry about that," Nicholas said, throwing the Chancellor's words back at him through gritted teeth. "I can promise you that you'll never see her again."

"Aniya, yes. And I wouldn't be so sure," the Chancellor said. His smile grew wider as Nicholas's eyes narrowed. "Relax. You are here as my guests, and I mean you no harm. We have much to discuss, and if I am right, not much time in which to discuss it."

"Why?" Roland asked. "Do you have somewhere you need to be?"

"Not really, but I assume Kendall knows you're here?"

None of them answered.

The Chancellor nodded. "Which means the Director knows."

Roland looked up. "Who?"

The Chancellor's gaze flickered to Nicholas. "You haven't told him? Well, you'll find out soon enough. In any case, he can't be too happy that I'm still alive. As soon as Kendall tells him where I am, I won't have much time left."

Gareth spoke for the first time. "What do you want?"

The Chancellor turned to him, his arms spreading open as he licked his lips. "What makes you think I want anything?"

"Don't expect us to believe you're going friendly on us now," Gareth said, his words coming out terse. "You ordered the death of thousands of people, including my family. You terrorized the Web for decades. Now you invite us over for dinner? What do you want?"

"If you think I'm bad, you don't want to meet the Director." The Chancellor laughed, but he quickly stopped and cleared his throat, and his face grew somber. "I need your help. Aniya needs your help. Everything you did below the Citadel—destroying the reactor, your survival, Aniya's gifts—"

"What?" Roland's heart stopped. How could he possibly know?

The Chancellor glanced at him and smirked. "Surely you couldn't expect such a thing to be kept a secret. Tell me, Roland. Do you really think such a miracle could be a mere accident? The Director meant for it to happen, all of it. That's why Kendall was here, to make sure everything went according to plan."

Roland shook his head. "No, there's no way Kendall could have controlled that. He was surprised as I was to find out that Aniya lived. Her gift, as you call it? We don't even know what it means. No, no one could have seen that coming."

The Chancellor leaned forward. "I predicted it. It was my life's work, after all. You really don't give me enough credit, you know. You make me out to be a horrible monster, but I finally figured out a better way to provide power, one that would end the use of that horrible machine below the Citadel. Never again would we have to rely on the Citizen Tax. I was the one who finally cracked the code, but the Director took my research and arranged my removal. I made peace with the fact that my job was a thankless one a long time ago, but this was the ultimate insult."

He gave a deep sigh. "It doesn't matter now. What's done is done. My only chance to stop it from happening was you, and that, unfortunately, did not work out."

"Me?" Roland frowned.

The Chancellor nodded. "That's why I let you go. It was too late to show Aniya reason, so I came to you. I knew if I helped you save her, I would be able to talk with you plainly without Kendall whispering in your ear. I counted on you to not let Aniya kill herself. But in the end, it was her, so now we must make do and proceed."

"We?" Nicholas shook his head. "We aren't going to do anything. Not with you. We can help her without your lies."

"I understand. Her safety is of the utmost importance. But

you don't understand. Aniya cannot be helped, not by you. All that energy inside her . . . She needs an outlet. She can't just let it out into the open without risk of harming those around her. She needs a way to safely release that energy, and thankfully, I know how to do it. But any attempt you make to help her will do nothing but pose a risk to your own safety."

"Well," Roland said, "if you're telling the truth, we'll know right where to find you. But, I'm sure you understand, we're going to try to help her without having to listen to a madman."

The Chancellor nodded. "As I expected. I don't blame you, to be honest. Believe it or not, we're on the same side. We both want what's best for Aniya, so I won't try to keep you here. But don't waste any time. The longer that energy builds up inside her, the more dangerous she'll be to herself and others. And don't think that Kendall can help you. Even if he could, you really shouldn't trust him. Oh, I know he helped you and your sorry band of rebels overthrow the big, bad Chancellor. But as you very well know," the Chancellor said, pointing at Nicholas, "he did so only at the order of the Director, who does not have your best interests in mind. And you should assume that Kendall does not either. He intends to use Aniya for his own selfish purposes."

Roland scoffed. "As opposed to you, who have nothing but Aniya's best interests in mind?"

The Chancellor grinned and darted his tongue over his lips. "At least she and all of you will be safe if you bring her to me. I can't promise the same if she falls into the hands of the Director, and even if he does help her, I assure you, he will not hesitate to remove any loose ends. As long as he gets what he wants, he doesn't really care what happens to you."

"And *you* care?" Roland glared at the Chancellor. "You kidnapped and tortured me."

"You're sure of that, are you?" He looked at Nicholas. "If Kendall hasn't told you, his puppet, what really happened in the Hub, that's a conversation the two of you need to have."

"Puppet?" Nicholas clenched his fists.

"Indeed. You blindly followed his every order, from start to finish. Oh, please don't misunderstand me. I'm not demeaning you in any way. Your loyalty is admirable, if not misplaced. I talk to you openly now because I trust that you will see reason and do what is best for Aniya."

The Chancellor folded his hands and peered at Roland. "Consider this. What reason would I have for your kidnapping? I knew where Aniya was. At that very moment, my Operative was securing her and bringing her back to me. What use would I have for you or the Scourge's daughter?"

Roland shrugged. "Why does an insane dictator do any of the things he does?"

"Kendall's plan was to attack me on multiple fronts, to divide my forces and weaken my response. I have to say, it worked all too well. If Salvador had not attacked me, I would have had the resources to stop Aniya beneath the Citadel. But there never would have been a battle if the daughter of the Scourge hadn't been kidnapped. My dear, old friend was happy to live out the rest of his days in the caves, with no thought or regard for any of the happenings in the sectors. Yet he came out to fight once again because his daughter had been taken. Why would I do such a thing if I knew it would only anger the Scourge? I remember his tenacity all too well. He may have been a fake, but he was an efficient fake. He played his part well."

Roland leaned across the table and slammed his fists down, knocking a plate of oranges to the ground. "He wasn't a fake. He was a great man."

"I can agree to that. He was a fraud indeed, but a great man. A fierce fighter devoted to his cause. And as such, I had no desire to meet him in battle. However, his daughter was conveniently kidnapped, and so he responded in a predictable fashion. I hope I don't seem foolish to you. I like to think that I am rather smart. Tell me, do you think I would be foolish enough to start a battle I know I cannot win?"

Roland simply stared at the Chancellor. Neither one moved or spoke. Every retort Roland could think of died on his lips. And the more he considered the Chancellor's explanation, the more it resonated with his own reservations when it came to the mysterious Kendall.

Maybe this insane dictator wasn't so insane after all.

Nicholas's response shook Roland from his reverie. "You're a liar," he said. "You're a liar and a murderer. Why would we believe a word you say?"

The Chancellor leaned back. "You don't have to. Just think about it. Think about it, and be careful when it comes to Kendall. And when he betrays you, when he stabs you in the back, when everyone you love dies, don't say I didn't warn you."

He stood up and winced again. "Now, if you don't mind, I must rest. Feel free to stay, but I'm sure you will want to return to Aniya soon."

Nicholas stood as well. "You realize we have to take you in, right? You're no longer a chancellor, just a war criminal."

The Chancellor smiled. "Be careful, Nicholas. I am letting you go, released of all consequence you have brought on yourself for your treason. Even Dr. Tigoro is free to leave Holendast and find whatever death he seems appropriate after his disturbing, violent history. Do not make me regret my gracious choice." The Chancellor gave a small wave with his right hand, and instantly, the large doors behind the group opened. Eight Silvers poured into the room and lined the walls, a rifle in each of their hands, pointed at the floor but ready for action.

"Now, if you will excuse me." The Chancellor turned and left as the Silvers flanked him and safely escorted him out of the room.

5

Kendall took a quick look back at Refuge before quietly slipping down the tunnel that would lead to the rebels' communications jammer.

The device had caused significant problems for the Lightbringers back in the days of the Uprising, and it was still an inconvenience now as Kendall had to manually disengage the electromagnetic interference anytime he needed to use the radio.

Thankfully, the tunnel was guarded only by a few tripwires, which Kendall knew to step over. According to Corrin, Refuge didn't assign manpower to guard this tunnel because access to Refuge was strictly limited to those with access codes to the giant steel doors that blocked off the rest of the Web. And only a select few had the entrance codes.

Kendall said a silent thank-you to Corrin as he stepped over a tripwire and into the small cavern with the jammer, quickly covering his ears and blocking out the annoying humming coming from the machine.

The device was rather large, and it took up most of the cavern. From the giant, yellow machine came at least a dozen wires that were thicker than Kendall's wrist, and they disappeared into the rock walls of the cavern in different directions.

Kendall almost caught himself admiring the foresight of the rebels to leech energy from a dozen sectors as well as the backup generator they had on hand, but he remembered that this was the original ingenuity of the Lightbringers.

With one last look behind him, he entered a code on a keypad on the machine, and a green light flashed. A small monitor above the panel read "Manual Override: Y/N."

He pressed the "Y" key at the bottom of the panel, then flipped a large switch next to the button.

The machine whined loudly, a long tone that receded in volume until the cavern was as quiet as the tunnel that had brought Kendall to it.

He slipped on an earpiece, pressed a button, and the voice came almost immediately.

"Report."

Kendall cleared his throat and spoke as calmly as he could. "Sir, there's been a complication."

"Proceed."

"It's the girl."

The voice hardened. "What happened?"

"She's alive, but she's in a coma. She went with my army to Ravelta to track down the Chancellor, and—"

"You let her fight?" The man's voice was on the verge of trembling. "I made it perfectly clear how important it is that she stay safe. I left no room for any misunderstanding."

Kendall spoke quickly. "It wasn't my intention that she fight. She was supposed to stay here, but she convinced the rebel leader to let her tag along."

"Are you not the rebel leader? Careful, Kendall. I trusted you to control that Web. If you cannot do so, you of all people know how easy it is to be replaced."

"Yes, sir."

The man's voice returned to its normal, calm state. "Now, what happened?"

"The girl has taken on some . . . interesting properties since the meltdown in the Hub. It seems that some residual energy is trapped inside her body." He hesitated. "Her capabilities are lethal, sir. It's a good thing most of my army had been forced into the tunnels because apparently, she took out nearly a thousand men in an instant."

"Interesting."

The man's tone revealed nothing.

"And now she's slipped into a coma, so it seems. Completely unresponsive."

"Then it's important that we move quickly, now more than ever. Perhaps I was wrong to let her stay in your care for as long as she has."

"I thought she needed to recover."

The man's voice revealed annoyance. "She did, but I counted on your ability to keep her stable and not run off into battle. Besides, I needed time to prepare her new home. Her actions and your negligence, however, seem to have progressed her condition significantly and therefore will force my hand. What of the boy?"

"He shows no sign of the same anomalies. Whatever happened down there, it only affected her."

"Interesting. Keep observing him."

"I will," Kendall said. "Both of them."

"Not the girl. The preparations are nearly complete. Bring her to me."

"She's dangerous. I'm afraid if we get too close to her, we'll trigger a lethal response from her. She took out one of her friends in the battle, so I don't think she's in control of her power."

"Then neutralize her."

Kendall froze. "Sir?"

"The operative I'm sending you will be carrying a sensitive package. Use it to kill the girl and safely transport her body."

"You don't want us to revive her? It worked last time."

"We can't leave anything up to chance. If you deem it too dangerous to move her in her present condition, then incapacitate her."

"Sir—"

"Bring her to me."

With that, the Director was gone.

6

Roland lay in his old cot in the Holendast clinic, staring at the ceiling. Nicholas had argued that it was pointless to start making their way to Refuge when they were all tired, so Gareth had agreed that they should stay the night here. But try as he might, and as tired as he was, Roland couldn't sleep. The Chancellor's words kept echoing in his mind. His accusations of Kendall, his defense of his actions, and his reference to the mysterious man called the Director.

Nicholas had refused to give any information about the Director, saying only that he wasn't sure who exactly that was. He'd avoided further questions and changed the subject, complaining of an unusual fatigue. He was now asleep on the exam table in the next room.

Roland didn't know what to think anymore. Kendall had not yet earned his trust, that much was clear. He had tried to argue the Chancellor's point of view with Nicholas and Gareth, but neither of them would hear it. Gareth, who was now sleeping across the room from Roland, had insisted that until there was firm evidence, there was no point in arguing. They needed to be on the same side, he'd said. It would only waste time and distract them from Aniya, who they all agreed needed their help. Roland had only agreed to let it go for now when Gareth said that once Aniya was taken care of, he would look into Kendall and promise consequences if there was any truth to the Chancellor's words.

To their credit, the more Roland thought about it, the more he accepted that, because the Chancellor was responsible for so much hurt in the Web, it was foolish to trust him.

But there seemed to be no way to fully know the truth. Roland knew it was unlikely that he would ever find out what really happened in the Hub.

Finally, the fatigue overwhelmed his racing thoughts, and his eyelids slowly drooped to a close.

Whether it was a second later or after a few hours of sleep, Roland didn't know, but it was the least of his worries as a cold hand clamped over his mouth, startling him awake and into a frenzy. His eyes flew open, but he couldn't make out the intruder's face in the darkness. He kicked and lashed at the person now holding him down by his chest, but the intruder's grip on him remained firm.

A sharp prick in his neck made him lash harder, but almost instantaneously, a heavy feeling forced his eyes back closed.

Roland opened them again to see a large, white room, furnished only by a chair five feet away.

"You're awake." A voice came from behind Roland, and a man in a white robe stepped to his front and sat down in the chair. "Good."

Roland glared at the Chancellor and started to stand, but found that he was securely bound to his own chair by steel handcuffs. "You know, for someone who's trying to convince us that they're not a kidnapper, you're going about it in the wrong way," he said, gripping the edge of the armrests firmly.

The Chancellor smiled. "I've only brought you here to speak with you. I come in peace and only wish to help you."

"*This* is helping me?" Roland nodded to his bound hands.

"I'm more than happy to free you if you remain calm. Just know that I have guards on standby."

After pausing for a moment to think, Roland nodded.

The Chancellor unlocked the handcuffs and tossed them aside.

Roland wasted no time, blurting out, "What do you want?"

The Chancellor sat back down. "You and your friends always seem to think I want something. Is it too outlandish to think that I simply want to help you?"

"It hasn't crossed my mind," Roland said.

"I'm not terribly surprised. After all, I haven't always been the best leader."

Roland rubbed his wrists. "That's an understatement."

The Chancellor seemed to ignore this. "Aniya needs our help. Specifically, she needs *my* help. And if the Director gets his hands on her, I promise you, her wellbeing will be the last thing on his mind."

"Who is he?"

"My boss. Well, Kendall's boss now. That's all you really need to know." He grinned. "Besides, if I share everything I know, you won't need me anymore."

Roland leaned forward, frowning. "And what does he want with Aniya?"

"I honestly don't know. When I came up with the idea of putting that much energy in one human, my goals were nothing if not altruistic. But the Director's goals, I believe, are far beyond anything I could have ever imagined. Far more ambitious, and far more dangerous. Aniya's potential is nearly limitless, after all. I have my suspicions, but again, I won't be sharing them at this time."

"If you're not going to tell me anything, what do you expect me to do? What do you want from me?"

The Chancellor's grin vanished as he licked his lips. "I need your help, Roland, just as much as you need mine.

The Director wants me dead, and he'll have Kendall come in here by force and execute me long before I ever get a chance to help Aniya. But with your help, it doesn't have to happen like that. I can help her and save her life."

Roland looked down at the floor. If there was any chance that the Chancellor was telling the truth, he had to consider it. He took a deep breath and shook his head.

"What did you have in mind?"

7

Tamisra woke up the next evening to a minor annoyance. Her hands were tingling, itching, but she couldn't make any move to scratch them and relieve herself. She opened her eyes to see a large man standing over her, his bushy beard obscuring most of the details on his face.

Whether it was due to her grogginess or simply because she hadn't met him, she didn't recognize the man. She had become familiar with all the medics in Refuge, few as though they were, but this man simply did not look familiar.

As the large man lumbered over to the other side of her bed, Tamisra got a better look at his face, and she became certain that she had never seen this man before. She groaned and closed her eyes, wishing away the tickling sensation in her hands, but she was startled as she realized that her shirt was being lifted. Cold hands found their way to her stomach, inching up toward her chest, and her eyes flew open.

"Who are you, and what are you doing?"

The hands retreated. "My apologies, young lady. I thought you were still sedated. My name is Gareth Tigoro, and I have been asked to examine you and your injuries."

"I don't care who you are."

Gareth frowned. "But you just said—"

"I don't care." Tamisra glared at him. "My chest is just fine. Put my shirt back."

"Of course, miss."

Her shirt was replaced, and she closed her eyes again.

"The damage does seem to be confined to your hands, thankfully. However, your injuries are quite severe."

Sighing in frustration, Tamisra opened her eyes again. "Hardly. I barely feel anything. Now, would you please let me sleep?"

"You don't feel much because you're on some painkillers that are quite powerful," Gareth said. "I'm afraid it will be quite some time before you can use your hands again."

Frowning, Tamisra pushed herself up and looked down to see that her hands were indeed wrapped in several layers of bandages. "What happened?"

"It seems that you got too close to Aniya," Gareth said. "I've been told she has developed some rather unique gifts, and while they appear to have saved your life from the Silvers, you touched her at a very dangerous moment, resulting in severe damage to your hands."

Tamisra grunted and laid back. "I was trying to stop her. She . . . She hurt Xander."

"I don't think much could have stopped Aniya, from what I'm told about the incident. Even before she took on these abilities, she couldn't be talked out of much." Gareth smiled. "Much like your father."

Tamisra's heart grew heavy. "You were close, weren't you? He talked about you."

Gareth nodded. "And I am heartbroken to hear of his passing. I'm very sorry for your loss, Tamisra. Salvador was a good man."

Tamisra drew in a sharp breath and shook away the thought of her father. "Why aren't you taking care of Aniya? The last time I saw her, she was unconscious."

"And she still is. I examined her as soon as I got here this afternoon, but there's nothing I can do to help her beyond putting her into a deeper sleep to stabilize her. I did just that, so she shouldn't get any worse, but I don't know enough about her condition to know if she'll recover on her own. We are looking into alternative treatments, but her situation truly is a mystery to me. As for your condition, you will heal in time. I can recommend certain ointments that will speed up the healing process, but in the end, all you can do is let it heal."

The door burst open, and Roland ran to her side. "Tamisra, are you okay? I'm sorry. I never should have left you. It's all my fault. I asked you to watch over Aniya. I'm so sorry." He finally took a breath and stroked her hair. "Are you in pain?"

Tamisra shook her head and grinned. "You shouldn't worry so much, pet."

Gareth cocked an eyebrow at this term of endearment. "I thought I told you to remain outside until she's ready, Roland."

"Trust me, I'm ready," Tamisra said. "I hate being stuck in bed, but the distraction is very welcome."

"You and Aniya will be up and at it in no time." Roland looked up at Gareth. "Right, Doc?"

Gareth looked doubtful.

"They told you about Aniya?" Tamisra asked, trying again to not focus on the incredible, insatiable urge to scratch at her hands. "Have you seen her yet?"

"Yeah, Gareth said I could see her while I was waiting for you to wake up. She doesn't look good."

Tamisra sighed. "And while we're on bad news, I don't have anything to report on you-know-who."

"Report?" Gareth frowned.

Roland froze.

"Yeah . . ." Tamisra drifted off as Roland shook his head slightly. "No?"

Gareth folded his arms. "Report about what and who?"

"Nothing," Tamisra said quickly, forcing a smile. "Just battle things. You know, wars. Guns."

Roland turned around slowly to face Gareth. "Please don't tell Nicholas. He's stressed out about this enough as it is."

"You asked her to spy on Kendall, didn't you?"

"Not so much spy as keep an eye on," Roland said.

Gareth sighed and shook his head. "I won't say anything, but you need to focus on the enemy you know you have rather than the one you're still not sure about."

"Speak for yourself, Grandpa," Tamisra said with a scoff. "The guy was a Lightbringer. We have reason enough to be cautious about him, especially now that he's made his home in the place my father fought to build and protect."

Roland nodded. "And if Kendall's the one who tortured us, it would have been to bait Salvador into a fight that eventually got him killed. If he's the reason Salvador is dead, then you and Tamisra have more reason than I would to hate—"

"Roland," Gareth said sharply. "A word?"

Roland stared at the doctor for a moment but finally stood up and followed him out of the room.

After several minutes, Roland came back inside and closed the door, but Gareth was not with him.

"Where did the doc go?"

Roland didn't answer.

"What's going on, Roland?" Tamisra growled. "I know, I know. We can't trust Kendall. You keep saying that. But what are you not telling me? What happened beneath the Citadel?"

Again, no answer.

"Why are you so set on turning Kendall into a criminal? If he did everything you're saying he did, you're right. It'd mean that he got my father killed. But they were on the same side, Roland."

"I'm beginning to think Kendall doesn't take sides. Only his own. Just him and this Director guy."

Tamisra frowned. "Director?"

"Kendall's boss. That's all I know about him. Apparently, he wants Aniya for something."

"Who told you that?"

Roland paused. "The Chancellor."

Tamisra laughed. "The same Chancellor we were fighting to overthrow? I understand not wanting to trust Kendall, but taking the word of a dictator?"

"It all makes sense," Roland said. He paced back and forth. "We wouldn't have been able to destroy the reactor if the Silvers weren't preoccupied with your father's army. And your father would never have fought if you hadn't been taken. You know that better than I do."

Tamisra nodded. "Sure, but I think it's a stretch to think that Kendall kidnapped and tortured us just so his plan would work."

"I don't know anymore. I don't know what to think."

"What are you going to do?" Tamisra asked.

Roland sighed. "I don't know that either. It's not like I can just ask Kendall if he tortured us. Just stay clear of him for now. As for me . . ."

Tamisra frowned as Roland buried his head in his hands. "What is it?"

It was a long time before Roland spoke again.

"I'm sorry for not telling you as much as I should," he finally said softly. "You've done nothing to make me think I can't trust you. But between Kendall, the Chancellor, even your father . . ."

Tamisra placed a numb, bandaged hand on Roland's arm. "What is it, Roland?"

"Nothing I'm about to do is going to make sense if you don't know the reason for it all." Roland took a deep breath. "It's time I told you what happened in the Hub."

8

Roland walked out of the clinic, leaving Refuge by way of one of the many tunnels branching off of the main cavern.

He had told Tamisra all of it, what happened to Aniya and everything the Chancellor said. But he didn't tell her about *this*. She probably would have tried to stop him.

He could hardly believe he was doing it himself. Just weeks ago, he would have laughed at the thought of it.

Whatever it takes to save Aniya.

Roland marched on, repeating this mantra to himself over and over again. If anyone ever found out, it would be his only defense. Surely they could see that. If no one else, Nicholas would understand eventually.

That is, if he could be trusted.

It was a long path down the tunnel, and Roland was thankful for the map he had copied from the war room. The random offshoots from this tunnel provided dozens of options, and he would have gotten lost for sure without directions.

He finally made his way to another cavern, this one much smaller but much louder. A giant machine took up most of the space in the cavern, emitting an annoying hum that drowned out any other noise.

Roland stepped over a thick wire that ran from the machine and into the walls, and he approached an access panel on the side of the machine.

He punched a code into a keypad, pressed a button, flipped a switch, and waited for the machine to wind down.

Roland took a deep breath and pulled the device from his pocket. It was different from any radio he had ever seen, but the concept couldn't have been that much different. He placed it in his ear, then pressed a button on the device.

"This is Roland. Do you copy?" He looked back toward Refuge. "It's time."

9

Aniya sat back in her home in Holendast.

For whatever reason, the ethereal purgatory she'd found herself in had most recently manifested itself as her childhood home. Sometimes, the scenery would change to Nicholas's roof, the locale of many late-night talks and the beginning of a dozen shenanigans. Sometimes, she found herself back inside the tank, deep below the Hub.

On rare occasions, she would catch glimpses of the real world. She'd seen Nicholas a few times, Roland once, both of them looking down at her with concerned expressions. A few times, she could make out speech from the world beyond the veil of the void, though it was always short-lived, and somehow it always sounded like gibberish.

But now, like most of the time she'd spent so far in this strange place, she was alone, sitting in silence in her blood-soaked home.

The room was exactly as she had left it, down to the tiniest detail. Her father lay on the ground, his throat slit open. Aniya's mother was next to him, a single shot through her head.

Even the flames Aniya had ignited just before her departure were still burning, a perpetual fire that consumed nothing.

If the fire gave off any heat, it didn't matter. Aniya felt nothing. Her body was completely numb, her senses dull.

She couldn't even hear the crackling of the flames. Every sound seemed to dissipate into the surrounding void. Aniya was grateful for this. The voices could have returned by now, but even if they did, she never would have known. She had already tried talking, but her voice had been muffled to the point where she heard nothing, only feeling the vibration in her chest.

She remembered how her home had smelled. The flames had started to burn away her parents' bodies, giving off a horrible stench. But Aniya smelled nothing now, and she was thankful for this as well.

And so she sat.

The only indication of the passage of time was her occasional blink into consciousness, just long enough to see someone different standing by her bed, checking her vitals or trying to talk to her. For all Aniya knew, she could have been in the void for weeks.

Her home began to twist around her, and as Aniya saw the floor drop out from beneath her, she instinctively reached out for something to grab. But there was nothing to grab, and all she could do was watch as her home morphed into the shape of Nicholas's roof.

As soon as this new location settled around her, a relieved smile spread across her face. It was a comforting sight, especially after being back in her burning home.

Growing up, whenever she felt the urge to run away from the heavy expectations placed on her by her family and the Lightbringers, she would retreat here. No matter how upset Aniya was, she could always count on the peace that this location provided.

The mere sight of it was enough to settle her heart, but

there wasn't anything special about the roof, even though she had said the opposite to Nicholas multiple times over the years. His smiling face would be the rock that grounded her. He was her landing place, her shelter.

On some level, Aniya knew that she had always loved him. She didn't know why she had rejected him when he verbally expressed his obvious feelings. Maybe because she was afraid of things changing. Maybe she thought they'd be better off as friends. Maybe it was too much to handle when there were too many other people to keep happy.

This last reason made most sense to her. After all, now that there were no parents to offer their well-meaning advice, now that there were no obligations for either of them, and now that they were out of the Lightbringers' grasp, all the extra noise seemed to be gone. She could think clearly now. And the more she thought about it, the more she knew it.

She loved him.

And all she wanted was to finally tell him. But the last few weeks had been hectic, what with preparing for war against the Chancellor and his remaining Silvers. Nicholas had always been in meetings of some kind, and Aniya had spent most of her time in clinics, being evaluated and re-evaluated in the aftermath of the incident beneath the Citadel.

As if her void were granting her a wish, Nicholas appeared in front of her, standing on the same roof where they had met hundreds of times.

She greeted him, ignoring the fact that her speech remained completely unintelligible.

He seemed to understand her, and he smiled back, talking back in his own muffled voice.

Aniya reached for him, longing for his embrace, but her feet were rooted to the ground, keeping Nicholas just out of arm's reach.

Then, Nicholas's smile faded. His mouth popped open, his eyes went dark, and his feet hovered above the ground.

They were back in the tank.

Aniya floated in the water, a tube attached to her mouth, watching helplessly as Nicholas's lifeless body drifted away from her.

The tube disappeared, and she now floated freely, but as she reached out to Nicholas, he disappeared.

She resigned to simply let herself drift aimlessly in the water, not bothering to fight for air. Even if she were drowning, she couldn't feel anything.

"Aniya."

The oppressing silence was gone, and one of the voices was back.

It was the warm one, the masculine one. The one that brought an unnatural peace to Aniya. The Stranger.

It was the only clear speech Aniya had heard since falling into the void. It had called out to her every now and then as she sat in her mental prison. It was the only thing that seemed real, and it always brought her to her feet, desperate to find its source.

But as she took a step to search for the voice, Aniya realized she was still in the tank. She fought to change the scene again, picturing Nicholas's roof and trying to leap there by will, but she remained trapped within the glass enclosure.

She clenched her fists and began beating on the tank, knowing the voice lay waiting on the other side, within reach if she could just escape the water. With each blow to the glass, sparks flew from her hands, shocking the water and zapping her body. It was the first sensation she had felt so far, and Aniya almost reveled in the pain. If nothing else, the minor jolts just urged her to beat harder, and so she did, beating against the tank with all her might.

Finally, the glass broke with a mighty explosion, sending shards flying away in slow motion, careening into the distance and disappearing in the black.

But Aniya was still in the water.

The liquid maintained its form, held up by nothing.

Aniya tried to swim out of the strange pool, but could not breach the outer wall. It remained a firm, jelly-like substance, bouncing and bubbling every time she touched it. She swam up, but the top of the water held the same rigidity, imprisoning her just as efficiently as the glass had.

"Aniya."

She began choking. Not on the water that threatened to invade her lungs, but on her own tearless sobs that came with every failed attempt of escape.

Then the water went still.

It remained a physically impossible prison, but the ripples ceased all at once as a deafening silence fell over Aniya's mind.

From out of the darkness walked a being shrouded in yellow light, nearly blinding Aniya as it appeared from nothing. The Stranger.

"Aniya."

She should have been afraid, but Aniya found herself in a deep calm as she watched the pillar of light approach her.

But the Stranger's light suddenly began to diminish as the Shadow appeared from behind it, quickly advancing and threatening to overtake the light.

She tried to shout and warn the Stranger bathed in light that the Shadow was coming. But the water flooded her lungs and silenced her.

"Aniya," the Shadow said with its dark, feminine voice that sent chills down Aniya's spine.

The blazing, yellow figure seemed to turn and stare at the approaching Shadow. All went still for a moment as the two beings remained at a kind of impasse.

Suddenly, the Stranger spun around, reaching out a fiery finger and touching the water that trapped Aniya.

Instantly, the wall of water collapsed and drained out into the void below. Aniya was free from the water, but she was somehow still floating in mid-air.

She looked around, and the cavern under the Hub was gone. There was only a black nothingness that surrounded herself and the two phantoms.

"Aniya."

The Stranger spoke again, this time tenderly, with what seemed like sorrow.

Her breath stopped. That voice was hauntingly familiar. Why couldn't she place it?

Aniya looked up and saw the Stranger and the Shadow standing in front of her, each of them extending a hand to her. She glanced between the two when both suddenly vanished, leaving her alone in the void.

"No!" she cried out as she looked around. "Come back!"

"My dear Annelise, I am here at your service."

Aniya froze.

A new voice had invaded her mind, echoing in the void with a sickeningly sweet tone.

This speech was not distorted like the two voices that continued to haunt her. It was clear and rich, and Aniya instantly knew the identity of the speaker.

What was worse was that Aniya heard the voice twice. Once in her mind, and once with her ears.

It was the Chancellor.

And he was in Refuge.

10

Roland jogged down the stairs, almost missing the last step. With an extra leap to keep his balance, he stepped into the war room in the basement of the Refuge tower.

Six men looked back up at him, each of them sitting at the large stone table.

"You're late," Kendall said, his eyes narrowed. "I thought Nicholas told you we were starting soon."

"I'm not sure why he's here at all," Malcolm scoffed. He was sitting between Corrin and Lieutenant Haskill. "I didn't realize we were inviting kids to help plan a war."

Corrin shot a stern glance at his son. "You're not that much older than he is, Malcolm. I suggest you don't raise questions of age. Besides, Roland has earned his spot at this table."

"Doesn't mean he can be late," Malcolm muttered.

Roland looked back at Kendall as he finished catching his breath. "Sorry. I was just checking on Aniya. She doesn't look great."

Malcolm laughed. "Doesn't look great? She's glowing, Roland."

Across the table from Kendall, Gareth looked down at

his lap. "I've done all I can, but I'm afraid her condition is beyond me."

"So getting your doctor friend was a waste of time," Malcolm said. "I knew it."

"It wasn't a complete waste," Nicholas said from the other side of the table as Roland sat next to him. "We know where the Chancellor is now."

Kendall nodded. "Indeed. It was a fruitful mission, even if it didn't give us the exact fruit we wanted."

"So what now?" Roland asked.

"Now," Kendall said, "we talk about the fact that you lied to me."

His tone was flat, unsurprised, as if he were stating a simple fact.

"The description Corrin gave me of Aniya's actions in Ravelta were incredible, unbelievable. Yet they explained much more to me than the story I got out of you after I had you pulled out from underneath the Citadel." He eyed Roland as if waiting for a response.

Roland glanced at Nicholas, but his friend was staring at the table, a bead of sweat sliding down his cheek.

"It is, of course, possible that you didn't have words to explain what happened. Would you like to try again, Roland?" After a few seconds, Kendall sighed. "I had hoped we would come to trust each other, Roland. Thankfully, I don't need your cooperation to help Aniya. Someone who obviously loves her more has already volunteered the information I need."

Roland looked up sharply, his nostrils flaring. He looked right at Nicholas, who was still avoiding all eye contact.

"You told him?" Roland asked with a trembling voice.

Nicholas finally looked up. "You want her to die? She needs help."

Roland stood quickly, shaking the table. "She trusted you. I trusted you. I didn't even tell Tami, and you told a guy who used to work for the Lightbringers."

"I had to tell him."

After a moment, Roland spun around and glared at Kendall. "Why did you bother acting like you didn't already know?"

"Nicholas wished that I not tell you."

"What, that he betrayed Aniya? That he betrayed me?" Roland clenched his fists. "I bet he did."

Nicholas stood and stepped toward Roland, placing a hand on his arm, but Roland recoiled sharply, thrusting his arm up and pushing his old friend away. Nicholas reacted as if he was punched, and he stumbled backward for a moment before regaining his balance. When he did, he grabbed the table and breathed heavily.

"Please, we need to move forward," Gareth said. "We can't change what happened. All we can do now is work together and help Aniya."

"I don't know why we're trying to help her," Malcolm growled. "I think we need to get rid of the threat. We'd all be much safer."

Corrin shot a look at Malcolm. "Quiet. She saved all of our lives."

Malcolm sank back into his chair as he mumbled, "Yeah, all of us but Xander. How are you okay with all this? My brother, your son, is dead."

"I never said I was okay with it. I miss him just as much as you do. But it wasn't Aniya's fault."

Malcolm struck the table with his fists. "Of course it was her fault. She attacked those men and got my brother killed. How can you say it wasn't her fault?"

Corrin placed a hand on Malcolm's shoulder. "If it wasn't for Aniya, you and I would both be dead. Xander was just in the wrong place at the wrong time. He was trying to help her."

"Helping her is what got him killed, and you want to do the same thing? I don't understand. How can you just let this go?"

"I have faith that you'll understand sooner or later, Malcolm. I just hope it's sooner."

"She needs to leave. She can't stay here."

"Do you think that's what Xander would have wanted?"

"It doesn't matter what Xander wants anymore. He's dead."

The room was silent for several seconds before Kendall spoke again. "Both of you are correct, in a way. Aniya is incredibly dangerous, but I believe she can be helped."

Lieutenant Haskill sighed as he shook his head, pressing his fingers to his temple. "For those of us not in the know, would you please explain what's going on? The way I see it, we're sitting a few hundred feet away from someone who could blow up and kill us all at any second. What exactly happened to her?"

Kendall glanced at Roland as if asking permission.

"You might as well tell them. No point in keeping it a secret anymore," Roland said, glaring at Nicholas.

"Very well, then," Kendall said, standing. "When we overloaded the machine beneath the Citadel, the energy from several thousand humans was temporarily inside Aniya, if only for an instant. That energy was to then be redirected back to the reactor and destroy it. Obviously, it worked. But it seems that Aniya inadvertently kept some of the energy for herself. Or it refused to leave. Or it replicated itself. I have no way of knowing. Whatever the case, there is now excess energy trapped inside her, and by nature, since it is not her own, it demands to be let out. Unfortunately, it seems to come out in a very corporeal type of light, and a lethal one at that. The only thing that leaves me puzzled is Nicholas's survival. He was in the tank with her, and his body had not been given a chance to acclimate to the conditions of the machine. From what I saw before the reactor blew, he died. I've asked Nicholas, but he has no memory of what happened after that." Kendall approached Roland slowly. "Do you have any light to shed on the subject?"

"We've already told him everything else," Nicholas said, wiping sweat from his forehead. "He needs to know. Don't you want to help Aniya?"

After a long pause, Roland sighed. "Is it possible that this energy has restorative power? It was all a blur, but I remember she touched him, and then he woke up."

"Well, the human body is, in essence, energy. That was the whole reason for using people to power the Web. I suppose if you think of it technically, Nicholas's body was without power, and Aniya transferred some of her own and resuscitated him. But this is all mere speculation." Kendall sat again, rubbing his chin. "What happened to Aniya right after she came out of the reactor?"

Roland frowned. "She was dead. Or at least she looked like it. I tried to resuscitate her, but I can't imagine that's what woke her up. She looked completely dead. And even when she came back, it wasn't Aniya. She almost brought the cave down on us, and I had to talk her down. Honestly, I was scared of her."

Kendall frowned. "I have some rudimentary scientific knowledge, enough to achieve an understanding of the reactor and the machine. But this is clearly beyond my expertise, and that of any clinician here in Refuge."

"There is someone else who might be able to help," Gareth said slowly, looking up at Roland.

Roland froze. He should have brought it up himself to avoid suspicion. Of course, it didn't matter anymore, but they didn't know that. He was shocked Gareth had mentioned it at all.

"Well?" Gareth raised an eyebrow. "I know you have strong opinions on this matter, Roland. I thought you would have said something by now."

Nicholas rolled his eyes. "Don't encourage him, Gareth."

"What is he talking about?" Kendall asked.

"The Chancellor," Roland said quickly, covering a crack in his voice with a cough.

Lieutenant Haskill cursed under his breath as Malcolm scoffed, but Kendall just gave a small smile. "Yes, Nicholas mentioned he tried to sell you on some story about how he was Aniya's only hope."

"He knew about her situation," Roland said. "We didn't have to tell him anything, and he already knew. If we had brought it up, he could have lied about it, but he said it first. Just like you, he said Aniya needs to release the energy inside her, but apparently there's a safe way to do it that won't get everyone killed."

Kendall gestured for Roland to continue. "Which is?"

"He didn't say."

Nicholas gave a short laugh, but it came out as more of a wheeze. "He was telling you what you wanted to hear, Roland."

"He didn't know what I wanted to hear," Roland shot back. "We were on the other side of the Web, and we didn't even know what was happening to Aniya. But he knew."

"Did he say anything else?" Kendall asked.

Roland nodded. "He said anything we try to do will only end up hurting her and ourselves."

"Which is true," Corrin said as he bowed his head. "Look at what happened to Tamisra and Xander. And every time our medics have tried to treat her, that light has flared up again and they have to back away."

"We can't trust the Chancellor," Nicholas said. "He's a murderer, a liar."

"You trusted *him* quick enough," Roland retorted, pointing at Kendall.

"Enough," Kendall said, frowning. "I don't believe our old friend knows how to help Aniya, but if he has any useful information, it's worth a try."

"A waste of time," Nicholas said, shaking his head.

Kendall cut him off, holding up a finger. "And if it's all a ruse, it doesn't matter. Capturing him will end the Lightbringers at last. We'll bring him in anyway and finally put a stop to all this."

"He won't go willingly," Gareth said. "He's nothing if not stubborn. We either play by his rules or not at all."

"Then we take him," Corrin said, shrugging. "We were going to hunt him down anyway, and he doesn't have to be willing in order to help us."

Roland shook his head. "If we take him by force, he won't help us."

"He will," Kendall said, smiling. "He won't have a choice. If he won't, I'm sure the information can be pried from him."

A chill ran down Roland's spine at this implication. *Just like you tortured me, Kendall?*

"But how can we hope to take him?" Nicholas asked. "Holendast is nothing like we left it. It's well-stocked and armed to the teeth."

Kendall shrugged. "We took the Hub. Surely we can take Holendast. We don't have a choice, after all. This is what we have to do to bring peace. And if he knows something that can save Aniya, we need to know it too."

"Why?" Roland asked. "She's my sister, she might as well be Gareth's daughter, and she's Nicholas's—whatever. What is she to you? Why do *you* care?"

"It's for the good of the Web," Kendall said. "It's clear that she holds great power."

"There it is," Roland said, rolling his eyes.

Kendall frowned. "I don't know what's going on with her, but she may as well be her very own nuclear reactor. If she dies, what do you think will happen to us? I'm not willing to find out. She poses a danger to all of us like this. We're fighting the Lightbringers to save the Web, but if we don't save Aniya, there may not be any Web left."

Roland folded his arms.

"If I had a little more time," Gareth said, "maybe I could—"

Nicholas cut him off as he let loose a loud moan.

Roland opened his mouth to ask what Nicholas was moaning about but stopped suddenly as he cocked his head. Voices were crying out somewhere above.

"Do you hear that?" Lieutenant Haskill muttered as he stood.

Nicholas tried to stand but faltered and had to catch himself on the table.

As the cries escalated, Roland's eyes widened, and he ran back up the stairs and out of the tower.

A red, pulsing light was coming from the other side of Refuge.

As the light dimmed, its source became apparent. It came from the clinic, which could barely be seen thanks to the blinding red glow that pulsed from within. Another pulse, and the light grew so bright that it completely hid the shack from view.

Roland's heart stopped.

"Aniya."

11

"What do you want?" Aniya asked, clenching her fists. She thrust them against the sides of her head, trying to drive out the Chancellor's voice. "What are you doing in my head?"

"Aniya, I do hope you can hear me, or I fear this is a waste of time."

"Get out!" Aniya shouted, waving her fists around, hoping to make contact with her sworn enemy. There was no sign of his smirking face anywhere in the void, and his voice seemed to come at her from every direction.

The Chancellor soothed his tone. "I know I'm the last person you would think to trust, but it is imperative that you listen to me right now."

"What do you think you're—"

But he cut her off. "I know what it looks like."

Aniya almost shouted again, but he apparently couldn't hear her. Instead, she stood, her arms folded, fuming at the man who had brought so much pain into her life.

"And I will be the first to admit that not all my actions were wise. But I did what I did for the safety of the Web, and now you must do the same."

Her anger boiling over, Aniya shouted again. "My family is dead because of you!" She knew he couldn't hear her, but it felt good to scream at him anyway. As she raised her voice to an all-time high, the pitch black around her flashed an angry red.

The Chancellor's voice grew softer. "Aniya, please calm down. I can't hear you, but the more agitated you grow, the more danger you bring to yourself and those around you. You've been given a great gift, one that is dangerous if you don't know how to use it. And one that certain people would take advantage of, if given the chance. Which is why you must leave the Web as soon as possible. There's a man coming for you. He'll tell you stories, lies. He wants to use you for what he thinks is the greater good, but please believe me when I say that his road will only end in tragedy for you and your loved ones. When you wake up, if you wake up, come find me. I can show you the way."

His voice continued almost lovingly. "You're a smart girl. Resourceful, talented, brave. I truly believe in you. You can make this world a better place, and if you honestly consider your options, you will eventually realize that I am right. You may not believe me now, but you will. I just hope that when you do, it won't be too late."

Aniya folded her arms. As angry as she was with the Chancellor, she was angrier that whatever kept her trapped in this awful state kept her from speaking to the man who had her family killed. She wanted nothing more than to tell him just how much she hated him.

"I don't have much more time, so I'll leave you with a warning. You can't trust anyone except Roland. Everyone else has been blinded by lies, and they will do whatever they think they need to do to serve their own selfish purposes. Roland, for whatever reason, is the only one who seems to have a mind of his own, and as a result, you can trust only him. As for

Nicholas, I fear he is too far gone. You must temper everything he says with a strict level of skepticism."

Now she *knew* not to believe a word the Chancellor said. Nicholas may have played the traitor at one point, but only to help her. If there was anyone she knew she could trust, it was Nicholas.

"It looks like I'm out of time, so just remember what I've said, and when I am proven correct, you'll know where to find me."

With that, the voice went silent, and Aniya was again alone.

She tried to calm herself down, but the more she attempted to clear her mind, the more she found herself focusing on the insane man who had ruined her life and now passed himself off as her friend.

He deserved to die, this much was clear. Forget talking to him. Aniya wished more than anything to wake up so she could kill him herself.

The void twisted and took shape as her imagination took over, and she suddenly found herself in a room alone with the Chancellor. She wrapped her hands around his throat and squeezed as hard as she could.

The Chancellor simply smiled, and Aniya screamed in fury as his grin grew wider.

She ignored the heat that spread over her body as the light flashed wildly, reflecting in the madman's eyes as she crushed his windpipe.

But throughout it all, he only smiled.

Aniya's scream escalated into a banshee's wail, and she raised a fist to begin pummeling her imagined captive, but everything suddenly faded away, and she was alone again.

She looked around, desperate to finish him off. But he was gone.

Pure fury consumed her, and she looked up into the black and let loose a howl of rage.

12

Roland burst through the clinic door and immediately raised a hand to block out the intense red glow. He peeked through his fingers but couldn't see anything. The blinding light pervaded every nook and cranny of the clinic, making it impossible to make out any details.

Intense heat filled the room, making the light look like it was twisting in visible waves and further impairing Roland's vision. But as the pulsing glow dimmed momentarily, he could make out a dark figure standing by Aniya's bedside.

With a running leap, Roland tackled the figure, dragging him to the ground and mounting him.

"Sedate her!" Corrin's voice came from the clinic entrance.

Gareth's burly, panicked voice was the next to rise. "I can't see anything!"

"Hurry." Kendall's voice was calm but firm. "She could take us all out if we don't act quickly."

Roland ignored the voices behind him. Instead, he strained his eyes through the pulsing red light, desperate to identify Aniya's attacker.

"Found it," Gareth said. Footsteps moved across the room. "I can barely see her body. I don't think I'm going to be able to find a vein."

"Do it blind," Kendall said. "We don't have any time."

Seconds later, the red glow slowly shrank and contained itself within Aniya's body. The heat dissipated as well, but it was still uncomfortably warm in the clinic.

Roland rubbed his eyes, and he could finally see. The Chancellor's emotionless face looked back up at him.

A horrible guilt gripped Roland's heart as his eyes flew wide.

This was *not* the plan.

"You lied to me," he hissed quietly. With a grunt, he punched the disgraced dictator in the face, knocking him out.

"How did he get in?" Kendall threw his arms in the air as he raised his voice. "Only a few of us have the entrance codes to Refuge, and we would know if he tried to tamper with the door."

Nicholas finally entered the room, gasping for air. He surveyed the room, and as his eyes landed on Aniya, he stumbled forward, reaching for her bedside.

Corrin placed a hand on his chest, holding him back. "You can't touch her. Not unless you want your hands burned off."

Malcolm pushed Roland aside and dragged the Chancellor away, firmly planting a knee in the dictator's stomach.

"She's red, Doc," Roland said as he stood up and looked at Aniya. "What does that mean?"

Gareth shook his head. "I know as much as you do, probably less. There's—wait a minute," he said, looking closer at Aniya's arm. "There's a second needle mark. Who authorized an injection?"

Roland crouched down next to the Chancellor and searched the pockets of his robe. His heart sank as he pulled out an empty syringe. He thought about hiding it, but there was no point.

"Here," he said, offering the syringe to Gareth as a cold feeling spread over his body. If whatever was in the syringe was harmful, he would never forgive himself.

Gareth took it and frowned. "There's no telling what was inside," he said.

Kendall shook his head. "I'm not sure that's true. We have the equipment to examine the molecular composition on any residue that might be left. We can test it and have the results in a matter of days."

"If we can wait that long," Gareth sighed as he handed the syringe to Kendall, who took it gingerly and placed it in a plastic bag from the drawers along the side of the wall.

Corrin crouched down by the Chancellor's side. "However he got in, he's here now. I guess we don't need to launch an attack after all."

"On the contrary," Kendall said, "now is the perfect time to take back Holendast. Without the Chancellor, they'll be in disarray, unprepared for an attack."

Lieutenant Haskill nodded. "I agree. It was only a matter of time until we made our way to that part of the quadrant anyway. Besides, if it's as stocked as Gareth made it sound, we'd be setting ourselves up quite nicely for the rest of the war. I can have our army there tomorrow."

"I'll take them," Corrin said, standing again. "As long as the Chancellor is in Refuge, I want him under your watch."

Kendall looked from the Chancellor to Corrin. "Do we have any holding cells?"

Corrin nodded. "Where we used to keep the Silvers. Malcolm, would you mind escorting the Chancellor to a cell?"

"With pleasure," Malcolm said, glaring at the unconscious man.

Roland eyed the Chancellor as Malcolm began dragging him away. The man owed Roland some answers.

Kendall stood up. "He's not the Chancellor anymore. He's a criminal. Nothing more. Nicholas, we need to send a message to the rest of the Web. The time of the Lightbringers is over. It's time to rebuild."

PART II

INTERVENTION

13

Kendall closed the cell door and sat down in front of the prisoner.

For almost twenty years, the prisoner had been Kendall's superior. Kendall had to assist and advise on all matters pertaining to the Web, whether they related to his mission or not. It had been quite the challenge to serve such a destructive dictator, helping the madman plan and execute his vision for the underground world while Kendall plotted to overthrow him at the same time.

Now, the man's reign of terror was finally over, and Kendall had no doubt that the Web would be a better place without him.

"So," the prisoner finally said. "I assume you have come to either ask for my help or kill me."

Kendall shrugged. "I have no use for you dead. And I don't believe you have any help to offer me."

"Then why are you here?"

"Because there are those who believe differently, and I want to do my due diligence."

The prisoner nodded. "Roland. I suspect I had quite the impact on the boy."

"Yes," Kendall said. "I'll give you one thing. In all your years as chancellor, you never did lose your touch for manipulating people."

"I often find that manipulation is quite unnecessary. Sometimes, the truth is a very effective motivator."

"The truth? After the hundreds of lies that I helped you craft over the years, you expect me to believe that anything you say is the truth?"

"As you say, *you* helped me craft them. I don't have you anymore, so all I have left is the truth."

Kendall scoffed. "Your silver tongue won't help you here, Noah."

"Might I suggest you listen to what I have to say and then decide for yourself whether or not it is the truth, rather than deciding I must be lying before I even speak my piece?"

"That's the only reason I'm here," Kendall said. "Believe me, I'm more than happy to let you rot in a cell and never see you again."

"I believe you," the prisoner said. "I'm sure you can't wait to move on and become the new chancellor, collect your thirty pieces of silver, complete your betrayal."

"I have no interest in being chancellor, but if that's what he needs me to do, then I will accept that responsibility."

"If the Director didn't promise you an underground world of your own to rule over, what *did* he promise you? What did he say would be your reward for a betrayal that took nearly twenty years to produce fruit?"

"A better world," Kendall said. "You know what it's like out there. You know what it's like, and still you decided to treat Level XVIII as your personal playground. You had people killed, tortured. I had the responsibility and obligation to make the Web a better place, and so I did. That's the difference between me and you. I understand what it means to have an entire world under my care, and I refuse to use it for personal gain."

"How incredibly naïve of you," the prisoner said. "You know how the Director works. Surely you don't think he orchestrated all this for the good of the Web? Perhaps your intentions are right and just. Perhaps all you truly want is for Level XVIII to be a better world. But do you really think that's what he wants?"

"It doesn't matter. I've succeeded. I've made the Web a better place, and that's enough for me. It was always enough for me."

"Just be careful, Kendall. You'll be handing over to him a limitless source of power, an incredible weapon. You'd better be sure that his intentions are as pure as you say yours are."

Kendall narrowed his eyes. "You asked me to hear you out. Are you going to talk or just keep wasting my time?"

The prisoner nodded. "I'll talk. Aniya, as I'm sure you know by now, has been transformed into an incredibly powerful conduit of energy. A living nuclear reactor, if you will. It was science that I theorized nearly twenty years ago, but no one took me seriously. Or at least, I didn't think anyone did."

"Get to something I don't already know, please."

"Well, she was supposed to be self-sustaining. A never-ending cycle of energy production and processing. But something seems to have gone wrong during her creation, and she doesn't function safely like she was meant to. She cannot process her energy herself. Therefore, she needs an outlet. She needs some way to safely release the energy that builds up inside her over time. If she doesn't, she will quite literally overload and cause disastrous harm to anyone around her. I believe she will destroy even herself in the process, but I'm not sure."

Kendall nodded. "We suspected this as well."

"Then you know how important it is that she is helped."

"And you've come here to do that, have you? What was in the syringe you used on her?"

"That served two purposes. First, it stabilized her just long enough for me to communicate with her. Second . . . well, you'll find out when the time comes."

Kendall glared at the prisoner. "The time is now, Noah. You're not in a position to play your mind games anymore. What did you do to her?"

"Nothing, really. Call it a contingency plan should the worst happen. I assure you, my only goal is to help her."

"And how exactly do you plan on doing that?"

"I'm surprised you haven't figured it out by now. It is a solution that will not only save Aniya and those around her, but it will benefit the entire Web."

Kendall stared at the ground.

"Now that such power is contained within Aniya, we no longer need the Citizen Tax. No more relocative servitude. Aniya can safely maintain the reactor all by herself. You're not a foolish man, Kendall. I'm sure this has crossed your mind."

"It doesn't matter," Kendall said, looking back up.

"Why, because the Director wants her for something else? Or because you already have plans for the machine?"

Kendall didn't answer.

"Both, then." The prisoner laughed. "You're no better than I, Kendall. You call me traitor, murderer, yet you plan to do the exact same thing."

"It's not the same thing," Kendall said, punching the ground and creating a small cloud of dust. "You were ruthless, merciless. I will do what has to be done."

"No, you blindly follow the orders of a voice over the radio. If you had any mind for yourself, you would use Aniya to power the Web instead of torturing tens of thousands."

"You would force her to be the Web's energy source without her consent?"

"She's proven herself willing to do it by choice. But if necessary? Yes." The prisoner frowned. "Desperate times, Kendall."

"That." Kendall said, pointing a finger. "That right there is why we removed you."

"Because I am willing to do whatever I must to maintain the Web? We're the same, you see? The only difference between you and me is that I think for myself. I don't need a voice in my ear telling me how to save this world."

Kendall held up a finger. "We have the same purpose, but not the same methods. I understand what it takes to make the world turn. It's the only way. But public executions? Whippings in the streets? There never would have been a war had your methods not been so barbaric. You could have continued on with the same secret under the Citadel and maintained a peaceful Web."

The prisoner shrugged. "Mistakes were made. Regrets were had. It's a waste of time to dwell on the past. All we can do is find a way to move forward. And the only way that guarantees the safety and survival of the Web is the sacrifice of one person who was already willing to give her life for those she loved. I don't see what's so criminal about asking her to do it again. And neither would you if you didn't have the Director whispering—"

"The Director has a plan, for her and for the Underworld."

"He always does, doesn't he? Tell me, what do you think that plan is? I know he didn't tell you. You've always seemed to be a good man, a noble one. Do you really think the Director's intentions are noble? How do you think he plans on saving Aniya? Are you certain he plans on saving her at all? Maybe he just wants to tie up his loose ends. Maybe he wants to use her as a weapon. If you send her to him, there is no promise of her survival, or that of the Web. You may just guarantee your own destruction. I offer you the chance to save her and the entire Web. You would be a fool not to take it."

Kendall stood up. "I would be a fool to trust you."

"Be careful in whom you place your trust, Kendall. I hope you find out who your real friends are before it's too late."

Kendall rapped on the cell door and turned to face the prisoner again. "Big words coming from a man with no friends."

The prisoner smiled as he licked his lips. "I have at least one."

The cell door opened, and Kendall left.

14

Nicholas studied the computer in front of him, impatiently watching a loading bar crawl across the screen.

"Are we ready to transmit, Nicholas?" Kendall asked as he put a stray hair back in its place, studying himself in the mirror.

"Not quite. Still rerouting power from the backup generators."

Kendall turned around, frowning. "Are you sure they wired us in correctly, Malcolm?"

Malcolm, sitting by the wall next to Tamisra, scowled. "Of course. I supervised them myself."

"Good. Let me know when you're ready, Nicholas. I want to start as soon as possible."

"You'll be the first to know," Nicholas said. He looked back at the computer, blinking rapidly as he shook his head. The exhaustion that had plagued him for the last few days was relentless. Even after getting some rest earlier, he was just as tired as he was before he slept, maybe more so.

Kendall picked up a piece of paper and scanned the page. "If I get off topic, don't be afraid to wave me down. The role of the Adviser was perfect for me, working behind the scenes, but public speaking was the Chancellor's gift." He handed the paper to Malcolm, then straightened his tie.

He was no longer in his bland, gray outfit. He was now in a white suit, and it gave Nicholas an unsettling feeling every time he looked at Kendall. It was too much like the Chancellor.

Nicholas checked the connection in the back of the computer for the fifth time. It was equipment that hadn't been used in years, but it seemed to be running fine, if not for a little more latency than he would have liked. He wanted to set up next to the generator, where a power and data line were close and the signal would be at its strongest. But at Kendall's request, they had set up on the ground floor of the Refuge tower, and Salvador's old base had been turned into a nest of computers and wires.

Kendall took a drink of water and cleared his throat. "Are you sure this will reach the entire Web?"

Nicholas nodded. "Every sector's sky ceiling will broadcast every second of it."

"Good. I don't want to repeat this. We'll be using a lot of power from the backup generators. Too much."

Nicholas only nodded again.

"Where is Roland, Tamisra? I thought he'd want to be here."

"He said he wasn't feeling well," Tamisra said.

"That's a shame. History is about to be made."

"Let's get on with it, then," Malcolm said.

The loading bar finally finished, and Nicholas turned to Kendall. "Ready."

Kendall stepped into a square that Nicholas had drawn in the dirt and looked into the camera that rested on a tripod, then at a screen directly behind it. "And this monitor will show exactly what the sectors are seeing?"

Nicholas double-checked the feed. Sure enough, Kendall's face showed clearly on the screen. "Yes, it's all set up."

"Good." Kendall took a deep breath and nodded. "Give me a countdown."

Nicholas turned back to his computer and held up his right hand, counting down on his fingers. "Five, four, three . . ." He let his fingers finish the countdown, and when his count reached zero, he pressed a button on the keyboard.

"Good evening, citizens of the Web." Kendall's smile shone brightly, successfully masking what Nicholas knew was nervous anticipation.

"As you can see, I am not your chancellor. Your chancellor has been removed from office. Many of you have had the misfortune of seeing his dark side. He was willing to manipulate, torture, even kill when he found it necessary. As such, he has been removed, and the Hub has been destroyed. The Chancellor, however, escaped to Holendast, where he tried to rebuild and start over, but we successfully captured him and brought him to justice.

"In the coming weeks, we will be clearing all sectors of Silver Guard that remain loyal to the ex-Chancellor. It will be a peaceful mission, and they will be given the opportunity to join our ranks. If we are met with resistance, we will not hesitate to remove it. With regard to the energy, it is regrettable that the power had to be disabled, but we are working on a plan to supply free energy to the entire Web once again."

Suddenly, the output display went dark.

Kendall looked at Nicholas. "Did we lose the backup generator?"

Nicholas examined the screen, then the computer. Everything was still powered on. There just wasn't any signal. "We've lost access to the transmission."

"How is that possible?"

Nicholas shook his head. "I don't know. It just—"

"Greetings, citizens of the Web."

Nicholas froze. He turned to the output display and was met by the Chancellor's smiling face.

"I thought I would take this opportunity to clear up some misconceptions regarding the state of the Web."

As the Chancellor continued to speak, Kendall pointed at the screen. "How is he doing that?"

Nicholas opened the transmission log and scanned the access logs. His eyes widened as he spotted the telltale signs of a direct line that bypassed the secure feed.

"He hacked into the transmission feed. He's tapped in somewhere directly."

Kendall groaned.

"I don't get it," Malcolm growled. "He wouldn't have the equipment or the knowledge to do this."

"Don't underestimate him," Kendall said. "He's a smart man."

Nicholas searched his mind for any explanation other than the obvious answer, but he eventually gave up and sighed. "Roland. He would have wanted to be here for this. Surely he would have made it even if he's not feeling well."

Kendall's eyebrows shot up. "You really think he would betray us?"

"He wouldn't," Tamisra said, shaking her head firmly.

"It's not any secret that he doesn't like Kendall," Nicholas said. "You tell me, Tamisra. Would you put this past him?"

Tamisra remained quiet.

Meanwhile, the Chancellor continued, "I made mistakes during my time as your chancellor. There is no denying that. Once I've spoken my piece, you can decide for yourselves if you wish to reinstate me as your leader. But before you make any judgments, I feel that you must know all the facts."

Kendall paced back and forth while Nicholas typed away at the computer.

"I was betrayed by my trusted adviser, the man that appeared just before me. However, he did not come up with this plan to overthrow me by himself. He's nothing more than a milquetoast yes-man, one that was sent here on behalf of a higher power."

"Done!" Nicholas pressed a key again, and Kendall's face replaced the Chancellor's on the output display.

Kendall gathered himself and spoke again.

"I deeply apologize for the interruption. It seems that your old chancellor has escaped once again. I assure you that this is not due to incompetence on my behalf. I believe that we have been betrayed."

Nicholas looked toward the door. *Roland, what did you do?*

"In any case, he will soon be found. I implore you, do not listen to him. You know who he was and what he did. A murderer, a liar, a manipulator like him cannot be trusted. Do not deceive yourselves into thinking that anything he says can possibly be true. Your old Chancellor is desperate, hiding now somewhere in the tunnels, clinging to whatever attention he can get. Do not give it to him. His time is over. We—"

The feed switched again.

"Attention? You really think I'm doing this just for attention?" The Chancellor laughed and ran his fingers through his unkempt hair. "If that were indeed my motivation, surely I would have bothered to dress up nicer for you."

Kendall rolled his eyes.

"History, they say, is written by the victors. Kendall has won quite the battle, I will admit. However, he has not yet won the war, and as such, I do think I should have some say in whatever history I live to see."

Kendall turned to Nicholas. "Any updates?"

"He's actively fighting the signal. He has to have help."

Kendall's eyes narrowed. "And you think . . ."

"I told you. Roland doesn't trust you. If he thinks that the Chancellor has a better chance of saving Aniya than you or the Director, I wouldn't put it past him to do whatever it takes."

"But Haskill was watching the Chancellor," Tamisra said. "And he would never disobey orders."

Nicholas shrugged. "Maybe Roland took care of him."

"Where are they?" Kendall asked.

"In the caves somewhere," Nicholas said, examining the screen. "I can't give you an exact location, but if he's tapped in directly, he has to be along our data line somewhere."

Kendall turned to Malcolm. "Trace the wire back through the tunnels until you find them. Take a gun."

"Is that necessary?" Nicholas asked.

"You tell me."

Malcolm nodded. He turned to leave, but Nicholas stood up with a grunt, gently placing a hand on Malcolm's chest.

"Don't hurt Roland. Please."

Malcolm pushed Nicholas's hand out of the way and left.

"Get me back online," Kendall said.

Nicholas sat back down and began typing again. Meanwhile, the Chancellor was still talking.

"I would like to take this opportunity to give my most sincere apologies to the citizens of the Web. I know that many of you suffered beatings at the hands of the Silver Guard and my operative. I do not claim that I was blameless, by any means, but please understand that my operative worked autonomously, and the Silver Guard were given perhaps too much power, often acting without consulting me first. What about the rebels that were executed after the Uprising, you might ask? You would be correct in saying that I did authorize their execution, but it was in order to prevent further war. A war which, if you remember, put the Web at greater risk than I ever did alone. Everything I did, I did to ensure your safety and the survival of what is left of the human race. I didn't—"

The feed switched again.

Kendall wasted no time, speaking quickly. "The safety of the human race? Criminals belong in prison, not lying in a ditch. Murdering anyone who challenges your authority is the work of a traitor to humanity. You would stand before them now and act like a benevolent savior of mankind, but it's too late. People have seen you for what you are. You have lost the moral high ground, as if you ever really had it. The Web suffered enough with you at its helm. It is now time to move on. Citizens of the Web, I propose to you a world where you don't have to live in fear. A world free of dictatorship, murder, where you can live safe and free. You will never see such a world so long as your old chancellor has any power. But if you work with us, we can and will have that world together. That is my promise. That is—"

The Chancellor's face appeared again. "Safe? Free?" His voice was now grating as his volume raised. "You dare promise them that? I don't suppose you've told the sectors how we supplied free power to them all those years. You never told them what we had buried deep inside the Hub, did you? And you were never going to. You know that the only way to restore power is to continue my work. Well, let's see how open they'll be to your precious free world when they find out what you have in store for them."

Kendall spun toward Nicholas. "Get me back. Now."

"But it doesn't matter. You're not going to fix the machine and keep abducting people, right?"

Kendall was silent.

Nicholas narrowed his eyes. "Right?"

It didn't matter. The Chancellor leaned forward until his face filled the screen. "The secret of the oh-so-Glorious Bringers of Light is that we used people."

Kendall turned back to the monitor, horror written on his face.

Even Nicholas felt a sense of dread crawling over his skin. Everything was about to change. The Chancellor was going to tell the entire Web the secret of the Lightbringers. And if the people chose to blame Kendall for it as well, it was going to make their work infinitely more difficult.

The Chancellor continued solemnly, "We used your fathers and sons as living batteries. We used you as a living nuclear reactor to supply power to the entire Web. The Citizen Tax was nothing more than glorified kidnapping for the sole purpose of powering a reactor underneath the Citadel that fed power into the entire Web."

Kendall held his face in his hands.

"And would you like to hear something truly ironic? The man who instigated this horrible tradition, a tradition that I would not have been able to stop even if I wanted to, is the same man who sent Kendall to betray the entire Web and plunge it into darkness once again, robbing you of your precious light, the one good thing you have. He calls himself the Director. You see, he really doesn't care what happens to the Web. You don't matter to him. Any of you. There's more to your world than you realize. There's a dozen other—"

The feed came to an abrupt stop, and Nicholas looked at the screen, expecting it to have switched back. But the Chancellor's face was still on the screen, frozen.

"What happened?" Kendall asked.

Nicholas fiddled with the wires in the back of the monitor, but the image of the Chancellor remained, his mouth hanging open and his eyes staring straight ahead.

He was convinced that the feed froze somehow, but the Chancellor suddenly blinked.

Then, blood started to trickle out of his open mouth.

The Chancellor turned around slowly, revealing a six-inch blade embedded between his shoulder blades.

Then, a dark figure appeared from the shadows behind the Chancellor and vaulted over his shoulders, landing between him and the camera. The shadow pulled the knife from the Chancellor's back and spun him around to face the camera once again.

A gloved hand plunged the blade into the Chancellor's belly, then almost instantly pulled it out and drew it swiftly across his throat.

Blood gushed from the Chancellor's neck, and he plummeted to the ground, dead.

15

"No!" Roland fell to his knees, dropping the camera from his hand. The Chancellor was sprawled out on the ground, staring blankly up at the cave ceiling, his mouth still hanging open.

A dark figure stood over the dead man, looking back at Roland.

Roland stared back, his grief mixing with anger.

It was a woman, but barely so. In fact, she couldn't have been much older than Roland. But her black bodysuit highlighted her matured feminine features, the spandex material clinging tightly to her body.

Roland quickly looked back up at the girl's face, and she smiled as she wiped blood off her knife and placed it in a sheath on her back.

"I don't know much about the guy," she said, "but I don't think he was worth crying over."

Roland stood up, clenching his fists. "You idiot! He was the only one who could have saved Aniya. Whoever you are, you just killed her last chance."

The girl was seemingly undisturbed by Roland's nose just

an inch away. The remnants of her smile still lingered on her lips. "I had my orders."

"Let me guess. Kendall?"

She shrugged. "Sure."

"The Director, then?"

The girl shrugged again as her smile grew wider.

Roland took a deep breath. "It's all the same. Both of them, just trying to control the Web with no regard for the people who live in it." He squared his shoulders and glared at the girl. "And I've had just about enough of it."

The girl frowned. "Careful there, boy. That sounded like a threat to me."

"And what if it was?"

She smirked. "You don't want to find out."

"Who are you?"

"I'm an operative. I believe you've met one of my kind before, from what I've been told."

"The murderous animal who killed my parents?"

"Sounds like him. What's your name?" she asked, drumming her fingers on his chest.

"Roland. Probably no point in asking what yours is."

"Correct you are. Don't even have one. Some call me Zeta, but you can call me whatever you like."

Roland glared at her. "I doubt you want me to do that, you wretched b—"

"Roland."

He turned to see Malcolm standing behind him in the tunnel, staring at the Chancellor.

"What have you done?"

"Don't look at me." Roland pointed at Zeta. "She killed him. I didn't do anything."

"No," Malcolm said. "You're just the one who helped him escape and put us all at risk. You're probably the one who got him inside Refuge to begin with. Do you have any idea how much danger you've put us in?"

Roland bristled. "I brought him to Refuge so he could help Aniya. He was the only one who could have saved her." He glared at Zeta again. "And now he's dead."

"Forget Aniya," Malcolm said. "You put our entire community at risk. If you had just waited, Kendall would have brought him back here himself."

"As you can see," Roland said, pointing at the dead man, "Kendall was never going to let him live. Why do you trust him? He's lying to us."

Malcolm shook his head. "It's hard to take anything you say seriously when you've betrayed all of Refuge. Where's Haskill?"

"Back at the cells. I knocked him out. He's fine."

"You assaulted a lieutenant? I knew they were wrong to trust you. Come with me. I'm taking you back to Refuge." Malcolm looked at Zeta. "And whoever you are, I assume you're with Kendall? I'm sure he'll want to talk to you too."

The girl only nodded.

Resigned, Roland sighed and let his arms fall limp. "Fine. It doesn't matter anymore anyway. Aniya is going to die, and there's nothing we can do about it."

Malcolm escorted the group back into Refuge, leaving the Chancellor's body behind.

The inhabitants of the hidden city had come to accept Roland as one of their own, and so they all smiled and waved at him as he walked by, unaware of his betrayal. He returned their waves, a small pang of guilt prodding him with each face he saw. With no sky ceiling to show them what had just happened, Refuge knew nothing of Roland's betrayal.

Malcolm led them to the Refuge tower, where Kendall had been pacing. When they entered, he stopped and glared at the group. Behind him, Nicholas looked at Roland with disappointment, and Tamisra was biting her lip, shaking her head.

"What did you think you were doing?" Kendall demanded.

Roland put his hands on his hips. "Whatever it took to save my sister."

"Not you. Shut up," Kendall said, spite dripping from his words. He pointed his finger at Zeta. "*You.* You murdered a man in front of the entire Web. The man who's been leading them for decades. Do you have any idea what kind of panic that had to have caused? We're in the middle of a war."

"Not anymore," the assassin said, smirking. "I think I took care of that problem for you."

"Even if we determined that he should die for his crimes, it didn't have to be like that."

"You were going to kill him anyway," Roland said to Kendall. "You were going to kill the one person who could save my sister."

"Shut up," Kendall said again. "We're in a very delicate situation right now, Zeta. The Web is without power, and we're trying to restore order, not sow panic among the people. I did my best to ease the situation as soon as I was in control of the feed again, but I don't know how well it worked."

Zeta shrugged. "Not my problem."

"But it is your problem. You were sent here to serve me, and I—"

"Wrong," she said coldly. "I was sent here at the order of the Director with very specific instructions. And if you get in my way of carrying them out, believe me when I say that I don't have a problem killing you either."

Roland rolled his eyes. "You're all the same, aren't you? Killing whoever gets in your way."

This time, the command came from Zeta. "Shut up."

"We can discuss this later," Kendall said. "I'm not going to get in your way, but the situation is more complicated than you might think. I'll leave it at that for now, but I'll explain later."

Zeta hesitated but nodded.

Roland threw his hands in the air. "Does no one care

about Aniya anymore? She's about to blow up and probably take us out with her, and no one is interested in saving her?"

Kendall and Zeta turned to him and spoke in unison. "*Shut up!*"

Kendall advanced toward Roland, continuing, "We will do whatever we can to save Aniya and protect the Web. The Director has a plan, and I need you to trust us. Whatever safety the Chancellor promised you, it was never a sure thing. In the meantime, I will have to detain you until we restore peace and a sense of normalcy to the Web. This is a very critical time, and we have to know that we can trust the people who claim to be on our side."

After staring at him for several seconds, Roland nodded. He was out of ideas. With the Chancellor dead, he had no idea how to save Aniya. As much as he hated it, everything was in Kendall's hands now.

"I understand. Just please, find some way to help my sister. That's all I care about."

Kendall sighed. "I know. I promise you, I'll do everything I can. I know you don't trust me, and I wish you did, but I am a man of my word."

Nicholas stood up slowly, grabbing his chair for support. "I'll make sure of it, Roland. You know I love her. I'll make sure she gets help one way or another."

"Me too," Tamisra said.

Roland nodded again.

"Malcolm?" Kendall said, gesturing toward Roland.

"Can I have a minute?" Roland asked.

Malcolm shook his head, but Kendall held up a hand. "You have two."

Roland led Tamisra just outside the tower. Malcolm followed but kept his distance, stopping in the doorway to watch them.

"I'm sorry, Tami," Roland whispered. "I did what I had—"

"Do you really trust Kendall to help Aniya?" Tamisra hissed. "Just like that? If you're right, he had us tortured. He—"

"I know. I don't trust him in the least. We probably don't have a lot of time, but remember what we talked about?"

Tamisra nodded.

"We may not have another chance. Wait until he's in one of his meetings. Then, you know what to do."

"I'll find out the truth."

"Be careful, Tami. And no matter what you find out, don't hurt him. If he can fix things with the Web right now, we might as well let him. Besides, we're going to need more than just the two of us if it turns out that Kendall needs to be dealt with."

"I'll wait. But Roland, if he had us tortured, I'm not going to hurt him. I'm going to kill him."

16

That evening, Tamisra quietly slipped into the Refuge tower, closing the door behind her. It was once her home, the huge shack that she and her father had shared her whole life. Neither of them enjoyed sleeping in the large tent that was just a half-mile away, but the tent was all Tamisra had now, ever since Kendall took up residence in Refuge and declared his need for a command center.

But if what Roland had said was true, if Kendall couldn't be trusted, Tamisra wondered if she had given up her childhood home to the man who had kidnapped and tortured her.

She made her way upstairs. The war room may have been in the basement, but Tamisra had been in there enough to know that there was no place to hide any sensitive information.

Kendall had made his home on the second floor, and that's where Tamisra was headed.

Each floor consisted of only one room, so when she stepped off the stairs, she was already inside what Kendall had made his bedroom. She was grateful for the building's simple design, since Kendall probably would have locked his room up tight otherwise.

It was a simple room. A bed in the corner, a map of the Web on the far wall, a closet just on the other side, shelves on the adjacent wall with dirty dishes sitting on top, and in the nearby corner, what looked like a filing cabinet. If she was going to find any damning evidence, it would be in there.

Tamisra approached the cabinet and tugged on the handle.

Locked.

She didn't really expect it to be unlocked, and normally it wouldn't be a problem, but with her hands still bandaged, she wouldn't be able to pick the lock.

Tamisra grimaced and examined her hands. Above a layer of gel mixed with herbs, bandages were wrapped tightly around her hand and around each finger. The new bandages Gareth had applied were formfitting, but it wasn't enough for something as dexterous as picking a lock. She would have to force her way in, a method that would certainly leave evidence.

She shrugged. Kendall wouldn't be able to find out who had trespassed in his room. Besides, if Roland was right, it wouldn't matter.

Tamisra took a knife from the dirty dishes on the shelf and pried it beneath the first drawer, leaning hard into it. But it wasn't enough to force the drawer open. She began striking the handle of the knife with a closed fist, but she winced as a stinging sensation shot up her arm.

The painkillers were wearing off.

Awkwardly, she raised her elbow and bashed it down on the handle of the knife, managing enough force that she was able to break open the drawer on the fourth try.

Inside were hundreds, if not thousands of papers, some of them labeled, some of them not. She sighed and began rifling through the documents, a task considerably difficult thanks to her bandaged fingers.

As Tamisra went through the papers, she quickly scanned

their contents, hoping that something would stand out to her, but most of it was either scientific or military jargon that meant nothing to her. She groaned in frustration and grabbed the knife again for the second drawer. Spurned on by annoyance and impatience, she was able to break into this drawer on her first attempt, and she began searching through the documents.

These papers, to Tamisra, may as well have been identical to the first set. Some formulas here, some medical reports there. Nothing that seemed of any use to Tamisra. She was about to work on the third drawer when she came across a folder that had just three words on the cover:

THE PHOENIX MANDATE

Frowning, Tamisra took the folder and opened it to find a complete profile of her boyfriend's sister, Annelise "Aniya" Lyons, complete with her picture clipped to the front page.

She turned to the second page. It was another data sheet, filled top to bottom with a bunch of letters that seemed to repeat. Nothing obviously special on this page except some highlighted sections.

She continued through the folder until she came to a page with legible sentences. The top of the page read "automated transcript," and Tamisra scanned its contents.

As she read, her eyes grew wide. Forget Roland's suspicions. The truth was far worse.

"If you wanted to know something, you could have just asked."

Tamisra dropped the file, and papers flew out of the folder. She spun around to see Kendall in the doorway, his arms folded.

"Most of my work here is done. Secrecy doesn't matter as much anymore."

"You knew," Tamisra said softly in disbelief. "You knew what was going to happen to Aniya."

Kendall winced and rocked his hand back and forth. "More or less. I didn't know that she was going to survive. The Director hid that from me."

"Who is the Director?"

"I think you already know. Our benefactor, the man behind the curtain, the one ultimately responsible for Aniya's survival and the liberation of the Web. You should be grateful."

Tamisra frowned, her eyes narrowing. "Grateful? After what you did?"

"What I did?" Kendall raised his eyebrows. "What I did was assist Aniya in overthrowing the Chancellor. What I did was implement a plan that led to the destruction of the Hub and the horrible machine that supplied its power. What I did was save you from the hand of a murderous dictator."

"Murderous? You of all people think you can accuse him after what you did?" Tamisra snarled and leapt at Kendall's chest, tackling him as she whipped a knife from a sheath at her side. She brought the blade to Kendall's throat and tickled his skin. "You used me. You used me and my father."

Kendall simply smiled. "Heard that, did you? I know that's not in the file you were just reading. Did the Chancellor tell you that? You should know by now that he can't be trusted."

"But you did it, didn't you? You took me and tortured me to bait my father into a fight just so your plan would work."

Kendall said nothing.

"Admit it," she said, digging the knife slowly into his skin, drawing blood. "You said that secrets don't matter anymore. So tell me. Tell me, or I'll cut your throat. You should know me well enough by now to know that I'll do it."

His smile remained, unmoving. However, he finally sighed. "I did."

Tamisra uttered a low growl. Tears begin to spill from her eyes, and Kendall winced as they slid over his open wounds.

"My father came for me," she said, her voice trembling. "He died in the Citadel because of you."

Kendall shook his head very slightly, pressing up against the knife. "Your father didn't step foot in the Citadel until after you were delivered safely to the border of the Hub. He came to talk to the Chancellor."

"Because he thought the Chancellor was the one who took me. If he had known it was you, you wouldn't be alive right now, I can promise you that."

Kendall smiled again. "No, I suspect I wouldn't be. You have every right to kill me. I know that. But I ask that you trust me. I ask—"

Tamisra laughed shrilly. The knife shook in her hands and dug deeper into Kendall's skin. "Trust you? You electrocuted me. You—"

"Technically, electrocution implies death. I only—"

"Shut up!" Tamisra screamed, hurting her own ears. "You electrocuted me and hung me by my toes. I would have died if the Chancellor didn't let us go."

"I never would have let you die. I needed your cooperation to—"

"My cooperation. That's all you do, isn't it? You use people. You used Nicholas, you used Aniya, and you used me. Forget it. You're done. You're finished. And when I'm through with you, there won't be—"

"Tamisra, what are you doing?"

She looked up to see Nicholas standing by the stairs. She grinned through her tears. "Oh look, your puppet came to save you."

Nicholas slowly advanced, his arms stretched out. "Tamisra . . ."

"Don't come any closer, or I'll paint the floors with his blood."

Nicholas froze. "I know what he did."

Tamisra's mouth slowly dropped open. "You knew he kidnapped me and you didn't tell me?"

Nicholas's eyes flew open. "He did *what?*"

"He's not as much of a puppet as you may think," Kendall said. "There are some things that he still doesn't know."

"Well," Tamisra said with a teary chuckle, "he knows now."

Despite her warning, Nicholas took another step. "I know that he used Aniya. I know that—"

"And you're okay with that?" Tamisra exclaimed in disbelief. To read it in the folder was one thing. To hear it come out of Nicholas's mouth was another. "He didn't know that Aniya was going to live until afterward. He thought she was supposed to die. And for all *you* knew, that's exactly what was going to happen. You were leading her to her death, and you knew it. It's a good thing your boss man had other plans."

"Aniya was supposed to live?" Nicholas frowned.

Kendall spoke slowly. "Like she said, I didn't know until after. But yes, it was the Director's plan for her to live."

"But you thought she was going to die," Tamisra said, glaring at Kendall, "and you let her step into that machine anyway." She looked up at Nicholas accusingly. "You knew it too."

Nicholas bowed his head. "Yes, I knew."

"I thought you loved her."

"I do."

Tamisra shook her head. "No you don't. There's no way you would trick her like that and get her killed if you truly loved her. You're just as bad as Kendall, using people in the name of a plan." She pushed the knife down on Kendall's throat, now pressing the flat of the blade against his Adam's apple. "Your stupid plan!" she screamed.

Nicholas took another step forward and winced as a pained sigh escaped his lips. "She had a choice. She didn't have to do it. She could have chosen to leave the Hub then and there. Instead, she chose to give her life for the Web. No one was ever going to force her to die."

"I'm not so sure about that," Tamisra said. "I don't know much about this Director, but I don't think he would have liked his plan being foiled." She looked down at Kendall. "He would have sent someone to trick Aniya into stepping into that machine, right?"

Kendall remained silent.

"Right?" Tamisra moved the knife out of the way and squeezed Kendall's throat with her other hand.

"Yes," Kendall croaked. "Probably."

Tamisra relaxed and sat up. She shook her head. "We trusted you. Aniya trusted you. And for some strange reason," she said, pointing the knife at Nicholas, "you still trust him, don't you?"

"We need him," he said, his words shaky. "At least for now. When the war is over, when things are as normal as they can be, we can hold him accountable for what he's done. But we need him right now."

"I refuse to believe that. Keeping him alive only puts us at risk. I say we put him on trial *now*. It's what my father would have done."

"Your father knew the plan," Kendall said. "Granted, he didn't know that I was going to kidnap you to force him out of hiding, but he knew everything else. Why else do you think—"

"No." Tamisra shook her head fiercely. "He never would have agreed to that. If he knew that you had thousands of people underneath the Citadel, slaves to your machine—"

"He knew. He knew eighteen years ago. We tried to stop it then, together. It was never supposed to go this far. We tried, and we failed. But it didn't matter. Aniya was what the Director was after all along."

Nicholas shook his head. "It was always going to be her?"

"It was always going to be her. And now, the Hub is in

ruins, the Citadel is destroyed, and the Chancellor is dead. It's all over now, thanks to her. And she's alive. You're alive. I'm sorry it happened the way that it did, but I only did what I thought had to be done. I will accept the consequences for it all when the time comes, but there is still work to be done. I only ask that you let me finish what we started."

"If Aniya was supposed to live, the Director still has some use for her, doesn't he?" Tamisra nodded at the file cabinet. "He wants you to bring her for examination, according to that folder. If we let you live, then you'll send Aniya to be with him."

"I have to," Kendall said. Before Tamisra could place the knife back on his neck, he held out his hands. "I don't know how to save her. I truly don't. This was always the Director's plan, and he never told me much. Only what I needed to know at the time. But I do know this much. If we let Aniya continue on like this, she will die. There's no doubt in my mind about that. And when she expires, she will take this entire civilization with her. At least Refuge, and in my estimation, many of the sectors. Possibly the entire Web. It's in her best interest and all of ours that she is brought before the Director. Please believe me. It's the only way I know to save Aniya."

Tamisra looked up at Nicholas.

Nicholas shrugged. "I don't see any other way. I don't like it anymore than you do, but none of us, not even Gareth, have any idea how to save her."

Tamisra sat atop Kendall for several seconds, simply shaking her head back and forth. Finally, she slipped off and to the side, letting the knife fall to the floor as Kendall slowly sat up.

Nicholas picked up the knife and placed it on the table. He stepped toward Tamisra with a visible limp. "If you don't trust Kendall, then trust me, Tamisra. I know you may not think so, but I really do love Aniya. At the end of it all, I lost my nerve. I couldn't go through with it, and I didn't want to see her die. I went down there to try to talk her out of it. I tried telling her that she didn't have to do it. She got in the tank anyway, and I got in with her to keep her awake so it would all work and she wouldn't die for nothing. I was ready to die with her because I love her."

Nicholas reached a hand down to Tamisra, who stared at the offered help for a second. Finally, she reached up and took his hand, but Nicholas made no move to pull her up.

Instead, he looked down at her with a vacant stare.

"Nicholas?" Tamisra frowned.

His hand slipped away from hers, made easy by the sweat that quickly covered his skin.

Nicholas blinked twice as the veins in his face slowly became defined, red tendrils of blood that spread over his skin. He opened his mouth and let out a wheeze, and when his breath ran out, he toppled over and crashed to the floor.

17

"Aniya."

The voice drifted across the void again, pricking Aniya's ears.

It had been quiet since the Chancellor's attack. Aniya had not seen the Stranger or the Shadow since his intrusion, and the surrounding void was all she had.

"Aniya."

She curled her fists in frustration. It was the Stranger, the soothing, masculine voice that used to warm her heart. It repeated her name now in a friendly, almost inviting manner, but she had grown tired of its constant nagging, with no way to find out what it was.

"Who are you?"

The voice simply responded, "Aniya."

Aniya rolled her eyes. "Is that the only word you know?"

In the distant black, a small red light appeared.

"Aniya," the Stranger said again, whispering.

"You couldn't have popped up a little closer?" Aniya grumbled and walked toward the light. The surface beneath her feet was nonexistent, but the world around her knew she was walking, and it brought the light to her slowly.

"Aniya," the voice came again, this time louder.

"Shut up, I'm coming." Aniya began to pick up the pace.

Then, in an instant, the light was in front of her. It was a humanoid shape, standing before her unmoving.

"Who are you?"

"Open your eyes."

The revelation that this Stranger could say something other than her name was lost on Aniya. Instead, she threw her hands in the air as her frustration escalated. "What are you talking about? My eyes are open."

Without a word, the phantom of light raised its finger and pointed directly between Aniya's eyes.

Then, the Stranger touched her forehead, and a red flash seared her vision. Her eyesight cleared, and her heart leapt. Now she knew why the voice was so familiar. She understood why, despite its ethereal quality, the voice was a warm beckoning, calling her home.

The specter was gone, and in its place stood her older brother that had given his life to save her.

"William."

18

Nicholas's eyes drifted open, almost of their own volition. Gareth was looking down at him, his face grim.

"Welcome back, Nicholas."

Nicholas tried to sit up, but found it impossible. He was, however, able to look around at his surroundings.

He was resting on a cot in the clinic, across the room from Aniya. She still glowed red with light that flooded the room and painted it a somber setting.

"What happened?"

Gareth shook his head. "You're dying, Nicholas. Your vitals have slowed to a crawl."

"Dying?"

"I had Gareth inject you with adrenaline so we could speak." Kendall's voice came from the other side of the room. Nicholas turned to see him sitting at a table across from Lieutenant Haskill, his expression downcast. "There's an important conversation we must have."

Gareth looked away. "It was enough adrenaline to wake up a hibernating mole, but you're still barely moving. To say this is not a good sign is quite the understatement." He sighed deeply. "It doesn't seem like you're able to synthesize energy, and as soon as you run out of whatever you have left, you'll simply cease to live."

Nicholas looked around the clinic. Tamisra was sitting against the far wall, eying him with pursed lips. Thankfully, there was no sign of Malcolm. However, Corrin was also missing, and given what Tamisra had just uncovered about Kendall, Nicholas was uncomfortable continuing without another authority figure present.

"Shouldn't we wait for Corrin?"

Kendall shook his head. "We can't wait for him to return from the siege on Holendast. Besides, he and his son are too emotionally compromised to take part in this particular discussion."

Tamisra growled. "Are you going to keep talking about talking, or are you going to get on with it already?"

"Yes, thank you," Kendall said. "Nicholas, as you know, the Director claims that he can save Aniya. I understand that some of you have qualms about trusting him, but we no longer have a choice. The only other person who *might* have been able to help is dead." He glared at Zeta. "We've run out of options, and it's time to act."

Nicholas nodded. "I agree. If there's even the slightest chance that the Director can help her, we have to take it."

"You'll just trust anyone, won't you?" Tamisra sneered. "I didn't think I could lose any more respect for you, but I guess you're full of surprises today."

Lieutenant Haskill frowned at Tamisra before turning to Kendall. "Our distrust for your superior aside, how do you suggest we move Aniya? We were able to get her back here after Ravelta with some discomfort, but ever since the Chancellor, it's been impossible to get near her."

Kendall nodded. "The Director has a solution for that as well, and I ask that you hear me out." He took a deep breath. "She has to die."

Nicholas looked up, his eyes wide.

But before he could speak, Kendall held up his hand. "Temporarily. Do you remember when we first brought you back from the Hub? She was practically dead. We were able to resuscitate her, and the Director plans to do just that again. If we can stop her heart—"

Tamisra threw her hands in the air. "You want to kill her? Just like that? Good luck getting any of us to agree to that. Besides, you said it yourself. If she dies, she takes out all of Refuge."

Kendall made a calming motion with his hands. "If we terminate her peacefully, she should stay stable long enough for us to move her."

Gareth spoke up. "And he's really making it seem much worse than it really is. We would be stopping her heart, shutting down normal body functions—"

"So, killing her," Nicholas interrupted.

"If Aniya dies peacefully, the energy dies as well," Kendall said. "I've been assured of that. Of course, when we resuscitate her, I suspect that it will come back in full force, but the Director is prepared for this. You must understand. If we don't do something about this now, all of Refuge will be destroyed, maybe even the entire Web."

Gareth placed a hand on Nicholas's shoulder. "I've thought about this time and time again. There truly is no other option."

"It sounds like you've already made up your minds," Nicholas said, folding his arms. "Why did you even bother waking me up?"

Kendall spoke softly. "Out of all of us, you are closest to Aniya. You would know what she would want to do. She trusts you. So whatever you decide, we will trust your judgment."

"So if I decide that we do nothing, then Aniya stays here and poses a threat to Refuge?" Nicholas shook his head. "That doesn't sound like much of a decision."

Kendall gave a soft smile. "Not exactly. Should you decide

to do nothing, we will evacuate Refuge and travel to the farthest reaches of the Web. That way, we have some chance of survival. Despite what your friend Roland thinks, I'm not a monster."

"And what makes you think I can decide this? If this doesn't work, if she doesn't make it . . ." Nicholas looked back over at Aniya. "I already led her to her death once. Sure, she made the choice in the end, but I paved the way. And now you want me to decide for her whether she lives or dies without ever giving her a choice?"

Gareth sighed. "You're deciding whether we *all* live or die. Aniya is an amazing girl, and I know you love her, but Salvador fostered this community for almost twenty years, rebuilding and creating a sustainable society after a terrible war. If they die now just as we win the Web back for them, all of his work was for nothing."

Nicholas closed his eyes. After the Hub, he'd sworn never to put himself in this position again. He thought this was all behind him.

Sacrificing Aniya meant saving the Web, just like before, but this time, a decision to do nothing meant the possible deaths of hundreds of thousands.

And then Nicholas realized who else was missing from the room.

Zeta, the assassin who had killed the Chancellor and seemed determined to take Aniya to the Director. If Nicholas decided to do nothing, surely she wouldn't just let that go without having something to say. She might even take matters into her own hands. And her methods would surely not be as gentle as Kendall and Gareth's.

There was no winning move. At least this way, he would have some control over the outcome. He opened his eyes and nodded.

"Do it."

Kendall stood up and bowed his head. "Thank you,

Nicholas. I promise that I will do everything I can to ensure her safe return."

"Just give me a few minutes with her."

Kendall hesitated but left the clinic, Tamisra and Lieutenant Haskill right behind him.

Gareth wheeled Nicholas's bed over to Aniya's side.

"Remember, you can't touch her," he warned before turning and leaving the clinic.

When the room was empty, Nicholas placed his hand on Aniya's bed, comforted by the warmth coming from her body and entranced by the crystal that hung around her neck. Apparently, Gareth had tried to remove it, but it shocked him when he tried to touch it. Now, it lay on her chest, sparkling with a blood-red light that danced on the ceiling of the clinic.

He took a deep breath, not sure where to begin. Finally, he just started speaking, uttering the first words that came to his mind.

"It was never supposed to be like this. You have to know that. When we left the Hub, I thought it was all over. I couldn't have been happier. I thought we could go back to normal. I thought . . . I thought you would forgive me when I finally told you everything. I kept putting it off because I always thought there would be a better time, but I guess I was wrong. Now it's too late. Wherever you are, if you can hear me, I'm sorry. I love you, and I'm sorry. I hope one day I get the chance to tell it to you in person."

Nicholas looked back up and tried to read a reaction from Aniya's face, but she remained steady.

"If you can hear me at all, give me a sign."

Nothing.

Behind Nicholas, the door creaked open.

"Are you ready?"

Nicholas didn't react to Gareth's voice, simply staring at his best friend and love.

"Nicholas, it's time."

This was it. Aniya would die all over again, once again thanks to his direct involvement. Nicholas wondered if his role in her life was forever cursed, limited to deciding whether she live or die, and never being the one she loved.

The warmth emanating from her body at least gave Nicholas some peace, even though it heralded impending doom. It reminded him of the passionate girl he had always known, a true friend.

Nicholas yearned for her touch. Even as friends, the touch of her hand had always provided a kind of home to him, a constant he could always count on, even in the darkest of times.

And this was surely the darkest of times.

Nicholas let his hand creep closer to Aniya's body. He knew the pain that waited for him if he touched her skin, but the warmth that enveloped his hand as he drew closer only filled him with an ever-growing sense of peace. And if he was about to die anyway, maybe there wasn't any harm in it.

"Nicholas . . ." Gareth cautioned, stepping forward.

As his hand drew ever closer, the warmth began to grow painful. If it was physically painful, Nicholas didn't know it. No, this pain was the simple fact that he was inches away from the girl he loved, yet he knew in his heart that he was the furthest he had ever been from her.

Finally, Nicholas could take it no longer. With one dart of his hand, he latched on to hers, crying out as an incredible heat began to travel up his arm.

"Nicholas, no!"

Out of the corner of his eye, Nicholas saw Gareth leap forward and attempt to pull his hand away from her, but as the doctor's hand grazed Aniya's skin, a crackle of electricity split the air, and Gareth flew backward into the wall.

The warmth from Aniya's body spread through Nicholas, and he began to burn.

19

"William?" Aniya's heart pounded. Surely this couldn't be real. She leapt forward and wrapped her arms around her brother. Instantly, her soul flooded with the most bizarre mixture of emotion. Her greatest joy and most awful pain manifested themselves in an instant, and Aniya let William go. For a split second, she thought she saw something in the distance.

She took a deep breath. This was a strange place, and she couldn't wait to get out. If she ever could, that is.

"What are you doing here?"

Her brother shrugged. "The same as you. I'm trapped."

Aniya examined him. He looked exactly the same as when she had last seen him, ravaged by three years of slavery in the machine, aged decades.

A twenty-one-year-old in a sixty-year-old's body.

"But you're dead."

"Yeah, I gathered." William grinned. "I don't mean to eavesdrop, but I can't help it."

"What do you mean?"

"Everything you see, I see. We all see it."

"We?"

He nodded. "Everyone who was inside the machine."

Aniya's head spun, and she looked around. They were alone. No sign of any other phantoms like William, and no sign of the Shadow. "How did you get here?"

"I'm not entirely sure how exactly it happened, but when you used the machine beneath the Citadel to destroy the reactor, I woke up here, in your head. From what I understand, you took in the energy of everyone hooked up to the machine."

"But you weren't hooked up to the machine." Aniya frowned. "You were outside."

William shrugged. "Yeah, I'm not sure on that part. I don't even remember that happening, though I've heard you and Roland talking about it. The last thing I remember from the real world is stepping into the machine for the second time, when Kendall tried to use me to take out the reactor. Anything that's happened after that I've learned from listening to you and wandering around in your subconscious. My guess is that the machine remembered me somehow."

"So it kept a copy of you?"

"I don't know," William said. "Like I said, I'm just guessing. I don't really know much more than you do."

"So the voices that I hear, those are all actual people?"

William nodded. "Most of them. There's one of them I'm still not sure about."

"The Shadow," Aniya said as she looked over her shoulder. It had to be the voice William was talking about. A chill ran down her spine just thinking about the phantom that had been taunting her.

Another nod. "Yeah, I have no idea who that is. But you're not the only one who's heard her. She talked to me while I was in the machine too."

"So it *is* a woman?"

"Sure sounds like it. I was getting real annoyed with her

blocking us from talking to each other. I'm sure it won't be long before she shows up again."

Aniya looked around again but saw nothing. "And the rest of them are people who were trapped in the machine with you? Why haven't any of them come to talk to me like you are now?"

"Well, none of them actually know you. Besides, I'm not sure they have the same physical connection as us. You're my sister, and you did take my pod, after all, the one I was in for three years."

"Makes sense, at least as much as it can." Aniya bowed her head as she said the words she had longed to say to her brother for the last several weeks. "I'm sorry you died, William. I did everything I could to save you."

"I know. And I'm not sorry. As I understand it, I died to save you, and you apparently saved the entire Web. It's a small price to pay."

"It's still too much."

Aniya was overcome with guilt, and she found herself stepping forward again to hug her brother, forgetting for a moment what had happened the last time. She threw her arms around him before she could even think, and once again the emotions came racing back. Tears flowed this time as love, hatred, peace, and anguish overwhelmed her.

Drawing no comfort from the hug, she released William and stepped back. This time, the figure standing over his shoulder in the distance was clear.

It was Xander, the boy she had killed in Ravelta. He was staring down at his blackened hands as he wept. He looked back up at her with fire where his eyes should have been.

She blinked and he was gone, but so was William.

An instant later, William was back.

Aniya looked around as she wiped her eyes. "What was that?"

"What was what?"

"You vanished."

"I did?"

The world began to shake around Aniya as the void lit up with flashes of red light.

Aniya turned to William. "Are you doing this?"

William shook his head.

Red light shone out of Aniya's fingertips, like lasers firing into the distance. As the world shook, Aniya began to drift upward while her brother remained below.

"Don't leave me!" Aniya shouted down.

"I'm not going anywhere."

Aniya's ascent quickened, and William grew small in the distance.

"No!" she screamed.

William's voice came back from below, faint now. "I'll be right here. You know where to find me."

Then his light blinked out, and Aniya was alone in the black again.

Her body began to convulse as the light pouring from her fingertips turned to tendrils that turned back on her and ran over her body in a swirling cyclone of light.

Something pulled at her in every direction, but rather than splitting apart, she felt herself expanding. As the surrounding glow began to turn white, Aniya let out a guttural scream as light flooded from every orifice, white beams shooting from her body in every direction. Details started to take shape around her.

Nicholas's face appeared before her, and Aniya froze. Her love was right in front of her, and she knew it was no apparition. Yet somewhere in the void behind was her brother, and she knew there was no guarantee she would ever see him again.

Aniya turned to dive back into the void, but with a sudden surge of energy, she was yanked upward as the black disappeared.

The void was gone, and she was awake.

20

Nicholas's body was burning.

At least, that's what it felt like. As he opened his eyes, he noticed that his flesh remained unscathed, and no flames licked his body. The burning sensation, however, was clear and very real. The heat from Aniya's body now poured into him at full force, and Nicholas's vision began to clear as strength poured back into his body.

Beams of light shot across Aniya's body, starting from her heart, racing down her arm, and into Nicholas, each one giving off a small electrical shock that buzzed throughout his entire body.

Behind him, the door flew open, and Kendall, Tamisra, and the lieutenant rushed inside. Tamisra and Haskill knelt by Gareth's unconscious body, but Kendall rushed to Nicholas's bedside, his gaze alternating between him and Aniya.

"What's going on?" Kendall's eyes widened. "What are you doing? You know she—" As he stretched forth his hand, a tendril of red light shot from Aniya's chest and wrapped its fingers around Kendall's body, pushing him backward.

Nicholas gritted his teeth as his skeleton vibrated. He couldn't let go now even if he wanted to. His hand, though it simply rested on top of Aniya's, was locked in place, held down by some unseen force that cemented their connection.

Much-needed energy kickstarted his body, and for the first time in days, Nicholas breathed effortlessly.

His white skin was slowly turning a healthy shade of pink once again. As warmth flooded his body, Nicholas looked back to Aniya and noticed that the red light had changed to a brighter yellow color.

Out of the corner of his eye, Nicholas saw Tamisra approach.

"How is she—"

Nicholas pointed a finger without turning. "Stay back!"

Tamisra stumbled backward as yellow lightning crackled from Nicholas's fingertip.

As the light around Aniya's body changed color again to a bright green, Nicholas not only felt normal again, but he felt stronger than ever before. He sat up and climbed off his bed, his hand still on Aniya's.

Finally, the light receded from his body back into Aniya, and he felt his hand come free once again.

Nicholas looked down at her. The light had diminished to a barely visible, green glow that covered her body. Her crystal hung around her neck, glimmering with an emerald shine.

Then, Aniya opened her eyes.

21

Aniya looked around the room. She was back in the Refuge clinic.

A number of faces looked back at her, but all she could think about was the one she left behind.

"No!" Aniya screamed, closing her eyes tight and wishing for her brother back again.

A hand clutched hers.

"It's okay. You're okay."

But she only squeezed her eyes shut harder, desperately trying to return to the void inside her mind.

"You're safe now."

After a moment, Aniya gave up. She went limp and opened her eyes to see Nicholas looking down over her. "I saw him."

Nicholas frowned. "Who?"

Aniya opened her mouth to speak, but speech faltered on her lips as she spotted Kendall looking over Nicholas's shoulder.

"Nothing." She looked again at Nicholas as a smile slowly returned to her face. As much as she wanted to see her brother again, she was glad to be back with Nicholas. It had felt like months that she was trapped in her living nightmare.

"I missed you," Aniya said as she squeezed his hand, and his smile warmed her heart.

But her mind was uneasy. As much as William had been able to explain back in the void, it had only made things more confusing. And now, rather than some dark hallucination, the nightmare she had just woken up from felt all too real, a part of her that was lurking, patiently waiting for her return.

If she concentrated, she could hear the voices, quietly repeating her name. She shivered as the Shadow's voice rose above the others and stretched her name out in a raspy breath.

Aniya shook herself and focused on Nicholas's face. "What just happened?"

"Not sure," Nicholas said. "That was like nothing I've ever seen."

Kendall stepped up to Aniya's bedside next to Nicholas. "Something unthinkable, it seems. You were very nearly dead."

"What I could see before I was knocked out," a voice came from the other side of the room, "was what seemed to be some sort of energy transfer."

Aniya turned to see Gareth climbing to his feet across the room.

"Gareth!" She grinned widely. "They got you back."

He nodded, holding a hand to his head. "They did indeed. I'm happy to see you alive and well. I just wish I had done something to help."

"An energy transfer, you say?" Lieutenant Haskill spoke, and Aniya craned her neck to see him pacing back and forth behind Nicholas and Kendall.

"Yes," Gareth said. "From Aniya into Nicholas. I didn't see much. I tried to intervene because I didn't want Nicholas to be harmed, but apparently Aniya disapproved."

"I disapproved?" Aniya frowned.

Gareth nodded. "I touched you, and you blasted me clear across the room."

"I don't remember any of that," she said. "What do you mean, an energy transfer?"

"A quite successful one, it seems." Gareth walked across the room and examined Nicholas, then Aniya. "Nicholas here was suffering from some form of energy loss, an advanced form of fatigue. He was almost as close to death as you were, I'd say. Though your problem was quite the opposite, an excess of energy. From what I've been told, you carry a great deal of residual energy from the Lightbringers' machine, and it seems to have transferred itself into Nicholas's body of its own volition."

"Just like in the Hub," Nicholas muttered.

Aniya froze. At Roland's request, they had agreed not to say anything to Kendall about the strange events beneath the Citadel. But as she looked at Kendall, she realized that he didn't look surprised at all.

"You told him?"

"I'm sorry, Aniya," Nicholas said. "We had to help you, and they needed to know everything."

Gareth stepped forward. "It's true, Aniya. Though, I must say, I was not able to help you like I had hoped."

Lieutenant Haskill stopped pacing and turned to Aniya. "So it seems the energy inside you is not only capable of destruction, but it is also a source of healing."

"Yeah, but it almost kills me," Aniya said. "And it's not like I can control it. I didn't know what I was doing back in Ravelta. It was like the light had a mind of its own. All I could do was stand back and watch it happen. All I could do was watch people die."

Xander's face flashed in Aniya's mind, bearing the same pained look he had when she had incinerated him, the same face with burning eyes. She looked around for Corrin and

Malcolm, but Xander's father and brother were not in the room. She wanted to beg for their forgiveness but didn't know how to start.

Maybe it was better that they weren't there.

"I don't want this," she said. "If I can't control it, I'm a danger to everyone around me."

"You just need to learn how to control it," Kendall said.

"I'm not so sure I want to."

"Nicholas, please come with me." Kendall suddenly turned to leave. "There's something I must discuss with you."

Nicholas nodded. "Just a moment." He turned to Aniya. "Please forgive me for telling him. I just wanted to help you."

"Of course. I understand."

"There's something else," he said as he shifted his balance. "I need to—"

Kendall cleared his throat. "Time is of the essence, Nicholas."

Nicholas turned to leave. "We'll talk about this later."

"Okay," Aniya said, confused.

Lieutenant Haskill turned to follow them out, but Kendall held up a hand.

"Just Nicholas, Lieutenant."

Haskill frowned as Kendall and Nicholas left the clinic. He looked back at Gareth, who shrugged. With a sigh, he exited the clinic, leaving Aniya with Gareth and Tamisra.

Tamisra stepped forward and placed a hand on Aniya's shoulder. "I'm glad you're okay."

"Where's Roland?"

Tamisra frowned. "Long story. I'll tell you later, but right now, there's something I have to do."

With that, she turned and left.

Aniya shook her head as Gareth began examining her body. "Strange girl."

Gareth only nodded.

"How's Corrin and Malcolm?" she blurted out. She still

wasn't sure what she would say to either of them, but she wanted to get it over with so the awful memory of Xander's death would stop haunting her.

"Another long story," Gareth said. "Corrin will want to see you when he returns, but I would stay away from his son if I were you. I haven't seen such an angry man since . . ." He bit his lip and went quiet.

Aniya resisted the urge to close her eyes, afraid Xander would be waiting for her in her mind. "I didn't mean to do it, Gareth. I would never—"

"I know," he reassured her. "You're not capable of doing such a thing on purpose. Whatever sentient energy is inside you seems to be in control, at least for now. From what I'm told, it's no one's fault that Xander died. Least of all yours."

However, Aniya was anything but reassured. And what was worse was her dreaded certainty that something like this would happen again.

22

Kendall paced in the war room, ignoring Zeta, who sat in Salvador's old chair and twiddled her thumbs. He glanced at Nicholas, who was just sitting down, and took a deep breath.

The next few minutes were crucial. His asset had gone along with every instruction, complied with every order. But *this* would be the true test of his loyalty.

Granted, the boy had already done the unlikely, leading the girl to her death. Minutes earlier, he had surprised Kendall by agreeing to let her die again. Given that Nicholas had proven his dedication to the cause, Kendall could not think of a single logical reason that the boy would now choose to no longer go along with the plan.

But, in Kendall's experience, love had never been logical.

Kendall continued pacing. He couldn't calm his nerves long enough to sit. A hundred different outcomes to this conversation played out in his head, and he only had one chance to choose exactly the right words to say.

"Aniya is still in danger," he finally said.

A solid start, Kendall reflected as he held back a satisfied smile. *The boy wants to fight for a better world almost as much as I do, but his weakness has always been the girl.*

"What do you mean?" Nicholas asked.

"She can't control her abilities. She said so herself. And if she goes into an explosive state every time her abilities manifest themselves, it won't be long before we're all in danger again."

Nicholas said nothing.

"Whatever happened in the clinic between you and her, the energy transfer—it seemed to make her better. But for how long? I think it's safe to assume that it was only a temporary solution." Kendall narrowed his eyes. "She healed you once before, yes? And she seemed normal enough in the days after the attack on the Citadel. Clearly, even though she looks normal now, we can't expect her to stay that way."

Nicholas sighed. "I'm all for a permanent solution. As happy as I am to see her awake, I don't want to see her wind up in another coma."

Kendall's eyes flickered to Zeta, whose face was emotionless as she stared at her fingers. He braced himself. "Then I hope you will agree that we move ahead with taking her to the Director."

"I know. I was thinking the same thing."

Kendall frowned. "You were?"

"Not until recently. Not until she wound up nearly dying in Ravelta. I thought she was fine, but now . . . You said he knows how to help her. And it sounds like Aniya wants to be helped just as much as we want to help her. I'll talk to her and see what she wants to do."

Zeta looked up at Kendall and raised her eyebrows.

"I'm afraid you don't understand," Kendall said. "We have to take her to the Director whether she wants to go or not."

"I'm not going to make her go if she doesn't want to."

"You have to. For our safety and hers, she has to be taken to the Director."

"What if we're wrong?" Nicholas leaned over the table. "What if she's just fine? What if she doesn't need his help?"

"What if we aren't, what if she isn't, and what if she does? If she needs our help but won't accept it willingly, you have to understand that it's our duty to help her." Kendall shook his head. "I don't understand, Nicholas. You were on board with this a moment ago. What changed?"

Nicholas folded his arms. "You're asking me to betray her. Again. I won't do that, Kendall."

"It's not worth the risk, waiting for her to realize that this is what has to happen. Besides, I have my orders. The Director expects her tomorrow." Kendall's voice hardened as he looked at the assassin at the head of the table. "Despite her brash actions, Zeta didn't come to kill the Chancellor, Nicholas."

Nicholas turned to Zeta, glaring at the girl. "So you just did that for fun, then? You operatives are all the same."

Zeta shrugged. "I killed the Chancellor because he talks too much, and the Director likes his secrecy."

"So if you didn't come to perform an execution in front of the entire Web, what are you doing here?"

"I came to take Aniya. And I'm not afraid to use force against anyone who stands in my way. Even if that person is Aniya herself."

Kendall turned to Nicholas. "You see? For her own sake, you have to convince Aniya to go peacefully. Surely you want what's best for her?"

"It's not a question of whether I want her to go or not. I already told you, I agree with you. If the Director can help her, she needs to go see him. But I think she should be given a choice."

"Not thirty minutes ago, you decided that she should die so that we could transport her."

"Yeah, well, she was in a coma then. If she can decide for herself now, she should."

Kendall sighed. *A different approach, maybe.* "If she refuses, a number of things will happen. First, Zeta will feel that she has no choice but to take Aniya by force. Am I wrong?"

Zeta only grinned.

"Let's say she tries that. If she succeeds, she will incapacitate Aniya and take her to the Director. No harm done. But as we know by now, Aniya is more than capable of defending herself. If she lashes out at Zeta using her abilities, chances are she'll end up in a coma again. Then, we will have to make the same decision that we just made thirty minutes ago. Worst-case scenario? Zeta attacks Aniya, and Aniya destroys all of Refuge."

Kendall finally sat down across the table from Nicholas. "You have to realize that we simply have no choice. Aniya must be delivered to the Director, and he will get his way no matter what you or I do. He always does. But if you help me, we can guarantee Aniya's safety and the safety of everyone in Refuge."

After a moment, Nicholas sighed and bowed his head. "I understand. How do I convince Aniya?"

"By any means necessary. First, tell her the truth. Tell her we can't guarantee her safety, and there is someone who has the knowledge and technology to help her. That alone should be enough to convince her."

"And if it isn't?"

Kendall shrugged. "Lie to her. Tell her that we know, without a doubt, that she will deteriorate again all by herself, whether she uses her abilities or not. Tell her that she will die if nothing is done to help her."

"I can't lie to her."

"You already did once. Besides, for all we know, this is exactly what will happen."

Nicholas looked away. "And what if she doesn't go for that?"

Kendall took another deep breath. Without a word, he took a syringe from his pocket and set it on the table.

Nicholas stared at the needle, his eyes wide. "Is that how you were going to—"

"Yes. This is what we were going to use to stop Aniya's heart in order to transport her to the Director before she woke up. It will have the same effect now if administered while she is awake."

Nicholas stood up, backing away from the table. "No way. I'm not going to kill her. Absolutely not."

"I'll do it then," Zeta said, standing up. "I don't have any problem taking her out."

Nicholas growled and clenched his fists. "If you touch her, I'll kill you."

"I'd like to see you try," Zeta sneered as she bared her teeth.

"Nicholas, Zeta, please."

Nicholas glared at the assassin as if Kendall were not in the room.

"It's not as bad as it sounds," Kendall said. "We would essentially be putting her in a controlled coma, unlike the one she was just in. Gareth and I have run the numbers multiple times. This *will* work, Nicholas. She won't completely die, I promise you."

Nicholas stopped and stared at Kendall. "Gareth agreed to using this on Aniya when she's awake? Why would he ever—"

"I had him do the calculations when we first discussed using it on her while she was in her coma. He asked why, and I told him that this might have to be done. His reaction was similar to yours, but in time, he agreed. He knows that this is best for Aniya and the Web. Please, Nicholas. See reason. Help Aniya."

After a long pause, Nicholas stepped toward the table and picked up the syringe. "As a last resort *only*."

Kendall nodded. "As a last resort only."

Nicholas shook his head as he placed the syringe in his pocket.

"You're doing the right thing, Nicholas."

Nicholas turned and walked toward the door. "I keep telling myself that."

Tamisra backed away from the trapdoor as she heard footsteps on the stairs, coming up from the war room below.

A horrible feeling crawled over her skin as she realized that Nicholas was going through with it. He was going to kill the girl he proclaimed to love.

Aniya had to know. Roland had to know.

And they were all running out of time.

She turned and left the tower just as the trapdoor opened, and she took off toward the clinic, running as fast as she could.

23

Tamisra ran across Refuge. She didn't know how long it would be before Nicholas came looking for Aniya, but she didn't want to waste any time. The only problem was that Tamisra had no idea what she was going to say.

If she exposed Kendall to Refuge, he would just claim that he was just trying to protect Aniya the best way he knew how.

If Aniya fled with her to the sectors, Kendall could send out another transmission, this one asking for help finding them.

If they stayed somewhere in the tunnels, it was only a matter of time until Kendall's Silvers found them.

Her mind racing, Tamisra decided to get Aniya first and decide on a course of action later.

She burst through the door of the clinic and looked at Aniya's bed.

It was empty.

Just then, Gareth came downstairs, carrying a few medical supplies.

"Where is Aniya?" she blurted out.

Gareth looked up, smiling. "Hello, Tamisra. Are you feeling better? I—"

"Where is Aniya?!"

He frowned. "I think she went to go see Roland."

Tamisra felt her nostrils flare. "She just woke up from a coma, and you let her go see her brother?"

But before Gareth could respond, she waved him off. "Never mind."

She almost left, but seeing Gareth with his supplies gave her an idea. She had no way of knowing what kind of trouble they would run into, and it would be smart to be ready for anything.

After Gareth left the clinic, Tamisra opened one of the cabinets on the wall and rummaged through it, grabbing anything she could carry. Not bothering to close the cabinet, she turned to leave and ran directly into Nicholas, who stood in the doorway. The supplies she had grabbed fell to the ground.

"Hey, Tamisra." Nicholas smiled, a sight that chilled Tamisra to the bone.

"Hey," she said, trying to brush past him.

Nicholas stuck out an arm and blocked her path. "Why are you looking for Aniya?"

"I'm not."

"That's not what Gareth said when I ran into him on the path just now."

Tamisra stared him down, trying to hide her contempt. "I just wanted to check on her. Wanted to make sure she's okay."

"I saw you running away from the tower, moving awfully fast for someone who just wanted to check on her." Nicholas advanced, and Tamisra slowly backpedaled into the center of the room. "You've already spied on Kendall once, so I can't help but wonder if you were listening in on our conversation."

She shook her head. "I don't know what you're talking about."

Nicholas reached into his coat pocket and slowly pulled out a syringe.

Tamisra's eyes widened, and she took another step back. "Stay away from me."

"So you did hear us," he said, his voice flat.

"No, I just don't like people threatening me with needles."

"You know this isn't any ordinary needle, don't you? How much did you hear?"

Tamisra glared at him for a moment. "Enough to know that I'm not letting you anywhere near Aniya."

"I just want to help her, Tami."

"By using *that* on her? How is killing her going to help her?"

Nicholas put the needle back in his pocket. "I only showed that to you to get you to start talking. I was never going to use this on her. I only told Kendall what he wanted to hear, but Aniya will have a choice. If she doesn't want to go to the Director, I won't make her."

"You made her sacrifice herself to end the Lightbringers, or at least you tricked her into it," Tamisra said. "I don't know what you will and won't do anymore."

"You don't know the full story."

"What else is there to know?" Tamisra sighed and let herself relax a little. "Look, I know you think you're doing the right thing. I know you think you're helping her. But Aniya deserves the opportunity to decide for herself, and I don't know if I believe you when you say you'll give her that choice."

"She needs help."

"You don't even know that. She could be just fine."

"If someone so much as tries to wake her up while she's sleeping, we could find ourselves in the same position all over again, wondering if she's going to explode and take out all of us with her."

"You don't know that."

"Kendall's not willing to risk it, and to be honest, I don't think I am either." Nicholas stepped forward again. "What would you do if Roland was in this position? If you knew that saving him was out of your control, that there was nothing you could do to help, wouldn't you do anything to find someone who could help him?"

"I wouldn't do anything he didn't want. I certainly wouldn't kill him."

Nicholas sighed. "I told you. I'm not going to use the syringe."

"You've lied to her—to all of us—so many times that you know I can't believe you."

"Please, Tamisra. Let me help her."

Tamisra shook her head.

Nicholas ran his fingers through his hair. "Please don't make me do this, Tamisra."

"Do what?"

"I would do anything to help her. And if I have to get you out of my way in order to help her, I will."

Tamisra clenched her fists as best as she could through the bandages. The only upside to her injuries was that she was still numb enough that she could punch Nicholas as hard as she could without hurting herself. She bent her knees, crouching down slightly as if ready to pounce. "Then do it."

Nicholas didn't move. He simply stared at Tamisra, blocking the doorway.

After several seconds, Tamisra couldn't wait any longer. She leapt at Nicholas, who sidestepped and thrust out an arm, letting her stomach collide with his fist.

She crumbled to the ground, clutching her belly in pain as she gasped for air.

"Please don't make me do this," Nicholas said again.

Tamisra growled and swiped at his legs with her arm, knocking his feet out from under him and sending him crashing to the ground. Without giving him time to recover, she rolled over and vaulted on top of him, pinning him to the ground.

"You just don't want to be beaten by a girl."

But as she taunted him, bending down toward his face, she got too close, and Nicholas head-butted her.

Tamisra held a hand to her head and let herself roll off his body, moaning in pain.

"We're on the same side, Tamisra." Nicholas stood up, standing over her as he grimaced.

She got up slowly, holding out her other hand to defend against any attack, but Nicholas simply watched her stand, shaking his head.

"Please let me help her. I love her more than you know."

Tamisra shook away her dizziness and held her fists out in front of her face. "Talk all you want. Nothing you say will convince me now."

"We're wasting time, Tamisra. If I don't do something right now, Zeta is going to come for her. Whatever you think I might do to her, I promise you, an operative will do all that and more. We don't have time for this."

Tamisra smirked. "What, you want to walk away now?"

"I want to help Aniya. Please let me."

But Tamisra didn't budge.

Finally, Nicholas shook his head slowly. "You're not going to stop, are you?" he asked as he raised his fists. "I'm sorry, Tamisra. I really am."

With that, he lunged forward and swung a fist.

Tamisra's hands were already in a defensive position, and the blow glanced off her arms as she delivered a punch of her own, an uppercut that landed on his jaw and sent him reeling backwards.

Without waiting, she dashed forward and punched him square in the chest. As he kept staggering backward, Tamisra continued her onslaught, lunging forward again and punching him in the face.

Finally, she delivered a swift kick to his stomach, and he doubled over. Tamisra pulled back her fist to deliver a devastating blow that would surely render him unconscious.

But as she punched, Nicholas looked up and reached out, grabbing her fist and stopping the punch cold.

Tamisra winced as his hand clamped down around her fist, just tight enough that she could feel it through the numbing agent. She tried to pull away, but her hand was stuck in his, locked in place beneath his fingers.

Her hand turned cold as blood drained away. She felt something pop in her hand, and she cried out in pain. All she could think about in that moment was how bad it would have felt if she hadn't still been partially numb.

She reached out at Nicholas with her free hand.

"Nicholas, please—"

But he swatted her hand away and grabbed her throat. As his fingers tightly wrapped around her neck, he lifted her off the ground, letting her toes reach helplessly for the floor as she choked.

"Please," she croaked out again, her voice barely above a whisper.

Nicholas simply stared at her as her vision began to go dark. The cold invaded every area of her body, and a new numbness settled over her.

But she kept flailing her arms wildly, and suddenly her left hand grazed something. She was so cold and numb that she couldn't quite tell what it was, but as she focused on the object, she reached out, wrapping her fingers around it. Finally, she had a firm grasp on the object, and with all her remaining strength, she pulled the object, letting it crash down on Nicholas's head.

Tamisra never felt herself fall, but as she opened her eyes and her vision cleared, she found herself on the floor, lying in front of Nicholas, who now lay still with his eyes closed.

The stand for the IV drip lay over his body, and a red mark was beginning to develop on his forehead.

As warmth returned to her body, Tamisra climbed to her feet, gasping for air that wouldn't come quick enough. After a few seconds, her breathing was not quite normal but close enough. She turned to Nicholas, who still lay on the floor, moaning.

Bending over, she picked up the stand and hit him over the head once again.

Nicholas went still, and Tamisra turned and ran out into Refuge. It wouldn't take long for Zeta to find out what happened, and Tamisra wasn't sure she could stop an assassin.

24

"That's quite the story," Aniya said, frowning. She looked up at the bars that surrounded them as she toyed with the crystal dangling from her neck, resting on her chest. The cell didn't look like it had been used or cared for much, and she took pity on her brother. She was just visiting, but he had to stay here until Kendall deemed otherwise.

Roland sat across from her. "It's true, all of it. To be fair, it's a whole lot more believable than you talking with William's ghost."

"I didn't say I didn't believe you. I believe you think you're right."

"So you think I'm wrong," Roland said, sighing. "I don't blame you. If you told me that the Chancellor, the guy we spent our whole lives hating, was trying to help us, I'd think you were crazy too. But you weren't there."

Aniya sighed. "I guess it doesn't matter anymore."

"Thanks to Zeta, no. I guess it doesn't."

"Yeah, she doesn't sound any more pleasant than the last operative. But the Chancellor, Roland? You let him inside Refuge after everything he's done?"

Roland shrugged. "I didn't have much of a choice, not if

I wanted to help you. I know it was dangerous, but I would have done whatever it took to save you."

Aniya gave a soft smile. "I know. I doubt he really knew how to help me, but I don't think that's why he asked you to help him get inside Refuge."

"Why else?"

"Who knows? Did they ever find out what he injected me with?"

Roland looked at the ground. "No. I was scared to death when I saw that. I would never forgive myself if he hurt you."

"Hopefully there's no harm done. Maybe I wouldn't have ever woken up if he didn't inject me with whatever it was. I could hear him clearly, so I was at least partially conscious."

"What did he say?"

"Mostly the same stuff he told you. Don't trust Kendall, don't trust the Director, and don't . . ."

As Aniya trailed off, Roland frowned. "Don't what?"

"Don't trust Nicholas."

Roland nodded. "Makes sense. Nicholas has pretty much been following Kendall blindly. To his credit, I think he's trying to help you in his own way."

"But don't trust him?" Aniya shook her head. "If I can't trust him, I can't trust anyone."

"Not even me?"

Aniya smiled. "Of course I trust you. What I meant was I couldn't imagine Nicholas betraying me."

"Didn't he kind of do it already when he was undercover with the Lightbringers?"

"That was different." Aniya leaned against the wall and folded her arms. "He didn't have a choice, and if the Operative had found me before Nicholas, I may not have made it to the Hub alive."

Roland held his hands up defensively. "I'm just saying, maybe it's best to keep your distance for now. Just until we know for sure."

"He jumped in the tank with me and died just to keep me awake so I could blow the reactor. I trust him, and you should too."

Roland sighed and shook his head. "Honestly, I'm just glad you're awake. As long as you stay that way, I'm happy."

"Me too. I didn't think I'd ever get out of there. I'm still not sure how much of it was real."

Roland grinned. "Considering you were seeing ghosts made of light and shadow, I'd say not much."

"Yeah, it was pretty surreal. I don't even—"

The entrance to the small prison burst open, and Tamisra stumbled inside. Her skin was pale, her eyes bloodshot.

She fumbled with the lock on the cell and opened the door. Her eyes darted between Aniya and Roland, and she spoke with a raspy voice.

"We need to go."

25

Aniya stood up and grabbed Tamisra just as she released the cell door and began to fall.

"What happened?" Roland jumped up and took Tamisra's other hand, pulling back her wet hair and scanning her face.

Tamisra looked up at Aniya. "Nicholas."

A tingling sensation raced over Aniya's skin, and the cell began to fill with a soft, green glow. Beads of light traced over her body and into the hand that supported Tamisra, shooting into the girl's body as she breathed heavily.

Seconds later, the cell went dark again, and Tamisra stood up straight, her eyes wide and her skin flush. She glanced down at her hands, which she flexed freely and stared at in wonder. "Was that you?"

"You said Nicholas did this?" Roland interrupted.

Tamisra nodded as she tore the bandages on her hands away, revealing clean, pink flesh. "He's coming for you, Aniya. Kendall still wants to take you to the Director, and he knows you'll trust Nicholas. And if you don't go willingly, he'll . . . He'll kill you."

"No way," Aniya said, shaking her head. "He wouldn't. He couldn't."

"We don't have time to argue. When he wakes up, he'll come for you. You can find out for yourself then, but it'll be too late to change your mind."

Aniya frowned. "Wakes up?"

"You were right, Roland," Tamisra said. "Kendall kidnapped and tortured us. He tricked my father into coming to the Hub and got him killed. And he clearly doesn't have Aniya's best interests in mind. You were right about everything."

Roland's eyes widened, and he turned to Aniya. "We need to leave, now. I've seen enough to know that Kendall will do anything for the Director, and I don't want to stick around long enough to find out if Nicholas feels the same way. We can sort it out later, but right now we need to get out of here."

Aniya looked between Roland and Tamisra for a moment before finally nodding. "Let's go."

She closely followed Tamisra and Roland out of the prison and through Refuge, hoping that the occupants of the hidden city were not yet aware that she was once again a fugitive, now from the very people who had fought to end the oppressing reign of the Lightbringers.

No one seemed to care. If anything, they got a lot of strange looks as they half-crouched, half-ran through the cavernous city. Aniya almost suggested acting normal, but she knew that if they were spotted by Kendall or his new operative, their escape would be over not long after it started.

Her mind raced. She could hardly believe that Nicholas would try to kill her. No, she couldn't believe it.

But Tamisra seemed so sure.

As much as Aniya wanted to find Nicholas and hear him out, give him a chance to explain himself, it was too dangerous. Even if it was a misunderstanding, even if he wanted to help her, this new operative definitely didn't. And Aniya had seen enough of their kind to know that Zeta was not someone she wanted to meet in person.

So she followed her brother's lead, counting on seeing Nicholas again soon to hear his side of the story.

They skirted along the edges of Refuge, but still far enough inside the cavern that they could use the hundreds of tents scattered across the ground as cover.

It would have been so much faster to cut straight across the cavern to the tunnel they needed to follow, but that would have meant walking right past the main tower, where she knew Kendall would be waiting for her.

Finally, they made it to the other side of Refuge without incident, and Tamisra guided them down another tunnel.

Several minutes later, they arrived in a large cavern, and a smile spread across Aniya's face as she realized they were in the stable.

Dozens of cages lined the walls, each containing a mole that stood about four feet tall. Aniya looked for Brisket, the creature she had befriended not long ago, but at this distance, she couldn't distinguish one creature from the next.

As she walked into the center of the cavern, she noticed that each of the moles turned and stared in her direction, watching her every move. They were unnaturally still.

"What are *you* doing here?"

Aniya turned to see Malcolm approaching them. He glared at Tamisra and Roland but wouldn't look Aniya in the eye.

"Malcolm, there you are." Aniya breathed a sigh in relief as she would finally get a chance to make amends for the horrible accident that had claimed his brother's life. "I'm so sor—"

"Aren't you supposed to be in a cell?" Malcolm pointed at Roland.

"We need a couple moles," Tamisra said, ignoring his question.

Maybe Malcolm hadn't heard Aniya. She tried again. "Malcolm, please. I need to—"

"Do you have authorization?"

Tamisra scoffed. "Authorization? Since when do we need authorization?"

"Since someone decided to let our greatest enemy inside, we have increased all our security measures," Malcolm said, scowling at Roland. "We even changed all the codes on the electronic locks and put them on a rotating system."

"Whatever. Look, we'll bring the moles right back."

"Sorry, Tamisra. Orders are orders."

Roland growled. "Do you know who her father was?"

"Her father is dead. A lot of people are dead that didn't have to die." For the first time, Malcolm looked at Aniya, and his frustration seemed to morph into pure hatred as she bowed her head.

"And more people will die if you don't let us take these moles." Tamisra sighed. "Look, Malcolm. We need to help Aniya get out of here."

Malcolm's eyebrows shot up at this. "I'm listening."

"She's in danger. The Director's operative is coming for her, and the only way we can get away from here fast enough is if we take the moles."

But Malcolm shook his head. "I'm sorry, Tamisra."

"Don't do it for her, Malcolm. Do it for me." She placed a hand on his arm as Roland frowned. "Do it for old times' sake."

"Really? That's the best you've got?"

Tamisra groaned and pulled her hand away. "Please, Malcolm. Just do this for me. You owe me that much."

After a moment, Malcolm nodded. "Fine, but don't tell anyone that I let you have them. Where are you going to take her?"

He glanced back at Aniya, and as she looked closely, she thought she caught a hint of grief in his steely eyes.

"I honestly don't know," Tamisra said. "There's still Loyalists in most of the sectors, people who would jump at the chance to turn her over to what's left of the Lightbringers. I don't know if anywhere is safe enough for her."

"Lyrindal," Malcolm said suddenly.

"The old rebel headquarters?" Roland asked. "There isn't any air. Any better ideas?"

"It's an abandoned sector," Malcolm said. "No Loyalists, no Sympathetics, no Silvers, nothing. And after all this time, air will have trickled in from the tunnels. The three of you would be able to stay there for a long time."

Tamisra frowned. "You want to take her to another quadrant? We know nothing about the tunnels on that side. It's hundreds of miles of unexplored territory. Even I've never been to Lyrindal, not with the Hub between us and it."

"We have everything mapped all the way to Lyrindal, thanks to Corrin," Malcolm said. "Once you get to the Hub, just follow the map."

Tamisra shook her head. "You want us to go through the Hub?"

"Why not? It's abandoned too."

"Yeah, and in ruins. Worse than Lyrindal, I bet. There'll be enough radiation in there to kill a person in days."

"Most of the reactor explosion was contained underground," Malcolm countered. "I checked it out myself last week with . . . with Xander. It's clear."

Tamisra paused. "I don't know. Taking her through the Hub, into territory we know very little about—too many things could go wrong."

"You don't have to listen to me if you don't want to." Malcolm's neutral expression gave way to his familiar scowl as he folded his arms. "But I'm telling you, it's the safest place I know. You know what happened in the war."

Aniya finally spoke up. "Let's do it. According to Tamisra, the operative won't be far behind us. We don't have time to look for any other option. Besides, the last place they'll expect us to go is toward the Hub. I think it's our best shot."

Roland nodded. "It might be our only shot."

"Fine," Tamisra said. "Lyrindal it is. Will you come with us, Malcolm?"

Malcolm shot a glance at Aniya. "I don't know."

"We don't know the area. Besides, if we run into trouble, you're the best fighter we've got."

Roland and Malcolm both gave a short laugh, but Aniya suspected they were for two very different reasons.

"Flattery's not a good look for you, Tamisra," Malcolm said. "But you're right that you could use the help. Do you have enough supplies for me?"

Tamisra looked away. "Well . . ."

"You don't have any supplies?" Malcolm folded his arms. "The Hub is not a short journey, and there's no guarantee you'll run into any mole small enough that the three of you can take down by yourselves. No one's looking for me, so I'll go get supplies for all of us and be back in less than ten minutes."

Tamisra nodded, and Malcolm turned to leave, but not before Aniya gently placed a hand on his arm.

"Can we talk?"

But Malcolm looked at her with what looked like confusion. "We have nothing to talk about."

"Please." Aniya looked down, her heart heavy. "I feel terrible about what happened to Xander. Can we just—"

"Don't say his name." With that, he yanked his arm away and took off down the tunnel.

Roland turned to Tamisra. "Old times' sake?"

Tamisra elbowed him, grinning. "Don't worry. You have nothing to be jealous about."

"I'm not jealous," Roland grumbled.

Aniya stepped away from her brother and his girlfriend and toward the cages that lined the wall. The moles had remained motionless the entire time, almost entranced by her presence. She walked along the row of cages, letting her fingers graze the metal and wood that held the animals inside, until she stopped in front of one particular cage.

"Hello, Brisket." Aniya grinned at the large mole. According to Tamisra, Refuge usually didn't try to tame the moles when they reached a certain size. Brisket had well surpassed that point, and he had remained wild, even dangerous until Aniya befriended him.

She unlocked the cage door and beckoned with her fingers, and the mole slowly stepped out of the cage, letting its snout fall into Aniya's open hands. As she twirled her fingers before Brisket's eyes, the mole followed her every move, staring at the twinkling lights that softly clung to Aniya's skin.

Aniya ran her hands over the loyal beast and nuzzled her own forehead against the creature's cheek. After a few minutes, Aniya pulled the mole's snout up to her eye level. "Ready for a ride?"

Whether Brisket understood or sensed her anticipation, Aniya wasn't sure, but the mole leaned down slightly as if inviting her to hop on.

"When have you found the time to train this guy?"

Aniya turned to see Tamisra watching them. She grinned and hopped on Brisket. "Jealous?"

"Yeah, a bit." Tamisra mumbled and unlocked another door, carefully leading a mole out with a rope. "Feel confident enough to ride one, Roland?"

He smirked. "I rode my own to Holendast. Pretty sure I can handle one today."

Just then, Malcolm came running back into the cavern, breathing heavy, a backpack slung over his shoulder. "Refuge is lit up. They know you're gone, and I'm guessing it won't be long until they figure out what you're planning."

Tamisra nodded. "Then let's go."

26

Aniya held on tight as Brisket galloped down the tunnel, leading Tamisra, Roland, and Malcolm toward the Hub.

Initially, Malcolm had tried to lead the way, but his mole had kept slowing down and turning to look at Aniya, staring at her with a blank expression. Roland had suggested that Aniya should lead the way after that.

They had stopped only two times in the last several hours for the sake of the other three moles. While Brisket had maintained boundless energy, the other mounts could only run for so long before they needed to stop.

Aniya had at first wondered at the incredible endurance that Brisket seemed to have, but she soon realized that she was the source of the mole's energy. A familiar buzzing sensation traveled down her legs and into the mole beneath her, and tiny, barely visible tendrils of green light wrapped themselves around the ropes in her hand and made their way to Brisket's neck.

The last time they had rested, Aniya asked Tamisra and Roland if they'd noticed this phenomenon. Roland confirmed that he could see the light around her, though just barely. Tamisra said she saw nothing.

Meanwhile, Malcolm remained their silence escort, taking up the rear without so much as a word to the rest of the group, especially not Aniya. Every time she glanced at him, he made a point to look away.

Finally, the group reached the last stretch of the tunnel, and they stepped into the abandoned Hub.

They stopped for a moment on the cliffside and looked over the sector.

It was unnaturally quiet and eerily dark. The fires of the factories had long since died away. The sky ceiling was no longer burning in pieces on the floor of the sector. There were no candles, no glowworms. The Hub was covered in a blanket of darkness that made it impossible to see more than a couple hundred feet away.

Through the sea of black came an awful stench. The smell of burnt flesh pervaded the air, reaching all the way to the cliffs, far above the massive plain where Salvador's men had waged war against the Lightbringers.

Aniya lit a torch, knowing that if only Roland could see her natural light, it would do Tamisra and Malcolm no good.

"Let's get out of here," Roland said. "No reason to stick around here any longer than necessary."

Malcolm spoke up. "According to the map, the fastest way to the opposite quadrant is straight through the center of the Hub."

"Whatever we have to do," Aniya said. "I'm with Roland on this one."

"Then let's go."

After carefully descending the cliffs and reaching the valley below, Aniya steered Brisket around bodies that lay scattered across the sector as they proceeded slowly through the Hub. Occasionally, she had no choice but to proceed over a fallen body, and she winced as Brisket's paws stepped into rotting flesh, brittle bones snapping beneath the weight of the animal.

They finally crossed the valley and entered the industrial grid, guiding their moles through smokestacks and factories. Their path was much more limited here, but there were far fewer bodies, to Aniya's relief.

As they approached the center of the Hub, the Citadel emerged from the dark, a massive obelisk that disappeared into the black haze above them.

A cold feeling tickled Aniya's spine as her hair stood on end. She looked away from the tower and glanced at Tamisra. As much as Aniya hated the thought of the horrors she had experienced in the Citadel, she knew Tamisra harbored an even deeper hatred for the tower.

Her father, Salvador the Scourge, had last been seen making his way into the Citadel, telling Corrin that he had important business to discuss with the Chancellor.

Aniya turned her mole to go around the tower when a door suddenly materialized from the silver building, creaking open slowly. A figure stepped out of the shadows and walked down the steps, stopping before the group.

Aniya's jaw dropped open as her best friend stood before her, a somber look on his face.

"Nicholas, what are you doing here?"

He took a deep breath as his gaze wandered over the group before settling on Aniya. "I've come to take you to someone who can help you."

A pit formed in Aniya's stomach. "It's all true, then? You were going to take me away, even if I didn't want to go?"

"It's for your own protection, Aniya. I was going to ask you."

"And if I said no?"

Nicholas looked back at the Citadel behind him, neglecting to answer.

Aniya shook her head in disbelief. "I don't understand.

I just don't. You say you love me, that I'm all that matters to you, but you want to manipulate me? You want to take me to this Director person so he can do God-knows-what to me? You want to kill me so you can save my life? How does that even work?"

"Please, Aniya. You have to believe me. All I've ever wanted is for you to be safe."

Tamisra spoke up. "Well, that's not true, is it?"

Nicholas glared at Tamisra, and Aniya turned toward her.

"You knew what was waiting for her in the Hub. You knew that in order for Kendall's plan to work, she had to die. You knew all that, and you led her right into the Hub anyway. What part of that is keeping her safe?"

Aniya's spirits fell. The thought had occurred to her once before, but she had instantly dismissed it as an impossibility. There were two things that Aniya knew Nicholas wanted more than anything else in the world: her, and a world without the Lightbringers. But now, she finally knew which one was more important to him.

"Tell me this isn't true. Tell me she's lying." Aniya choked on her words as her eyes grew wet. "Tell me she's wrong."

Nicholas looked at the ground.

Tears began to fall now, and Aniya's voice dropped to a whisper. "Were you ever going to tell me?"

"I never got the chance. I wanted to tell you so badly, but there was never a good time."

"Never a good time? You could have told me at any time before Kendall asked me to die for the Web. You could have told me before you tried to kiss me that night in the Hub. You had your chance. You had plenty of chances. But you didn't tell me because you didn't think I would agree to it, right? You didn't want to sacrifice your mission and lose the chance to end the Lightbringers? Because as much as you claim to love me, all that really matters to you is winning your silly war."

Nicholas stepped forward, reaching a hand out toward her.

"Don't." Aniya spat out a warning, and Brisket growled viciously as if it sensed her anger. "We're done. I'm leaving."

Nicholas shook his head, and Aniya ignored a tear that slid down his cheek. "I'm afraid you won't get very far."

"If you try to stop me, I'll run you over." Aniya sat tall on Brisket, glaring at him. "Get out of my way."

"I won't try to stop you," Nicholas said.

"Good."

Nicholas took a deep breath. "But she will."

A dark figure fell from above, as did two long daggers that drove deep into Brisket's neck.

The beast swayed beneath her and toppled over, sending Aniya tumbling to the ground.

27

Aniya winced as she sprawled out awkwardly on the pavement. Somewhere above her, Tamisra let loose a pained cry as Brisket crashed to the ground.

She rolled over and looked up at her attacker, a girl in a black bodysuit, armed with two knives that dripped with blood. The girl grinned down at her.

"Aniya, right? I'm Zeta. Nice to meet you."

Struck with shock, Aniya struggled to find words.

"Where are your manners? I was told you were a nice girl. Don't disappoint me."

Meanwhile, Tamisra jumped off her mole and ran to Brisket's side, running her hands over the animal.

Zeta wiped the daggers on her pants before spinning them in the air, catching them and returning them to their sheaths. She walked back over to Nicholas, a spring in her step almost making it look like she was dancing.

"What do you see in her? If you ask me, she looks kind of helpless." She tapped her fingers on Nicholas's chest and pranced around behind him, wrapping her arms around his chest. "She doesn't talk much, does she?"

Aniya glared at the assassin. "You're doing enough talking for both of us."

Zeta laughed heartily. "She does speak! And with some attitude, I might add."

Tamisra stood up, her cheeks wet with tears. "He's dead. Why would you do that? Was it fun to you?"

The operative shrugged. "I couldn't let Aniya leave."

"So you killed an innocent animal?"

Malcolm rolled his eyes. "Calm down, Tami. It's just a mole."

"Too true." Zeta smirked and approached Malcolm. She turned and glanced at the dead animal. "If nothing else, he'll make a fine dinner."

Tamisra growled and charged at the assassin's back, but Malcolm jumped off his mole and tackled her.

Roland dismounted and rushed to help Tamisra, but Zeta reached out a leg and tripped him, then delivered a casual kick to his stomach.

"Thank you, Malcolm. You're proving yourself to be all sorts of useful today, aren't you? It would have taken me and Nicholas some time to track them down if you hadn't told us exactly where they'd be."

Tamisra struggled against Malcolm's arms. "What is she talking about?"

Malcolm sighed. "I'm sorry, Tami. Taking Aniya to another part of the Web so she can blow up a different quadrant is not enough. Whether she means to or not, she's a danger to innocent people. She has to be taken care of."

Tamisra went still. "What does that mean?"

"Whatever it has to," Malcolm said softly as his grip on her seemed to relax.

Tamisra took advantage of Malcolm's guard being dropped, and she lashed out with an elbow, striking him directly in the nose. Without bothering to watch him fall, she turned toward Zeta. "What are you going to do with her?"

The operative folded her arms. "I'm taking her with me. I was given an order, and I intend to obey it. You really should reconsider your unquestioning loyalty to the girl, though. I'm sure all of you have found out by now what happens when you get in our way." She turned toward Aniya. "The choice is simple. Come with me and let us help you, or resist and watch your friends die."

"If your boss really wanted to help me, he wouldn't have sent an assassin."

Zeta gave a small smile. "He had to make sure that I would do whatever it took to bring you back."

Behind the operative's back, Roland slowly got up from the ground and pulled a gun from his side, nodding at Aniya.

"How about a third option?" Aniya put her hands on her hips. "You go back to wherever you came from and leave us alone."

Zeta laughed. "I'm not going anywhere without you, Aniya."

"Fine." Aniya nodded toward Roland.

In a flash, Zeta spun around and kicked the gun out of Roland's hands. As soon as the assassin turned, Aniya dashed toward her, but Zeta turned back around and sidestepped her attack, wrapping an arm around Aniya's neck and holding her tightly like a shield.

Tamisra took one step forward, arms outstretched, but with her left hand, Zeta pulled a knife from its sheath and threw it with deadly precision, driving the blade deep into Tamisra's shoulder.

"No!" Aniya screamed. She felt heat bubbling inside her, and as she clutched at the arm that held her captive, she noticed that her hands were glowing a deeper green.

Zeta shook her head. "Now, now, Aniya. You could have just come with me and avoided all this. Please don't make the same mistake again."

Vibrations rattled Aniya's skeleton, and pins and needles

tickled her body from head to toe. She wanted more than anything to let loose the power inside her and fry the snarky assassin, but as she looked down at her glowing hands, she noticed that the black fabric on Zeta's arm was glowing with orange lines, as if it somehow absorbed her energy. She reached back toward Zeta's face, but the operative kept moving just out of reach.

"Aniya, please," Nicholas pleaded. "I just want to help you. That's all I've ever wanted."

"You took me to the Hub so I could die," Aniya spat, green sparks shooting forth from her mouth. "How was that helping me?"

"She won't go willingly, Nicholas," Zeta said. "It's time for your last resort."

"Not yet."

"Hurry up," Zeta growled. "She's getting warmer."

Nicholas took a step forward. "Aniya, you have to trust me. Forget everything you've been told, everything you've heard. You think that I'm not going to give you a choice. Well, here it is. I'm giving you that choice now. Come with us to the Director and let him help you, or don't. The choice is yours, and I'll go along with whatever you say."

Aniya simply glared at him. After all the lies he had told her, after everything he had put her through, he was daring to offer her the illusion of choice now?

"Aniya, please. No matter what you believe, I love you and want the best for you. I believe that means taking you to the Director to help you. But if that's not what you want, then I will respect that. But you have to make a choice, and you have to make it now."

For an instant, Aniya let herself consider his words. If the Director could really help her, if he could keep her from deteriorating again and putting the entire Web at risk, wouldn't that be the right choice? No one else seemed to have any other solution. He was the only one who seemed to be able to help her. Could it be worth it to at least hear him out? Besides, thanks to her new abilities, Aniya knew that she was strong enough to walk away if the Director's intentions were malicious, before he could so much as lay a finger on her.

But as Aniya looked at the dead mole, then at Tamisra bleeding out on the ground, it didn't seem likely that the Director could have pure motives. Even if he wanted to save her, it had to be for his own selfish purposes. He had sent an assassin to retrieve her, after all. He wanted her for something, and Aniya guessed it wasn't to heal her or help her.

She looked back up at Nicholas and shook her head. "I'm not going."

Nicholas sighed. "So be it." He pulled a syringe from his pocket and approached Aniya.

Aniya's heart sank. As much as her mind had told her otherwise, she'd wanted to believe that Nicholas was offering her a real choice.

"Nicholas, please," she begged as her voice turned to a whisper. "Don't make me go there. Don't do this."

Nicholas shook his head. "I'm sorry, Aniya." He plunged the syringe toward her, and Aniya fell as a great weight crashed over her body.

28

Aniya moaned as a jarring pain reverberated throughout her body. A heavy weight was on her, a black film covering her vision. In the shock of the moment, she didn't have enough strength to stand back up, but she was still conscious.

But the weight was suddenly lifted off her as the black film slid away, and she was free.

She rolled over and turned around to see Zeta's body spread out on the ground next to her, convulsing in tremors. Nicholas's syringe lay embedded in her neck, empty of the clear fluid that had been inside.

Aniya looked up at Nicholas.

"What . . ."

He shrugged. "I said I would give you a choice."

"What did you do?" Malcolm scrambled to his feet, holding his bleeding nose. But as soon as he stepped forward, Roland jumped to his feet and delivered a swift punch to the exact same spot. This time, Malcolm was knocked out instantly, and his limp body fell to the ground.

"That's for Tami," Roland said before kneeling by his girlfriend's side again. Tamisra was lying on the ground, gripping the knife embedded in her shoulder and moaning in pain. Roland leaned over her body, speaking in hushed tones as his eyes grew wet.

Zeta reached for a dagger but couldn't grip the handle. It looked like she was trying to speak, but the only thing that came out of her mouth was white foam.

Within seconds, the assassin was still, her empty eyes staring up into the darkness.

Aniya dashed to Roland's side and crouched down next to Tamisra. She placed her hands on the girl's shoulder, right below the protruding dagger, and took a deep breath.

The energy moved somewhere within Aniya, but it was latent, hiding beneath something else. She tried to focus, but too many things were fighting for her attention. It was too confusing, all of it. The assassin, Nicholas's apparent betrayal, her brother with his dying girlfriend.

Aniya closed her eyes to block it all out, but Xander's face was there in the black waiting for her, staring at her with those burning eyes.

Shaking away the mental image, Aniya opened her eyes again and stared intently at Tamisra's bleeding shoulder. A slight buzz awoke in her hands, but she couldn't manage to squeeze the light out and into the wound. Something else raged within her, a churning, swelling feeling, a mix of emotion that almost felt like she was about to vomit.

Aniya kept trying for a few more minutes, but nothing seemed to happen. She looked up at Roland, shaking her head. "I don't think I can help her."

Roland shook his head as tears began to form. "I don't understand. You healed me. You healed Nicholas. You healed Tamisra before we left Refuge."

"Not on purpose," she said, biting her lip. "I can't control this. If I could, I would do it again, I promise. But I can't make myself do it."

"Please, Aniya." Roland was whimpering now, and his

trembling lips broke Aniya's heart. "This is bad. The blood loss alone . . ."

Aniya placed her hands on Tamisra's shoulder again and tried harder, but all she did was make her head spin. With a gasp, she relaxed with a sigh and looked back at Roland, her own tears beginning to fall. "I'm sorry. I can't."

Roland buried his face in Tamisra's shoulder and cried into her clothes for several seconds. Finally, he looked back up at her, his eyes red. "You need to get out of here. I'll take her to Gareth."

Nicholas held out a hand toward Aniya.

"Come on."

Aniya took his hand and stood up. "I knew it. I knew you wouldn't do this to me. It was all a trick, wasn't it? You had me brought here so you could get rid of Zeta without Kendall interfering."

Nicholas nodded.

"This was your plan all along. You knew what was going to happen. Even in the Hub, you knew I wasn't going to actually die." Aniya grinned widely. "I knew it. You would never lead me to my death like that."

Nicholas remained silent.

"Right?"

Aniya's smile faded.

"Right, Nicholas?"

Nicholas ignored the question and tugged on her hand. "We don't have much time."

But Aniya shook her hand free. "Nicholas, did you think I was going to die? Did you take me to the Hub, believing all along that I was going to die?"

He turned away and joined Roland at Tamisra's side, but Aniya grabbed his arm and pulled him back toward her. "Nicholas, answer me!"

"Yes, okay? I knew you would die. I knew exactly what

would happen, and that's why I made sure Kendall gave you a choice. You didn't have to do it."

Aniya backed away from him, shaking her head in disbelief.

Nicholas sighed. "But it doesn't matter. You're alive now, and I'm going to help you escape. I told you I would let you choose, and I did. Do you not trust me now?"

Aniya gave a short laugh. "Trust you? It's too late for that, Nicholas. I'm grateful that you didn't make me go to the Director, but it doesn't change the fact that you lied to me, that you betrayed me, that you led me to my death."

"Fine. Don't trust me. But you have to come with me if you don't want to wind up where I was going to take you anyway. It won't take long for another operative to come along for you. You don't have to trust me. Just come with me."

"Where would you even take me?" Aniya folded her arms.

"Out of the Web."

"What? You mean back into the tunnels?"

Nicholas shook his head. "To another Web."

"What are you talking about?"

"There's more to the Underworld, Aniya." Nicholas stepped forward, but Aniya instinctively took another step back. "Several layers, actually. We're on the eighteenth level, and I'm going to take you to another one where no one's looking for you."

Aniya's mouth dropped open. She looked back at Roland. "Did you know about this?"

"First I've heard about it. But he's right, we don't have time to talk about it. Tami needs help, and you need to get out of here."

"Please, Aniya." Nicholas again reached for her hand, which Aniya quickly pulled back. "It's the only way you'll be safe. Just let me take you away from here, and then you can do whatever you want, go wherever you want."

Aniya looked at Roland, who nodded.

"Go, Aniya."

"No, you have to come with us." Aniya looked up at Nicholas. "I can't trust him."

"You have to go without me. Wherever he plans to take you, I don't know if there will be anyone with the tools or knowledge to save Tamisra. But Gareth can help her." Roland's tears seemed to melt away as his eyes turned to steel. "And when we've taken care of her, we have to take care of Kendall."

Aniya nodded. She joined Nicholas, but as an afterthought, she knelt down by Malcolm's side.

He was still unconscious, sprawled out on the ground and lying atop a dead soldier unceremoniously.

"I'm sorry, Malcolm," Aniya said, gently pulling him off the dead body and onto solid ground. "I'm so sorry. I never meant to hurt Xander, and I know I can never make things better. Please just know how much I hate what happened, and I don't blame you for anything you've done. I deserve it. Just know that I'm sorry."

Aniya took a deep breath, stood, and turned to her oldest friend. But she didn't know what Nicholas was to her anymore. She had been overjoyed to awaken from her coma and have his face be the first thing she saw, the face of the man she loved. But now, confusion and anger drowned out any positive emotion toward the man who said he loved her but had betrayed her.

She pushed the feeling aside, knowing that Nicholas was her only ticket out of here, no matter what she felt toward him. She would have to take this leap of faith.

"Let's go."

Nicholas gave a nod and turned around. He didn't offer a hand to her, and while Aniya was relieved, it also sealed the pain in her heart with a finality that crushed her spirit.

There was no going back.

PART III
LEVEL I

29

Aniya didn't know exactly how Nicholas planned to get her out of the Web, but she definitely didn't expect him to walk straight up the stairs of the Citadel and open the front door.

"What are you doing? I thought you were going to get me out of here."

Nicholas nodded. "And this is the fastest way out."

She frowned but followed him inside.

They walked through the scorched, darkened halls of the Citadel. The entire building looked like it had been burned, but there seemed to be no structural damage, as if the tower had been ready for just such an incident.

Aniya stepped over dozens of dead bodies that littered the hallways. Melted flesh sagged around their skeletons, and she shuddered as she imagined Salvador's body in a similar state, somewhere in the building.

Nicholas stopped in front of a dead end and pressed a button on the wall. Three sets of six-inch doors opened, revealing a pristine, white elevator.

"How was this not touched by the fire?" Aniya asked.

Nicholas knocked on the large doors that jutted out slightly from the wall. "Blast doors."

They stepped into the elevator, and the doors closed behind them.

"How does it still have power?"

"I don't know for sure, but I have a guess," Nicholas said. "Did Roland tell you that Holendast has power again?"

She nodded.

"Same source, probably." Nicholas gestured to the massive panel of buttons on the wall. "Take your pick."

"I don't understand," Aniya said. "We're going to hide in the Citadel? I thought we were leaving the Web."

Nicholas shook his head. "This elevator goes beyond the tip of the Citadel and below the cavern where the machine was. See this right here?" He gestured to a row of buttons second from the bottom. A button near the end of the row was lit up yellow. "That's us, what Kendall calls Level XVIII. Everything above and below our row is a different web."

Aniya's jaw dropped open as she looked over the rows of buttons. All her life she had been told that the Web was the final remnant of civilization, the last million or so people left on Earth. At least, that's what she had been taught in Assembly, based on a curriculum approved by the Lightbringers. It was unsurprising that this was yet another lie, but after hearing the same thing her whole life, this was still a shock.

"How long have you known?"

"Not long," Nicholas said. "Kendall told me recently because he wanted me to take you to the Director, who is in a different web."

"Which one?"

He pointed to a single button above the massive grid. "Just don't hit that button, and we'll be fine. I recommend the twelfth button in any row so we end up on the ground floor of a different Citadel. We don't want to end up in the middle of another massive tower that we'll just have to escape from."

"So which one should we go to?"

"That's up to you. I don't know anything about them. They could be just like ours or totally different."

Aniya scanned the array of buttons.

"Whatever you choose, do it quickly. As soon as the Director finds out that his operative is dead, it won't be long before someone else summons the elevator, and I don't think either of us want to find out who that'll be."

She nodded and pressed the twelfth button in the top row, right beneath the button that would apparently lead to the Director. She took a deep breath, but nothing happened.

"Sorry." Nicholas took a thin plastic card from his pocket and placed it in a nearly invisible slot beneath the array of buttons. "Apparently, in order to move between different webs, you need one of these. Courtesy of Kendall." He nodded toward Aniya. "Go ahead."

She pressed the button again, and the elevator began to rise at an incredibly fast pace.

"Why so close to the top?" Nicholas frowned.

Aniya shrugged. "No one will think to look for us there."

"Good call."

As the rapidly ascending elevator began to pick up even more speed, Aniya's stomach plummeted, and she sat down on the floor of the elevator to keep herself from falling over.

Nicholas sat down next to her, and the ride continued in silence for several minutes.

Aniya closed her eyes and listened to the mechanical hum of the elevator. After a while, the vertigo became her new normal, and she almost found herself enjoying the feeling of racing through the air.

She almost found peace just as Nicholas finally spoke. "Aniya, I'm sorry. I—"

"Don't." Aniya shook her head.

"You don't understand. They—"

"I don't want to hear it."

Nicholas sighed.

After a pause, Aniya opened her eyes and turned to him, unable to resist. "Answer me this. Do you really believe that I can trust you now? After everything you've done, do you honestly think that I owe you that?"

When he didn't answer, she leaned back against the wall and closed her eyes again. "I didn't think so."

A few seconds later, Aniya felt something slip into her hand. She opened her eyes and looked down to see the key card that Nicholas had used to operate the elevator.

"There. Now you can leave whenever you want, and you don't have to take me with you." Nicholas bowed his head. "I did what I said I would. I got you out of there. What happens after that is your call."

Aniya held the card up in front of his face. "And just like that, I'm supposed to trust you again?"

"That's up to you."

She huffed and shoved the card in her pocket, then leaned back and folded her arms, turning away from Nicholas for the remainder of the journey.

Eventually, the elevator slowed its ascent.

"So?" Aniya asked, turning to Nicholas. "What's the plan?"

Nicholas shook his head. "Now you know as much as I do. If it's anything like our Web, my first instinct is to get out of the Hub as quickly as possible."

Aniya nodded and turned back to the doors as the elevator came to a halt.

"Aniya?" Nicholas asked as they stood.

She looked back at him.

"Are you with me?"

After staring at him for a moment, Aniya turned again, facing the doors as they opened.

"For now."

30

Aniya and Nicholas stepped out into a white hallway. Unlike the dead Citadel in their own Web, this tower was pristine, brightly lit with powered, fluorescent lights.

But this building also seemed to be empty.

Aniya looked around the interior of the tower. It looked just like their own had before she destroyed it. "So if they have their own Hub and Citadel, does that mean they have their own version of the Lightbringers?"

Nicholas grimaced. "They're all Lightbringers. The Chancellor, Kendall, the Director, they're all part of the same organization."

"So you lied about that too? Teaming up with Kendall was just to take out the Chancellor? We weren't ever fighting against the Lightbringers?"

"I thought we were. At the time, I thought the Chancellor was the leader of the Lightbringers. I had no idea that there was more than one web, more to the Lightbringers. But isn't it just semantics? We got rid of the Chancellor, which is what we really wanted."

But Aniya wasn't listening. Sacrificing herself to destroy

the reactor, Salvador's death in the battle in the Hub, even the war her parents started, it was apparently all for nothing. There would always be more to the Lightbringers. There would always be someone else waiting to take over.

"Why overthrow the Chancellor at all?" she asked. "If Kendall is part of the Lightbringers, wouldn't he be shooting himself in the foot?"

"I don't know. In case you haven't noticed, Kendall keeps a lot of things to himself."

Aniya frowned. That seemed to be a common theme. "Who takes over our Web now? Kendall? Another chancellor?"

"I don't know, Aniya."

She sighed, and as they both fell silent, Aniya realized that the faint sound of muffled speech was drifting down the hallway. She looked back at Nicholas.

"Do you hear that?"

He nodded.

Aniya looked back down the deserted hallway as she began to proceed slowly through the building. "Where is everybody?"

Nicholas shrugged and joined her, walking down the white hallway. "If it's anything like our Web, most of the factories in the Hub are run by robotics. The Citadel is staffed by very few people and holds mostly servants of the Chancellor. There'll be several of the Silver Guard in the barracks, but other than that, the population of the Hub is quite small."

Aniya froze, letting Nicholas continue on ahead.

He turned back toward her. "What is it?"

"If this level is exactly like ours, with its own Hub, its own sectors . . . does that mean that they have a machine below the Citadel? Do they have the Citizen Tax and relocative servitude here?"

"I don't see how they could survive without it," Nicholas said softly. "That's how we produced our power, and as you can see, this level has all the power it needs. They probably do the exact same thing here."

Aniya's mouth dropped open. There were more levels, more webs, each with tens of thousands of people held captive, hooked up to a massive machine, doomed to be tortured forever in a never-ending cycle of death.

"We have to help them."

Nicholas shook his head. "I hate it as much as you do, but there's nothing we can do about it. There's no Kendall waiting for us here to help us destroy the reactor. We would be on our own. And what could *we* do? You can't control your abilities, and even if you could, there's no way to know if you would be able to take out the machine without someone like Kendall managing the process."

"But they're being tortured. We know it's happening, and we have to do something about it."

"I'm sorry, Aniya. Even if we tried, it would draw the attention of the Director. You want to stay hidden from him, right? We have to lay low."

Aniya looked down at her toes.

"Come on," Nicholas said.

They made their way to the main exit, and Nicholas opened the door for Aniya, who glared at him as she stepped through and into the Hub.

But her feet turned to cement as she stared out at the street in front of the Citadel, where there were standing two long lines of people, split almost perfectly between boys and girls. There had to have been hundreds of them, and each one of them was looking directly at her.

A row of Silvers standing on the steps of the Citadel turned around to face them, and one of them stepped forward, pointing a rifle at Aniya and Nicholas.

"Well, now. What do we have here?"

31

Aniya stared back at the Silver pointing a gun at her. She forced herself to take a breath to calm her nerves and hoped that the sweat she felt beginning to form on her head would not be visible. Feeling at her chest quickly, she was relieved to find that her glowing necklace was still safe under her shirt, out of view of the Silvers.

"Surely you know the penalty for dodging the Citizen Tax," the Silver said. "It is a great honor to be chosen for servitude, and you should be proud to serve your Web in such an honorable capacity."

He moved behind them and pushed Aniya toward the two rows of people lined up in the streets of the Hub. "Now, get back in line, and I'll forget this happened."

She obeyed the officer, and she walked with Nicholas down the street, avoiding the judgmental eye contact of hundreds of boys and girls, and soon joined them in the back of the long lines.

They turned, and Aniya realized what the source of the muffled speech had been.

A man was standing on the third-floor balcony of the Citadel. He was dressed in a white suit, and as his stern gaze vanished, a large smile spread across on his face. Unlike the Chancellor's thin smirk, this man's smile was wide, and his eyes seemed to gleam. A man in a black cloak stood behind him to his left.

"I trust there will be no more interruptions," the man in the white suit said. "As I was saying, I welcome you all to the Hub, my home. For many of you, it is your new home as well. As your president, let me offer you my most sincere gratitude in advance for your payment of the Citizen Tax."

The two lines of children burst into applause, and as Aniya quickly joined in, she turned to Nicholas and mouthed, *President?*

Nicholas shrugged.

The applause finally died away, and the President continued, "Relocative servitude is the greatest sacrifice we ask of our citizens, and we do not take your service lightly."

Aniya shuddered and looked at the ground, imagining the giant reactor below their feet.

"As such, each year, this is a day to be celebrated, the day when many of you come here ready to pay the ultimate price. But it is also the day that the future of the Web is secured by your actions. We will never forget the heroes that have gone before us, and we will never fail to celebrate those who come after us."

The President raised a hand toward his head and thrust it outward. "To our heroes, we salute you."

In a snapping motion that echoed throughout the Hub, each member of the group raised their hands and saluted back. Aniya quickly raised her hand to avoid singling herself out more than she'd already done.

"And to the rest of you who will serve the entire Underworld as members of our esteemed Silver Guard, get ready to embark on the most challenging yet rewarding ten weeks of your lives." The President glanced at the man in black to his right. "General Addington has assured me that this will be

Sector F's best training class yet, and I look forward to the results, as he has never failed to develop a team of high-caliber peacekeepers."

The President raised his arm again. "Safe travels, good luck, and all hail the Glorious Bringers of Light."

"All hail the Glorious Bringers of Light," the group of teenagers said again as they saluted. Aniya raised her hand but did not speak.

The children applauded again, and the President turned and walked back inside the Citadel, letting the doors close behind him. The man in the black cloak remained on the balcony, watching the proceedings below.

One of the Silvers walked up the steps of the Citadel and turned to face the group, pulling out a long sheet of paper. "Please form two lines as I call your names. Group A, you will stand to my left. Group B, to my right."

Aniya shot a look of panic towards Nicholas, who returned a similar glance.

"Bradley Abernathy, group A. Fallon Ackerman, group B. Quinn Afsel, group B. Naomi Allers, group A."

The panic diminished for just a second as Aniya frowned. So far, there was a girl in each group, one going to power the reactor and one serving in the Silver Guard. Apparently, they did not only choose boys for relocative servitude here.

As the officer continued down the list, Aniya looked around rapidly, searching for an exit. Unfortunately, the entire group was surrounded by the Silver Guard, and the one that had caught them earlier was still keeping a close eye on them.

"Matthew Ribbles, group B. Nicollete Ridor, group A."

Aniya considered making a run for it, but she knew how the scene would play out. The Silver Guard would try to stop her, and she would either break free and be shot or turn into a nuclear bomb that could level the Hub and kill hundreds of innocent children.

There was no escape.

"Jeffrey Yersen, group A. Callie Yorsef, group B."

Aniya hung her head and waited for her inevitable fate.

Sure enough, just a moment later, Aniya and Nicholas were the only ones left. They stood facing two long lines of steely eyed children, surrounded by Silver Guard, totally exposed.

"And that's the list." The officer reading the names frowned. "It seems we have two extra. What are your names?"

"Aila Tigert," Aniya replied after a brief pause.

"Nikolai Radmilovic," Nicholas said with a short laugh. "Not sure what happened. They drew my name and made sure I got on the train."

The officer studied the list again. He sighed. "This happens occasionally, where someone sneaks aboard the train. We understand that it is a great honor to serve the Lightbringers, but you were not chosen."

"I don't think they snuck on," a voice came from the side. "They were the ones that were trying to escape."

Aniya winced as the Silver that had stopped them at the door stepped forward.

Nicholas gave another laugh. "Can you blame me? I would have much rather stayed with my family than work here for the rest of my life."

A ripple of murmurs passed through everyone standing before them. Up on the balcony on the Citadel, the man in black stared back down at the two of them, folding his arms.

The lead officer frowned. "You dishonor your family by attempting to leave. Why would you shun such an honorable destiny?"

Aniya spoke up. "It doesn't matter. It didn't work, and we're sorry we did it."

Nicholas nodded. "Look, I don't know why our names aren't on there. But does that mean we can go?"

The lead officer craned his neck, looking up at the man in black on the balcony above.

After a moment, the man gave a short nod.

The officer looked back down and sighed. "You said it yourself. There must have been some mistake. If someone forgot to write your name down, that's unfortunate, but you're here now, so you get to serve the Lightbringers for the rest of your life. If you're not on the list, we haven't prepared pods for you, so both of you will be assigned to group B."

Aniya sighed both in relief and resignation and followed Nicholas to stand in front of the indicated group.

The officer gave a single clap and smiled. "Thank you, everyone, for another exciting induction ceremony! We applaud your bravery and admire your sacrifice."

The Silver Guard began to applaud, and the children joined in. This time, Aniya watched the boys and girls clap, and she was surprised to see genuine excitement on their faces. She looked back up at the Citadel, where the man in black gave another nod and disappeared into the building.

The officer gestured toward the edge of the Hub, where a train was waiting in the distance. "Group B, let's head out."

32

Nicholas sat across from Aniya on the train. There was plenty of room for everyone to spread out, so they had chosen a booth far away from any neighbors.

Although thirty minutes had passed since they left the Hub, not a single word had been shared between them.

Every time Nicholas looked at Aniya, she was staring out the window, obviously making a point not to look in his direction. Each glance at her face put a heavier weight on his heart. He had seen her angry before, even livid, but this was something new.

Aniya had always been headstrong. She'd always made a point to let others know that she was angry and why. It had always frustrated Nicholas.

But now she was silent. The sight nearly terrified him, and it left Nicholas feeling empty. He couldn't decide if it was worth apologizing again. Would she even hear it? Could it ever change anything?

For all he knew, Aniya wasn't even angry. Maybe she didn't think it was worth the energy to be angry at him. Maybe she had decided that there was no place for him in her life anymore.

And Nicholas agreed. There wasn't. Not as her lover, and not as her friend. He had broken her trust and betrayed her. There was no coming back from that.

And so, even as the guilt kept nudging him, prompting him to say something, anything, Nicholas remained silent.

He didn't deserve her, and she didn't need someone who continually led her into danger.

Nicholas stood up and stepped away from their booth.

"Where are you going?"

Aniya spoke for the first time in nearly an hour, but Nicholas got the impression from her tone that she didn't really care where he was going.

"I'm going to talk to some of the other recruits. See what I can find out about this level."

"What do you think you'll be able to get out of them without giving away the fact that we're not from here?"

Nicholas shrugged. "Whatever I can."

He turned and walked down the train car, scanning for anyone sitting alone who would be able to talk with him quietly, reducing the risk of anyone overhearing a potentially dangerous conversation. It wasn't long before he came across a blonde girl sitting by herself, staring out the window blankly.

Nicholas cleared his throat to get her attention. "Excuse me. Can I sit with you?"

The girl turned toward him, and her eyes seemed to come alive as a small, charming smile appeared. "Sure."

Nicholas sank down in the seat across from the girl and extended a hand. "I'm Nikolai."

"Quinn." She smiled and shook his hand. "You're one of the ones who was left behind after they called out the list, right?"

He nodded.

"Did you really sneak on?" The girl said with a laugh. "That's what they're saying."

"No. I guess they just forgot to put me on the list."

"I'm surprised they let you in."

"I know," Nicholas said, sighing. "Rotten luck, right?"

Quinn's eyes widened. "Rotten? To have the good fortune to be chosen to serve the Lightbringers? I know dozens of people who would've loved to take your place."

Nicholas looked at her quizzically. "You *want* to serve the Lightbringers? I don't think they have anything pleasant planned for the other group."

"What do you mean? You know exactly what they have planned for them. Everybody knows."

Nicholas raised his eyebrows. "They do?"

"You don't?"

He stammered. "I mean, of course I do. I just didn't think it was common knowledge."

The girl shrugged. "Sure. My best friend is underneath the Hub right now, supplying free energy to the rest of the Web."

There was a brief pause as Nicholas squinted at her. She seemed not to care about the torture her friend must have been going through at that very moment. "And you don't think there's anything wrong with that?"

"Why would there be anything wrong with it? She's serving the Glorious Bringers of Light, the entire Web."

"Wait, so why are they sending girls?"

"Are you saying only boys should be able to serve the Web? That's not very fair, don't you think?"

Nicholas searched for words. "What I mean is, I guess she's not as lucky as you."

She smiled. "That's true. She would be *so* jealous if she found out that I got to be a member of the Silver Guard, that I get to serve the entire underworld and not just one level."

Nicholas looked away to hide his surprise as he realized that there were no secrets here. Here, being drafted for relocative servitude seemed to be cause for celebration, induction into the Silver Guard an annual ceremony, starkly compared to Level XVIII, where the Silvers would forcibly kidnap children on the day of their eighteenth birthday. For a very brief moment, he caught himself wondering if the President got it right on this level. If using humans to provide power was truly the only way, maybe they should have done it like this back home.

"I'm not looking forward to the training, though," Quinn continued. "I've heard it's brutal. Though, I'm glad I didn't have to wait longer than most people after they find out they get to serve. My birthday was last week, so I lucked out."

"Happy birthday," Nicholas said. The words felt wrong. Back home, the eighteenth birthday was never celebrated. There was too much tension surrounding the unknown fates of children for there to be any joy.

"Thanks," Quinn said with a grin.

Before Nicholas knew it, her hand was on his knee. He looked down in surprise, then back up at her. Her eyes were twinkling.

A twinge of guilt lingered in the back of his mind, but he quickly banished the feeling. Aniya had made it abundantly clear that things were over between them.

She had moved on.

And so could he.

33

Aniya stared out the window of the train, distracting herself with the view, doing everything she could to push Nicholas to the back of her mind.

The scenery was breathtaking. Each sector they traveled through seemed to be flourishing. Buildings of glass and marble decorated the grassy hills and valleys of Level I, covering the sectors in pure beauty.

Even the tunnels between sectors were flawless chutes of steel, well lit by hundreds of bright, white lights that appeared as seamless lines of light due to the sheer speed of the train.

The beauty had lulled her into a welcome peace, but as Aniya glimpsed Nicholas down the aisle, laughing, her calm vanished. Over his shoulder, she caught a flash of long, blonde hair.

Aniya's fingers tingled and grew warm. She could feel anger brimming within as her temperature rose, but as she looked away, she found that her fury was slowly dampened by apathy as she found herself wondering if there was any reason to be hurt by this betrayal.

Their relationship hadn't lasted long, even though it felt like it due to their lifelong friendship. And now that it was over with such a resounding finality, now that he had betrayed her so completely, was there really any reason to let it break her heart?

The thought tore at her. The fact that there was no longer a relationship at risk made things easier, but was it really all over, just like that?

She moved closer to the window until she could no longer see Nicholas out of the corner of her eye, and she pressed her forehead into the glass, trying to wipe the image of her old friend away.

Her fingers wandered to her chest, where she grabbed at the crystal that was hiding under her shirt and squeezed it, distracting herself in whatever way she could.

As she enjoyed her first quiet moment in hours, Aniya allowed her mind to wander. She wasn't terribly surprised when the voice came again, but it didn't make the surprise any less unsettling.

"Aniya."

Here in the waking world, she couldn't tell whether it was William or the Shadow. Whatever it was said her name again, and Aniya found herself drifting off, letting the cadence of the train machinery rock her into a deep slumber.

She opened her eyes again and saw black.

Immediately, a nauseating feeling turned in her stomach. She wasn't in a coma anymore, and she could feel herself in the real world. She felt the leather cushion of the train booth beneath her. She heard the engine humming. She felt the glass of the window on her cheek.

But she was standing in the void, surrounded by the empty black.

"Welcome back."

Aniya turned around, and the nausea, the anxiety, even the apathy instantly vanished as she saw her brother. She smiled. "I didn't think I was going to see you again."

"I wouldn't let that happen." William reached out and took her hand.

And in an instant, it all came rushing back in a horrible wave of emotion. Aniya saw Xander's face materialize over William's shoulder, and she let go of his hand quickly.

Warmth returned, and Aniya sighed as William frowned.

But he nodded as if he understood. "I couldn't bear the thought of not seeing you again. That's why I keep calling for you. I was beginning to think you couldn't hear me."

"Oh, trust me. I heard you. It didn't sound like you, though. It sounded like hundreds of different people all at once."

"Thousands. Tens of thousands. It's hard to get your attention while you're awake, so I have to be loud. There's a lot of us in here, and as long as they have no interest in talking to you, they're just sitting there doing nothing. Might as well put them to use."

Aniya looked around. "Where are they?"

"Around. I haven't actually seen any of them, at least not like I'm seeing you. They're throughout your entire body, inside and out." He shrugged. "I could be like them if I wasn't so insistent on finding a way to talk to you."

"So back in Ravelta, that was you? All of you? I don't get it. Why did you let Xander die?"

"It wasn't our choice, Aniya."

Aniya put her hands on her hips. "It wasn't mine either."

"I know. And I know you think we're in control, but we're really not. I'm just as much of a spectator in this as you are."

"So then who or what is controlling the light?"

"I have no idea."

"Thanks. You've been very helpful."

"What do you want me to say, Aniya? You've not been very gracious with people lately."

She looked up sharply. "Are you talking about Nicholas?"

"Maybe."

"I need time. Until then, nothing is going to change."

"You need to forgive him."

"Don't talk about things you don't understand."

William sighed. "I do understand, Aniya. I see and hear everything you do. I know exactly what he did."

"Then you know why I can't forgive him."

"No. I know why you *won't* forgive him."

"Same thing."

"No." William's voice was calm but firm. "I understand that he betrayed you. I'm not too happy about it myself. But you have to believe that he wants the best for you despite his lapse in judgment."

Aniya clenched her fists. "You're telling me to ignore his betrayal and act like it never happened."

"That's not what I said."

"That's exactly what you're saying." The void flashed green as Aniya growled. "Words are only as good as actions. Nicholas can tell me he loves me all he wants, but when he tricks me into dying for his stupid cause, that tells me a whole lot more."

William's voice grew quiet. "He gave you a choice."

Instead of lowering her voice as well, Aniya shouted, "That doesn't make it better! He lied to me until it was too late. How can you not see that?"

"Aniya," he said, placing a glowing hand on her shoulder.

She forced herself to take it this time, staring at William's eyes and avoiding Xander's burning gaze as he reappeared. Pushing away the wave of painful emotion, she chose to focus on the love that radiated from his touch. As she let the warmth become all she knew, her childhood home materialized around them, building itself up piece by piece until they were standing in their tiny shack. There was no sign of their parents' bodies, no blood. For the first time in a long time, Aniya was home.

William squeezed her shoulder as his voice softened.

"You've known him for a long time, but I've known him even longer. He can be quite foolish at times, but he loves you more than anything. Who do you think he talked to when you rejected him? I got so sick of him talking about you like you were the best thing in the entire Web. Trust me, he loves you. If he could have taken your place and died in the Citadel, he would have. I have no doubt about it."

Aniya finally took a breath and matched William's tone. "You can say what you want, but I don't see any way to get back to where we were before. It's over, William."

He studied her face for a moment before shaking his head. "I don't understand, Aniya. You were always stubborn, I know that. But you were never so unforgiving, especially not toward Nicholas. He's your best friend."

Aniya couldn't find the words to respond. Was he still her friend? The memory was still there, lying on his roof and watching the stars. It brought her a hint of serenity, the faint echo of peace that had once warmed her heart. But she couldn't for the life of her imagine ever feeling that with him again.

She closed her eyes. It did no good, as closing her eyes only enhanced the illusions of the void. She watched as her home fell apart around them, piece by piece. The warmth vanished, although William's hand remained on her shoulder, and Aniya looked past him, surrendering herself to Xander's piercing stare.

He was holding out his burning hands toward her. His mouth opened and moved, but no sound came from his lips.

It didn't matter. Aniya knew what he was saying.

"I know," she said as William faded away. It was just her and the boy she had killed, staring at each other. "I know it's my fault. I don't deserve your forgiveness. Or Malcolm's. Or Corrin's."

Glowing, red tears fell from Xander's flaming eyes as his

expression twisted in pain. His face flashed, showing Nicholas's face for an instant.

Aniya shook her head. "And he doesn't deserve mine."

As her heart turned cold, Xander faded away, and the void was all that remained.

That, and William's voice echoing in her ears.

"He's your best friend."

But Aniya sighed and bowed her head. "Not anymore."

She felt the void melt around her, and she opened her eyes to find herself back in the booth, the train still zipping through the Web.

"Never again."

34

The train finally began slowing down, and Nicholas stood up and made his way back to Aniya. To his surprise, she spoke first as he sat down.

"Talk to anyone interesting?"

Nicholas paused, realizing that a silly grin was slathered on his face, and he wiped it away before responding. "Not really."

"Find out anything?"

"A bit. Enough to know that this level is very different from our own. It's almost like the people have been brainwashed. Did you get some rest?"

Aniya nodded.

"Did you sleep well?"

She shrugged.

Nicholas sighed and wondered if he could ever have a casual conversation with her again. "It's never going to be like it was, is it?"

She looked out the window and took a deep breath. "What are we going to do once we get off the train?"

"I guess we have to play along. Something tells me it's not going to be easy to just slip away. If they want to train us, maybe we have to let them."

"So that's it? We settle in, become Silvers, start new lives as goons of the Lightbringers, terrorizing citizens all over the Underworld?"

"What do you want me to do, Aniya?"

She didn't move.

Nicholas sighed. "Look, Aniya. Let me just take you to the Director. If he can help you get better, we can go back to our own Web and help them rebuild. We don't have to constantly worry about—"

Aniya's head snapped away from the window as she glared at him. "You gave me a choice, and I made it. I don't trust the Director, so I'm not going. I feel fine, and if nothing changes in a few months, I might even go back. But I'm not going to the Director."

"*You* might go back?" Nicholas frowned. "What happens to me?"

She looked away again as the train finally came to a stop.

"Aniya . . ." He stretched a hand toward her, but she stood up and walked past him down the aisle. Nicholas bowed his head and followed, exiting the train and stepping out onto a platform overlooking the sector.

Unlike the sectors they had passed on the train, the landscape was nearly completely silver. What light came from the sky ceiling was reflected off the silver buildings, resulting in a shining, sparkling view that was difficult to look at for any great length of time.

Instead of a sun, a giant digital clock was in the center of the sky ceiling, displaying the time in massive, yellow numerals. Right now, it read 1340.

After the last recruit stepped off the train, the train zipped away, leaving the hundreds of young adults spread throughout the trainyard.

The station was unnaturally silent. Nicholas thought that such a massive group of teenagers would have begun talking by now, but the entire group quietly waited for instructions.

All of them seemed to be facing generally the same direction, so Nicholas turned and found himself staring at a dozen Silvers standing before them in two neat rows. The man in the black cloak that had been in the Hub was in front, his hands behind his back.

"Welcome to Sector F," he said. "I am General Caspian Addington. For some of you, this will be your home for the next three years. The remainder of you will be here for six. What determines the length of your stay is a ten-week evaluation that takes the form of a fighting tournament, pitting you against your peers."

A horrible thought came to Nicholas's mind as he glanced at Aniya. If she was forced into fighting, the light could come back with devastating results. It would not end well for any of them. Her pale face revealed that she had come to the same conclusion.

"We do this to learn your strengths and weaknesses, and so that we know how much attention you need. If you lose a fight, however, don't be discouraged. We do this so that by the time you leave Level I, you will all be evenly matched. However, the best of you will be placed in our advanced program to train to be a part of an elite squadron of fighters."

Nicholas frowned. Kendall had made no mention of an elite squadron, and Nicholas had never seen any evidence of one.

The man's gaze traveled over the group. "These competitions have proven to be quite intense in the past, and serious injury occurs. Not to worry, of course. We have the best medical facilities in the entire Underworld, and even the most devastating injury can be treated and remedied in days. In some rare cases, the fights do turn lethal, and while that is quite unfortunate, we can't deny that it is an effective method of weeding out those that are unfit for this lifestyle. All other pertinent information will be distributed throughout the week."

The man broke his somber demeanor as a small smile spread across his face. "But as for today, we need to find out where each of you are so we can develop a custom training plan for each of you. Report to the arenas in the middle of the sector in one hour to be sorted off into groups. Your training begins now."

35

"Doc, we need your help, quick!"

Roland staggered into the clinic, Tamisra's body in his arms. The knife still protruded from her shoulder, and dark blood freely dripped to the ground below, creating a trail to the post outside where he had tied his mole.

Gareth had been talking to Corrin and Lieutenant Haskill on the far side of the room, but at Roland's cry, he spun around, his eyes wide.

"Are you okay?" Gareth asked as he rushed to Roland's side, helping him gently place Tamisra on a bed. "What happened?"

"Zeta," Roland said. "We were trying to help Aniya, but she tried to stop us. Malcolm, too."

"What do you mean?" Corrin asked as his skin turned pale.

Lieutenant Haskill interrupted. "How long has she been like this?"

"Twelve hours," Roland said, fighting back tears. "I couldn't treat her. We didn't have any medical supplies."

"Quiet," Gareth growled as he ripped away part of Tamisra's shirt. "I need to work."

Roland nervously paced for several minutes as Corrin and the lieutenant watched Gareth tend to Tamisra. It wasn't long before the door opened again and Kendall stepped inside, his hand on Malcolm's shoulder.

Malcolm was staring at the floor, holding a hand to his nose, which was covered in blood.

"What's going on? Why is there a mole in Refuge, and why was Malcolm tied to it?" Kendall looked at Gareth and Tamisra. "What happened to—"

That was all Kendall got out before Roland dashed across the room and tackled him.

"What's going on?" Corrin's voice came from behind, and Roland spun around, placing Kendall between himself and Corrin. Kendall reached back wildly, but Roland wrapped an arm around his throat and clamped down tightly.

Lieutenant Haskill approached slowly, stretching a hand out toward them. "Roland, let him go."

"He tried to have Aniya killed. He used Nicholas against her." Roland squeezed harder as Kendall began to croak. "He kidnapped me and Tamisra, tortured us, and got Salvador killed."

"We don't know that," Gareth said, looking up from Tamisra. "Let him go, Roland."

"Yes, we do. He admitted to it."

"Is this true?" Corrin froze and glared at Kendall.

"So what, you're going to kill me?" Kendall's voice was barely above a whisper. "Your girlfriend might stoop so low, but you're better than this, Roland."

"You're right, she would," Roland said, hissing in Kendall's ear. "And she can't because your assassin nearly killed her. Don't think for a second that I won't finish you off for her."

Gareth stepped forward and held up a hand. "Roland, that's enough."

His voice boomed throughout the small shack, and after a

moment, Roland finally released Kendall, who rolled away, wheezing and gasping for air.

Roland glared at Gareth. "You said he would pay for what he did. You promised."

Gareth nodded. "And I meant it. But right now, Tamisra needs my help, and I can't concentrate if you're in here trying to start another coup." He turned to Kendall. "Go to the war room. We'll deal with you momentarily."

"You are here because I asked Nicholas and Roland to bring you here." Kendall choked out. "You can't—"

"Now," Lieutenant Haskill commanded, pulling his shirt aside to reveal a handgun strapped to his pants.

Kendall's gaze alternated between the four angry men. Finally, he turned and left the clinic.

Roland pointed at Malcolm. "Him too."

"Why Malcolm?" Haskill asked.

Roland glared at Malcolm. "He betrayed us. He said he was going to help us get Aniya to safety, but he led us right to Zeta. It's his fault Tami's hurt."

"Malcolm, no," Corrin whispered. "Tell me you didn't do this."

Malcolm looked down at the floor. "She had to leave. She was too dangerous."

"That's what we were doing," Roland said. "We were getting her out of here."

"It wasn't good enough," Malcolm spat, looking back up swiftly. "Moving her to another part of the Web? Nothing would have changed. She needed to be taken care of."

Roland growled. "Taken care of? You didn't want her gone. You wanted her dead."

"Malcolm, what did you do?" Corrin spoke softly.

"I did what had to be done," Malcolm said, folding his arms. "She killed Xander. She murdered him, and I'm tired of you acting like it never happened."

Corrin shook his head and rested his face in his hands.

Gareth sighed. "Go to the war room with Kendall. We'll decide what to do with you later."

As Malcolm left the clinic, Gareth returned his focus to Tamisra, and Roland moved to her bedside.

"Kendall can't stay here, Doc. I don't know what he wants, but he's not on our side. We can't—"

Gareth spoke without looking up. "Don't make me ask you to leave as well. I need to concentrate."

Roland sighed and sat down by Tamisra's side. "Sorry, Doc. It's been rough even before you got here. And now with the Chancellor dead, Aniya and Nicholas only God knows where, Tamisra getting—" Roland's voice faltered, and he stared at the knife sticking out of her shoulder. He nearly vomited as Gareth withdrew the knife swiftly, sending blood gushing from Tamira's open wound.

"I understand, Roland." Gareth placed a rag on Tamisra and nodded toward Roland. "Hold this."

"I don't," Lieutenant Haskill said. He paced back and forth, glancing in the direction of the Refuge tower. "What happened out there?"

Roland opened his mouth to speak but glanced at Gareth. He was still focused on Tamisra, and Roland didn't want to risk distracting him.

But the doctor sighed and waved a hand.

So Roland recounted everything that had happened in the last day, and when he was done, Corrin and the lieutenant took several minutes to process it all. No one seemed to be terribly shocked that there was more than one web, which baffled Roland.

Finally, Corrin spoke again. "If what you say is true, then we have a serious problem. We waged war against the Chancellor eighteen years ago because he was manipulative and dangerous. It doesn't seem like Kendall is any different. And we just let him inside Refuge, giving him access to all of our men and resources. We need to take care of him before we end up exactly where we were with the Chancellor."

Gareth shook his head, still looking down at his work. "No one is taking care of anyone. Whatever his motivations, Kendall helped us overthrow the Chancellor, something we never could have done on our own."

Roland threw his hands in the air. "You think he should just be allowed to carry on, doing whatever he wants after this?"

"I didn't say that. We can't kill him is what I meant, but you're right. He can't stay here either."

"What are your orders?" Lieutenant Haskill asked, turning to Corrin. "My inclination is to try him and imprison him if necessary."

But Corrin turned to Gareth. "What do you suggest, Doctor?"

Gareth tied the last stitch and wiped his bloody hands on a nearby rag. "We ask him to leave."

Roland scoffed. "And if he says no?"

"Then we make him."

36

Aniya stood in the stands of the silver coliseum, shifting in place for two reasons. First, the silver jumpsuit she had been given by the Silvers was uncomfortably tight. Second, she knew that her turn was coming up next.

It was about time, too. She had been waiting in dreaded anticipation since the day before. There were so many recruits that the first round of fights had to take place over two days. By next week, she had been told, half of the fighters would be knocked out of the ten-week tournament, so starting then, each round of fights would be held in one day.

Aniya had secretly hoped she would lose her upcoming fight. She would still be in the training program like the rest of the defeated, and no extra attention would be placed on her. But two recruits had already died in the last day, and Aniya didn't want to imagine how brutal her defeat would be.

In the end, she decided that she was going to try to win. Not try so hard that she would accidentally activate her dormant power, but enough that she could stand some kind of chance. But as she watched the fighters now, she found herself wondering how much of a chance she actually had.

In the arena below, a boy and a girl circled each other in

the dirt. Occasionally, one would lunge at the other, but it would never result in any great injury.

But it wasn't for lack of skill that the fight didn't seem to escalate. Rather, the teenagers seemed highly competent in combat and held their ground, seemingly without effort.

A vicious strike would come from one of them, but the defender would always sidestep and answer with an attack of his or her own, which would then be quickly deflected by the initial attacker.

Aniya guessed that unlike her own Web, the Lightbringers encouraged fighting at a young age here, hoping to develop combat skills long before their formal training began.

Finally, the girl in the arena below rushed forward, but rather than defending again, the boy jumped high, spinning in the air and delivering a kick that struck the girl's face with a loud, sickening crack that echoed throughout the arena.

The girl fell to the ground and went still.

Aniya's jaw dropped. The fight had lasted for mere moments. This was the level of competition she would be facing, brutal fighters trained from birth that could incapacitate her with one blow.

Her shock remained until the next fight began at 1645. She hoped that this match would be different and give her some hope of survival for her own battle.

The fight was indeed different, but not any less skilled. Two girls met in the center of the ring, and after bowing to each other, one of the girls immediately rushed forward and locked the other in a tight embrace, forcing her to the ground.

This match lasted longer, but only because the two girls fought at much closer quarters than the previous fighters, making it difficult for either opponent to land any finishing blow.

But within minutes, one of the girls had managed to get behind the other and wrap her arms around her opponent's throat, squeezing down tight until her victim passed out.

And just like that, it was Aniya's turn.

She had almost forgotten that she was up next, and she had to scramble back to the entrance of the arena when they called her name.

The officers at the entrance wordlessly searched her for weapons before waving her on to the center of the arena. Aniya was relieved that she had left her crystal necklace in her dormitory. Surely they would have considered it to be some kind of weapon.

As she readied herself, a young man came from the other side of the ring of dirt. He was smiling at her, and he even seemed to give her a small wave.

Aniya frowned as she realized that the boy's smile was a friendly one, with no trace of contempt or spite. Much to her own surprise, she found herself waving back.

The boy wasn't quite buff, but he was in good shape. Thanks to the tight, silver jumpsuit, Aniya could see highlights of his well-developed muscles.

They met in the center, the boy's smile still wide and almost amusing.

They bowed, and when Aniya looked back up again, the boy's smile was gone.

Before even a second had passed, Aniya found herself on the ground under the weight of the young man. She tried to take a breath in recovery, but the boy's fist smashed across her open mouth, and she howled in pain as she felt a tooth come free and drop down into her throat as blood rushed after it.

Aniya coughed, choking on her blood and tooth. She opened her eyes again just in time to see the boy's other fist come down on her left eye.

Heat spread throughout her body, a tickling sensation that buzzed her insides from head to toe. Strength stirred deep within, and as her body quickly warmed, her heart turned cold.

The boy reared back for another assault, and with a shriek

of anger, Aniya yanked her right hand free from underneath the boy's legs and swung her hand across his face, her fingernails deeply raking his skin.

Without pausing, she whipped the same hand back the way it had come, the back of her hand knocking the boy off her body and to the side.

Aniya climbed to her feet before the boy could retaliate and spit blood and her tooth out on the ground as she finally breathed freely again.

The throbbing pain in her mouth fed to the rage that boiled inside, and as energy swelled deep within her, pumping strength into every limb, she shuddered in anticipation.

All she had to do was attack now, and her opponent would soon fall.

But as the raw power surged through her body, Aniya looked at the boy, who was still struggling to stand again. Blood poured from his face, and where a smile had been just a minute earlier, his face read nothing but pure agony.

She looked down on her right hand, the one that had dug the wounds in the boy's face. Her fingernails were covered in his blood, which dripped to the ground and mixed with her own. But what drew her attention was the light that glowed faintly from her skin. The shimmer had turned from a rich emerald to a sickly yellow-green.

Aniya took a deep breath, doing her best to calm herself. Continuing to attack the boy would only end poorly. If things escalated, she could accidentally kill him, expose herself, and possibly let loose a barrage of light that would incinerate everything in sight.

As her anger rose, she closed her eyes and held her breath, trying her best to push the light back down to wherever it came from.

A noise stirred her focus, and she opened her eyes just as the boy rammed into her chest, sending her flying backward.

She landed roughly and immediately rolled to the side in

anticipation of the boy's next attack, and she let a grin slip loose as she heard the boy fall right where she had just lain. She jumped to her feet and steadied herself, taking advantage of this reprieve to let herself breathe again.

Within seconds, the boy had recovered and was rushing her again, but Aniya just stepped to the side and let him run past her.

The boy turned and rushed her once more, and with another sidestep from Aniya, he again stumbled right past her.

"Fight me!" The boy shouted, baring his teeth as blood dripped from his open wounds into his mouth.

He rushed again, and this time Aniya stuck out a foot as she dodged his attack, sending him tumbling to the ground.

It was too dangerous to engage him. Dangerous for him, for her, for everyone present. The best she could hope for was tiring him out and incapacitating him carefully, without getting too excited.

Familiar laughter came from the stands above as Aniya dodged yet another attack, and she risked the brief distraction as she looked up at the coliseum seating.

Her gaze made its way to Nicholas, who was near the bottom of the stands. However, he didn't seem to be watching the fight. His eyes were instead on an attractive, blonde girl standing next to him, who was staring back at him with a look that made Aniya's stomach churn.

She looked down to see their joined hands at their sides, then back up just in time to see the girl laugh at something, then stroke Nicholas's arm.

Suddenly, Aniya's lungs closed as she was lifted off the ground. She clawed at the hand around her neck as her vision grew fuzzy, but even as she reached to free herself, all she could see was Nicholas, who leaned in closer to the girl as she whispered in his ear.

The world began to go black, and her field of vision tightened to a circle around Nicholas.

Then, the girl kissed him on the cheek.

Blazing heat erupted from deep within Aniya as the black edges of her vision were replaced by a film of yellow light. With a roar of fury, she gripped the arm that held her and squeezed tight.

She barely heard a scream and the snap of bone as she forced herself free and threw the boy to the ground.

His silver jumpsuit was black in the place Aniya's hand had gripped him, and a faint wisp of smoke rose from the cloth. He writhed in pain, squealing as he kicked his legs.

But Aniya barely noticed. She mounted the boy and punched him in the face, not even flinching as blood flew forth from his mouth and splattered over her.

A second punch, and the boy's nose bent at a sickening angle.

Somewhere in the back of her mind, Aniya felt herself reel in disgust. Nausea rose within her, but it was quelled instantly as she delivered another punch.

She just couldn't stop.

Another punch, and the boy's cheekbones shattered, skin hanging loosely around his mouth.

"Aniya!"

Her heart stopped as she looked up.

Nicholas was no longer looking at the girl. He was staring at Aniya with horror written on his face.

Clarity suddenly returned, and Aniya took a deep breath, shuddering as the heat receded back inside her body.

The yellow light faded from her eyes, and she let herself fall backward as her heart slowed. From somewhere far away, she heard an announcer call her, "Aila Tigert," the winner.

Applause woke her from her stupor, and as Aniya looked around the arena, her disgust deepened. No one seemed disturbed by the bloody display. It was just another fight to them.

Her eyes landed on Nicholas again, the only one who

wasn't clapping. His skin had turned ashen, and he looked like he was about to vomit over the railing into the arena. The other girl's hand stroked his shoulder, and Aniya's rage returned instantly, in full force.

She walked past the bloody heap on the ground and straight to the edge of the arena, glaring at Nicholas as he stared back at her.

Without pausing, Aniya reached over the railing and grabbed Nicholas by the collar. With her other hand, she slapped him across the face.

A jolt of electricity erupted from her palm as Nicholas's head was forced to the side. He held his hand to his cheek and turned back to Aniya.

"Aniya, what—"

She slapped him again, and he visibly shuddered as another jolt of energy raced out of her body.

Nicholas looked back at her in shock as yellow energy flashed over his eyes. The light morphed to green, and as it faded, Aniya felt the warmth in her body subside somewhat. But the rage remained. All Aniya could think about was the other girl's lips on his cheek and the fact that he had betrayed her, that he had led her to the Hub to die.

"This isn't you, Aniya!" Nicholas held out a hand, pleading. "Snap out of it!"

Aniya heard him, but the words didn't make any sense. She had to punish him. He deserved so much worse. He deserved to burn. She pulled her hand back for another swing, but her grip on Nicholas's collar was forced away, and she was dragged backward. She looked behind her to see three Silver Guard pulling her away from the stands. One of them pulled out a plastic device and jammed it up against her neck. Sparks flew from the device, and Aniya shook, but when the device switched off, she only staggered for a moment before recovering and rushing toward Nicholas again.

The Silvers grabbed her, and the device was used again.

This time, the other two officers pulled out gadgets of their own. With another sparking device on her arm and another on her chest, Aniya was forced into convulsions.

After several seconds, darkness spread over her vision, and she fell backward into their arms, limp.

37

Kendall fumed as he passed the Refuge tower and kept walking through the massive cavern.

No good deed goes unpunished, right?

If Tamisra hadn't been so curious, if they had never found out about the necessary evil he had to commit in order to bring about change, they would be praising him now. He had destroyed the Hub and ended the Chancellor's reign, saving the entire Web.

His were the accomplishments of a hero who asked for nothing in return, someone who would do anything to see the Web move on and heal after generations of oppression.

But the cost had been great.

He had kidnapped and tortured children to bait a warlord.

He had convinced a girl to sacrifice herself.

He had asked a boy to temporarily kill the girl he loved in order to save her.

It sounded insane, he realized, knowing they would never understand.

It was Kendall's curse, it seemed, to do everything he could to save people and change the world, only to be forced to stand idly by while others ruin his progress and make him a pariah.

He sighed as he left the Refuge cavern and began walking down a tunnel.

Maybe the Director was right. Maybe he *was* the wrong man for the job. Everything he did seemed to backfire, and every move he made to improve the Web only dug a deeper hole for himself that these well-meaning fools would bury him inside.

Then again, maybe it wasn't Kendall. Maybe it was just this Web. Almost every other level lived in peace, without needing an emissary of the Director to influence things for the better. And it wasn't Kendall's fault that the Chancellor was a sanctimonious, power-hungry man who didn't understand his role.

But Kendall had believed he could make a difference here. Of course, if he had known that this was the inevitable outcome when he was first asked to take on the role of Level XVIII's adviser, he never would have agreed to the mission. The stakes were too great to fail.

And fail he had.

There was no coming back from this. The rebels would give him the exact same treatment as they had the Chancellor, determined to either kill him or exile him, ruining his chance to turn this Web into what it was always supposed to be.

There was no winning scenario.

If Kendall fought back and forced them into submission, he would become the dictator they already thought he was, taking the place of their old nemesis. But Kendall came to save the Web, not simply change the regime.

If he went along with their wishes and left Refuge, the Web could still be saved, but there would be an entire society in Refuge left without a home in the sectors, still living in awful conditions while the rest of the Web healed in the wake of the Chancellor. And there was no guarantee that the rebels would let him fulfill his mission in peace. They might follow him to the sectors and make his life incredibly difficult.

And if he were to plead his case and tell them the truth from beginning to end, that meant giving up the Director, exposing the outside influence that guided the Underworld. Kendall had told them what they needed to know, but there was so much more he held back, information that would best case save him, worst case condemn him. And even if he told them everything, he knew it wouldn't be long before the Director silenced him.

Kendall finally made it to the electromagnetic emission device and shut it down. He pulled his earpiece from his pocket and grimaced. He hated delivering such unpleasant news to the Director.

Right before he could press the button on the side and begin speaking, Malcolm arrived in the cavern and leaned up against the rock wall with a huff.

Kendall turned, annoyed. "Why did you follow me?"

"They don't like me any more than they like you right now," Malcolm said as he rolled his eyes. "We're stuck together for now."

Kendall paused. Maybe not all was lost. "What happened out there?"

"They asked me for help getting out of here. I told Zeta, and she said to lead them to the Hub."

"Yes, she told me," Kendall said, waving a hand. "Where is Zeta now?"

"Roland jabbed her with a syringe. She's dead."

Kendall frowned. "The syringe, did it have clear liquid in it?"

Malcolm nodded.

Maybe this wasn't a complete waste.

"Did Roland search her body?"

Malcolm shrugged. "I don't think so. He was focused on Tamisra."

"Good. And where did Nicholas and Aniya go?"

"I don't know." Malcolm looked away, his face turning nearly as red as the dried blood below his nose. "They attacked me right after they killed Zeta, and I don't remember anything."

Kendall thought for a moment. Despite how bad it all looked, maybe the asset had managed to turn things around. He had killed the operative, but Kendall couldn't bring himself to fault the asset for that. He didn't like the assassin either. But maybe it was because the boy wanted to ensure the girl's safety. Maybe he took her to the Director after all.

He raised a finger to his lips and activated his earpiece, and within seconds, the Director's calm voice answered.

"Report."

"Has the asset arrived with the girl yet, sir?"

"No," the Director said coolly. "I'm beginning to wonder if you can handle such a simple assignment."

Kendall's heart sank as he winced and held a hand to his forehead. So much for optimism. "The asset has turned, sir."

A long pause followed, and the Director's hissing breath was the only sound for a moment.

"You assured his loyalty."

"I did," Kendall said. "And I was wrong. In my defense, I couldn't have foreseen this. The girl is going to die without your help, and he has no reason to—"

"Don't bother defending yourself. You failed me. It's as simple as that."

Kendall bowed his head. "What now?"

"Now, we move on. The operative is more than capable of—"

"The operative is dead."

"How?" The Director's voice changed, a gravelly texture lining his words that made Kendall shiver.

"The asset turned on her and injected her with the serum you prepared for Aniya."

The Director's tone relaxed slightly. "Good. Have someone bring her to me."

"I was thinking the same thing." Kendall glanced at Malcolm. "She probably still has her key card on her body. I'll have her sent to you right away."

"Where are the asset and the girl?"

"They took the elevator, sir. They could be anywhere."

"Together?"

Kendall frowned. "I assume so, sir."

"And you ran diagnostics on the asset, correct? He shows no trace of the residual energy?"

"None. In fact, he seems to be getting weaker. The machine seems to have taken quite the toll on him."

"Yes, I thought this might happen. Send scouts to search the Underworld until we find them. The other levels are too highly regulated for them to remain hidden for long."

"Yes, sir." Kendall paused. "Meanwhile, we've run into problems in this level."

"Such as?"

"The insurgents are about to turn on me. They know everything. Well, almost everything."

A long, slow sigh came over the line. "Perhaps you misunderstood the nature of what we do, Kendall. We are *éminences grises*, the hidden power that keeps the Underworld under submission, ensuring their continual production without making our presence clear. Subtlety is key. Secrecy is vital. If they have found out anything, then you have failed more colossally than I could have imagined. Now that the Chancellor is dead, your job is simple. Production must continue. The Web must be restored. It's not a difficult task."

"But the girl—"

"Leave the girl to me, Kendall. It is clear now that you are incapable of handling her. Focus on the work you were sent to do."

"And what of the insurgents?"

The line went silent for a moment. "Send the girl's brother to me. If the girl cannot be retrieved, he could be a suitable alternative. He shares the same potential."

"Yes, sir. And the others?"

"Eliminate them."

Kendall froze. "Sir?"

"Progress cannot be halted, and if they pose a threat that will keep you from doing your job, they must be removed."

"But sir—"

"Kill them."

With that, the feed went silent.

It was the fourth option that Kendall swore he'd never use. The one he never seriously considered. He had tortured Salvador's daughter. He had sent Aniya to her death. He had ordered Nicholas to kill his girlfriend. He had encouraged wars that resulted in the deaths of thousands. But his actions had always served a greater purpose.

Committing genocide, however?

Maybe it was the only way.

"So, what now?"

Kendall looked up at Malcolm, who was still standing by the entrance to the tunnel.

"Now, I do my job." Kendall reached up and activated his earpiece again. He pressed a few buttons and waited a moment.

Soon, a voice came over the earpiece. "Sir?"

"Yes, Commander. I need a squadron sent to my location. Tell the rest of your men to gear up and be ready for a fight. Approach at my signal."

"Aye, sir."

"A fight?" Malcolm's eyes widened. "What are you talking about?"

Kendall didn't respond but simply placed the earpiece back in his pocket.

Malcolm stood up. "I can't be a part of this."

"You made your choice, Malcolm."

"Forget it. I'm not going to betray my people."

"It's too late for that, isn't it?"

"That was different. That was Aniya. This is my home, and I can't let you hurt anyone."

"I need you to trust me."

Malcolm shook his head. "After everything you've done? You know I can't—"

Footsteps came from the tunnel, and Malcolm fell silent. After a moment, Corrin stepped inside the small cavern, followed by Lieutenant Haskill, Gareth, and Roland.

"What are you doing here, Kendall?" Corrin's voice was cold. "You were instructed to wait in the war room. Decided you had to step away to speak with your Director?"

Kendall took a deep breath and readied himself. He knew that the outcome of this discussion would determine the fate of the Web.

38

Nicholas shivered slightly in the cool of the evening as he waited for the fight to end.

He was about to be subjected to a one-on-one battle that would put his physical prowess to the ultimate test. And unlike Aniya, he had nothing but his natural strength to protect him from the vicious fighters of Level I.

The coliseum was a much different setting at night. Hundreds of stadium lights hung from the sky ceiling, lighting the dirt arena brighter than it had been earlier that day when the fights took place under the artificial sun.

A roar from the crowd signaled the end of the current fight, and after a moment, the two Silvers at the entrance waved him through the main gate.

Nicholas stepped just inside the arena, looking over the stands at his fellow trainees. Most of them had been training long before he had arrived in Level I. They had already gone through this ritual, and they seemed more than happy to watch as the new recruits were subjected to it. Every one of them would soon be cheering, whether he managed to come out victorious or be beaten to a pulp.

However, as intimidating as the upcoming battle was,

all Nicholas could think about was the look in Aniya's eyes earlier when she had attacked him.

A terrifying hatred had burned in her eyes as she slapped him. There was something inside her, a horror that probably would have done a lot worse to him if the Silvers hadn't intervened. They took her away without giving him a chance to speak to her, and he hadn't seen her since.

Nicholas was nudged forward gently, and he walked across the dirt floor, ignoring the rising roar of the crowd.

From across the arena came another boy. The first thing Nicholas noticed was that this was unlike any recruit he had seen so far. Most of them had been fit, some of them with rather larger muscles that were obvious through their clothing.

But this recruit was a monster.

He was a hulking brute, with over-developed muscles nearly bursting through his silver jumpsuit. Blue veins raised from his skin and lined his neck. He stood nearly five inches taller than Nicholas, with a frame that seemed to grow an inch with every step he took.

Nicholas's eyes grew wide, and he turned back around to the entrance just in time to see the massive portcullis sinking into the ground. His heart plummeted to his stomach as he turned again to see the large boy grinning widely at him.

The fight ahead played out in Nicholas's head over and over again as he reluctantly approached the center of the arena.

Even with the element of surprise, if he rushed this guy, it would do nothing. It would be like running into a brick wall. He would be handing himself over to his opponent and ending the fight quickly.

Nicholas considered using his speed against the boy. Surely a boy that large wouldn't be able to keep up. But no matter how far Nicholas could outrun him, all he would do was tire himself out, leaving himself exhausted and vulnerable for his opponent to simply walk up to him and finish him off.

All that was left was to fight him directly, but that would end just as tragically. The boy's fists seemed to be nearly the size of Nicholas's head. If the boy managed to land even one punch, Nicholas wasn't sure he would get back up again.

This fight was suicide. Nicholas knew it, and as the fans grew more raucous, he realized that they knew it as well. They didn't come to see a fight. They came to see a beatdown.

He looked for Quinn in the stands. With Aniya gone, she would be the only one in his corner, the only one cheering for him in these impossible odds. But if she was there, Nicholas couldn't single her out in the sea of silver.

The only winning move seemed to be a surrender, but Nicholas doubted that was an option. The Lightbringers had these fights for a reason, and they seemed to always get their way no matter what web they were in.

Nicholas would be leaving this arena either unconscious or in a body bag. There was no other way out.

As they reached the center of the arena, the large boy cracked his knuckles and laughed, a hearty chuckle booming from his massive chest.

"Really?" Nicholas sighed. "Could you be any more stereotypical?"

The young man didn't look like he knew what the word meant, and all he did was laugh again.

Nicholas shook his head. "Let's get this over with."

The beast of a boy nodded slowly, the blue veins on his neck pulsing and scrunching up as his head moved.

They bowed to each other, and when they rose back up, the massive recruit simply stood in front of Nicholas, a grin still on his face.

The two boys stared at each other for a moment. Neither of them seemed willing to make the first move. Nicholas's hesitance was out of fear, but he knew his opponent had no reason to be afraid.

"What are you waiting for?" Nicholas laughed, trying to mask his shaking voice. "Come and get me."

The recruit simply shrugged, making no move forward.

Nicholas started circling the boy impatiently. It was a strange feeling. He wanted to get the fight over with, even though he was in no hurry to get his face smashed in by his giant opponent.

The boy turned slowly, keeping one eye on him.

Nicholas sped up and finally placed himself directly behind his opponent, and he instantly took advantage and jumped toward his enemy, lashing out with a flying kick at the boy's head.

But the boy turned just as the foot approached his face, and he grabbed Nicholas's ankle in the air and slammed him back to the ground.

Nicholas landed roughly, forming a cloud of dirt on impact that began to seep into his eyes and lungs. He coughed violently, grasping desperately for a handhold as the boy began to drag him backward.

His foot was suddenly released, and he scrambled to his feet only to be grabbed by the collar and pulled backward as a massive fist crushed into his spine.

Nicholas's eyes flew open as an awful cracking sound came from his back, and he howled in pain. The boy released him again, and he slumped to the ground.

Somewhere in the distance, the crowd was probably cheering even louder, but the ringing in Nicholas's ears escalated until it was all that he heard. He didn't even hear the boy step to his side and deliver a slow, vicious kick to his stomach.

Nicholas saw stars as he gasped for air. The metallic taste of blood invaded his mouth, and he coughed again, a mere wheeze now that came out as a sharp whistle.

A shadow fell over his face, and a massive boot appeared out of the corner of his eye as he suddenly felt an intense pressure fall on his cheek and begin to grind his face into the dirt below.

Nicholas flailed at the boot that pressed down on his body, but could find no relief against the overwhelming pain as he began to shriek in agony. He managed to grip his opponent's ankle, but the boy's foot remained unmoving, firm. With one last, desperate move, Nicholas squeezed down on the boy's ankle with whatever strength he had left.

Black began to creep over Nicholas's vision, the pain vanishing as a numbing sensation fell over his body.

Then nothing.

As the life drained from his body, all Nicholas could think about was the girl, that beautiful girl, the one whose kiss still lingered on his lips.

The one he had betrayed.

The one he knew would never love him again.

More than anything, Nicholas yearned for one more chance. A chance to atone for the hurt he had caused her, a chance to tell her how much she meant to him, a chance to show her that he was the same boy who used to lie next to her for hours, pretending to sleep as he watched her stare in awe at the stars.

A tingling sensation brought him back to reality as energy buzzed through his arm, stirring the cold blood in his veins.

Air trickled into his lungs, the pressure lifted from his cheek, and a warm strength flooded his body. A loud crack came from his back, and after a brief stabbing pain, Nicholas felt relief.

The shadow lifted, and Nicholas turned to see the boot coming away from his face.

The boy was staggering backward, his foot still in Nicholas's hand. He waved his arms wildly as he toppled to the ground, crashing into the dirt.

The stadium fell silent.

Nicholas released his opponent and slowly stood up with

shaking knees. He looked around at the quiet stadium, his blurry vision sharpening as his head cleared.

He turned to the boy, who was also recovering and just now standing. But he looked just as unsure on his feet as Nicholas, and he stumbled backward before regaining his balance.

The boy jerked his head violently, as if shaking away exhaustion, and he looked at Nicholas with a frown on his face. His face contorted, his frown morphing into a scowl as he growled.

Nicholas readied himself again, and this time, the boy refused to wait, charging him as fast as his massive frame allowed. He swung a fist as he lumbered forward, smashing into Nicholas with an incredible force.

But the boy stopped dead in his tracks as his fist collided with Nicholas's open hand. His jaw dropped open as Nicholas wrapped his fingers over the boy's knuckles and squeezed tightly.

He looked as surprised as Nicholas was as his fist turned white, blood draining as veins bulged from his skin. The boy's locked arm buckled, and he stumbled forward.

Nicholas grabbed the boy's throat, wrapping his fingers as far around as he could.

Shock flooded the boy's face as his mouth dropped open. His face turned pale, and a gagging sound escaped his throat as he reached out limply with his free hand.

Nicholas ignored the hand and dug his fingers into the boy's throat.

The blue veins on the boy's neck turned a ghostly white as energy coursed throughout Nicholas's body, feeding him with a power that reverberated down to the ground and shook the dirt beneath his feet.

As a blinding heat seared his vision, Nicholas found himself more of a spectator in his own body, watching himself crush the boy's lungs. With a growl, he lifted the massive boy off the ground, letting his feet dangle inches above the dirt.

The boy's desperate flailing turned to mere twitches as his eyes grew dark.

Within seconds, the boy's body turned limp, and he hung above the ground loosely, his head draped over Nicholas's hand.

With a roar of fury, Nicholas watched himself slam the boy into the ground, a loud cracking sound shaking the arena as dust exploded from the ground in a massive cloud.

Panting, he turned to face the stadium, which still looked on with a silence that was deafening.

Then, as if on cue, the stadium burst into a roaring cheer, shaking the earth.

Nicholas turned away from the boy's dead body and left the arena.

39

Kendall cleared his throat as he stared at the men blocking the way out of the small cavern. "Before you begin, let me—"

"No," Haskill said. "We've heard enough from you. There is no excuse for what you've done, and now you must answer for your actions."

Just as Kendall had suspected, they wouldn't even give him a chance to explain himself. "If I could just—"

"Forget it," Roland said. "You tortured me and Tamisra, you used Aniya and nearly got her killed, and then you told Nicholas to kill her if she wouldn't go along with your plan. There's nothing more we need to know."

"There's more to it than that. The Director—"

"If the Director wants to come and explain himself, he can feel free to do so," Gareth said, narrowing his eyes. "We've never seen this Director, and I personally have my doubts as to whether or not he actually exists. We are here to discuss what *you* have done, not this so-called Director."

Kendall sighed. "Fine. Let's talk about what I've done." He turned and paced back and forth. "You're right. I kidnapped and tortured Roland and Tamisra, but only to get

Salvador to bring his army and destroy the Chancellor's Silvers. I convinced Aniya to sacrifice herself in order to destroy the reactor and end the Chancellor's true source of power. And I told Nicholas that he might have to temporarily disable Aniya in order to get her to the Director, all so that Aniya could be helped and the Web could be saved from her destructive nature. You see? It was all for the good of the Web. Everything I've done, I've done to create a better world for you."

"We never needed you or your good intentions," Corrin said. "If Salvador had fought the Chancellor without you, we would have defeated him and had all the access we needed to shut down the machine. Maybe not destroy it in the same way, but disable it permanently. If we had done this on our own, Aniya wouldn't be in her condition, and we never would have needed to find a way to help her. She never would have posed a danger to us. This Web never needed you. All you've ever done is create problems for us."

"If I didn't inspire Salvador to action, he never would have fought," Kendall said. "You knew him eighteen years ago when he was ready to fight, when he led a band of rebels against the Lightbringers and almost won. But at the end of his life, he was not that man anymore. You know that better than I do. Salvador never would have made another move against the Lightbringers if I didn't do what I did."

"That doesn't make it right," Roland said. "It doesn't justify anything you did."

"I know, and I'm sorry. I was only doing what I knew I had to do."

Lieutenant Haskill folded his arms. "Say you were telling the truth. If you had succeeded and made the Web a better place, there would be no place for you. Not after what you've done."

Kendall nodded. "You're right. There's no place for a man like me in the Web I worked so hard to improve. But that was never the point. I had the power to make it a better place for all of you. When I was done with my work, I was going to return home."

"Home?" Roland asked. "Where is home for you?"

Kendall smiled. "Far away from here."

"You understand we can't allow you to stay here," Gareth said. "So you might as well go home now."

And there it was.

His work was about to get so much more difficult.

"My work is not done, but I understand. I will take my men and leave for the sectors immediately."

"No," Gareth said. "You can't stay in this Web."

Kendall shook his head. "I'm afraid I can't agree to that. I came here to save the Web. There are certain standards that must be met before I return to the Director. You might be able to stabilize the society, but there are certain things that you do not have the power to bring about."

Corrin raised an eyebrow. "Like what?"

"That's privileged information. Suffice it to say that you need me."

Gareth guffawed. "Just like that, we're meant to believe that we need you? You can't say why, but we just do? We survived without the Lightbringers. We can survive again."

"I'm not so sure about that," Kendall said.

"That's it, isn't it?" Roland said slowly. "You're going to fix the machine. You're going to restore the power, aren't you?"

Kendall bowed his head.

Roland clenched his fists. "After what we did to put an end to that, you're going to reinstate the Citizen Tax all over again? Why did you even bother overthrowing the Chancellor?"

"Even the Lightbringers were hesitant to enact relocative servitude and the Citizen Tax in the first place," Kendall said. "But they are necessary evils. As for the Chancellor, there were many aspects of his rule that were unsatisfactory to the Director, and so he had to be removed. The Web will be a safer place now that he's gone, and the people will be happy once again. But we have to supply power. It's what we're here for."

Roland stepped forward, jabbing a finger into Kendall's chest. "You know, you almost had me fooled. I believed for a second that you actually do care about the Web, that you do want to make it a better place. But you want to endorse the torture of thousands of people just so we can have electricity. You don't care about the Web or anyone in it. You never have."

Kendall held up a hand. "Roland, I—"

"He's right," Corrin said "Roland is absolutely right. If you have another place to go, great. But you can't stay on this level."

Lieutenant Haskill took a step forward and placed a hand on the gun at his side. "And if you don't go willingly, we will remove you by force. You'll have to kill us all to stay here."

Kendall sighed. He was so close.

Oh, well.

He raised his voice and shouted down the tunnel, "Commander?"

Heavy boots echoed down the tunnel, and in seconds, ten Silvers marched into the cavern, weapons drawn.

Haskill made a move to pull out his gun, but Corrin stopped him.

"What, do you want to get us all killed?" Corrin hissed.

"I have a job to do," Kendall said. "If you don't understand that, then I suppose there's nothing I can say to convince you. And I will do whatever I must to finish my work, including the removal of those who stand in my way."

Roland smirked. "So to protect us all, you'll kill us? Yeah, spoken like someone who truly has the good of the Web in mind."

Kendall stared at Roland for a moment. He had to take a breath to keep his annoyance with the child under control.

Besides, the boy would be forced into submission soon enough when the Director got a hold of him. Kendall had the manpower to force his cooperation now, but taking him in front of his friends would likely result in a firefight that wasn't worth it. He could be retrieved later.

"I'm not going to kill you. I really meant it when I said that I've come to help the Web. I don't think killing you would accomplish anything or help anyone, though there are those who believe otherwise. However, I can't allow you to stop me. I will continue restoring the Web with or without you. But I beg of you, don't try to stop me. Because then, I truly will have no choice."

"Get out, then," Roland spat. "And take your lackey with you," he said, nodding toward Malcolm, whose eyebrows shot up.

"Absolutely not," Corrin said as Malcolm shook his head rapidly. "You won't be taking my son anywhere."

"Take him," a weak voice came from the other side of the cavern, and Kendall turned to see Tamisra standing in the entrance, holding on to the rock for support.

"Take him with you," she said, pointing in Malcolm's direction.

Roland rushed to her side and wrapped an arm around her. "What are you doing out of bed? You need to be resting."

"Blame Gareth." Tamisra gave a small grin. "He leaves his painkillers just sitting around."

Kendall glanced at Malcolm. "I have no need for him."

"And we have no want for him," Tamisra croaked.

Corrin stepped forward. "Tami, I know what he did, and I will deal with him later. But we don't exile our own."

"I don't care. I want him gone. He almost got me and Aniya killed."

Malcolm stepped away from the wall of the cavern and approached Tamisra. "I didn't mean to hurt you, Tami.

I could never do that to you, not when I love you just as much as when we—"

He stopped short as Tamisra spit on his face.

"Get out of my city," she said, growling. "Now."

"Drop it, Tami," Corrin said. "He didn't—"

"I'll go."

The cave fell silent.

Malcolm looked at the ground as he spoke quietly. "You're right. I don't deserve to be here after what I've done. I'm sorry." He turned and joined Kendall. "I'll go."

"So be it." With that, Kendall turned and left the cave, surrounded by Silvers, with Malcolm at his side.

40

Aniya's eyes drifted open to see blue skies above, a warm sun smiling down at her. A fresh breeze drifted over her skin, and a peaceful feeling settled in her heart.

She sat up and looked around. Sand surrounded her, and a vast expanse of water lay a stone's throw away, stretching off in front of her as far as she could see. The water was unnaturally still and looked like little more than a flat blanket of blue that extended from the shore.

Other than that, Aniya saw nothing. She stood up, but she almost fell back down in surprise as a palm tree appeared over her head, providing shade from the warm sun.

Aniya turned around as several other trees began to sprout from the ground, materializing in the landscape before her and quickly growing to full height.

The flat landscape shook slightly as mounds of sand began to rise from the ground, forming dunes every several hundred feet.

A splashing noise alerted her, and she turned around to see the ocean before her now gliding into the shore in waves, sending water rushing toward her gently.

But as the water splashed over her skin, Aniya felt nothing, even as the water trickled over her skin, back to the sand and toward the ocean.

"Oh, good. You're already awake."

Aniya turned away from the water.

A man stood before her, clothed in a simple black robe. It was the man who had given them their brief orientation to Sector F, the one who had been standing by the President in the Hub.

He sported a short, black beard that was trimmed perfectly, forming a strange design on his face. It gave him a look that Aniya first deemed evil, then later decided it was more enigmatic.

Something about him was eerily familiar, but Aniya couldn't place it.

"You caught me as I was just putting finishing touches on the landscape." He smiled. "Do you like it, Aila?"

"General Addington, right? What is this place?" Aniya looked around again, partially in an effort to conceal her momentary confusion upon hearing her fake name. The landscape looked incredibly real, but she knew this couldn't possibly be the case.

The man gestured at the world around them, and the sands seemed to shift in response as his hand danced through the air.

"This is a world I've made just for you. In order to achieve maximum focus, I have created a place in which you can feel utter peace. Of course, I could only do so much given that we've never spoken, but most people feel quite at ease in this atmosphere. Here, we can explore your mind without any distraction. And, please. Call me Caspian."

Aniya frowned. "Are you . . . in my mind? Am I dreaming?"

Caspian laughed. "Of course not. This isn't a mind trick, and you are very much awake. This is simply a virtual reality, a hologram-based technology over which I have complete control. And as long as we are here, I am your guide."

"My guide? For what?"

"Your own mind. We need to find out the source of your anxiety and quell it."

"Anxiety?"

Caspian began pacing in the sand. "Immediately following your first fight, you attacked a boy in the stands. It was quite peculiar behavior, the kind that the Lightbringers strongly discourage among its trusted protectors. I must discover if you can be rehabilitated, made fit to serve the Underworld to the best of your ability."

Aniya's eyes narrowed. "You're my therapist?"

"If you think of it like that, I suspect we won't get very far." Caspian smiled warmly. "Please, Aila, think of me as your friend."

Aniya slowly nodded. She didn't know what would happen if he decided that she wasn't fit to be part of the Silver Guard, but she didn't want to find out. She was safe for now.

"Good. Then let's begin." Caspian approached her and gazed into her eyes. "It's my belief that you acted out of passion. Premeditative acts of violence are quite rare in the Underworld due to the suppressant gas, so unless you have any objections, we can safely rule that out."

Aniya tried to hide her shock as she realized why the citizens of this level submitted to the Lightbringers' laws and regulations so strictly. There was something in the air, some kind of calming agent that softened willpower. And judging by Caspian's casual reference to it, everyone knew about it.

"But even acts of passion are rare, so I suspect that your motivations were strong. Misplaced, perhaps, but guided by a love or hatred so strong that it overcame the neural pathways that have developed in your brain since birth."

"So the suppressant doesn't block everything?"

"Have you already forgotten your studies from Assembly?

The suppressant itself blocks nothing. It simply serves as a facilitator, a chemical that weakens the strength of raw emotion. All it does is give you more control over your feelings, allowing you to choose logic over instinct. And because attacking another recruit in full view of the Silver Guard is foolish, your passion was clearly strong enough to overwhelm your logic."

"Makes sense."

"Good. Because I have the tough job of finding out the extent of your problem and remedying it so you can act in a manner appropriate of a Silver Guard of the Glorious Bringers of Light." Caspian kept a stern look on his face before breaking loose with laughter. "Sorry, even I have to follow the script sometimes."

Aniya was put at ease by his warm demeanor, and she found a smile of her own slowly growing on her face.

"Let's get started," he said. "The first step is for me to understand the reason for your anxiety."

"I thought you said it was passion?"

Caspian shrugged. "Probably so. But negative passion is formed from a place of fear. Even love, when expressed in such a violent manner, is born out of a place of anxiety. Passion is good, Aila. We would have died out long ago without it. But we must control our fears and anxieties so that we are masters of our emotion. Now, what are you afraid of?"

"Nothing," Aniya said quickly.

"As I suspected. Not that I really believe that you are afraid of nothing, but I did not expect you to know your own mind as well as others I have trained. I just asked to see if we could dive straight into the main issue. Tell me, what does the boy mean to you?"

Aniya took a deep breath. Where to begin? Nicholas was the primary source of stress in her life, that much was certain, but how much could she share without giving them both away?

"Nikolai," she said, making sure to use his assumed name, "is special. Or at least he was. We came from the same sector." She looked down. "We were in love once."

Caspian nodded as if he expected this. "What happened?"

"He lied to me. Betrayed me. And then . . ." Aniya shook her head as she imagined the girl at Nicholas's side in the arena.

"Yes?"

She barely managed to get the words out. "He found someone else."

"And this hurts you because you still love him?"

Aniya shook her head firmly. "Not after what he did."

Caspian smiled. "If you don't love him anymore, why would it hurt so much that he's found someone new?"

"Because we were in love just days ago. Since then, he's betrayed me twice, broken my heart, and replaced me. It's too much to handle all at once. I definitely don't love him anymore."

After a moment, Caspian nodded again. "We'll see. I don't believe that your head is clear enough to understand your own emotions and put them into words, so we will put a pin in that. For now, we will focus on housekeeping."

Aniya frowned. "Cleaning?"

"Housekeeping is what I use to mean tidying your mind and decluttering your emotions. We could wait days, weeks, months, however long it takes for you to move on and let go of Nikolai, but we don't have time for that. We need to find the mental stumbling block and remove it directly."

"Directly? Like surgery?"

Another laugh from Caspian. "Okay, maybe not that directly. You could describe it as a surgery of some sorts, but no one will be cutting into your brain. Instead, you will be descending into the depths of your own mind and removing the block yourself."

"Like removing my memory of him?"

"Your memory will remain intact. What we will be doing is making up for the apparent shortcomings of the suppressant gas. Unfortunately, it is too late to alter the way you react to the emotion, so we must remove the emotion itself."

"Hate?"

Caspian shrugged. "Or love, whichever one it is. Whatever the emotion, you must neutralize it if your mind is to be normalized."

Aniya knew it was hate, but she didn't bother to argue. What was more disconcerting was the thought of altering her brain in such a way that was obviously never meant to be disturbed. "Will I ever feel that emotion again?"

"Not until I deem its restoration safe," Caspian said. "If it is indeed hatred, you may choose to continue to block it. Such a raw, negative emotion has consequences on your health, both mental and physical. But if the emotion is love, then you may one day decide that you wish to utilize it."

Aniya frowned. The Lightbringers were training an army to regulate the rest of the Underworld, carrying out brutal public punishments without a second thought. Surely hate would be more valuable to them.

"What happens if none of this works?" Aniya asked. It was a fair question, she thought. Thanks to the suppressant that the rest of the recruits lived with since birth, she would be biologically different from the rest of them. Whatever technique Caspian wanted to teach her, it might not even work.

"It will work. This is the training I have given to every operative, who now have ultimate control over their emotions, making them the most efficient weapons in the entire Underworld. If you've ever had the privilege of seeing them in action, you know that my work speaks for itself."

Aniya shuddered as she recalled the ruthlessness of the two operatives she had the misfortune of meeting.

"Are you ready?"

She honestly didn't know. When she didn't respond for several seconds, Caspian spoke again.

"If not, we can come back tomorrow and try again. But we must proceed and at least begin our sessions by the end of the week. You must be kept in your placement matches so that we do not delay your training, but we have to make enough progress in here so that I can make a formal decision on your status soon after your final match."

Aniya sighed in relief. If she remembered the training timeline correctly, this gave her ten weeks to figure out her next move.

"Let's do it."

Caspian grinned. "Good. Have a seat."

Aniya sat down on the sand, and as her hands touched the ground, she noted the warm feeling of thin carpet rather than the coarse texture she expected.

"You said I'm going inside my mind. What am I going to see?"

"I can't tell you because it's different for everyone. Now, close your eyes."

Aniya hesitated, unwilling to drop her guard around someone who trained killers for a living. But as far as she knew, Caspian had no reason to suspect her true origins. Besides, if he was going to hurt her, he could have done so when she was unconscious. So she eventually sighed and closed her eyes, embracing the dark.

"I'm going to increase the frequency and volume of the waves of the ocean. This is typically a noise that induces an enhanced calming state that should put you at greater ease. It also carries subliminal radio waves that will aggravate you just enough to bring your negative emotions to the forefront of your mind. Let me know if it's too much."

The sound of moving water fell upon Aniya, and even though she knew the virtual water was at her side, the noise surrounded her and engulfed her in a pleasant bath of sound.

From somewhere in the distance came a squawking sound that was unfamiliar, but somehow comforting.

"Now, take deep breaths. With every wave that washes over the shore, breathe in, then breathe out with the next."

Aniya breathed with the rhythm of the water as her nerves calmed.

"What do you see?"

"Nothing. How long will it take?"

"There's no way to know. It's difficult to reach that level of peace on your first try. I believe it will come, but I don't think you will be able to hold it for very long. For now, just focus on the waves."

Her eyes were already closed, but Aniya tried to close the eyes of her mind, ignoring the dark that surrounded her. She focused on her hearing only and once again breathed in time with the waves.

"Good. Just keep breathing."

Aniya continued to focus for several minutes, doing her best to ignore the void.

It seemed like an hour later, but finally Aniya saw something in the black. A tiny green light shimmered in the distance, almost beckoning for her.

"Caspian, I see something."

"What is it?"

Aniya felt herself walking toward the green sparkle. "A light."

"Go to it."

"I am."

As she neared the light, she realized that it was William, and her heart swelled.

"You're smiling, Aila. This light is your friend, something positive that we did not come here to face. You need to focus on the negative emotion that's disturbing your calm if we're going to find out what it is."

"But I don't want to."

"That's not an option, Aila. Now, focus."

Aniya's smile faded as she turned away from the green light, feeling William's presence shrink away into nothingness. She waited for the inevitable appearance of the mysterious, feminine voice of the Shadow and the cold feeling of dread that accompanied her.

But it never came.

"I don't see anything else, Caspian."

"Patience. Remember what it felt like to see your love betray you."

Caspian's words echoed in her mind, and the black morphed around her as the canvas of her mind was painted over with broad brushstrokes.

Aniya was back in the arena. As she looked around, she realized that this stadium was empty, save for two people sitting in the stands. It was Nicholas and the girl, looking at each other.

His eyes were smiling, gazing at the girl before him with a look Aniya once thought belonged just to her.

The girl was looking back at him, her eyes wide, her hand traveling over his shoulder and down his back.

As Aniya's heart sank, the void went cold, and the scenery took on a blue tint. Then, as she clenched her fists, her heart racing, the blue arena went red, colorized crimson by a light that grew from behind Aniya, casting a long shadow in front of her.

"Talk to me, Aila," Caspian's voice came from the distance.

Aniya turned around to face a blazing pillar of red, an angry phantom that crackled and hissed. This wasn't William. It wasn't even the Shadow. It was a new presence, one that scared her more than the Shadow ever could.

"I see it," she said with a trembling voice.

Caspian's voice was hushed, almost excited. "What is it?"

Open your eyes, Aniya.

William's words came back to her, and she closed her eyes and took a deep breath, forcing herself to stretch her hand forward into the light.

As her hand entered the pillar of flame, her bitterness turned to pure hatred, and she opened her eyes again, ready to turn back to Nicholas and slap him all over again.

But the arena was gone. She was alone in the void with the red light, a beacon that was now a cyclone of flame, swirling in front of her until it suddenly settled into a recognizable form.

It was the man in a white suit, standing before her with a broad grin on his face. He licked his lips and grinned widely as his body was licked by orange flame.

"Hello, Annelise."

Then, the Chancellor lunged forward and grabbed her throat.

41

"We have to fight him," Roland blurted out. "He wants to restart the machine and put us back in slavery all over again. We'll have come all this way for nothing."

He had spoken immediately upon entering the war room of the Refuge tower, and he ignored a stern look from Gareth as most of the room's occupants sat at the table.

Corrin gently waved his hands. "Sit down, Roland. We'll get to that."

"No," Roland said, still standing. "There's nothing else to discuss. We don't have a choice. You fought eighteen years ago against the Chancellor's oppression, but Kendall's going to do the exact same thing. We have to stop him before he gets the chance."

"Roland," Gareth said sternly. "Sit down."

After a moment, Roland collapsed in his chair with a huff. A soft hand on his arm caused him to turn, and his temper soothed slightly as his eyes fell on Tamisra. Gareth had wanted her to remain in the clinic, but she'd insisted on being present for the meeting.

Lieutenant Haskill stood nearby, the last of the gathered

group, and he pored over the map on the table, ignoring the conflict around him.

Corrin eyed Roland for a moment, then cleared his throat. "You all know the problem we face, the one by the name of Kendall. Lieutenant Haskill reports that his scouts saw Kendall heading toward Quadrant I, but he could be anywhere in the Web by now. With him is my son—"

Tamisra gave a short scoff at this, though she apparently paid for it as she winced in pain.

Corrin glanced toward Tamisra, then continued, "Whom I would very much like back. But it seems he has made his choice. As such, it seems we are at an impasse. Without knowing Kendall's location, there's nothing we can do."

"Are you kidding?" Roland's eyes widened. "You're just going to let Kendall take over the Web?"

"Even if we did know where he is," Haskill said, "we're in no position to fight him. He has an army with him."

Roland stood up again, unable to contain himself. "No, he has a bunch of armored goons. They're not supposed to be soldiers, you know. Just lawkeepers. I'd say we're in the best position to fight him. He wouldn't expect it, that's for sure."

"And what do you think we have, Roland?" Corrin folded his arms. "We were once an army, yes, but those days are long gone. Salvador trained the next generation to defend Refuge, not to launch full-scale battles against a horde of Silvers."

"It worked well enough when we sacked the Hub," Roland said.

Lieutenant Haskill shook his head. "A surprise attack with a man on the inside is hardly a fair fight. Against Kendall, we would be fighting blind with no such advantage."

"You agreed quick enough to attack Ravelta when we were looking for the Chancellor," Roland said. "And you were ready to storm Holendast to capture him."

"We had the Silvers on our side both times," Corrin said. "To fight without them now is suicide."

Gareth nodded. "I agree. We can't afford to pick a fight with him right now."

Roland clenched his fists. "We can't afford not to. He's going to enslave the Web again. He's going to torture thousands of people just to restart the reactor and generate power. If we have any chance of stopping him, we have to do it. We have to try."

"But we have no chance, Roland," Gareth said gently. "Kendall has an overwhelming supply of resources. Not only ammunition, but technology, people, an entire web at his disposal to use against us. We're hiding in a cave, barely able to defend against invasions. If we tried to fight him, we would be slaughtered. We're no more to him than a nuisance, not much more threatening than a mole."

"Then let's fight like moles."

The room fell silent as Tamisra spoke for the first time. Her voice was quiet, her speech weak, but it was enough to demand attention.

She looked around the table and spoke raggedly, but clearly. "We've spent our entire lives in the dark, sneaking into sectors and helping people escape from under the thumb of the Lightbringers. We're invisible to them, and that is a weapon that they've underestimated time and time again. We've made the shadows our home, and until Kendall restarts the reactor, the entire Web is in shadow."

Tamisra slowly stood, pushing Roland's helping hand away. "I'm with Roland. This is the best time, maybe the only time, when we can fight back. I loved my father, but he spent half his life hiding from the Lightbringers after vowing to destroy them. We can finish what he started, but if you hide now, you're no better than him. And if we fail, so what? We'll have gone out fighting for the Web. What greater purpose is there?"

As she finished, she sat back down again and slumped forward slightly. Her staggered breathing was loud enough that Roland placed a hand on hers, stroking it gently for support. He wanted to say something to back her up, but there really was nothing more to say.

After a long pause, Corrin spoke again.

"Your father would be proud of you, Tami. You have grown into a worthy successor, and the name of Salvador would suit you well."

Tamisra gave a small smile.

"However, it is simply too dangerous, and I have no reason to believe that we would be even remotely successful against such a threat." Corrin bowed his head. "I must make a decision for the safety of Refuge, and so we will remain here and reevaluate our position at a later time."

Roland's heart sank. He opened his mouth to speak, but Corrin held up a hand.

"My decision is final."

With that, he turned and walked back up to the ground floor.

Roland sank back into his seat, and not even Tamisra's comforting hand could bring him any solace.

42

Aniya's eyes shot open as electricity jolted her body awake, her heart pounding.

Gone was the Chancellor, the void, even the sand and sunny sky. She was lying on the ground in a large, white room, empty except for her and Caspian.

"Well done, Aila." Caspian smiled down at her. "Sorry for the rude awakening. I had to pull you out."

Between her heavy breaths, she retorted, "Well done? He almost killed me!"

Caspian offered her a hand. "Sit up. Let's talk about it."

Aniya swatted away his hand as she pulled herself up.

"Who is 'he'? What happened in there?" Caspian sat across from her, crossing his legs and folding his hands.

"I did what you said. I thought about what it was like to see Nikolai with another girl, and I got angry. Then I saw . . . *him*."

"Who?"

Aniya shifted. "Someone who hurt me."

"More than Nikolai?"

She nodded.

"It's not uncommon for people to project all their negative

emotions on one individual," Caspian said. "I think we've found who yours is."

"Great," Aniya said, frowning. "Now what?"

"Now you must confront him."

"You want me to fight him?"

"I didn't say that. Fear is not conquered by victorious altercation but by understanding. You must talk with him."

Aniya shook her head. "I can't do that. He attacked me last time."

"He's nothing more than a part of you, Aila." Caspian smiled warmly. "He attacked you because that's what you expected him to do."

"What should I expect him to do, chat about the weather?"

"Just give him a chance to talk. Are you ready?"

Aniya frowned. "What, now?"

"Yes, now. You're forgetting that I have to approve you before you set foot in that arena again." Caspian pulled a device from his pocket and pressed a few buttons, and the white room rippled and morphed into the same beach scene in seconds. "Close your eyes."

With a sigh, Aniya did so and instantly found herself face-to-face with the Chancellor again.

The same smirk was on his face, but he made no move to attack her.

"You're back," the Chancellor said. "Sooner than expected, I might add. You hurt my feelings."

"What do you want?"

"What do I want?" He shrugged. "You tell me. Why did you bring me here?"

"Me? Trust me. If I had the choice, I would never see you again."

"Yet here I am." The Chancellor spread his arms open. "I'm not your brother. I can't come and go as I please. It takes a little effort on your part to summon me."

He took a step forward and Aniya backed away. "Summon you? You're not real. Unless——" She froze. "You injected me with something. When you came to Refuge, you put something in me."

The Chancellor laughed. "I have no idea what that old coot did. I am not the actual Chancellor, Annelise. I'm merely a manifestation of your hatred. Of course I'm not real. But I'm real enough that you're still talking to me, and that's good enough for both of us, it seems."

Aniya took another step back and looked behind her. "Caspian, I'm ready to come out now."

"Oh, he can't hear you." The Chancellor waved a hand dismissively. "I imagine you're not willing to discuss certain things around him, so I made sure we have some privacy."

"What did you do?"

"Technically, I didn't do anything. I'm a part of you, remember? That means that part of you wants to be here with me, which means there's something you've been dying to talk with me about. Now, please, what can I do for you?"

Aniya's skin crawled as he smiled again. "Why is it you? Your operative killed my parents, but all my fear and anger looks like you?"

"Do you want me to look like my operative?" The Chancellor frowned. "Very well."

His face began to twist into a grotesque mess, and as it began to take shape again, his clothes turned from white to black. As the details settled and Aniya saw the first hint of the Operative's wicked grin, she waved her hands.

"No, please, don't."

Instantly, the Chancellor's body normalized and settled.

"I thought as much," he said, grinning again. "I suspect you see me rather than my operative because he was my puppet. For all you know, I gave the order to have your parents killed." His grin disappeared as he suddenly looked bored. "Now, why am I here?"

"I need to talk to you." Aniya turned away and shuddered as the words left her mouth. "But I don't know what I'm supposed to talk to you about."

"Whatever you want, I suppose. Ask me what you will, Annelise. I am apparently at your disposal."

After a moment, Aniya turned back around. "What happened in the arena? I saw Nicholas, and I just lost it. Everything that happened after that, hurting that poor boy, hitting Nicholas—I saw it all happen, but I wasn't in control."

"I'm sure you had some control. You can't blame your emotions for everything, after all. But you're right. You were always hotheaded, a wild child, and it seems this power has only made things worse. Now, whenever you lose your temper, I get to come out and play."

"How do I ignore my emotions?"

The Chancellor smirked. "You can't. Your emotions rule you. They always have. You make decisions without regard for logic. It is a strength in the right circumstances, but in most, it is your greatest weakness. Especially now that they are your key to accessing the terrible power within you."

Aniya shivered. "So to use these abilities, I have to use my emotions? I have to get mad?"

"Yes, dear. You must embrace your emotions if you hope to use your power at will."

"But then I have no control."

He shrugged. "Some things are not meant to be controlled. The only thing you can do is learn to access the power when you need it and trust that your emotions will guide you."

"By using my feelings?"

"Exactly. Try it now." The Chancellor rubbed his hands together. "Stir up your emotions and let's see if we can't get a little light out of you, eh? Nothing too crazy. You don't want to fry poor Caspian."

Aniya turned away from the Chancellor and stared into

the black. As she focused, the canvas before her once again turned into the arena. Nicholas and the girl appeared in the stands, and her heart instantly quickened as her blood began to warm.

"A little too much, Annelise. Try something a little more tame."

She focused on Nicholas, and the rest of the scenery faded away until it was just him standing before her.

He turned and looked at her, a smile on his face. Aniya clenched her fists, and she glared at him, a mix of emotions bubbling inside.

"Pick one feeling and stick with it. Focus your emotion."

Aniya made her choice, and she took a deep breath as spite filled her mind. As her temper rose, Nicholas's face began to contort into a smirk that made her hair stand on end.

"Are you going to punish him for the rest of his life, Aniya?"

She froze as William's voice came from Nicholas's mouth. His body slowly changed, and within seconds, her brother's body had taken Nicholas's place.

Aniya glanced behind her. Surely the Chancellor would have something to say about this, but her old enemy was frozen in place, the same stupid smile still on his face.

"He loves you, Aniya. He's loved you for years."

She turned back to William. "He betrayed me. He lied to me."

"I know. And he knows. But he's begged for your forgiveness. Don't you think it's time to move on?"

"Move on to what? There's nothing between us anymore, and I don't think there ever could be again."

William smiled. "If you feel this strongly about it, that means you care enough about your relationship with him to fix it. It means there's still something there."

"Maybe," she said slowly. "But I don't know if I want that anymore."

"That's your choice. But you have to find a way to move forward. You can't live the rest of your life hating him."

She smirked. "You really think so?"

"Okay, maybe so. But I don't recommend it. Just think about—"

William's voice suddenly died away as everything went dark.

The void was a black place by nature, a vast nothingness that stretched on in every direction. And yet it seemed to grow darker still as a Shadow fell over Aniya, filling her with a cold dread.

"Aniya," the voice came.

It was the feminine voice of the dark phantom, the one Aniya had not heard for a long time. The one she had hoped was gone for good.

But it was back now, and as Aniya tried to look around for its source, she felt every muscle freeze until she was locked in place.

"What are you?" she shouted, barely able to move her mouth.

It was a pointless question. The voice had only ever said her name.

But this time, the voice came back, uttering new words.

"Your destiny," the Shadow said with a hiss, drawing out the second word.

Aniya blinked in surprise. It had to have been because she was in the void by choice this time, that she was intentionally diving into the depths of her mind. That's the only explanation she could think of for how the phantom could finally say more than just her name.

"Neither of these men are your future," the Shadow said as Aniya looked in William's petrified eyes and felt the Chancellor's gaze on the back of her head. "Let them go, Lightbringer. Only then will you be ready."

Aniya squeezed her eyes shut, but it was pointless. The

void was there waiting for her, unchanged in her closed eyes. She looked at William, still standing before her. His face flashed and morphed into Nicholas's again.

"Join with him, Lightbringer," the phantom shrieked suddenly. "It is the one true path to peace."

The Shadow was gone in an instant, and the void returned to whatever normalcy Aniya could expect from it. She looked around, but there was no sign of the hissing phantom. In fact, with every second, Aniya became more convinced that she had hallucinated the strange being's voice.

"Well, what are you waiting for?" The Chancellor's smooth voice came from behind, making Aniya jump.

But Aniya ignored the Chancellor and pushed back her bitterness as Nicholas's haughty expression slowly faded into a neutral stare.

Once upon a time, he was the one constant in her life, the one she could always turn to in the worst of circumstances and know that she would always be welcome, always feel loved.

It seemed so long ago that she could look in his eyes and feel an overwhelming peace settle over her. It wasn't a feeling she could conjure up now. She could barely even remember it. Even in the caves, when she had tried to kiss him, her heart had been going a million miles a minute, her feelings battling between distrust and desperation in the midst of running for their lives.

No, the last time she had felt at ease with him was weeks ago, before William had shown up in Holendast, back on Nicholas's roof.

As she pictured it, the scenery changed to her home sector in the dead of night. Aniya and Nicholas stood on his roof, the twinkling stars and massive moon hanging above them, painting Nicholas's face in a glow that couldn't help but calm Aniya just a little.

He reached a hand out to her, and as she took it, a smile

crept over his face, a warm and gentle expression of friendship. Forget romance. She couldn't bear to think of that right now. No, this was pure platonic love, one that she had relied on for years.

And as her soul warmed, her hand buzzed. Aniya looked down to see her hand glowing green. As she squeezed Nicholas's hand, the light grew, quickly encompassing her entire body.

She swung back to the Chancellor and smiled.

When he spoke to her, his voice carried a soft feminine echo. "Well done, Annelise."

43

Roland looked down at Tamisra and smiled. "You feeling any better?"

Tamisra pulled her shirt down and peeled back a bandage just far enough to reveal a large, purple bruise and a set of stitches decorating her shoulder. "What does it look like?"

"Just thought I'd ask." Roland sat down by her side as she replaced her shirt.

"I know." Tamisra's voice softened, and she sighed. "I'm just tired of being in this bed."

"How much longer does Gareth think it'll be?"

She shrugged. "Apparently, Zeta was not kind enough to clean her knife before throwing it at me, and I got infected with something. So it could be days. Could be weeks. I just hope I'm better before it's too late."

Roland frowned. "Too late for what?"

"Come on, Roland. Do you really think I'm going to go along with Corrin's ridiculous plan of sitting here and hiding? I thought you knew me better than that."

"Tami, don't do anything stupid."

She stuck her tongue out. "I was kind of hoping you'd do it with me, actually."

"Corrin doesn't want to send an unprepared band of cave-dwellers to fight an army, so you think it's a good idea to take them on with two people? I think you should wait until the meds wear off before you think up any more grand ideas."

"Are you with me or not?"

Roland grinned. "How about you just let yourself heal, and then we'll talk?"

"Talking is for people like Corrin and Haskill." Tamisra folded her arms and winced. "I'm not going to sit around and watch Kendall turn the Web into the living hell it was with the Chancellor."

"You'll be sitting around anyway. It's not like you can do anything like this."

Tamisra's eyes flashed. "Wanna bet?"

"No. I don't want to watch you hurt yourself." Roland placed a hand on her arm. "Please, Tami. Just wait."

"Wait for what? For when we talk to Corrin again and he still says no?"

Roland took a deep breath. "Tami, you're Salvador's daughter."

"Gee, thanks, Roland. I had no idea."

"But you don't. You don't know what that means. Now that Kendall's out of the way, once you recover, you'll be taking over as the leader of Refuge. Not Corrin. When the time comes, he won't have a say in what we do. You give the word, and we can attack Kendall without Corrin being able to do anything about it. He may lead the army, but he still has to follow your orders."

Tamisra gave a short laugh. "Really? They'd let me take over, just like that? They know what I want to do, and they'd still let me lead them?"

"You're Salvador's daughter," Roland said again. "They know what it means, and they respect that. I talked to Corrin about it. He already knows it'll happen eventually. Of course, Haskill voiced his objections."

"I bet he did. What did he say?"

"That you're emotional, vindictive."

Tamisra grinned. "And what do you think?"

"Well, I can't say I blame him." Roland smiled back at her. "But Refuge needs someone like you to lead them."

"I don't want to lead Refuge. I've never wanted it."

He shrugged. "If you really want to fight Kendall, you have to do it. They won't listen to you otherwise."

"By the time I recover and take over, it'll be too late. It won't matter anymore. Kendall will have restarted the reactor and be untouchable. We have to fight him now, Roland."

"That's not an option. Corrin has made that very clear."

"Then Corrin can stay here." Tamisra turned toward him and stared with unblinking eyes. "Promise me you'll go with me."

"Go where?"

"To kill Kendall."

Roland sighed. "Tami, I don't like him any more than you do. I don't necessarily disagree with you that he deserves to die. But do you really think we can get to him? He has an army, and we don't even know where he is."

"I'll do whatever it takes, Roland. You know that." Her voice dropped as she looked toward the floor. "I owe it to my father."

"Tell you what. If we find out where he is, I will do whatever I can to find a way to get to him and make sure he pays for what he did to you and your father. You have my word."

Tamisra shook her head. "I have to kill him myself."

"Tami—"

"Roland. I have to."

After a moment, Roland nodded. "Okay. When the time comes, I'll make sure you have your chance, as long as you wait and do it the right way. No rushing off on your own."

Tamisra smiled. "Thank you."

"Get some rest, Tami." Roland forced a smile and stroked her hair before leaving the room and closing the door behind him.

He walked down the stairs and tried not to regret lying to her. But if that's what it took to make sure she didn't get herself killed, Roland would tell her as many lies as necessary.

The ground floor of the clinic was silent. Gareth had taken up residence in Kendall's old room in the tower. He had intended on staying in the clinic until Tamisra recovered, but she insisted that he make himself comfortable in an actual bed.

So, alone, Roland climbed inside one of the beds and blew out the candle.

Every time he had tried to sleep in his own tent, he found himself tossing and turning, unable to stop thinking about Tami in the clinic and the fact that she slept alone, with no guard nearby. Of course, now that Kendall and the Silvers had left Refuge for good, there was no danger, real or perceived, but Roland had almost lost her once. He wasn't willing to risk losing her for good.

He was just on the verge of sleep when his eyes flew open as a rag was placed over his mouth, cutting off his airflow and pressing down tight.

His lungs filled with a sweet taste, a calming one that very nearly put him at ease, but the dark figure that loomed over him kept him from relaxing fully, and he thrashed his body even as his senses began to dull.

Roland opened his mouth as wide as he could, and a hand slipped between his teeth, fingers reaching so far into his throat that he gagged and nearly choked. The hand began to pull away, but Roland bit down hard, trapping flesh and cloth in his mouth as a faint shriek of pain came from above.

The hand and rag finally managed to wrench themselves free, and a dark figure staggered toward the center of the room as Roland stumbled out of bed. As soon as his feet hit the floor, his weak legs gave out from under him, and he fell.

Roland desperately gasped for air as he tried to climb to his feet, but the room spun around him, making it impossible to see clearly, let alone regain his balance.

Another shriek rang through the air, this one so jarring that it snapped Roland from his daze. He looked up just in time to see his attacker stumble for a second, then fall forward, his face crashing into the hard floor as blood poured from his head.

Tamisra looked up from atop the man's back and spat an ear from her mouth as blood trickled down her chin. "Are you okay?"

Roland tried to speak, but it came out as no more than mumbling. His eyes widened as another figure appeared from the shadows and placed a hand on Tamisra's shoulders. He scrambled to his feet, but his balance failed him yet again. This time, however, he managed to fall directly on the man behind Tamisra, bringing him to the ground.

"Roland!"

He spun around to see Tamisra pinned down by another man, his hands wrapped around her throat.

Roland drove his elbow into the man's back beneath him and stood again, taking just a second to steady himself before running across the room.

But he didn't quite make it to Tamisra's side. Instead, he was kicked from behind, and he sprawled out on the floor, his back aching. Before he could even look up, he was grabbed by the armpits and dragged through the open door of the clinic into the main part of Refuge.

Tamisra's screams were suddenly cut short, and Roland's heart sank. He kicked violently and thrashed his body, but his attacker kept a firm hold of him as he was dragged through Refuge, which was dark for the night, lit only by a few sporadic torches.

Roland resorted to screaming as loud as he could, hoping to garner the attention of the sleeping cave-dwellers. But his screams were quickly muffled by a gloved hand over his mouth, and he soon stopped trying in an effort to save his energy.

Then, everything froze as the immediate area lit up.

"Stop!"

A voice boomed throughout Refuge, and Roland's attacker ceased his retreat.

Roland looked up to see Corrin, Lieutenant Haskill, and Gareth blocking their path. Behind them, people began to exit their tents to find the source of the commotion.

"Let him go," Corrin said.

The man released Roland, but only with one hand. With the other, he pulled a gun from his side and pointed it at Corrin. "I can't do that."

"I know you," Gareth said, stepping forward. "You're one of Kendall's men."

"So?" The man cocked the gun and now pointed it at Gareth, who stopped his advance.

Corrin nodded toward Roland. "So what does Kendall want with him?"

"Doesn't matter," the man said. "Now, let us pass."

"How did you even get in?" the lieutenant asked. "We changed the codes when Kendall left."

"You didn't think he would leave without making sure he could get back in, did you?"

Before anyone could respond, a scream came from behind, and Roland was violently yanked to the side as the man spun around.

Tamisra leaped through the air as the man fired his gun. His grip on Roland was released, and the man fell to the ground under the weight of the shrieking girl.

Roland quickly climbed to his feet, his head finally clear. He turned to see Tamisra bashing the man's skull on the ground repeatedly, blood spurting from his head in tiny streams.

"Tamisra, stop!"

Corrin's command apparently fell on deaf ears, and Tamisra showed no signs of letting up until Roland stepped forward and wrapped his arms around Tamisra from behind, forcing her away from the prone man.

She kicked and screamed for several seconds, even in Roland's arms, but he held on tight until she calmed down, panting heavily while Gareth examined the man on the ground.

"What happened to the others?" Roland asked, carefully releasing Tamisra when she finally went limp.

Tamisra sat up and looked down at the ground. "Dead."

"The others?" Lieutenant Haskill frowned. "How many were there?"

She held up three fingers.

"He's alive," Gareth said, standing up. "Barely. Think we can get any information out of him?"

Corrin shook his head. "Doubt it. The Silver Guard has always been resilient against our interrogations in the past, and I have no reason to suspect that's changed."

"So Kendall is trying to kidnap Roland, just like before." Tamisra stood up, her fists clenched. "And you're still willing to sit here and hide until he succeeds?"

"Forget it, Tami." Corrin folded his arms. "We don't have the manpower to fight Kendall. Nothing's changed."

"You're wrong," Gareth said.

Everyone turned to the doctor.

"Everything's changed. We decided to wait it out and reevaluate our position based on the knowledge that although Kendall knows where we are, he can't get to us and wouldn't bother even if he could." Gareth pointed at Roland. "For whatever reason, this is not the case. Not only does

Kendall still have access to Refuge, but he cares enough to attack us and kidnap Roland. We're not safe here."

Gareth turned to Corrin. "Tamisra was right. He doesn't expect us to attack him. It should be the last thing on his mind. If you want to protect Refuge, the only way is to eliminate the threat."

After a pause, Lieutenant Haskill shook his head. "It's suicide."

"Maybe," Tamisra said. "But at least we'll go out fighting rather than waiting for him to come kill us in our sleep."

"And this way, we'll at least take some of them out with us," Roland said. "And if you still don't want to do anything about it, then I know there are some people who won't wait for your permission." He glanced at Tamisra. "I, for one, don't want to wait for them to come after me again."

Tamisra grabbed his hand and squeezed.

Finally, Corrin nodded. "I can't believe I'm doing this. Fine. Let's go pick a fight."

PART IV
CLASH

44

TEN WEEKS LATER

Kendall studied the stack of papers on the desk before him. Everything was finally falling into place. The raw materials needed to repair the machine had been gathered and processed. All that was left was to install it.

Of course, that presented him with a dilemma. Between him and the Hub was a band of rebels that had proven to be quite frustrating over the last several weeks. It seemed like every day that he was getting reports of another weapons cache blown to pieces, another scouting party gone missing.

The rebels couldn't hope to beat him in open battle, and apparently they knew it. Instead, they resorted to guerrilla warfare, vanishing back into the tunnels before Kendall could manage a counter attack.

His patience had already worn out. As much as he hated the idea of unnecessary killing, he had sent scouts to Refuge to start planning an attack, but they had come back reporting that the town had been evacuated, the caverns completely empty. The rebels had found a new home, either in another tunnel or another sector.

All efforts to track them had turned up nothing. All Kendall could do was send reinforcements to each sector to protect his resources. Of course, not knowing the location of the rebels made this strategy as dangerous as it was potentially helpful. Sometimes, the reinforcements radioed back and confirmed their arrival. Sometimes they didn't.

None of this would matter much if Kendall could just get to the Hub, but there was apparently no safe route there. Even if he took his entire army, they would have to pass through either the train tunnels or the mole tunnels. Either way, such a tight path would provide the rebels with the perfect bottleneck to whittle away at his men.

Kendall had the supplies to gas out the tunnels. It wouldn't be difficult. One press of a button, and every living thing still inside the caves would be dead in mere hours. But the risks were too great. If a tunnel exit was left open, the gas could get back into any number of unknown sectors.

Besides, who was to say that the rebels were even still in the tunnels? More likely than not, they were hiding out in another sector across the Web. And even if Kendall knew where they were, it was still preferable to keep them alive, even after all the damage they had done.

And then, of course, there was the Director breathing down his neck. Kendall had already had a rather uncomfortable explanation with his superior, having to explain why the rebels were still alive and why Roland was not in his possession. The Director had expressed his disappointment with Kendall in no uncertain terms, giving orders not to bother contacting him until any progress was made.

Kendall knew there was a limit to the Director's patience. If he didn't deliver soon, the Director would find someone else to do his bidding. Something had to happen, and it had to happen soon.

"Sir?"

Kendall looked up. A Silver stood in the doorway, his helmet in hand, the light still on and swaying slightly.

"Come in, Commander."

The man did not enter but stood just outside the room, shifting back and forth.

"At least turn your light off." Kendall rolled his eyes and looked back down at the map. None of the Silvers had spoken to him much in the last several weeks. He couldn't blame them. Their last leader had been an emotional one, prone to outbursts upon receiving bad news. Now, with every small rebel victory, they seemed to get more on edge as if expecting him to snap any second.

"Report," Kendall said, gesturing with his hand in a hurried circular motion.

"They got another one, sir."

Kendall let out a heavy sigh.

"Please forgive us, sir. We didn't—"

"It's not your fault." Kendall stepped away from the table and began pacing. "What sector was it?"

"Fyrhaust."

Kendall nodded slowly.

The man took one step inside. "I don't get it. There doesn't seem to be any pattern to their movements. Every week, it seems to be a random sector."

"It's not random. They're targeting our smallest weapons depots. Building their way up, making sure they have the weapons to fight us."

"But how do they know which sectors to hit?"

Kendall shrugged. "They probably send an advance party to scout out the sectors to make sure they can handle it before they actually attack. They're stockpiling."

"Surely they have enough weapons by now. Do you think we'd lose a battle if they found us?"

"Oh, absolutely not." Kendall smiled. "They may have

more numbers, but we still have more resources. However, I don't want to fight them if I can help it."

"So you've said. You still want to talk to them after everything they've done?"

"This Web belongs to them, Commander. We owe it to them to give them a chance to keep on living in it, don't you think?"

The man shrugged.

Kendall sighed and turned back to the map. "Besides, we have other things to worry about, namely the reactor. They don't realize it, but they're quite effectively keeping us from going anywhere near the Hub. Until they're dealt with, we can't do our job and restart the machine."

"So we force our way through. Whatever it takes, right?"

"Commander, I'm convinced that there's a better way to solve this, a strategy in which everyone wins."

The man folded his arms. "In a timely fashion? You said yourself that the Director won't wait forever, and we don't even know where the rebels are."

"You're right. They could be anywhere in the Web."

"So what can we do? Sit around and wait for them to find us?"

Kendall shook his head. "I think there's a much simpler way."

"Yes?"

"We need to bring them to us."

45

"This suit itches."

Roland looked to his side to see Tamisra attempting to scratch her back at an awkward angle, but stopping short as her reach was limited by her armor. With a growl, she yanked her arm forward again, but the metal wouldn't bend at this angle, and her arm twisted and locked in place as she yelped in pain.

Stifling a laugh, Roland turned her around. "Let me get that for you."

He unhooked the metal and spun the silver braces around until Tamisra could pull her arm forward.

"Thanks. Stupid shiny costumes."

Roland held a finger to his smiling lips. "We're undercover, remember? Let's try to act like it."

"Easy for you to say. You've lived in the sectors all your life."

Roland looked around. Basradur was nothing like his home sector of Holendast. It was nice, classy, far from the gravel roads and wooden shacks of the Hole. This sector was almost sophisticated, at least as far as he could tell. White spires decorated the landscape, beautiful pinnacles that gave the sector a very geometric design. They looked impressive even with the power out, and Roland knew that with the lights on, the sector would be simply breathtaking.

"I'm not sure that counted," Roland said. "The Hole wasn't much of a step up from Refuge. I've never seen anything like this. Even the Hub wasn't as fancy."

Tamisra rolled her eyes. "Careful, buddy. We're here to spy on them, not move in."

"What, you don't want to live in one of those shiny buildings?" Roland grinned.

"I hate shiny," Tamisra said. She jerked her arm and forced the armor to shift unnaturally, prompting another snicker from Roland. "How do you know how to work these things so well?"

"I like to wear actual clothing, not the crazy leather jumpsuit you made yourself."

"How do you know I made it?"

"I don't know anyone else that . . . creative." Roland stuck his tongue out, and Tamisra shoved him to the side, but he didn't even lose his balance as her blow was limited by the stiff armor.

Roland laughed until a glint of silver flashed in his peripheral vision. He grabbed Tamisra's arm and steadied her. "Silvers."

She looked down and continued walking with him along the paved road. Roland noticed that her posture was unnaturally stiff, and he was worried for a moment that she would try to blend in too much.

But as they passed the Silvers and continued on, he sighed in relief that they had gone unnoticed.

"We need to be careful," he said quietly. "If Kendall is here, then it wouldn't take long for the news to get to him. He'd be gone long before we even got close."

"And if he isn't, then we're wasting our time." Tamisra's speech was just as quiet, but her frustration was audible.

"We've already let him run around the Web for over two months now. We're losing whatever advantage we may have had."

Roland shrugged. "I don't know about a waste of time. We've destroyed a lot of their supplies and caches. We have weapons now, and plenty of them."

"We could have done that in a week. We didn't need to keep attacking their outposts. Kendall is still alive and out there somewhere."

"We're fighting all of them, Tami. Not just Kendall."

"He's the only one that matters. If he dies, his army has no one to answer to."

Roland's eyes narrowed, and he stopped in the middle of the street, turning to her. "I know why you want to kill him. You can say whatever you want to Corrin, but please be honest with me."

"If you know why, then stop trying to convince me that killing him isn't important." Tamisra turned away and kept walking. "You're not going to change my mind. You should know that by now."

They continued in silence until they arrived at the town hall, where they agreed Kendall would be if he was anywhere in Basradur. Roland tugged at the door handle, and he and Tamisra both frowned as the door opened freely.

"Doesn't mean he's not here." Tamisra pushed past him and walked inside.

Roland followed her, closing the door behind him.

The halls were empty, though the faint sound of people talking indicated that the building was not completely vacant.

Tamisra began walking ahead of Roland but stopped abruptly as her heavy boots resounded through the empty halls with dull thuds.

"So much for the element of surprise," Roland whispered.

Tamisra shot him a glare. "They'll find out soon enough

anyway." With that, she drew her gun and proceeded down the hallways with rapid steps.

"Easy, Tami," he hissed, jogging to catch up. He pulled his own gun out, checking quickly to make sure it was set to tranquilizer pellets. He thought about asking Tamisra whether she checked her own ammunition, but he knew what her answer would be.

"Relax," she said, not bothering to whisper. "Do you really think they're going to hear a footstep and instantly think they're being attacked?"

Almost instantly, a man stepped into the hallway directly in front of them. He was clothed in the standard gray compression suit that the Silver Guard wore under their armor, but none of the silver pieces that comprised the outer shell.

"I do now," Roland said as he raised his gun. But before he could fire, Tamisra snapped her arm up and fired a bullet into the man's forehead.

The man fell to the floor, his mouth hanging open in the same confused expression he had when he first looked at them.

The shot echoed throughout the building for a few seconds, and Roland took the opportunity to turn to Tamisra, saying, "What was that for? Are you trying to get us caught?"

Tamisra shrugged. "They'll all have heard that."

"Yes, that was my point."

"So if Kendall's here, we can expect him shortly." Tamisra cocked her gun again and grinned.

Roland growled as he switched the ammunition type on his gun. Tranquilizer pellets would be nearly useless in a firefight. "Yeah, if we're not dead first."

Sure enough, the thundering of boots replaced the echoing gunshot. The noise reverberated throughout the entire building, making it impossible to tell where the sound was coming from.

Roland pulled Tamisra into the room the man had exited, then reached back out and dragged the dead man inside before closing the door.

"If you keep this up, the only person you'll end up killing is yourself," Roland fumed. "And quite possibly me."

"Maybe." Tamisra's grin did not fade. Instead, she leaned over and kissed him on the cheek. "Or maybe I just have good faith in your aim and our ability to handle ourselves in a fight."

"We don't know how many there are, Tami."

She shrugged. "We'll find out soon enough."

"That's—"

Roland was cut short by the door slamming open, revealing several armored men standing in the hallway. The blood trail must have given them away.

Tamisra tossed something through the open door, and Roland raised his gun but almost immediately fell backward as an explosion shook the building, fire bursting from the hallway and into the room before dissipating.

His ears ringing, Roland finally sat back up after several seconds. An awful smell lingered in the air as the blood in the hallway burned into a black mess. He turned to Tamisra, who was sporting a triumphant grin.

"Told you those explosives from Dryfen would come in handy," she said.

But her celebration lasted for only a moment, and as she turned to the door again, her smile vanished. Roland followed her gaze to see a young man standing in the doorway, looking down at the bloody mess with pure shock written on his face.

Roland looked back at Tamisra, whose gun was already drawn, and he held up a hand up, shouting above the ringing in his ears.

"Tami, no!" Roland kept his open palm facing her, and he turned back to the man and raised his gun slowly with his other hand. "Drop your weapon."

The man followed Roland's order, and he stepped into the room slowly, raising his hands to his head.

"Please don't shoot."

Roland stood, keeping his gun trained on the young man. "We won't as long as you cooperate. Are you alone?"

The officer nodded, staring at the blood at his feet. His eyes glazed over as he muttered, "That was all of us. I was cleaning my gun, so I had to assemble it before joining the others. If only I had been here . . ."

"Then you would have been blown to bits with the rest of them," Tamisra sneered.

"Tami, please." Roland turned to her. "Go make sure we're alone."

She growled in the boy's direction before exiting the room, hopping over a smoldering hunk of flesh in the doorway.

"What's your name?" Roland asked.

The young man looked up abruptly, almost as if he forgot Roland was there. "Hitta."

"Hitta," Roland repeated. "Who's in charge here?"

"General Redmint."

"And where is General Redmint?"

Hitta grimaced and pointed at one of the mutilated bodies in the hallway.

"Sorry about that." Roland winced as he realized how insincere he must sound. "So Kendall isn't here?"

Hitta shook his head.

"Do you know where he is?"

The boy looked up and frowned. "Even if I did, why would I tell you?"

"Because you'd be helping the Web you've sworn to protect." Roland dropped his gun slightly. "Kendall plans to take over as chancellor, but it will be just as bad as before, maybe worse. If you care at all for the people you guard, you'll tell me where he is."

Hitta shrugged. "He'll do what he has to in order to restore the Web."

"You don't understand," Roland said. "I know you think the Citizen Tax is necessary, but they don't tell you what they do with those people, do they?"

"Sure they do. Those who serve the Lightbringers and give power to the world are the most valued and fortunate citizens of the Web."

Roland shook his head. "It's torture."

"It's sacrifice." Hitta looked around the room. "And if you value human life so much, why are you so quick to end it?"

"Because your death means a peaceful world." Tamisra entered the room, her gun drawn and pointed at Hitta once again. "And I'll kill every last one of you myself if I have to. Now, where is Kendall?"

Hitta looked like he was about to break, but he closed his eyes and clenched his jaw, shaking his head. "I can't tell you that."

"Then I can't promise your safety," Roland said. "I don't want to kill you, but I can't stop her. If you don't have anything to offer, then there's nothing I can do."

Tamisra grinned and cocked the gun.

Hitta stared her down for a second before shrinking away, throwing his hands up in front of his face. "All right! All right."

Roland's eyebrows shot up as he looked as Tamisra. Out of every sector the rebels had raided, they had not found anyone willing to give away any information regarding Kendall.

"Well?" Tamisra stepped forward again and placed the barrel of the gun on Hitta's forehead. "Where is he?"

Hitta sighed and let his arms hang loose at his side. "He's in Holendast."

Roland clenched his fists. It was bad enough when the

Chancellor took over his childhood home. But Kendall? This was somehow so much worse.

"Are you sure about that?" Tamisra pushed her gun into Hitta's skin, and the boy slipped on the blood and fell to the ground.

"Yes," Hitta said, looking down at his blood-covered hands. "I'm sure." He stood back up carefully and wiped his hands on his compression clothing.

Tamisra smiled sweetly. "Thank you."

A shot fired, and Roland stared in shock as the defenseless boy dropped back to the ground, a hole in his head.

"Well," Tamisra said, tucking her gun into her holster, "I guess you're going home."

46

Aniya kicked out behind her with a grunt, sending her opponent tumbling. She turned to attack the girl, but her enemy had already climbed back to her feet and was ready for her.

The girl delivered a swift uppercut, sending Aniya reeling backward in pain. She followed up with a low kick, and Aniya's legs were knocked out from under her as she fell to the ground.

"Anytime now," Aniya mumbled as she rolled over and back to her feet.

Her sessions with Caspian had been productive, and she was learning to better manage her anger, but it was difficult to find the right balance. She had to let herself get just angry enough to activate the dormant power in her without getting too emotional and losing complete control.

The girl jumped on top of her, but Aniya thrust her legs up and pushed the girl over her body and into the dirt behind her.

Aniya jumped to her feet but stumbled forward again as a foot landed square in the middle of her back. Blinding pain shot through her body, and as she growled in frustration, green light flickered over her body.

"Finally," she said, grinning as she turned again to face her opponent. The girl lashed out with a fist, and Aniya ducked under it, lunging forward with a punch of her own. Her fist connected with the girl's stomach with a green spark and sent her opponent flying backward a few feet.

Aniya took a deep breath as her heart rate quickened. She knew she only had a few seconds before she would lose control to the light. She had to make this quick.

So before the girl could get back up, Aniya leapt on top of her opponent and punched the girl in the face with a glowing fist. The girl's head snapped to the side, and she went still.

Ignoring the roar of the surrounding crowd, Aniya pushed herself off the girl and closed her eyes, taking deep breaths until her heart rate slowed.

Finally, she opened her eyes again and glanced at her opponent. Still breathing.

"Well done."

A voice came from above, and Aniya looked up to see a Silver standing over her, a blank stare plastered on his face.

"Please come with me," he said plainly.

Aniya got up and followed the man out of the arena, even as the stadium continued to cheer for her. They walked to a small building just next to the entrance, and the man ushered her inside before closing the door behind her.

Choosing to ignore this oddity, Aniya grinned widely. She had done what she thought was impossible. She had managed to continue to fight over the last ten weeks without blacking out and completely surrendering control to the light again. And she had won all of her matches as a result.

As it turned out, meeting with Caspian three times a week for guided meditation was a huge help. Something about his office made it easier to concentrate, and in that time, she had learned to step into the void at will. Her negative emotions would always be waiting there in the form of the Chancellor, but she was getting better at allowing them in small doses, giving her the opportunity to practice using the light without harming herself or others.

It was easier than she had thought, but probably because she had not seen Nicholas once in the last ten weeks. She hadn't actively tried to avoid him, and she wasn't sure if he was reassigned to a different training class or even transferred to another sector, but his absence did help her to focus her emotions more clearly. She was, however, immensely frustrated that the thought of possibly never seeing him again saddened her.

Aniya paced back and forth in the room for several minutes. After the adrenaline and the thrilling feeling of victory wore off, she began to wonder. Each of her other fights had ended with her returning to her dormitory and preparing for another week of training. She didn't know what she'd expected to happen when the fights were over, but it wasn't sitting in a room alone. What was this?

She recalled the introduction they had received ten weeks earlier. They had mentioned that the best fighters would be moved to a higher level of training.

Was it in another sector, and this was where they would keep her until it was time to leave? Was this simply where they would keep all of the day's winners?

Aniya sighed and sat down. There was no point in speculation, she reasoned.

She didn't know how long she would be waiting, so she closed her eyes and let her mind go blank. It took some time to fully focus, but not nearly as long as it had been when she first started. In addition to her sessions with Caspian, she would practice in her room alone. Of course, those times proved to be the most important time for her to focus on blocking out her feelings, or else her mind would wander without Caspian's help, and it would usually stray to Nicholas.

As she took another deep breath, Aniya found herself in the void. No one came to greet her, so she wandered around in the black, killing time until William decided to show up.

Sure enough, the familiar green light called out to her in the distance, and Aniya ran toward her brother, grinning. As soon as she got close enough, she reached out and touched the light to reveal William's true form, but she stumbled backward as the Chancellor's smirking face appeared instead in a flash of red light.

"Hello again!"

Aniya frowned. "What's with the tricks? Don't I tolerate you enough as it is?"

"I'm sorry, my dear." The Chancellor gave a pouting stare. "But I have a bone to pick with you. When I taught you how to access your power, I had hoped that you would rely on me a little more than you have. I resort to trickery because I don't feel like I've been given the attention I deserve."

Aniya's heart raced, and she turned away before she could get too upset. "You know what will happen if I let you out for more than a second. I don't feel like getting anyone else killed."

The Chancellor's face materialized in the shadows in front of her. "Let me out, Annelise. You're missing out on something truly wonderful."

"What could I possibly be missing out on other than the risk of killing everyone around me?" Aniya put her hands on her hips. "You're a part of me. My negative emotions, right? What could you have to offer me that I don't already know?"

The Chancellor grinned. "Your true potential. Do you have any idea what you're capable of?"

Aniya shuddered as she imagined Xander's pained face. "Trust me. I have a good idea of the damage I can inflict."

"You're going to need it, Annelise. The Director won't stop coming for you. You know that. You need to be ready for when he comes, and your mere dabbling with this power will not help you. It won't be enough to stop him, not even enough to slow him down."

"And what would you suggest?"

The Chancellor spread open his arms as a red glow spread across his body. "Let me out to play. Use me. Show the world, the Director, that you are not to be used."

"And let you take over?" Aniya turned around, shaking her head. "I don't think so. I like having control over my own body."

"You won't have control if you let him take you. He'll use you in the worst way possible unless you stand up and fight."

Nicholas and his new girlfriend appeared in the void before her, their joined hands gently massaged by each other's thumbs.

"Stop it," Aniya said, waving a hand in front of her, dismissing the image. She spun around and glared at the Chancellor as the light began to buzz within. "What are you trying to do, force me to use you?"

The Chancellor shrugged. "I'm only trying to help you, Annelise."

"Well, I don't need your help."

Aniya felt a hand on her shoulder, and she forced open her eyes, banishing the void. She looked up to see the man in the gray uniform standing over her.

"Are you ready for your next fight?"

"I thought that was my last one." Aniya stood up, frowning.

The man turned and opened the door. "This is the last *day* of matches. We continue the fights until there is one victor."

Aniya simply nodded and followed the man out of the room. This caveat was probably explained at some point during the orientation, not that she was listening.

She let the man guide her back into the arena, and she stepped out on the dirt as the crowd began to shout.

From across the arena approached her opponent, and Aniya stopped suddenly as the details of his face became clear.

It was Nicholas.

47

Nicholas stood across from his childhood friend, his mouth hanging open.

The roar of the crowd fell on his deaf ears as he stared in horror at the girl he had spent the last several years pining for.

He had intentionally avoided watching Aniya's fights, but he had heard the rumors of a surprise contender, an unassuming girl whose triumphs seemed effortless, no matter how uneven the odds were stacked against her.

Nicholas knew this mystery girl had to be Aniya, even though he kept telling himself otherwise. He had a good idea of her potential after the way Malcolm had described her lethal powers, but Nicholas hadn't expected her to be able to use them at will, let alone control them.

But Nicholas's own strange abilities had helped him get to this point as well. No matter how bad a fight would get, as long as he could get a firm grip on his opponent, something would kick in, sucking the life out of his enemy and making Nicholas stronger.

However, when this power awoke, it would always render Nicholas a prisoner in his own body, forced to watch as his opponent slowly died in his hands. Only after releasing them would he find himself in control of his own body yet again.

As useful as this power was, it terrified Nicholas at first. He avoided all contact for days after his first fight, not knowing if he would accidentally end up killing someone he brushed up against. He even broke everything off with Quinn for fear of hurting her. It took him weeks to realize that the power only seemed to manifest itself when he was in danger.

Now, Nicholas appreciated its potential as a weapon, one that could prove useful against the Lightbringers if they ever came for him and Aniya.

Today, he had stepped in the arena feeling confident, knowing that this mysterious power would mean another easy victory. Indeed, his fight just a moment ago had lasted mere seconds. He was so confident in his newfound power that it didn't even faze him when the Silvers said he would be fighting another opponent immediately after.

But now, he stood rigid in shock.

He knew that neither he or Aniya would actually fight with any real force, but even if they pretended to fight and put on a show for the Silvers, the same power he had come to rely upon could end up hurting, maybe even killing the girl he had loved for years.

And what if Aniya wasn't actually in control of her own power? It might betray her and kill him before he had a chance to defend himself. And this was assuming she didn't still hate him. Whatever anger she probably still felt toward him would certainly not help matters.

The ideal solution was a truce, but it wasn't like they could choose not to fight. This was the final round, the ultimate fight that the entire sector gathered for. This was the biggest event of the year. As Nicholas looked in the stadium, he spotted a man in a white suit. Even the President came out to see the results of Sector F's newest training class.

The Lightbringers expected to see a fight, and they would make sure they got one.

Nicholas looked back at Aniya, who seemed just as stunned. She stared back at him with wide eyes, her head shaking slightly. Neither of them had approached the center yet, but instead stood about fifty yards apart.

A long buzzer sounded, and Nicholas realized that they had been motionless for quite some time. He shook away his daze and realized that the roar of the crowd had escalated immensely as he had been contemplating his options.

He walked to the center of the arena, where Aniya met him.

"What do we do?" Her eyes were shifting quickly. Gone was the rage he had seen when she slapped him so many weeks ago. She was once again the nervous girl he had comforted on his rooftop when William returned from the Citadel, putting this horrible chain of events into motion. That was only a few months ago, but it seemed like a lifetime.

Nicholas had so much he wanted to say to her, but he only shrugged. "We can fake it. I learned how to pull my punches when I trained with Roland."

"You think they'll buy it?"

"No idea." Nicholas looked around. "Aniya, there's something I need to tell you. Something keeps happening to my body when I fight. I—"

The buzzer rang out again, and Aniya visibly jumped.

"Later," Aniya said. She bowed to him, and he bowed in return.

"Aniya, you have to know. I keep—"

Nicholas's breath was sucked out of his lungs as Aniya kicked him in the stomach. He doubled over in pain, gasping for breath as he dropped to his knees.

"Are you okay?" She knelt next to him and placed a hand on his shoulder. Her voice was concerned, but it carried a cold edge to it. "I'm sorry. I don't think they want to wait on us."

He nodded and held up a thumb. "No, I get it. Good job selling it," he said hoarsely.

"Good." With that, Aniya thrust her knee into his throat. This blow was not as forceful, but it still was enough that Nicholas toppled over, grasping his neck.

"Come on," she said. "I can't do all the work."

Nicholas looked up and almost forgot where he was. Aniya was looking back at him with the mischievous smile he had fallen in love with years ago. He hadn't seen that smile in months, and he'd forgotten how much it put him at ease. That same smile warmed his heart now, and it was almost like nothing ever happened between them. He chose to ignore the fact that there was an odd twist at the end of her lips, mutating her familiar smile into something new.

He grinned back at her and climbed to his feet. "If you say so. Just remember. You asked for it." With that, he stepped forward and kicked Aniya's legs out from under her, sending her toppling to the ground.

But she vaulted back up, nearly flipping to her feet with a grace Nicholas marveled at. "That's it? We're fighting here. Do you really think *that's* going to sell it to them?"

"Maybe they'll think we're toying with each other."

"Like playing with our food before we eat it?" Aniya laughed. "That might keep them entertained for a few minutes, but that's not what they want to see."

"I know." Nicholas sighed. "We have to make this look real, which means that at least to some extent, it has to be real. You know that, right?"

Aniya's face grew somber. "I can't do that."

"You have to. Just don't mess up my face too much. And make it quick, okay? No need to drag this out." Besides, Nicholas solemnly noted to himself, the faster she knocked him out, the fewer chances he had to accidentally retaliate.

"Wait, you're not going to fight back?"

"Of course not. I couldn't do that to you. Now, hit me. Really hit me."

Aniya thought for a moment but shook her head. "Please don't ask me to do that."

"One of us has to win, Aniya, and I would rather it be you. I've already hurt you enough."

The buzzer came again, this time louder and longer.

Nicholas took a deep breath. If pushing her was what it took, he had no choice. "Fight me, Aniya. I know you're angry. I betrayed you."

"Don't do this, Nicholas." Her head shook faster now, a tear breaking loose from her cheek and falling to the dirt.

"I knew you would have to die, and I lied to you to get you to go to the Citadel."

"I would have gone anyway, Nicholas." The steely tone to Aniya's speech was gone, and her voice cracked. "William was there. Please, stop."

Nicholas took a step forward. "You haven't forgiven me, though, have you? I know you still hate me for what I did."

Aniya retreated.

"I handed you over to a stranger because I wanted to start a war. I broke your trust and signed your life away."

More tears began to fall from her cheeks.

"Hit me, Aniya."

Aniya's cries were audible now, a whimper escaping her mouth.

"Hit me!"

Her cries suddenly escalated into a shriek, and a searing pain lit Nicholas's face aflame as her fist crashed into his cheek.

Nicholas stumbled backward, barely managing to maintain his balance. The blow was much more than he was expecting, and it very nearly knocked him out instantly. Somehow, he stayed on his feet, shaking his head to chase away the stars that clouded his vision.

He looked back up at Aniya just in time to see her leap on his chest, tackling him and driving a knee into his ribcage.

Without a word, Aniya punched him again and drove his face into the dirt.

Nicholas coughed, spitting blood on the dirt and puffing out mini clouds of dust next to his mouth. "Aniya, stop. Just a second. I—"

She grabbed his hair and pulled his head up before slamming it back into the ground.

"Just choke me out, Aniya. You don't have to—"

Another blow to his stomach, and Nicholas looked back up at Aniya to beg one more time, but his words died away as he gasped.

Her eyes were blazing with golden light that flickered wildly.

"You're wrong, Nicholas."

When the being spoke, it confirmed Nicholas's fear. Whatever was mounted atop him was not Aniya. Not anymore.

In place of Aniya's soft yet commanding tone was a new voice, a host of timbres and pitches that combined into an unearthly, terrifying voice. It was like the words that came from Aniya's mouth came from a thousand different voices, none of them hers.

She snarled and spoke with a deep growl. "You couldn't be any more wrong. I *do* have to do this."

With that, Aniya yanked Nicholas's head up to meet hers, bashing their foreheads together.

Nicholas fell back to the ground as she released him, and he moaned in pain as his vision began to blur.

There was no telling what would happen to him now. If the lethal power inside Aniya was now in control, she might just kill him without even knowing it.

He had to fight back. Whether Aniya killed him or not, her power might escalate and lash out at the spectators, meaning the deaths of thousands of recruits. And even if it wasn't that bad, it would surely draw the attention of the Director.

If Nicholas used his own power, he might be able to render Aniya unconscious, saving himself and countless others. The real trick would be keeping his own power from going too far and killing her.

As Aniya's fist smashed against his cheek again, Nicholas made a decision. It went against his every instinct, but he knew what he had to do.

He reached out with his right hand and grabbed Aniya's throat, clenching tightly.

Aniya froze, and as the light in her eyes began to dim, tendrils of yellow light slithered out of her body and into Nicholas's arm.

As the light made its way to his chest, Nicholas gasped as raw energy flooded his veins. It was more potent than any energy he had stolen from his opponents thus far. He could feel vibrations rock his entire body, tensing up every muscle and tickling every nerve.

A new tooth forced its way through Nicholas's gums as he spat out an old one that was still under his tongue. His rib cage stitched itself together with a crack, and the dent in his forehead slowly expanded back into place.

Nicholas felt Aniya's body relax, and he sat up, pushing her away as he stood. The light still raced over his body, streams of gold dancing over his silver jumpsuit and reflecting against the material.

Somehow, unlike every other fight so far, Nicholas was still in control. He was lucid, awake, and he knew what he was doing.

He took a deep breath as the light settled and dissipated, all visible traces vanishing. His heart slowed, and he exhaled gently, letting the buzzing sensation slow to a crawl.

Aniya looked down at her hands, a low growl emanating from her lungs. She looked back up at Nicholas and clenched her fists, staring at him with glowing eyes that now shone more green than yellow.

"Aniya, wait." Nicholas held up a hand. "It's me. It's Nicholas."

Her growl escalated. "I know," she spat, sparks shooting from her mouth. With a running start, she jumped at Nicholas again, leading with a fist aimed directly at his face.

Nicholas stretched forth an open hand. It had turned out to be a powerful stopping force. At some point during his fights, he could always expect a punch to his face, and because he was waiting for it, he could get a grip on their hands and start draining their energy before going in for the finishing move on their neck.

But this time, in the instant Aniya's fist contacted his open palm, a flash of yellow erupted from their touching skin and surged back on Nicholas, sending him flying backward and to the ground.

Yellow lights danced on a black canvas.

As far as Nicholas knew, his eyes were wide open. But all he saw was a black expanse, yellow spots pulsing in and out of view.

His vision cleared over several seconds, and he eventually sat up carefully, his head still spinning.

Aniya was in the same position, sprawled out on the ground several feet away. She was turning, moaning, and had not yet sat back up.

Nicholas stumbled to his feet and approached her, kneeling next to her side. "Are you okay?"

She finally opened her eyes, her normal black pupils restored, and looked up at him with wide, unblinking eyes. "Nicky. I didn't—"

But Nicholas had placed a hand on her cheek, and in the same instant, the angry yellow glow returned. Nicholas scrambled to get away from her, but it was too late.

Aniya kicked out at him viciously with both feet, knocking

him back to the ground just as he stood. Without waiting for him to react, she grabbed him by the ankles and lifted him in the air, swinging him like an ax.

Nicholas gasped as his body swung high in the air, up and over Aniya. The searing heat in his legs almost distracted him from the impending pain, but as he looked toward the advancing ground, he could only close his eyes in anticipation.

His body swung back to the ground with an exponentially increasing force, driven by Aniya's supernatural brute strength. His face smashed into the dirt, followed by the rest of his body, and his screams were muffled by the cloud of dirt that exploded around him.

As he wailed in agony, he turned around slowly, looking up to see nothing but a swirling cyclone of dust that lingered over him.

Aniya appeared out of the thick cloud and reached for his arm, perhaps for another devastating swing over her shoulder, but Nicholas swatted her hand away and pulled her down by her collar.

She toppled over him, and Nicholas dove to the side and then back on top of her, mounting her and forcing her into submission. Not wanting to risk any more significant injury, he reached for her neck to end the fight.

But as his fingers touched her neck, a thin beam of yellow light shot forth from Aniya's eyes, piercing through his silver jumpsuit and searing through his right shoulder.

Nicholas clutched his body and gasped, the burning pain too much to even manage a scream.

A horrible chuckle escaped Aniya's lips as her eyes morphed to a blazing red, and Nicholas was close enough to see white lightning flash in her irises and highlight her crimson pupils with streaks of silver.

He reached out and grabbed her neck again, but as red light began to race over his arm, a shrieking wail came from Aniya, and she thrust his body away.

Nicholas expected to land roughly in the dirt next, but Aniya met him in mid-air with a vicious kick, sending him careening into the wall of the arena. Something in his spine came loose, and pain reverberated throughout his back as he slumped to the ground.

He opened his eyes just as Aniya descended on him, a snarl on her face. She landed on him roughly and immediately began punching him everywhere she could reach.

His hands were pinned down by Aniya's legs, leaving no way for him to defend himself, so punch after punch, all Nicholas could do was lie down helplessly as she beat him to a pulp.

Nicholas began to lose consciousness, the roar of the crowd turning to a ring in his ears and a slight vibration in the dirt below. It was almost comforting, and the pain began to vanish as he went numb.

A slap to his face startled him back awake.

He was hanging off the ground, suspended by Aniya's tight grip around his neck. She was glaring at him with scarlet eyes, a fire crackling inside that nearly hypnotized him.

Small streams of energy began to poke at his nerves and wake his body up yet again, but the recovery was minimal. The damage that the light inflicted on his body far outweighed the healing it provided.

"I'm not done with you yet," she growled.

Nicholas gasped, and as her grip loosened the tiniest bit, he swallowed some air. "I'm sorry."

She cocked her head to the side.

"I'm sorry for everything. I hate the Lightbringers, and I thought I was willing to do anything to end them. But I love you more than I could ever hate them."

Aniya's eyes shifted, and the red began to flicker.

"Before you stepped in the tank, I wanted to tell you that you didn't have to do it. I didn't want you to do it. Even if it meant the end of the Lightbringers, I couldn't imagine losing you."

The red in Aniya's eyes began to dim, and the fingers around his throat shifted slightly as her grip loosened further. Gone was the crushing pain, and relief instantly shot through his body in waves.

"I'm sorry, Aniya. Please know that. I'm sorry."

Nicholas's toes touched the ground as the light in Aniya's eyes faded completely, and she let go of his neck, letting him breathe freely again.

He looked around the stadium, which had gone silent. Any second now, Nicholas knew the buzzer would force them back into a fight. There was no winner yet.

But if they kept fighting, there was no telling how bad it would get. Nicholas wasn't sure he could stop Aniya this time if she lost control again. And if she got too much worse, she would lash out at anyone in reach. If they fought again, it could mean the death of thousands.

He had to stop this. Now.

"I love you," Nicholas said, his voice cracking as he placed a hand on her cheek.

As soon as he touched her, Aniya's eyes shot open in alarm. Thin, white streaks formed on her cheek and spread across her face as power surged through Nicholas's body.

"Nicholas, stop!" Aniya's pained cries came out shaking, pleading for relief.

But he simply bowed his head as tears began to fall. "I'm sorry."

Despite her begging, Nicholas's hand remained glued to her cheek, sucking the energy from her body relentlessly. He wasn't sure he could have removed it even if he tried.

Nicholas looked up to see the red in her eyes return, only to morph back to yellow, then green.

He felt his own power within demand to take over, to fully drain her of her life force and feed him with ultimate power.

The only thing that kept him from closing his eyes and surrendering control was the fact that he couldn't take his eyes off her. If she didn't survive this, it would be his last chance to look in her eyes.

Finally, the light in her eyes dimmed, and her head lolled to the side.

Nicholas instantly withdrew his hand from her cheek, not wanting to touch her any longer for fear of further harm.

After remaining suspended in mid-air for a split second, Aniya's limp body crumpled to the ground.

48

Roland knocked on the heavy steel door at the end of the tunnel. As he waited, he snuck a glance at Tamisra, who was wiping blood from her silver chestplate.

Not much point in that, he thought to himself. Her silver body armor was covered in blood, except for one of her arms.

A hole appeared in the middle of the large door, through which Roland could see a man's face.

"Password?" the man asked.

Roland cleared his throat. "*Lumen ad mortem.*"

He was grateful that they had never told the old rebel passphrase to Kendall. Lieutenant Haskill had suggested it at one point, but Corrin and Roland had both been quick to shut that idea down.

The face vanished from the hole in the door, and then the hole closed itself up.

With a loud creaking noise that echoed down the tunnel behind Roland and Tamisra, the large door slowly swung open, allowing them to exit the tunnel and step into Lyrindal.

The abandoned sector was in ruins.

Like the Hub, very few buildings were left standing, most

of them nothing more than piles of blackened rubble scattered throughout the sector.

But unlike the Hub, there was no lingering smell of burnt flesh. Whatever bodies had been left behind after the Uprising had long since decomposed and became part of the dirt beneath their feet.

Their bones were left behind, but Roland had been surprised to see that there weren't even that many skeletons left. He had seen maybe ten since Refuge's arrival in Lyrindal. He had asked about this, but Corrin had grown unnaturally quiet at this question and refused to say anything.

Tents with four-fingered hands had overrun the old rebel headquarters. The streets of Lyrindal were littered with them, and the sector, though it was easily five times the size of Refuge, was beginning to resemble the rebels' old home.

And it wasn't just Refuge that had moved in. Corrin had been diligent about sending out scouts for recruitment since the sectors in Quadrant III were ripe with fresh blood, as Tamisra had put it. Salvador had only ever sent scouts to the surrounding sectors back in Quadrant I, and so each time Corrin's scouts went out now, they always came back with dozens of people at a time.

Though there were hundreds of new mouths to feed, finding enough food for everyone had been easy. Back in Quadrant I, Refuge had apparently scared away most of the giant moles. Here, the animals were not used to being hunted, and they provided Lyrindal with more than enough food to go around.

It was the most abundance the people of Refuge had ever seen, and Corrin expressed his reluctance on more than one occasion to risk it all by picking a fight with the Lightbringers again.

"Where are you going?"

Tamisra's question snapped Roland out of his reflections,

and he realized that she had started walking in the opposite direction.

He nodded across the sector. "The Lyrindal clinic. Gareth finally cleared away most of the debris the other day, and he wanted me to help salvage as much equipment as we can."

"We have to be debriefed," she said, frowning. "Gareth can wait."

Roland quickly let his gaze travel up and down her blood-soaked body. The sight reminded him of her merciless attack on the Silvers in Basradur.

"I'm sure you'll do fine yourself," he said, looking away. "I'm not feeling well."

"Fine. I'll let you know what Corrin says. Now that we know Kendall's hiding in Holendast, we'll want to move on him as soon as possible."

With that, she turned and left, leaving Roland to walk across Lyrindal alone.

He smiled and nodded at the people of Refuge, politely saying a quick hello to a few of them when they tried to speak to him.

Roland was rather famous now. Somehow, people had come to know that he was the reason they were finally out of Refuge. Of course, no one had wanted to leave their home at first, but now that they were in Lyrindal, with plenty of room and plenty of food, most of them were thrilled.

Even here, in a sector that was in ruins, they were more than content. Roland couldn't wait until the Lightbringers were gone so the people of Refuge could move to another sector and have real, normal lives.

He eventually arrived at what was left of the Lyrindal clinic, which Gareth had brought him to when they first arrived in Lyrindal and introduced Roland to his old home.

Most of the Uprising instigators were from Lyrindal, Roland remembered from the stories. Somewhere toward the center of the sector were the remains of his parents' old home, but according to Gareth, it had been so thoroughly destroyed that there was nothing left.

But here, farther out from downtown, Gareth's old clinic was only partially destroyed, and Roland had spent the last several weeks helping him excavate what was left of it.

The doctor was standing over it now, his arms folded. He heard Roland coming and turned, a small smile on his face. As he moved, he revealed a girl standing behind him, her sleeves rolled up and dirt covering her cheeks. Though she was covered in sweat, Roland couldn't help but notice that she was rather attractive. She turned and met his eyes, a wide smile on her face.

"Welcome back," Gareth said. "How was your trip to Basradur?"

"Productive," said Roland simply, staring at the girl.

Gareth looked back at the girl. "Ah, my apologies. Roland, this is Dawn. She's been helping me in your absence."

The girl's smile grew wider, and she stuck out a hand.

Roland shook it and was slightly amused to find that though her hand was stained by dirt and ash, it was smooth.

"I've begun training her to take your place," Gareth said as he folded his arms.

"My place?" Roland raised his eyebrows. "Where am I going?"

Gareth chuckled. "Nowhere, I hope. But you have become quite the clinician yourself, and you will need an assistant like you were mine. We'll need all the help we can get with so many people coming in from the sectors."

"Fair enough," Roland said. He shifted in place awkwardly, not knowing whether he could tell Gareth everything in front of this new girl.

Dawn seemed to catch on, but her smile didn't fade. She nodded quickly to Gareth and said cheerily, "I'll see you tomorrow!"

Roland lowered his voice and stepped toward Gareth as Dawn left. "We found out Kendall's hiding in the Hole."

Gareth cursed. "First the Chancellor, now Kendall? The Lightbringers seem determined to ruin every home I've ever had."

"That's what I thought. Speaking of," Roland said, nodding toward the clinic, "did you find anything? It looks like you've already started without me."

"Come." Gareth gestured for Roland to follow as he stepped into the ruins of the clinic.

It was larger than the clinic back in Holendast, but not by much. It was a simple, two-room building, whereas the Holendast clinic was only one room. But it had been well furnished, replete with supplies and equipment that was now lying crushed and rusted.

"I don't think we're getting much out of here, Doc," Roland said with a grimace.

Gareth ignored this comment and pulled a defibrillator from underneath one of the collapsed beds. It looked untouched, but it couldn't have still worked. "I'm sure most of it is indeed useless, but you never know what we'll find."

"I guess." Roland took the device from Gareth and put it in the corner.

Reaching back under the bed, Gareth pulled out a half-empty bottle. He glanced at its contents, shrugged, and took a sip.

"Doc!" Roland frowned. "That can't be any good."

Gareth grinned as he pulled the bottle from his mouth and licked his lips. "It certainly wasn't bad. But those days are long behind me." He tossed the bottle over his shoulder, and it shattered against the wall.

They continued scouring the clinic until Gareth came across another item he stopped and stared at for several seconds.

Roland peered over Gareth's shoulder. "What's that?"

Gareth was holding a scrap of fabric, yellow with a blue flower on it. Dried blood was spattered on the flower.

He shook his head and leaned against the wall, staring at the fabric. He didn't speak for several minutes.

Roland let him sit there in silence as he continued to search the clinic. He eventually came back to Gareth, who didn't seem to have moved.

"Doc, what is that?"

Gareth finally looked at Roland again. "There are many stories I never told you about the Uprising, Roland. And for good reason."

Roland waited patiently.

"Do you love Tamisra?"

The question came out of nowhere, and Roland found himself unable to answer immediately. Even as he thought for a second, he couldn't manage to spit out any words at all.

"She's not the same girl she was, is she?" Gareth smiled softly as he placed the yellow fabric in his pocket. "I've not known her for long, but just long enough to see her change over these last few months into something you don't seem prepared to handle."

Roland looked at the floor. "I don't know what to do with her. All she wants is to get revenge on Kendall. More than she wants to be with me, I think."

Gareth nodded absentmindedly. "I've seen what revenge does to a man. It drives him mad, eats at him until he is a mere shadow of the man he used to be. You wouldn't believe . . ." He trailed off as he shook his head.

"How do I get her to stop?"

"Stop?" Gareth looked back at him in surprise. "There is no stopping a thirst for blood like that. It blinds a man, makes him insensitive to logic and reason. Why do you think I was so firm with you when you seemed hell-bent on blaming Kendall, even though it was indeed his fault? Had I known then what kind of person Tamisra is, I would have spent my warnings on her instead. No, Roland. I'm afraid all you can do is love her through it and hope she steps out on the other side knowing what she has done to herself. And when that time comes, you must forgive her and help her heal. That is when she will need you the most."

Roland gave a small laugh. "When did you become so wise?"

"Have you considered I've always been this way? Children rarely think the best of their parents until they have seen the harsh reality of the world and look back at all the times their parents tried to prepare them for it. Then they begin to see the wisdom of it all."

"Well, I appreciate it, especially since my parents are dead."

Gareth looked away. After a moment, he spoke again. "To be honest, I have not always been the best steward of wisdom. I was a fool as a child. I've told you of my heroics before, but perhaps I should have spent more time telling you of my failures. I was a coward, roped into a rebellion I wanted no part of. The war changed us all. Lieutenant Haskill, for instance, is completely unrecognizable, a totally different man from what he used to be. I changed as well, and I embraced a more courageous path, but not before it was far too late. Not before my greatest failure and my darkest hour."

Roland shivered as Gareth's dark tone conjured up brutal images of war.

"Whatever wisdom I do have, I encourage you to heed it while you still can," Gareth said after a moment, turning back to Roland. "So you can save yourself and the ones you love."

"What if . . ." Roland's voice died away. He cleared his throat and spoke slowly. "What if I can't save her?"

Gareth sighed. "She's started down a dark path that few have broken away from. If she has her revenge, she may be lost forever. Never give up hope, and you can try to bring her back, but the decision is hers alone to choose a better life.

If that is what she decides, you can help her heal, but if she succumbs to darkness, you must be prepared to let her go. Such a weight will only drag you down a dark path of your own."

It was several minutes before Roland spoke again.

"I do love her."

Gareth only nodded.

Without a word, they returned to their work, not speaking again until Tamisra appeared in the open entryway to the clinic.

"It's happening," she blurted out without so much as a greeting.

Roland looked up at her. "You told them?"

She nodded as a wide grin spread across her face. "We attack in three days."

And then she was gone again.

Roland turned to Gareth, who placed a hand on his shoulder. "She's not gone yet, Roland. Have hope."

He nodded and turned back to his work, but he knew it was too late. Tamisra would have her revenge, and she would never be the same again.

The girl he had come to love, as he knew her, would be dead in three days.

49

Aniya couldn't bring herself to open her eyes when she woke back up. It's not that she didn't feel like it. She simply could not summon the physical strength to lift her eyelids.

But there was no pain, and even in the strange sensation of numbness, Aniya felt peace. Ever since she woke up under the Citadel with these strange new abilities, the voices had plagued her mind nonstop, constantly assailing her with unintelligible whispers.

Everything was quiet now, at least until one voice returned.

"Aniya."

A voice came as if from far away, and she frowned, unable to tell if it was William or the Shadow.

"William?" Whether she spoke out loud or simply in her mind, Aniya couldn't tell, but her voice was weak, little more than a whimper.

"It's Nicholas."

Aniya felt an aching sensation in her chest at the sound of his voice.

Memories flashed in her mind, harrowing images of

brutal violence that she had directed at the man who had once been her best friend. She couldn't imagine ever doing such horrible things, but she found herself wondering if she had truly lost control in the arena to a sentient energy inside her or if the darkest version of herself had come out to play.

"Go away," she moaned.

If he left her, all Aniya would be left with was the black. And with her power suddenly absent, she suspected that there would be nothing waiting for her in the void, whether it be William, the Chancellor, or the Shadow.

But given that the only thing Aniya felt in the numbness was guilt in the aftermath of her brutal battle with Nicholas, she was okay with being alone.

"Are you all right?"

Aniya didn't know how to answer that. She didn't miss the strange power that had constantly churned inside her body, always keeping her on edge. But the thought of never seeing William again was too much to handle right now. She had to think about something else.

"What happened?" Aniya asked, remembering how Nicholas had pulled the light out of her. "How did you hurt me like that?"

"I'm not sure. I think the machine did something to me too. If I touch someone, it's like I can suck their life away."

What a pair they made, she thought to herself. She was an unpredictable, uncontrollable nuclear weapon, and Nicholas was a human leech.

She mentally searched her body, looking for any sign of the tingling sensation that had been constant for the last several months.

Nothing.

"You took the light away."

Nicholas paused before replying. "I'm sorry, Aniya. I had to keep you from hurting anyone. I don't think you were in control."

"I wasn't." Aniya recalled the damage she had inflicted, her unrelenting assault. "I'm sorry, Nicholas. I never meant to go that far."

"I know. I'm sorry too. I can't quite control my own power, and I almost killed you. They didn't think you were ever going to wake up."

"How long have I been out?"

"Two days now. They almost decided to pull the plug on you, but I convinced them to give you a little longer."

Aniya finally mustered the strength to open her eyes, and she found herself in a simple white room, filled with hospital equipment. No one besides Nicholas was in the room with her.

She turned back to him. The raw hatred she had grown accustomed to was absent, and now she looked at her childhood friend as if seeing him clearly for the first time in weeks. It was all the more shocking as she recalled how angry she had been with him. She'd been mad at him before, angry with William, annoyed at Roland. But as she looked back down, she was ashamed with herself. For the first time, she wanted to understand what he did. Had she been punishing him for nothing? Or did he truly deserve it?

"Why did you do it, Nicholas?"

He looked up, frowning. "What?"

"Why did you take me to the Hub when you knew I was going to die?" Aniya looked down at her lifeless hands. "I thought you loved me."

Nicholas smiled softly. "I do, Aniya. I never stopped."

"But why?"

"You know how much I hate the Lightbringers. I would've done anything to get rid of them, and I guess I kind of did."

She stared at him blankly. "Why didn't you tell me?"

"I don't know. I kept telling myself that this was the only way, that you wouldn't even consider giving your life for the Web unless you were in the position to do so. If I told you any sooner, maybe we never would have made it to the Hub." He looked down at the floor. "Maybe I knew if I told you, it would be all over between us, and I wanted to put it off as long as possible."

Nicholas looked back up, tears in his eyes. "I can't imagine life without you, Aniya."

"I know."

It was all Aniya could say. Anything more, and she didn't know if her words would be true. She was distracted by a tingling feeling in her body, and she was relieved to find that it was simply the numbness fading away and not her power waking up again.

But another feeling quickly washed over her, the realization that she may have inadvertently given their position away to anyone still looking for them.

"What are we going to do, Nicholas? I can only imagine what we looked like in the arena. That was no ordinary fight, and it won't stay a secret. And if the Director is anything like what you make him out to be, he'll find out. He'll be coming for us now."

"I don't think so. The Silvers know you're strong, exceptionally strong. But I don't think they could tell what was going on down there, especially with all the dust flying." He took a deep breath. "However, they want to move me to an advanced training program because I technically won the tournament. That means constant supervision. I wouldn't get the chance to talk to you again or help you even if you wanted me to."

"So what now?"

He shrugged. "If you want to stick together, then I guess we have to go into hiding. Maybe go to a different level. I had no idea this entire level was dedicated to training Silvers, or I never would have let it be an option when you picked it. But if we're going to get out of here, it has to be soon, and you don't look like you're in any condition to travel."

"Give me a few hours," she said, wiggling her fingers. "I'm feeling better already. They've got some serious drugs here."

"Do you still have the key card for the elevator?"

"Of course. It's in one of the jumpsuits in the closet in my room. You'll need a girl to get you inside the dormitories, but I'm guessing that won't be a problem?"

Nicholas's cheeks turned red. "Yeah, I could talk to her."

"I guess she was good for something after all."

Nicholas shifted in his seat and looked away.

"I'm sorry." Aniya sighed. "I just . . ."

"I know." He stood up. "I'm going to get the card. Just sit tight."

"Can you get my crystal too? It's hanging in the closet, and I don't want to leave without that."

Nicholas nodded and turned to leave, but Aniya stopped him.

"If I'm still not strong enough when you come back, how are we going to get out of here?"

Nicholas paused at the door. "I really don't know. We'll cross that bridge when we come to it."

50

Aniya fidgeted under her blanket, jumping at every sound that came from the hallway.

Besides the fights in the arena, she had felt safe in her last ten weeks in Level I. She had no real reason to suspect that anyone had caught on to her presence here in that time, but now that she was about to leave for another part of the Underworld, and especially after her fight with Nicholas, she felt like her every move was being scrutinized. It felt like she was on the run all over again, even though no one was chasing her.

At least not yet.

Nicholas couldn't get back soon enough.

To make matters worse, Aniya wasn't recovering as quickly as she'd hoped. There was no guarantee that she would be strong enough to leave when it came time. Her only hope of recovery was the light she knew was now gone. It had completely left her, the vibrating sensation missing for the first time in months. The only buzz came from wires strapped to her skin and running to the life-support machine at her bedside.

She was completely powerless.

Aniya could do nothing but wait, and it was beginning to set her on edge. She would have meditated, but now that the light was gone, there wasn't much point, with nothing waiting for her in the void except her own mind.

It was a relief, really. As useful as the light had become, it came with a constant anxiety that never fully disappeared. Now that it was gone, she would no longer be at the mercy of her emotions, struggling to keep herself from harming those around her. Now, she would be free again.

And so when Caspian entered the room a few minutes later, Aniya shook her head.

"Sorry, Caspian. I'm not up for another session right now."

But he sat by her bedside and grinned. "That's not up to you, Aila. Thanks to your valiant efforts in the placement matches, I'm recommending you for elite training once you recover, but I still have to give you a final sign-off before you leave. You've made great progress, but we need to talk about what happened with your last fight."

Aniya moaned. "What did you expect from me? I was forced to fight my ex."

"I know. And you nearly killed each other. If he hadn't won, I'm not so sure he would still be alive."

"It was a hard fight, Caspian. It would have been the same thing if it was anyone else."

"Are you sure?" Caspian's eyes narrowed. "Because there were multiple times during that fight when you could have finished it. But you let him recover and then continued to beat him. Quite brutally, I might add. You wanted him to suffer, Aila. You wanted him to pay for hurting you."

Aniya gritted her teeth and stared at the ceiling.

"Am I wrong?"

Finally, she turned back to him. "It doesn't matter. The fights are over. I'm being transferred."

"And so is he. I don't have all the details, but it's probably to the same sector. You'll be working with him in the future, and I need to know if you can do that in a professional manner." Caspian leaned back and folded his arms. "And even if you never see him again, I have to be sure that similar issues don't crop up with other people."

"And if I don't do as well as you hope?"

Caspian shrugged. "Worst-case scenario, they keep you here. It's not like they're going to send you home after all the effort they've put into training you and all the money I've been paid to 'fix' you, as they put it. They might even go through with the transfer anyway without my approval. You've raised a lot of eyebrows."

"Fine." Aniya relaxed as best as she could and closed her eyes. With the light gone, she knew she wouldn't see anything, but this could work out in her favor. If there was nothing to resolve, Caspian might leave satisfied. On the other hand, if she didn't find anything and just wandered around aimlessly, he might deem it a wasted session and declare her unfit to leave.

But it didn't matter. Aniya simply couldn't find the void. It was black simply because her eyes were closed, but she didn't seem to be able to place herself in the depths of her mind. It had been easy, almost natural, when the light was in her. It was like it wanted her to be a spectator of her own consciousness. But now, all she could do was stare into her eyelids and listen to the humming of the machinery near her bed.

Caspian seemed to read her mind, and Aniya felt two devices slip in her ears. Within seconds, the beach sounds were gently playing.

"Just relax, Aila. Remember, deep breaths."

"I know," she mumbled. "I've been doing this for ten weeks now."

"Then breathe."

Aniya rolled her eyes, but she began breathing deeply, trying to match her breath to the cadence of the waves.

Several minutes passed, and as Aniya continued to breathe, she soon forgot that Caspian was in the room with her. Eventually, the canvas before her turned to a beach scene, almost identical to the virtual space back in Caspian's office. She was standing on the sand, staring into the waters. She could even feel the crisp wind around her, leaving the taste of salt on her tongue.

"I was beginning to think you weren't coming back."

Aniya spun around to see William reclining on a sand dune, his elbows digging into the sand to prop him up.

She let herself forget for a moment what this must mean, and she smiled widely and ran to his side, stopping just short of an embrace.

"I didn't think I'd ever see you again," she said. "I thought you were gone for good."

"You can't keep me away for long," he replied, a mischievous grin on his face.

Aniya's smile slowly disappeared as her heart sank. "Does that mean the light is still in me?"

"I'm still here, and I'm part of it, so I guess so. Isn't that a good thing?"

"It's a good thing that you're here, but honestly, I was relieved that I didn't have that power anymore. To watch myself hurt Nicholas like that . . . I may be mad at him, but I could never do that to him. Not willingly."

"I know," he said, frowning. "I had to watch it all myself. You have to figure out how to control it, Aniya. Surrendering to your emotions like that is dangerous."

"You think I don't know that?" Aniya nearly shouted at her brother. After a moment, she shook her head and sighed. "I'm sorry. This isn't easy, you know."

"It's been a long time since you've yelled at me. I kind of miss it."

"Really?"

"No, not really. I just miss you." He smiled softly for a moment, then looked away, seeming to ponder the issue. "Have you tried controlling your emotions?"

She laughed. "What do you think I've been doing?"

"Blocking them out," William said simply. "That's not the same thing as controlling them."

"Fine." Aniya folded her arms. "But until I figure out how to control them, I have to block them out. It's the only way to keep everyone around me safe."

"Have you considered that moving on will make it easier to control your emotions, and therefore, the light?"

"Moving on?" Aniya narrowed her eyes. "You mean forgiving Nicholas?"

"Is it so hard to imagine?"

She looked down at the sand beneath her feet. "Not anymore. At least I know why he did it now. But I don't know if I'm ready to forgive him."

"I understand." William lay a hand on her arm. "Just make sure you do it before it's too late."

"Too late?" Aniya frowned. "What do you mean?"

"I think you know," he said. "If I'm right, there's a reason he pulls energy from you. He can only—"

"Aaand you're done."

A smooth, sing-song voice filled the beach, chilling Aniya's spine as sand spiraled into the air, drifting for a second before freezing in place.

William was also unnaturally still, his mouth stuck open mid-sentence.

A red glow fell over the beach as the sand burst into flame and the water disappeared. In seconds, the fire was extinguished, leaving nothing behind but a floor of glass that remained suspended in the black. The glass softened and shifted around Aniya and William, curving around them and joining above their heads, imprisoning them in a sphere that dangled in the void.

Heat fell on Aniya's back, and she slowly turned to face the Chancellor.

"I must thank you, Annelise. It was quite nice to get out and stretch my legs again, not to mention fun." The Chancellor's eyes flashed red as the surrounding void turned from black to crimson.

"You're not welcome here." Aniya turned back around and let herself fall into a deep focus, refusing to let him take over. She would never make that mistake again, not after what happened with Nicholas.

After a long moment of silence, she opened her eyes again to see the Chancellor an inch away from his face.

"Boo."

Aniya fell backward onto the sphere as the Chancellor laughed.

"Get out," she said. "This is my mind, and I decide whether you stay or leave. I say leave. Now."

The Chancellor's laugh only grew louder.

This couldn't be happening. She had mastered the art of drowning his voice out, pushing him back to a far corner of her mind.

"Go!"

"You don't have that authority anymore, Annelise. You surrendered yourself to me when you let me take over back in the arena. I've seen every inch of your mind. I know your tricks. I'm here to stay."

Aniya turned to William and shook his shoulders.

"He can't help you, dear. I've made sure of that."

"What do you want?" Aniya spun back around and clenched her fists.

The Chancellor opened his arms. "I want to be with you, Annelise. I don't like being ignored."

"What does that even mean? You're a part of me,

my emotions, right? How are you doing this?" Aniya shook her head. "*Why* are you doing this?"

"If you bottle up your feelings long enough, they will fight back. You should know this by now. And are you even sure that I am just a part of you? I don't think you really believe it."

"It doesn't matter," she said. "You're in my mind, nothing else. I don't care what you are. I just want you gone."

He shrugged. "Fine."

Instantly, his form changed to that of the Operative.

Aniya closed her eyes, but somehow she just sank to a deeper level of her mind, and she was instantly trapped in the same glass sphere, staring at the same man in black that had killed her parents.

"Stop it," she said. "I don't want to see you either."

She blinked, and the Operative was gone, replaced by Kendall.

"How's this?" Kendall asked, smirking.

Aniya spun around, only to face the same mocking phantom.

"Go away," she growled.

Kendall spun in a circle, and by the time he faced her again, he had changed to Zeta, the playful assassin that Nicholas had killed.

Aniya swiped a hand at Zeta, her temper rising as her hand phased through the girl's face.

"Go away!"

"That's not very nice, Aniya."

Mock pity dripped from the girl's voice, but that wasn't what Aniya noticed first. Something changed. Her voice had a different quality to it. It seemed to come from two places at once, both from the girl before her and from somewhere in the distance.

Aniya frowned and stepped forward, but Zeta vanished

into the void. The glass sphere melted and sank into the black, and she was alone with William once again.

She turned to her brother and opened her mouth, but lost her voice as he slowly vanished.

Zeta's voice returned from somewhere beyond the void.

"Wakey, wakey, Aniya."

Aniya spun around. The voice came from all around her, echoing in the black and pricking the hairs on the back of her neck.

Suddenly, her throat constricted as a cold hand wrapped around her neck.

"I said, wake up."

Aniya's eyes shot open to the waking world. She was back in the hospital room.

Five men in black armor stood in front of the door, all of them watching her. At their feet was Caspian's unconscious body.

And on the other side of her bed was a girl in a black bodysuit.

Zeta grinned and lifted her hand from Aniya's throat.

"Hello again, Aniya."

51

Aniya couldn't move.

She had the strength, but she was now paralyzed in fear, staring up at the assassin that was peering down at her horrified face and grinning widely. Behind Zeta, five armored men stood stiffly by the door, their arms at their side. Their body armor, like the assassin's outfit, was sleek black, no silver to be seen.

Her eyes dropped to Caspian, who was lying motionless on the floor. She found herself feeling sorry for the Lightbringer general.

"What, no hello?" Zeta curled her lip and frowned. "I'm hurt, Aniya."

Aniya finally mustered the strength to speak, though her words came out shakily. "You can't be here. You're not real. You're dead."

"If I'm dead and you're seeing me, then you have bigger problems." The assassin grinned. "But since I'm not, then you have nothing to worry about." She paused and thought for a moment. "Well, I wouldn't say *nothing*."

"How did you find me?"

Zeta turned and tinkered with the monitor next to Aniya's

bed. "You caused quite the ruckus and got the attention of someone who very much wants to speak with you."

"I'm not going anywhere. Even if I wanted to, I can't. I'm hooked up to life support for a reason."

"You and I both know that you're more than capable of healing as fast as your body needs. I don't have time to wait, and I don't feel like carrying you, so let's speed things up a little, shall we?"

With a flick of her finger, Zeta turned the computer off.

As a whining sound came from the machine, the electric buzz dissipated, giving way to a crushing pain that quickly took over Aniya's body and sent her into convulsions as she lashed out with her limbs in agony.

Zeta stepped back and rolled her eyes. "Oh, get over it."

But as the pain intensified, it was all Aniya could do not to unleash a tortured scream.

A hand struck her across the face, and Aniya's body went still as her limbs grew warm. A new buzz spread through her body, this one coming from somewhere within. The pain slowly receded as she felt her body come to life. She looked down and was relieved to see a green glow slowly spread over her skin.

It was back.

But with her relief came horror, knowing that she was once again a danger to anyone around her. Of course, the closest person to her right now could use some incinerating, so maybe it wouldn't be the end of the world.

"There you go." Zeta smiled again. "You just needed a little encouragement."

Aniya growled as the warmth reached her face, choosing to ignore the dreaded feeling spreading through her and embracing the energy the light gave her. "Hit me again. See what happens."

"I'm not that stupid. Now, get up."

"Make me."

The smile disappeared from Zeta's face as she leaned in and brought her nose to level with Aniya's. "I said I don't want to carry you, but I will kill you and drag your cold body out of here if I have to." She stood up straight again and ran her hands down her bodysuit, smoothing out a few wrinkles. "You've wasted enough of our time already. Don't make this any more difficult than it needs to be."

Aniya closed her eyes and embraced the rage she felt toward this cruel girl as she dove into the void. She hated her, more than enough to kill her with her bare hands.

A red pillar of light raced toward her from the distance, and as it neared, she saw the Chancellor's grinning face as he opened his arms wide.

But the surrounding void vanished as a cold, metal needle pressed against her neck.

"Come back, Aniya," the assassin's sing-song voice came again. "Don't make me kill you."

Aniya opened her eyes to see Zeta holding a syringe to her throat. Slowly, the rage diminished as the light was quelled.

"Last chance, sweetie. Your choice."

She sighed and opened her mouth to respond but was interrupted by the door opening.

"All right. I got the key card and—"

Aniya and Zeta looked to the door, where Nicholas stood, frozen in place and staring at the intruders clothed in black.

After a full second, the men surrounding the door grabbed Nicholas, who thrashed wildly yet unsuccessfully against his captors.

Zeta stepped away from the bed and approached him, her grin returning. "So good of you to join us. You saved us the trouble of tracking you down."

"How—"

"Let's get straight to the point then, shall we?" Zeta said as she pressed a finger to Nicholas's lips. "We entrusted a job to you, Nicholas, and you failed us. I have to clean up your mess now. So I trust that you'll step aside so I can do your job for you."

Nicholas shook his head. "I can't let you do that."

"There are a lot of things you can't do, Nicky, but I'd say the one you can do least successfully is stopping me." Zeta spun the syringe around her fingers.

"Watch me." Nicholas clenched his fists and crossed his arms, grabbing at his captors' wrists and closing his eyes.

Within seconds, the two men that held Nicholas staggered slightly, their eyes rolling back in their heads.

But as soon as they showed signs of disorientation, Zeta took one step forward and delivered a high kick to Nicholas's face, sending him stumbling backward as he released his captors.

"Let go of him," she said.

The men in black released Nicholas, who fell to the ground, grabbing at his jaw.

Zeta knelt in front of him. "So you were affected by the machine too. The Director suspected as much. Thank you for your ill-conceived demonstration. I'm sure we'll be interested in your abilities at a later date."

She stood back up and approached Aniya again. "But for now, all I need is your girlfriend."

"Don't touch her!" Nicholas jumped to his feet but was immediately knocked back to the ground by one of the men.

"Stop!" Aniya cried as blood spilled from Nicholas's mouth onto the white floor.

Zeta shrugged. "That's up to him. If I walk out of here with you, he can stay here, alive and well. We won't kill him. You have my word."

"You expect me to believe you? You'll kill him just like you'll kill me."

"I would never dream of permanently harming you. You hold a very special place in the Director's heart. And even though your boyfriend technically killed me a few months ago, and that doesn't exactly fill me with the warm fuzzies, I don't have the authority to kill him now that I know he has power of his own. The Director may want to use him. Of course, if he attacks us again, I suppose my boss can't blame me for defending myself and exterminating him."

Nicholas slowly climbed to his feet, but he made no move to attack the men that surrounded him.

"So, for what I hope is the last time, what is your decision, Aniya? Come with me and spare his life, or resist, watch him die, and then come with me anyway?"

Out of the corner of Aniya's eye, she saw Nicholas clench his fists again and dig his feet into the floor.

Zeta saw this as well and turned to Nicholas. "Very well. Just know that you chose this."

"Wait." Aniya pulled herself out of bed, grunting in exertion. She stepped on the cold floor and carefully balanced herself, keeping one hand on the guard rail. "I'll go with you."

"Good," Zeta said, turning back to Aniya with a smile. "You made the right choice."

"No, Aniya," Nicholas said. "You were right. You don't know what the Director wants with you. I only wanted to take you to him when I thought you would die if you didn't go. If you don't need his help, it's not safe for you to go to him."

"It's not me I'm worried about, Nicholas." Aniya gave a sad smile.

Zeta approached Nicholas and held out her hand. "I'll be needing that key card, by the way. Can't have you wandering around the Underworld with that."

With a sigh, Nicholas reached into his pocket and produced the key card, slapping it down on Zeta's open palm.

"Let's go." Zeta placed the card under the neckline of her bodysuit and gently prodded Aniya forward. When they stepped into the hallway, Zeta turned back to the armored men. "Take care of him. Just don't let him touch you."

Aniya spun around as Zeta closed the door. "You said you wouldn't hurt him."

"I said I wouldn't kill him," the assassin said, grinning. "But we need to keep him under close supervision in case the Director wants him. My men are going to place him in captivity here, and how much he gets hurt depends on how much he resists. Now, move."

Zeta pushed her again, harder this time.

Aniya looked back at the room as she walked down the hallway. Nicholas had power too. Even against five men, maybe he stood a chance. Maybe he could overpower them and come for her.

But from behind the closed door, she heard blows land and cries of pain, and as Nicholas let loose an agonizing scream, Aniya bowed her head, leaving her childhood friend behind.

52

Kendall rewound the tape again, turning up the volume on the speakers so that the officer's voice filled the room.

"He's in Holendast."

Kendall grinned as Tamisra pointed a gun at the camera and fired.

It would only be a matter of time now.

Refuge would be at his front door soon, and he had one more chance to make peace with them and ensure the future of the Web.

But this time, it would be different. This time, he would tell them everything. The Director wasn't in any danger, not where he was. If Kendall spilled his secrets to the rebels in a final attempt to secure peace, surely it was better than executing them all. Besides, it would take some time for word to travel back to the Director that Kendall had spilled his guts. Plenty of time for him to finish his mission and retreat to another level.

And if rebels still resisted after Kendall told all, if they still insisted on fighting him, then he would do what he had to do.

After all, better a few thousand rebels die than the entirety of Level XVIII.

It would all soon be over. There would be peace, one way or another.

He picked up his earpiece and pressed the button on the side.

After waiting for few minutes, he tried again.

This wasn't particularly unusual. The Director was a busy man and didn't always immediately answer when Kendall radioed for a report.

But this time was different. It was several more minutes before the Director finally answered, and when he did, his voice took on a new tone.

"Yes, Kendall, what is it?"

Kendall had heard the annoyed speech of the Director before, and this was similar. But there was a new edge to it, one that sounded almost like boredom.

"The rebels will be on their way to me shortly," he said proudly, brushing aside the strange feeling the Director's voice gave him. "It'll be over soon."

"Good," said the Director after a second. His voice usually didn't carry much emotion, but this time it almost felt apathetic.

Kendall frowned. Maybe the Director hadn't understood what this meant. "I'll soon have the boy for you."

"The boy? Oh, yes. Don't hurt yourself trying to get him. He is no longer needed."

"Why not?"

The Director's voice shifted, and now it was the familiar annoyed tone. "It's not any of your concern, Kendall. You always were bad at staying focused on the task at hand."

"I'm sorry, sir." Kendall sighed. "I'll take care of the rebels and report to you when it's done. Are your orders the same?"

"What orders?" The Director growled. "I have given you no reason to think any of your instructions have changed."

"You said to eliminate the rebels if they get in my way. What if I can get them to see reason? Must they still be killed?"

The Director gave a long sigh. "Do whatever you want, Kendall."

And with that, he was gone.

Kendall sat down in utter shock. Never, not once in his entire career with the Lightbringers had the Director ever left any major decision to his subordinates. Never had he spoken with such lack of interest in or care for the matters of the Underworld.

It was confusing, curious. But more than anything, Kendall was truly terrified of what this could possibly mean.

53

Aniya stepped in the elevator and leaned against the railing for support. The train ride had given her time to rest, but the walk from the station to the Citadel had already worn her out.

The light was back, but it was returning gradually, slowly giving her more and more strength, and Aniya had not fully recovered yet.

Zeta followed her inside the elevator, and the doors closed as she pressed a button. "Feel free to sit down if you need to. It's going to be a while before we get there."

With a grateful sigh, Aniya sank to the floor as Zeta pulled two keycards from her bodysuit. She took one of them and slid it into the slot under the buttons before placing both cards back in her suit. The assassin pressed the very top button, and the elevator began to rise.

Zeta sat down across from Aniya and crossed her legs, smiling. "I'm glad you finally decided to join us upstairs. You're really going to like it."

"Really?" Aniya scoffed. "I've been in two webs now, and neither of them were particularly appealing. I can't imagine this one being much better."

"Who said it's a web?" Zeta's smile grew. "You were just in Level I. What do you think is above that?"

"Then what is it?"

Zeta didn't respond.

Several minutes later, the elevator stopped, and Zeta stood.

"Are you ready?"

Aniya shrugged. "I guess."

"That's the spirit," Zeta said, rolling her eyes.

The doors opened, and Aniya climbed to her feet.

They exited the elevator, stepping into a small wooden shack, empty save for a shaft of dust swirling in light that poured in from a solitary window.

Aniya followed Zeta to the door and walked outside, where she froze in place.

They had stepped into the open air of a paradise. A bright, yellow sun beamed down through dense trees overhead, bathing the floor of a beautiful, green forest with a glowing shimmer. Beyond the trees in the distance were hills of lush, green grass, populated with a blanket of blooming, multicolored flowers. A cool breeze drifted over the landscape, bathing Aniya's face in a refreshing wave of clean air, the first air she had ever tasted that didn't carry the metallic tint of air purifiers.

"Welcome to the Overworld."

Aniya turned to Zeta, who smiled widely and stretched her arms wide, embracing the warm glow of the sun. It was a strange sight. The assassin, with three visible knives strapped to her body, spun slowly in an open display of joy and comfort.

"How is this possible? The sun died centuries ago."

Zeta nodded as she dropped her arms to her side. "Oh, it did. And it's still dying, getting worse every day."

"Then what is all this?" Aniya waved her arms at the beautiful landscape.

"A mixture of synthetic material, holograms, and the same skydomes you use in the Underworld. The perfect combination of technology to create a paradise in the middle of a dead world. Thousands of these all over the world have joined together to make a living, breathing world just like it was in the Age of Glory. Isn't it amazing?"

"That's one word for it," Aniya mumbled.

Zeta frowned. "Be grateful you can't see what it actually looks like. It's not nearly as pretty."

"Whatever. Where's your boss?"

"The Director?" Zeta waved a hand. "Follow me."

Aniya turned and let the assassin lead her behind the wooden shack, where a large, metallic sphere waited for them. It was remarkably similar to the sphere underneath the Citadel in Level XVIII, the one that had taken her to her death.

She couldn't help but wonder what this one was taking her to.

"What is this?" Aniya ran her hand over the surface of the sphere. It was smooth and cold, without any tangible grooves or imperfections.

"We call it the Terrasphere," Zeta said as she opened a door on the side, motioning for Aniya to enter.

The interior was an off-white cream, a simple design with only four padded seats and a few dozen unlabeled, multicolored buttons on the wall.

Zeta sat across from Aniya and pressed one of the yellow buttons. The door closed by itself, and the sphere took off, hovering over the ground and gliding at an impressive speed. Zeta pressed a white button, and the surrounding walls turned transparent, allowing Aniya to watch the ground fly beneath their feet.

"How do people live up here?" Aniya frowned. "They told us in Assembly that there was nothing up here but radiation, that we'd die in seconds."

"Tell me, Aniya, do you always believe what the Lightbringers tell you?" She smiled. "I think I know you well enough to know that's not the case."

"But if it's safe to live up here, why do we live in the Underworld?"

Zeta waved her hand. "Better to let the boss explain all that. Just enjoy the journey."

Aniya was quiet for a moment, but her curiosity nagged at her until she relented. "Why is the elevator in a wooden shack out in the middle of nowhere? Doesn't sound very secure."

"If you think about it, it's probably even more secure *because* it's out in the middle of nowhere. No one would think to look for the entrance to the Underworld in a wooden shack in the forest. Besides, why would anyone go looking for something that no one cares about?"

Aniya's head spun. "How can they not care? It's twenty layers of massive underground worlds. Are people not curious?"

"You ask too many questions. Don't worry. The Director will answer all of them and more. Just be patient."

"If you know me at all, you know that's asking too much."

Nevertheless, Aniya leaned back in her seat and stared out the window.

Suddenly, the landscape rippled and changed. The view through the transparent walls changed from a dynamic, three-dimensional view to what looked more like a flat projection. Of course, the beautiful display was still detailed enough that if Aniya hadn't been watching when the view changed, she may not have ever noticed.

Zeta seemed to notice Aniya's confusion. "We're in a tunnel."

Aniya shook her head in wonder.

The Terrasphere took them out of the forest and abruptly into a desert landscape, sand dunes replacing hills of grass as the sun seemed to double in size.

Several minutes later, the display expanded again, and their surroundings shifted into a much more realistic atmosphere, a brilliant display that could have fooled Aniya all over again.

The sphere slowed to a stop next to a two-level, white building, and the doors opened, allowing an arid heat inside the floating transport.

"We're here!" Zeta hopped up and stepped outside.

Aniya frowned but followed. "This is where your Director lives? No massive tower?"

"He doesn't share the egos of the presidents that govern the Underworld. A simple laboratory is more than enough for him to conduct his work. Besides, there's a few more levels underground."

The Terrasphere doors closed behind Aniya as she stepped out on to a sandstone walkway. It was a short walk to the entrance of the building, and Zeta ushered her inside.

Aniya followed Zeta through the white hallways. It may not have been a monolithic tower, but the plain, white design of the laboratory reminded her of the citadels at the heart of the webs. At least the layout of this building wasn't as confusing. Every door had a label that clearly stated what was inside. Aniya noted rooms such as R&D, Testing, and so on.

This building also seemed to be more active. It didn't seem to be terribly busy, but people walked the halls casually, most of them dressed in white lab coats and staring down at papers. Every once in a while, someone would look up at Aniya, and they would always smile and nod at her knowingly.

Finally, Zeta led her to a door marked "Director" and knocked.

After a moment, a large man in a black suit opened the door. He looked at Aniya and scowled. "Hello, Annelise. We've been waiting for you."

Aniya glared at him, placing her hands on her hips. "Forgive me if I wasn't itching to get here just as fast as I could. I was too busy trying to protect my friends from you."

The man stepped toward her menacingly, and Aniya instinctively took a step back.

"You're lucky we let you live as long as we did." He glared back and curled his right hand into a massive fist.

"Is that any way to treat our guest, Bruno?"

Aniya froze as another, calmer voice came from farther in the room behind the giant.

"Please let her in. Our meeting is a long time coming now."

The beast of a man scowled at her, a quiet growl escaping his throat. Finally, he stepped aside.

"Thank you, Bruno," the voice came again. "You are dismissed."

Before Aniya could enter, the brute pushed past her and stormed off down the hallway.

"Charming guy," Zeta muttered. She prodded Aniya forward.

Aniya walked in the room and looked around. It was a small room filled with computers and file cabinets, unsurprisingly, but what gave her pause was a grounded train set that ran amongst it all.

There was barely enough room to walk, and Aniya followed a narrow, curving path to a desk at the end of the room, in front of a large window.

A man sat behind the desk, fiddling with a colorful puzzle. He wore a simple black t-shirt and blue denim pants, a much less intricate outfit than Aniya had expected, given the wardrobes of the Underworld's leaders.

He was a rather handsome man, perhaps forty-five. His silver-speckled stubble revealed someone who either didn't care to shave or simply forgot to. But Aniya suspected that it had been intentional, as it gave him a rather striking look.

Then, her analysis of the man stopped immediately as he looked up at her.

Those eyes.

Aniya's heart stopped as his overwhelmingly kind eyes peered into hers, twinkling with a light that took her breath away. Their corners crinkled in a hauntingly familiar way, and Aniya suddenly forgot who she was staring at.

They were unequivocally her father's eyes, eyes that always managed to carry a smile in them. Eyes that Aniya would have given anything to see again.

Aniya's anger and frustration faded instantly as the man gave a simple, soft smile that matched his eyes. And as he stood, offering his hand, Aniya found herself taking it.

"It's so good to finally meet you, Ms. Lyons. My name is Todd Lambert, but around here, I'm known as the Director."

PART V

THE DIRECTOR

54

Aniya shook the man's hand warily. "*You're* the Director?"

"In the flesh," he said as his smile grew. "Why, what were you expecting?"

Aniya realized she had no idea what she'd expected. A dramatically evil man with a curly mustache? A mad scientist?

"I don't know. Just not . . . you."

His smile remained, and he released her hand. "I must say, you're in a better mood than I expected. I thought you might hate me. You have every right to do so, at least from your perspective. After all, I more or less had to have you kidnapped just to see you in person."

Aniya's guard slowly began to raise again as her voice hardened. "That's exactly what you did."

Zeta rolled her eyes and pointed toward the door. "Can I go? I've been listening to her whine all day."

"Of course, Z." The Director gave a small wave. "Thank you for all your hard work. I appreciate your bringing her here before the flares."

Without another word, Zeta turned and left.

"I'm sure you have questions," the Director said before

Aniya could speak. "It's only fair that I answer them, so go ahead."

Aniya paused. She had more questions than would be possible to ask, but one burning inquiry was at the forefront of her mind.

"Why me? Why have you gone to such great lengths to bring me here?"

The Director nodded slowly as if this question was exactly what he had expected. "That's a long story."

"You're not going to tell me?"

"Of course I'm going to tell you. I was just warning you that it's a very long answer." He stepped back around his desk and motioned to an office chair across from him that was buried under stacks of papers. "Have a seat. You can toss the junk on the floor."

Aniya carefully placed the indicated papers on the Director's desk, but he grinned and tossed the stack to the ground.

"Those probably weren't important anyway. Now, where to begin?" The Director leaned over the desk as he tapped his chin and stared up at the ceiling. "Ah, the beginning."

Aniya resisted the urge to roll her eyes.

"The Underworld was originally home to what was left of the human race. It was our refuge against the nuclear fallout and the dying sun that ruined the Earth's surface. I suppose that's as much as you know. Anyway, our ancestors predicted the war that ended the Earth and sun, so we were prepared. We survived with the help of fission energy that we redirected from the surface into the world below. After a few centuries, we were brave enough to venture aboveground again, and our technology allowed us to construct sheltered sanctuary cities all over the world. The Underworld was abandoned, and we began to rebuild.

"However, as society grew, so did crime rates. We barely had enough room in the sanctuary cities as it was, and it was an arduous process to expand our territories back then, so we began condemning our criminals to the Underworld, and we sent our own men to act as lawkeepers. Everything was going just fine. But then we began to run out of uranium, a critical key to the production of fission energy. We began researching new ways to produce energy, and within a few years, we discovered the ultimate source of energy, a resource that would not so easily be used up. This, of course, was humanity.

"Of course, we couldn't just share this discovery publicly, so we turned the Underworld into a power generator for the entire world, taking condemned criminals and giving them a productive role in society again. We told everyone that we simply dug deeper and found more uranium. Everyone was happy. Except, of course, for those used for power in the Underworld."

Aniya glared at the Director. "Can't imagine why."

"We did what had to be done," the Director said softly. "Besides, they were criminals. Humanity thrives now above ground and below it, and it is thanks to the sacrifices of the Underworld. Over the centuries, the Underworld simply forgot its origins, and its people now live peacefully underground as if they had never touched the surface. It was challenging at first because older generations told stories of the surface world, and legend was passed down through their descendants. We found a way to work around that, though."

"Let me guess," Aniya said. "You killed them?"

The Director laughed. "I know some of my more . . . enthusiastic followers have given you reason to think otherwise, but we're not monsters. No, we developed a nerve agent, a suppressant that promotes submission, and we filtered it into the air processors in the Underworld. Crime decreased to an all-time low, and the Underworld finally had peace."

Aniya frowned. "Peace that you forced them to have."

"I can see how you might think that, but the suppressant doesn't block or force anything. It merely trains the brain to think in a more submissive way, hindering the more destructive primal urges. It's unfortunate, the lengths we go to in order to make a better world, but the end result, I daresay, is worth it. Wouldn't you agree?"

Her every instinct prompted her to answer with a firm negative, but she found the words stuck in her throat.

The Director continued. "In any case, this system worked wonderfully for a very long time. As the Underworld grew and thrived, our lawkeepers were promoted to presidents, governing entire worlds and responsible for the lives of millions. With a few exceptions, all was well until one of our emissaries decided he wanted more."

"The Chancellor," Aniya said.

"Yes. He decided the job we gave him was too easy. I believe his exact words were that governing people who don't have unfettered control over their mental faculties is not leading, but babysitting. He disabled the nerve agent and chose to lead Level XVIII the hard way. Sure enough, he faced revolution within mere weeks. To make matters worse, the adviser I sent to his level defected."

Aniya nodded. "Salvador."

"Correct again. The Uprising that ensued was a devastating war, and it cost us dearly, even though we won in the end. It was a blessing in disguise, however. That war was the inspiration your chancellor needed to achieve his true purpose. You see, the presidents of the Underworld were given another task, a secret one. An ultimate goal that, if successful, would restore this world to its former glory. We had theorized for centuries that we could engineer the perfect human to provide an endless supply of renewable energy, that we could abandon the Citizen Tax and power the entire world with one human. Of course, no one is meant to carry such an incredible amount of energy, and as much as we tried to retrofit the human body to handle such a capacity, we failed at every turn. We hypothesized that we needed to begin the process as early as possible, preferably during gestation.

I cannot tell you how many times we tried to accomplish this. Each attempt was closer, but the end result was never fully viable. Your chancellor finally figured it out in the heat of the Uprising, so when I sent Kendall to your level, one of his first missions was to prepare you for your future work as the world's savior."

"What are you saying? That you did this to me on purpose?" Aniya's head spun. "And you did it before I was even born?"

The Director smiled. "That's exactly what I'm saying."

"But getting in the machine and destroying the reactor had nothing to do with . . . all this," Aniya said, waving her arms. "I only got in there to end the Lightbringers. I was supposed to die."

"We couldn't just ask you to do all this. What would you have said if I came to you and told you then what I'm telling you now? Would you have even let me get this far?"

"Probably not."

"Exactly. Everything had to look like the natural course of action. I went to great lengths to direct the steps of your level, down to the finest detail." The Director leaned back and folded his arms. "I think I did a pretty good job, all things considered."

"So it was all a lie? Kendall tricked me into the whole thing?"

"Not exactly. Our true purpose is known only to myself and the presidents. Kendall still doesn't know what the endgame is. He simply followed my orders and used you to destroy the machine in Level XVIII. He had no idea that you were going to make it out of the Citadel alive. He had no reason to think so. The process that gave you your power killed you, like anyone would think. It doesn't seem possible to the ordinary human how anyone could come back from that."

"But you said Kendall's first mission was to prepare my body before I was born. He didn't suspect anything?"

"He didn't know what he was doing. He didn't even know who you were. It was a simple series of radiation treatments that only took a few days. Kendall is used to following orders without question, and this was no different."

Aniya took a moment to think. "You have me now. You won. What now?"

"You don't understand. It's not my victory that matters. What happens next can save the entire world. But I'm not going to force you into anything. I never have, and I never will. You have a choice, just like you always have. You can walk out of here freely, or you can sacrifice yourself so that billions more can have their own future."

"I get it," Aniya said, scoffing. "You brought me here to guilt-trip me. If I want to live, I'm selfish. If I buy into your grand plan, I'm a hero. A dead hero, but a hero nonetheless."

The Director leaned forward again. "You're a good person. I brought you here because I believe that you'll do the right thing, just like you did when you stepped in the tank to save the ones you love. And besides, you won't be dead. You won't be in pain, either. It's just like sleeping."

"Tried it yourself, did you?" Aniya narrowed her eyes.

"I'm not going to argue with you. All I can do is present you with your options and let you choose."

"And if I choose to leave?"

"Then we'll continue on just like we always have. The entire Underworld will continue to dedicate hundreds of thousands of people every year to servitude so that the world can survive." He reached over the table and took her hand again. "But know that you have the chance to help millions of people, in the Overworld *and* Underworld."

Aniya pulled away and folded her arms. "It looks like the Overworld is doing just fine to me."

A solemn look fell over the Director's face as the twinkle in his eyes faded. He spun around in his chair and looked out the window.

Aniya followed his gaze. Even this desert biome was a thing of beauty. The sun fell on the sand in a wave of amber sparkles. The dunes of sand peaked like waves of water, suddenly meeting a clear, blue sky.

The Director pressed a button, and it was all gone.

Aniya was now staring at an empty expanse, a void with not a single star in sight. In the middle of it all hung a black sphere, only visible because of red jagged lines that crossed over each other on its surface.

"It may look beautiful up here, but the sun is not completely dead, and therefore is incredibly dangerous." The Director spoke softly, staring at the black sky. "We experience occasional solar flares that pierce through our skydomes and cause incredible damage. We're due for another one soon, as a matter of fact. Our ecosystem barely holds back the radiation that covers the Earth in an ever-present haze. The population is overworked in an effort to sustain the infrastructure that barely keeps us alive. But your sacrifice will be enough to make our progress permanent. If all goes well, the Underworld will be abolished, and its population will be migrated to the Overworld to enjoy the world that we have revived and revitalized for them. You can make that happen."

Aniya paused. The choice was clear. She knew what she had to do, but she couldn't bring herself to say it out loud and accept what she knew was her destiny. Months ago, she had made her peace with dying so that her loved ones would be safe, along with thousands of others. Why was this such a hard decision now?

"I understand if you need time," the Director said. "Feel free to take as long as you need. There are dormitories on the floors below us, and I can have someone set you up comfortably until you reach a decision. If you want to leave, we will safely escort you back to the Underworld, no questions asked."

"And if I agree to be your human battery?"

The Director smiled warmly. "There are some calibrations we need to make, some final tests to run, but we can get you set up and ready to go within a day or so. If you want to return to the Underworld briefly to wish your friends goodbye, we can arrange that, but I strongly discourage it. I doubt they would let you go easily. Better for them to move on and enjoy the new world that your sacrifice provides them."

"You're right about that. If Roland had any idea what you were telling me, he would fight tooth and nail to 'rescue' me from you, no matter what I say. And Nicholas . . ."

As Aniya trailed off, the Director continued.

"This is your decision alone. They cannot choose this for you. And if you choose to do this, they will indeed not understand now, but they will one day honor your sacrifice and forever be indebted to you. You truly are our greatest and only hope, Annelise. You and you alone can be the light of this world."

Aniya's heart stopped again when he said her name in the exact same inflection her father used to say it. It was the first time in years that her full name had been said out loud and she hadn't immediately corrected the speaker. And in the strangest realization, Aniya found that it felt right coming from the Director now.

This was right.

"Again, take all the time you need," he said. "I won't push you to any decision, and if you—"

"I'll do it."

Aniya found the words slipping from her mouth almost unintentionally. Her compliance almost pushed itself out, and she found herself more at peace with her choice than she thought possible.

The Director cocked an eyebrow. "Are you sure?"

Aniya nodded. "I'd be selfish, stupid even, to say anything else."

"As you wish." The Director stood up. "As I said, you will

be well cared for until final arrangements have been made." He bowed his head. "I truly admire your bravery, Annelise. And from the bottom of my heart, I want to thank you for your incredible sacrifice."

Aniya wasn't sure what to say to this.

Thankfully, she didn't have to answer him. The door to the Director's office opened, and the massive manservant stepped inside as if he had been listening at the door.

"Bruno, please escort Annelise to a private room on the ninth level."

The large man grunted.

With one last look at the Director, Aniya turned and left his office, taking a deep breath.

It would finally all be over.

55

Nicholas sat in a dark room, chained to the floor, which was damp and sticky with his blood.

Zeta's men had beaten him senseless. And since he'd had no chance to grab on to any of them and leech their lifeforce, he was now depleted of energy, devoid of strength.

His only source of comfort was the crystal he had retrieved from Aniya's room. It hung around his neck now, tucked under his shirt. As long as it was touching his skin, the gem somehow provided a warmth that trickled into his chest and slowly crept through his body, and with the heat came an energy that was just enough to keep him conscious.

Of course, it meant more to him than the tiny stream of energy it gave off. The crystal was all he had left of Aniya, whom Nicholas was sure now he would never see again. Even if he managed somehow to survive this prison and escape, Aniya was surely in the hands of the Director now, and Nicholas found himself unable to even guess her fate. All he knew was that this was the end of the line for him.

And he deserved it.

He had lied to Aniya, betrayed her, kept so much from her all in the name of changing the world.

But Nicholas didn't want to live in that world without Aniya.

The crystal around his neck buzzed harshly, and he looked down. The glow was brighter now, covering the inside of his jumpsuit in a pulsing light that turned his entire outfit green.

Nicholas pulled the necklace out of his shirt and stared into the gem. The light was bright enough to flood the entire room in an emerald wash, but he found that he was able to look directly into the light without discomfort.

He massaged the surface of the rock with his thumb, imagining Aniya's hand in place of the gem. "I'm sorry, Aniya. I'm so sorry."

The light pulsed suddenly, sending stronger waves of energy buzzing through him.

"If I could do it all over again, I would." A glowing tear trickled down Nicholas's cheek. "I don't want to face this world without you, and I would do anything to be by your side right now."

The gem pulsed again, and Nicholas gasped as fresh air flooded his lungs, despite the fact that he was trapped in an airtight room.

"It wasn't worth it. Beating the Chancellor, destroying the machine, none of it. It will never be worth it without you."

Another pulse, and Nicholas's bruises slowly faded as the pain that covered his body dissipated.

"Wherever you are, I hope you're okay. I hope you find a way to move on and be happy, even if that means forgetting me."

He lay down on the ground, looking up at the ceiling. His injuries were gone, but worse now were the tears that wouldn't stop coming. "I hurt you so much, lied to you, did so many things I never dreamed of. You didn't deserve any of it, and I know you still hate me for it. You deserve better than me, and I hope you find it."

Green light massaged his face, evaporating his tears as they left his eyes.

"I just want you to be happy, Aniya. I just want you to have a life again." He closed his eyes tight, refusing to let the light take away the pain that he so deserved. If she died in the hands of the Director, it would be his fault. He deserved the hell he found himself in now.

But he couldn't stop himself from admitting his truest desire.

"More than anything," he said as his voice cracked, "I just want *you*."

Nicholas rolled over and cried into the blood that covered the ground. As his tears mixed with his blood, he beat the floor with his fists, splashing warm liquid over his face.

"I love you."

The words spilled from his mouth between sobs, and he continued to bash his fists into the ground until the fresh energy provided by the light was spent.

Finally, he collapsed, not caring that his face was now covered with his own blood, sweat, and tears.

He slipped into a deep sleep, repeating those three words over and over.

"I love you."

56

I love you.
"Nicholas!"

Aniya jolted up in bed, breathing in rapid heaves. Her dreams had been plagued with visions of Nicholas, dark omens that tugged at her heart and filled her with dread.

She heard every word as if he were sitting right next to her. The light still boiled inside her, reminding her of his stinging betrayal. But seeing him like this, at his most vulnerable, his heart aching only for her—if in reality he felt the same way as in her dream, maybe their relationship could be restored.

But even if he really did feel this way, it didn't matter. Aniya had accepted her fate, and she knew she would never see him again.

Ironically, this did make things easier. Because of her impending fate, Aniya would never have to deal with the difficult conversations that would come if she spoke with him again.

Besides, Aniya didn't want her dream to be anything close to reality. If her dream was to be believed, Nicholas was bleeding out in a dark dungeon, slowly dying.

No, it was better to believe that he was alive and well, even if it meant their relationship was over for good.

Once her heart calmed, Aniya considered lying back down, but it was too late. The adrenaline had taken full effect, and she was wide awake.

She got out of bed and stretched. A quick glance at the clock by her bedside showed that it was 0442. She wouldn't lose a lot of sleep by waking up now, even though she knew it didn't matter. Today would be the last day of her life as she knew it.

So she got dressed in jeans and a shirt, her first time in normal clothes in ten weeks, and left the room.

The subsurface levels of the building were just as dark as her room and just as silent. She remembered the building being full of doctors and technicians, but apparently their schedules allowed for a full night of sleep.

Aniya made her way to the end of the hall and walked down the staircase. She knew that her fate was waiting on the lowest level, and she wanted to get a good look at what she had agreed to.

She reached the bottom level and entered another long hallway, this one with only a few doors. As she walked, she read the placards on the wall: "Generator Room," "Security," "Communications," and an unmarked door at the end of the hallway shortly before the path forked left and right.

This had to be the room she was looking for, but when she tugged on the handle, the locked door remained firmly closed.

Frowning, Aniya continued down the hallway and turned right at the fork, revealing another long hallway. There was only one door in this hall, at the very end on the left. When she finally reached the door, she examined the placard on the wall next to it.

"Lucifer."

The word was familiar, yet Aniya couldn't place it. It was reminiscent of something ominous, and it was almost enough for her to turn around and go back the way she had come.

But curiosity won out, and she pulled the door open. She stepped inside, and her jaw dropped.

This was the room where she would spend the rest of her life.

A massive machine was standing in the middle of the room, steel arms protruding from its frame and hanging loosely, as if waiting for something to grab onto. Cables as thick as Aniya's legs jutted out from the steel frame in various places, snaking around the machine and racing along the floor into various terminals that were spaced throughout the room. A dozen glass tubes surrounded the machine, each filled with green liquid that bubbled quietly. And at the bottom of the machine was a circular platform, where Aniya knew a tank would rise from the floor, her new home.

She would be floating in the machine's tank for thousands of years to come, floating limply, braindead, energy constantly being sucked from her body and fed into generators to power the world.

Shuddering, Aniya turned and quickly made her way back to the door. If she stayed here much longer, she knew she would probably change her mind, so she stepped into the hallway again and closed the door behind her.

Breathing deep, she forced herself to focus on the tiles beneath her feet as she walked rather than the massive, life-sucking machine that waited in the room behind her. She turned at the fork in the hallway but stopped suddenly as the unmarked door opened before her, the one she had tried to open earlier.

Aniya panicked. The Director had seemed friendly enough the day before, but she didn't know what his reaction would be to finding out she was wandering around the building without an escort.

Quickly ducking back into the hallway leading to the

machine room, she hid behind the corner as a man in black armor exited the door and immediately began walking away from her, toward the stairwell as the door slowly closed behind him.

Aniya breathed a sigh of relief, but stopped as she realized that the door would still be open for another second. If she managed to make it inside before the door closed, she could find out what the Director might be hiding.

She knew she shouldn't care. She was about to spend the rest of her life unconscious. But if the Director would leave the door to such a powerful machine unlocked, what could he possibly bother to lock away?

Her curiosity won out again, and she darted out from behind the corner and ducked inside the door just before it closed.

Aniya found herself in another dark hallway, seemingly no different from the rest of the building. But as she slowly walked, the white walls changed to bars that ran from ceiling to floor. She grabbed at one of the bars and shook gently. It was solid steel, unmoving. An image from her dreams flashed in her head, and she shook away the unnerving feeling crawling over her skin.

She continued on, her way lit only by the light barely emanating from her body, until she came to the end of the hallway. It seemed that she had wasted her time.

The hallway was empty.

Aniya very nearly turned back and left if it were not for a large pane of glass to her left. A quiet humming noise came from the glass, and she reached a hand out to touch it when something moved behind her.

As she turned and peered into the darkness, the natural green light from her body grew to give off enough light that she could see a boy huddled in the cell before her. His body was lying slumped on the ground in a puddle of blood, his clothes torn around his body.

Aniya froze as she realized her dream had come to life before her. Then, her heart beat quickly as she pressed herself against the bars, desperately reaching toward the huddled man.

"Nicholas, are you okay?"

The figure turned to face her, and Aniya saw the weary face of the boy who had betrayed her.

The one whose brother she had killed in a blind display of rage against the Lightbringers.

"Malcolm?"

57

"You think he's really here?"

Roland almost didn't hear Tamisra's voice over the sound of thousands of footsteps. It didn't help that she was in front of him on the mole and throwing her voice down the tunnel ahead.

He shrugged, even though he knew she couldn't see him over her shoulder. Pulling on her waist to bring himself closer, he leaned toward her ear and responded.

"He'd better be. It'd be a huge waste of time if he's not. Besides, we've made everyone else walk for miles, so I'd feel pretty bad if we just had to turn around and go back."

Roland glanced behind him. Just beyond the dozens of mole-mounted cavalry marched five thousand foot soldiers, half of them trained fighters. And bringing up the rear was nearly a thousand mothers and children.

It was quite the risk, bringing everyone with them through the tunnels, but they didn't have a choice. In order to win such a battle, Refuge needed every available fighter, which would have left no one to take care of the defenseless.

Therefore, the entire population of Lyrindal had joined them on their trek to Holendast, where the rebels would finally have the chance to end the Lightbringers' presence in the Web.

And now, after marching on and off for two days, they were finally arriving at the tunnel entrance to Holendast.

Corrin stepped ahead of the group and accessed a hidden panel near the rockslide. Roland remembered Nicholas using the same panel several weeks earlier when they had come for Gareth.

With a press of a button, Corrin motioned the all-clear.

"The quakes are off," he said. "We're safe to proceed."

Gareth proceeded past Roland and dismounted. "Are you sure you don't want to rest before the attack? We've been marching for two hours now."

"We can't risk it," Corrin said, shaking his head. "If Kendall has placed any sensors nearby, he'll know we're here, which means he'd be getting ready right now. We can't give him the chance to prepare."

"You can rest if you want, Gareth," Tamisra said. "But if you do, I'll go in without you. I'm not waiting any longer."

Roland nodded. "Corrin's right. Our only shot of winning is surprising them. It's now or never."

"Then let's do it." Gareth said, taking a deep breath. "Are the explosives ready?"

"Right here." Lieutenant Haskill emerged from the mass of people packed into the tunnel, carrying a large package. It was strange seeing a native of Refuge wear the armor of the Silver Guard, but the mud slathered over the armor gave the metal a brown color, a more suitable look to the people of Refuge.

The entire army, including Roland, wore the same armor, stolen from supply depots and painted over to better reflect their nature and differentiate themselves from Kendall's silver army. The only fighter who didn't wear armor was Corrin, who believed that his traditional, weaker Refuge garb would inspire bravery in his men.

Corrin looked over the bundle. "And the other one?"

"Still on the payload. I'm surprised you agreed to that, Tamisra."

Tamisra bowed her head. "If that's what it takes to win, then that's what it takes. Trust me, I'm not happy about it, but it is an effective strategy."

"Deploy the explosives, Lieutenant," Corrin said. "We're wasting time."

The lieutenant nodded and carried the package to the mouth of the tunnel, which was still blocked by a massive mound of debris.

After a moment, he stepped away from the device, carrying a device in his hands with a button on top. "Let's move back," he said. "The positional firing mechanism should send everything out into the sector, but there's no point in taking an unnecessary risk."

"Agreed," Corrin said. He shouted into the tunnel, "Retreat fifty paces. Those not fighting, retreat a hundred and stay in the tunnels until we come back for you."

A few minutes later, everyone was in place.

Gareth turned to Corrin. "Do you want to say anything?"

Corrin looked back at the thousands behind him. With a solemn smile, he looked back at Gareth. "*Lumen ad mortem.*"

"*Lumen ad mortem,*" Gareth responded with a grin of his own.

Corrin turned to his lieutenant. "Whenever you're ready."

Haskill gave a countdown on his fingers and activated the detonator.

With a deafening boom, the tunnel entrance exploded, shooting most of the debris away from the tunnel and into the sector ahead. Though the blast was pointed well enough to protect them from harm, enough dirt showered over the rebels that even as Roland held up an arm in front of his face, dust still managed to get in his mouth.

Corrin probably ordered the attack, but Roland couldn't

hear anything over the ringing. Instead, he saw Corrin kick his mole and race through the cloud of dirt, and Roland grabbed Tamisra as their mole followed.

The army charged into the trainyard of Holendast, which was still as bright as Roland remembered it. But as soon as the first mole cleared the cloud of dust, the sky ceiling suddenly cut out, leaving the sector completely dark.

A panic raced over Roland as he looked around wildly. They had talked about using an electromagnetic pulse bomb to disable the lights, but Haskill had determined that they didn't have the materials left to construct one. Someone else had turned off the power, and it wasn't the rebels.

"Lights on!" Corrin shouted.

Roland reached up to his helmet and switched on the headlamp, and the sound of a thousand clicks came from behind as light after light turned on.

But as their headlamps switched on, the light only bounced back at them, reflecting off a wall of silver armor. The more lights that turned on, the brighter the reflection got, and Roland winced as he held a hand in front of his eyes.

Finally, one massive light flashed on above the Silvers, bathing the rebels in a light brighter than the skydome.

Roland turned around to see all of Refuge holding their hands in front of their faces to block the light. His heart sank as he peered down the tunnel to see several more lights flashing on beyond the sea of people lying in wait in the caves.

They were surrounded.

"Get the payload ready," Corrin said grimly. "We might have to use it right now."

"And kill all of us?" Tamisra muttered.

Lieutenant Haskill lifted his chin and sneered at the wall of Silvers. "Better to go out on our own terms."

A black form stepped in front of the blinding lights, silhouetting itself against the wash of white light. It came closer until the light from Roland's headlamp lit his face clearly.

Tamisra shrieked in fury and tried to dismount the mole, but Roland held on tight, forcing her to sit still.

Kendall sighed and folded his arms across his chest. "We need to talk."

58

Aniya stared at Malcolm as an awful feeling stirred in her stomach. She found herself at a complete loss for words as he stared back at her, his face twisted in an expression she couldn't quite read.

"Aniya? What are you doing here?"

"I was going to ask you the same thing." She looked back down the hallway, making sure they were alone. "Their operative brought me here. She's still alive."

Malcolm nodded and looked at the ground. "I know. Kendall had me bring her up here, and the Director revived her."

"What are you still doing here?"

"Zeta wouldn't let me leave," he said. "I've been in this cell for weeks now. But even if I could get out, there's nowhere for me to go. Refuge banished me and Kendall."

Aniya's eyes widened. "They banished you both? I guess that was Roland's idea?"

"He definitely had a hand in it."

"But wait," Aniya said, confused. "You helped Zeta, then she locked you up? That doesn't make any sense."

"She said she had no more use for me for now. She

thanked me for my help, then put me in here. I guess until she needs me again."

"For what? Are you sure the Director knows you're in here? It really seems like he's trying to fix the world. He wants me to help him supply power so we don't need the machines underground anymore."

"He doesn't want to help anyone, Aniya. Zeta put me in here without hesitation."

"Zeta did," Aniya clarified. "Not the Director?"

Malcolm's eyes narrowed. "She works for him, Aniya. You really think he doesn't know about this? Whatever he wants with you, it's not for anything good. He has to know how much power you have. He has to know how . . . dangerous you are."

His voice grew quieter as he said this, and Aniya bowed her head.

"I'm sorry about Xander. It was an accident. I didn't—"

"Later," Malcolm said shortly. "We need to get out of here."

"But they need me. I can help everyone if I stay here."

"Do you really think the Director is telling you the truth?"

Aniya shrugged. "He told the truth about everything else. I don't think he has any reason to lie."

Malcolm sighed and let his forehead fall against the bars. "So you're going to leave me here?"

But Aniya couldn't do that. Every time she looked at him, she was reminded of Xander. She may never see Corrin again, but could she really do that to him, kill one son and abandon the other?

"I didn't say that," she said. "I've pretty much agreed to die for him, so he'll have to forgive me for this. And if he doesn't, I doubt it'll change anything."

Malcolm gave a small smile, a strange look for the brash young man. "Thank you, Aniya."

"How do I get this thing open?" Aniya looked for a lock but found nothing.

"The computer," Malcolm said, nodding to the other side of the hallway.

Aniya approached the thin pane of glass behind her and touched it. The display came to life, showing a blue background with unfamiliar white characters scrolling down the screen.

"How do I work it?" She scanned the display, shaking her head.

"I don't know. Just press buttons."

It didn't seem like a good idea, but Aniya didn't have a better one. She touched random parts of the glass until the display changed to an array of video feeds. It looked like various rooms of the building, but Aniya didn't see the cells anywhere on the screen. She swiped her finger across the glass a few times until several green-tinted feeds appeared before her, and in the corner was a display that showed Malcolm standing by the bars of his cell and Aniya's right arm in the very edge.

She touched the feed, which expanded to fill the display. Several more buttons appeared by the side, all of which populated with more indecipherable characters. She touched each one until the bars of Malcolm's cell slowly descended into the floor, and Aniya turned around and smiled triumphantly.

"Sorry it took so long."

"That's okay," he said, stepping out of the cell. "I've been sitting here for weeks now, so a few extra minutes wasn't too bad."

His smile grew slightly, but it vanished as a loud siren rang out, nearly deafening them both.

Red lights flashed rapidly as Aniya clutched her ears in pain. She barely heard Malcolm shout over the sirens.

"Looks like they're coming for us. How do I get out of here?"

Aniya waved for him to follow and ran back down the long hallway. The door at the end wasn't locked from this side, and they stepped into the now-lit hallway, the white walls washed red from the strobing lights.

She guided Malcolm down the hallway and into the stairwell, and they ran up the steps, taking them two at a time, but they froze as the sound of several footsteps came from above them.

They turned to run back down the stairs, but it was too late.

Dozens of men and women in lab coats turned the corner and ran past them down the stairs. In seconds, they had all passed, and Aniya and Malcolm were left in the stairwell, alone again, staring at each other in confusion.

Aniya shrugged, and without a word, she turned and continued back up the stairs, Malcolm right behind her.

Soon, they were on the ground floor again, and they stepped out into the hallway and ran directly into Zeta.

The assassin stumbled backward, and her eyes opened wide, darting between Aniya and Malcolm. She opened her mouth to speak but was cut short by Aniya's fist slamming into her chest, sending her flying backward into the wall with a flash of green light.

"Come on," Aniya said, grabbing Malcolm's hand and running to the entrance.

The front door of the laboratory burst open as Aniya and Malcolm fled the building. They took exactly one step outside before being immediately knocked to the ground by fierce winds. The sound of the sirens vanished, drowned out by the raging gale.

Sand swirled in the air in a massive cloud, blinding Aniya and reducing her visibility to just a couple feet.

Malcolm shouted something, but most of his words were lost to the wind. All Aniya caught was "flare."

Aniya held a hand up in front of her face as she struggled

to stand to her feet. The swirling sand that surrounded her turned green as the light from her body grew stronger, and slowly, the sand was pushed away from her. Her light pushed out in a sphere around her and Malcolm, creating a bubble of green light that encompassed them. The noise of the wind quickly became muffled, and the sand beneath their feet settled.

"Whoa," Malcolm said, standing up and looking around.

Aniya took a cautious step forward, and the bubble moved with her, expanding slightly to keep Malcolm within the spherical shield.

"Are you doing this?"

"Kind of," she said, knowing that this convenient relief from the winds was unintentional. "Follow me."

She led him a few yards to the Terrasphere that Zeta had used to bring her to the laboratory. As they stepped inside, the green light receded back into Aniya's body as the winds began to beat against the transport. The sphere stood firm, however, and didn't budge against the strong gale.

"I can make it from here," Malcolm said. "You don't have to come with me."

"I wasn't planning on it, but I can't be sure you'll be safe unless I stick with you for a bit. They'll wait for me, I'm sure." She pressed the white button that Zeta had used, and the walls turned transparent, revealing the raging sandstorm. "It looks like they have bigger problems anyway," she said as she pressed the button again, turning the walls back opaque.

Malcolm pressed one of the green buttons, and the Terrasphere took off.

"How did you know which button to press?" Aniya looked back at Malcolm, who sat back in his seat.

"Kendall gave me a quick rundown on how to operate this thing. I had to come back up here with a dead girl, so I had to know how to get around." Malcolm pointed at the yellow button Zeta had pressed to take her to the Director. "This one will take you back to the lab when you're ready, if you still want to go back there."

"Thanks," Aniya said. She leaned back and watched the storm outside.

They rode in silence for a few minutes before Malcolm finally spoke.

"I'm sorry," he said slowly.

Aniya turned to face him, taking a deep breath. "For what?"

"Don't make me say it." He looked away.

Aniya nodded. "I get it. You thought I was dangerous. I could have killed someone else if I stuck around there for much longer."

Malcolm shook his head. "As bad as it sounds, I didn't care that you could hurt anyone else. I was just angry because it was too late and you already hurt someone. I just wanted my brother back, and every time I looked at you, I got angrier." He glanced at her before immediately looking away. His voice quivered and lowered. "I still do."

"I'm sorry, Malcolm." Aniya placed a hand on his arm, but he pulled away. "I never meant to hurt him, believe me. Please, forgive me."

After a long moment, Malcolm looked back at her. His eyes were narrow, his lips taut. His face shook, a barely perceptible detail, noticeable only because the single tear running down his cheek took a jagged path, vibrating as it slid down his skin and dropped to the floor.

Suddenly, the Terrasphere shook violently, knocking Aniya to the floor. A loud crashing noise came from outside as the transport rocked back and forth.

"What was that?" Malcolm braced himself by clutching his seat, ignoring Aniya's prone body.

Aniya stood back up carefully and punched the white button. The walls disappeared, revealing that they were back in the forest. The winds shook the trees hard, and leaves flew through the air in a cyclone. A red light shone from somewhere, covering the landscape in a crimson hue.

The horrible crashing noise came again, this time much louder, and as the sphere trembled, Aniya stumbled forward and grabbed the invisible walls of the transport before she could fall again.

But with another crash, the sphere broke free from its path and crashed to the ground, tumbling carelessly across the forest floor.

Aniya and Malcolm rolled with the sphere as the transparent walls flickered, and their bodies crashed into each other, then the walls, over and over again until the sphere collided with something, sending their bodies into the wall one final time and knocking Aniya unconscious.

59

The convulsing ground was what stirred Aniya into consciousness again, shaking her awake to the decaying world.

She sat up and was immediately slapped in the face by a gust of wind, accompanied by leaves flying through the air and whipping across her skin, cutting her in several places.

Grabbing her face in pain, Aniya let herself fall back to the ground, behind the safety of a large hunk of metal. She pressed her back up against the debris and looked around.

A scarlet light had painted the forest red, an ominous yet fitting sight considering the horrible earthquakes that still shook the Earth.

The Terrasphere had broken apart, and smoldering pieces of the metal transport were scattered throughout the forest.

Malcolm was next to her, still unconscious.

Aniya looked up and saw the source of the red color. The sky ceiling was blood red, pulsing gently as if giving off some sort of alarm.

A moan came from Aniya's side, and she turned to see Malcolm slowly turning over to face her.

"Are you okay?"

Malcolm ignored the question and sat up slowly. "Where are we?"

"Close to the elevator shack, I think. But it won't matter if we don't find shelter soon." Aniya touched her face and looked down at the blood on her fingers. "The quakes are getting worse. I don't think we want to be out here for much longer."

"Zeta mentioned solar flares," Malcolm said, looking around. "This has to be one of them."

Aniya shrugged. "Guess so. We should be fine as long as we get underground before it gets any worse."

Suddenly, the wind ceased. Leaves that flew through air stopped abruptly and drifted gently to the ground.

The world was deathly quiet.

Malcolm slowly stood up, looking around. "Is it over?"

"I don't know. I don't want to stick around to find out, though."

"Do you remember the way back to the shack?"

"Not really, but the transport was heading this way." Aniya pointed past the tree. "That's our best bet."

"Let's go, then."

They took off, jogging through the forest. The crunch of the leaves beneath their feet was the only sound that echoed against the trees.

Aniya noticed Malcolm sweating profusely and grinned. "Out of shape?"

"No," he said, growling. "It's just really warm. Aren't you hot?"

Aniya shrugged. "Not really."

Malcolm swiped his arm across his dripping forehead. "It's getting pretty bad. I don't think it's over, Aniya."

"Then you'd better run faster." Aniya sped up, hoping that it would encourage Malcolm to pick up the pace. As she looked forward again, she spotted the shack that housed the elevator, and her hopes soared. "We're almost there!"

But she tumbled to the ground again as a deafening roar blasted throughout the forest, shaking the ground violently. She looked up at Malcolm, who had stopped abruptly and was waving his arms around wildly as he nearly lost his balance.

A loud cracking sound ripped through the forest, and the ground opened up beneath Aniya. She fell backward into the gap but managed to grab onto a small rock that jutted out from the ground. It was just big enough for her right hand, and she dangled in the air wildly as she reached for another handhold. But every time she grabbed at a rock with her left hand, it would break free from the wall and fall to the depths below.

Motion caught her eye, and she looked up to see Malcolm jump over her body to the other side of the gap.

"Malcolm!" she shouted above the quakes.

His face appeared above her, and Aniya reached for him.

"Help me up!"

He stared at her for a moment, as if considering his options.

Finally, he reached down to grab her hand, but the ground beneath his body collapsed and crashed over Aniya, who held an arm above her head as rock and dirt rained down on her.

When the debris stopped falling, she looked back up to see Malcolm again. He had managed to back away to solid ground just in time, and though he was now farther away, he was still within reach.

"Malcolm!"

Aniya's cry was drowned out by the rumbling, which grew louder as the gap grew wider. She looked over her shoulder, and her eyes grew wide as the bottom of the pit was no longer visible.

Panicking, she reached within for the light, desperately searching for the power to pull herself out of the gap, but nothing came. She could feel it, somewhere within, but she couldn't concentrate.

Between the horrible noise, the shaking earth, and Malcolm's face—there was too much to take in, and Aniya found herself incapable of channeling the light, like she had practiced for the last several weeks.

"Are you going to help me?" she shouted up at Malcolm, glaring at him as he stared down at her.

He made no move to reach for her. In fact, he looked over his shoulder toward the elevator shack just a few yards away.

Aniya's heart sank as Malcolm stood up and turned away from her.

"What are you doing?" she begged. "Help me!"

As she cried out, the earth shook again, and the ground beneath Malcolm's feet suddenly gave way. After teetering back and forth on the edge, he fell backward into the pit, somersaulting through the air as he plummeted into the depths.

"No!" Aniya screamed as he fell. He was gone, and with him her last hope of being absolved from her guilt.

She reached again for another handhold to pull herself up, but the shifting rocks provided no stable anchor. She had to save herself, but it was an impossible task without the light.

Breathe, Aniya.

Caspian's words came back to her, even above her pounding heart and racing mind. She took a deep breath, but it came out ragged as she watched a tree topple over and fall directly toward her.

Aniya closed her eyes, knowing it was her last chance. She forced herself to take another breath, and instantly, the noise around her stopped. The shaking sensation ceased.

But there was still the strain in her arm as she held on for dear life.

There was only one thing left to do, and in one instant

of pure desperation, she let go of the rock and let herself fall into the gap.

She was alone in the void again.

"Hello again."

Aniya turned to see the Chancellor. She waved her hand. "Go away. I need to see my brother."

The Chancellor smiled. "No, you don't. Your brother can't help you, and you know it."

"He can help me more than you ever could." Aniya turned around, but the Chancellor was there behind her already.

"You can't control your power, Aniya. You need to accept that and stop trying. Until you can master your emotions and keep them in check, you will always be a slave to them. And because you have no other choice, right now, you need to embrace them. It's the only way you'll make it out of this alive."

Aniya snarled and lashed out at the phantom before her. "Go away!" Her anger only escalated as her fist passed through the Chancellor's body. As she overextended, pain pulsing through her arm, her fist flashed green.

"Very good," he said as his smile grew. "Again."

"Why are you always grinning like an idiot? Even when I'm hallucinating, falling to my death, you always manage to have that ridiculous smile on your face."

He only smiled.

"If you're trying to make me angry, it's working." Aniya clenched her fists.

"Good."

Aniya rolled her eyes and turned again, but the Chancellor, of course, was there waiting for her.

With a cry of rage, she leapt at the phantom, passing through his body. Spinning around, she swiped at him repeatedly.

"Where is my brother?" she screamed as she attacked the

untouchable Chancellor, the light surrounding her body turning a bright yellow color.

The Chancellor grinned broadly. "That should do it." Suddenly, he vanished.

Aniya was alone again.

But even as the void fell apart around her, the Chancellor's voice came drifting across the black. "Remember. Don't trust the Director."

Aniya's eyes flew open.

The tree was still above her, careering toward her rapidly, and Aniya realized that no time had passed.

She held up a hand, and the tree burst into flame, incinerating around her.

The yellow light grew to a large halo that spun around her body, and Aniya's body began ascending slowly. But even as the surface was within reach, she looked down into the pit below.

Malcolm was down there somewhere.

He was probably dead by now, but Aniya couldn't help but think about Corrin, now childless, without so much as a body to remember his sons by. And what if Malcolm was somehow alive? If she abandoned him to his death now, Aniya knew she would never forgive herself.

But as much as she knew what she had to do, her body continued to ascend against her will. Aniya knew it was egged on by her anger at Malcolm for betraying her. And now that he had just refused to help her up and nearly got her killed, her anger evolved into hate.

He didn't deserve to be helped. He made his choice, and now he had to pay the price.

Aniya's heart quickened as her blood boiled. Malcolm had been willing to let her die. She shouldn't feel guilty about letting him suffer his well-deserved consequences.

But as she closed her eyes to block out her doubts, Xander's burning body appeared before her, and he stared at her with eyes of fire. As flames consumed his body, he reached out to her, speaking unintelligible words in a voice that filled her with dread.

"I know," Aniya managed to say as she choked on a sob. "It's my fault. I did this to you. I'm sorry. I'm so—"

Another sob came, and this time it was too much. Tears spilled forth as she lost the air to speak. She bowed her head, crying softly into her hands.

When she finally looked back up, Xander was still reaching toward her with hands licked with flame, and this time, Aniya reached back. The instant she touched his melting flesh, the flames vanished.

Xander still stood before her, but his body was now restored. Now, Aniya could see his eyes, untouched by fire. They weren't filled with rage, as she had always assumed. He didn't look angry at all. In fact, he was staring at her with an expression more like pity.

"I know you didn't mean for this to happen," he said softly. "You're a good person."

This broke Aniya, and she fell to her knees, sobbing uncontrollably.

"I forgive you, Aniya."

The words fell on her ears, accompanied by a wave of warmth.

After all this time, begging for forgiveness, someone had finally given it to her.

But it wasn't enough.

She still felt terrible, like she was crushed under a heavy weight that his words should have lifted.

"Will you forgive yourself?"

Aniya looked back up slowly as something inside began to give. It was like a vice on her heart was being loosened, slowly starting to relieve her of an awful pressure that had tortured her for months.

"Will you forgive Malcolm?"

It seemed so easy now. She knew in her mind that Malcolm had done something truly horrible, and she had every right to hate him. But all of a sudden, she didn't want to anymore.

Instantly, the pressure vanished. Her heart could beat freely again. Whatever was tearing her apart inside was now gone.

Aniya suddenly realized Xander was also gone, and she opened her eyes to see the light around her flicker wildly as her mind battled against her emotion. Her ascent slowed to a halt, and the light vanished.

Then, she began to fall again.

This time with a purpose.

Aniya spun in the air to face downward, and her descent quickened as she straightened her body. As she fell, still seeing no end to the pit, she realized the very real possibility that Malcolm could still be alive. Her determination to save him grew stronger, and somewhere inside, it translated into some emotion that fueled her passion yet again.

The light exploded around her in a brilliant yellow halo and pushed her down into the pit at an incredible pace.

Finally, she saw Malcolm's body in the distance, still falling. Without even thinking about it, Aniya's descent slowed as she grabbed his body.

She watched as yellow light twisted around her body and exploded beneath her feet, sending her flying upward just as quickly as she had fallen. Rock and dirt fell over their bodies, but the debris was incinerated by a shield of light that formed over Aniya's head.

As she was propelled back to the surface, Aniya looked down at Malcolm's body. He wasn't dead, but he was unconscious, probably from the sheer shock of falling. She smiled, knowing that he would be fine.

They reached the surface again, and their bodies continued to hover for a moment as they moved away from the fault line and to safety several yards away, right next to the elevator shack.

The ground still shook, but Aniya turned her attention to Malcolm as the light continued to surround them, shielding them from falling trees and boulders that tumbled toward the opening in the ground.

She lay a hand on Malcolm's head, and tendrils of yellow light wrapped themselves around his body. After a few seconds, he opened his eyes and looked up at her.

"Are you okay?" Aniya asked, removing her hand.

Malcolm only nodded, his mouth hanging open. His eyes grew wide, and Aniya realized he wasn't looking at her anymore.

She turned to see the forest taking on an orange hue as trees began catching fire, quickly turning to a blaze that spread into a massive wildfire, rapidly consuming the forest.

The shaking stopped abruptly, and all was still again.

Then, with a deafening crash, the skydome above them burst open, large pieces of metal and machinery falling freely, and Aniya saw the real sky for the second time.

And this time was so much worse.

Before, the sky had been black, void of seemingly any celestial bodies.

This time, the sky was on fire, the earth's atmosphere bathed in red flame. Red lightning split the air, bursting through black clouds that spun in spirals. A bleeding, black sphere in the middle of the sky flashed wildly, orange bursts of light arcing from it. And with every flash of light, Aniya felt an incredible heat fall upon them, washing over the protective bubble as white sparks flew.

The light from Aniya's body turned blood-red, and she felt her muscles tense as the light raged on, seemingly determined to protect them from harm.

After several more seconds, the sky finally calmed and turned black yet again. The arcs of orange light ceased and receded back into the sun as the dying star now hung above the sky ceiling motionlessly, once again a black sphere with cracks of red visible across its surface.

Aniya and Malcolm sat in the bubble for several minutes, speechless in the aftermath of the horrors they had just witnessed.

Then, the ground shifted around them, revealing several small holes in the earth. White smoke shot up through the holes and quickly filled their surroundings as it expanded rapidly.

A stinging sensation made its way through Aniya's bubble, and she realized that the smoke was far below freezing temperature. Sure enough, as the smoke continued to spread, the fires throughout the forest were quickly extinguished.

With a sigh, Aniya's light retreated back into her body, leaving nothing but thin, red beams of light that trickled across her body with an audible buzz.

Malcolm, his head still in her lap, looked back up at Aniya with wide eyes.

"Thank you," he said. "You didn't have to come back for me."

Aniya gave a soft smile. "Yes, I did."

Malcolm stood up slowly, his legs shaking. Aniya stood with him, offering a hand for support, which he readily took.

"Then there's something I have to do." He looked down at the ground. "Aniya, I—"

But that was all he got out before he fell to the ground, a bullet in his chest.

60

Aniya knelt by Malcolm's side as he winced, grabbing at his chest and gasping for air.

She heard footsteps behind her, but all she could think about was the blood that poured from Malcolm's chest, coursing over her hands as she looked down in horrified helplessness.

"I don't know who's luckier that you survived," a female voice came from behind. "You or me."

Aniya finally turned to see Zeta, standing behind her with a gun pointed at them. A squadron of soldiers in black armor stood behind her, guns ready.

"I'd probably be put out of commission if the solar flare had killed you," she said. "You know, I admire you. You're a survivor. But your friend here? I can't let him live, so please move."

Aniya dared to push the gun away, staring up at the operative in anger. "Why do you care if he dies? You were going to keep him in a cell for the rest of his life."

"Where we could keep an eye on him. He knows too much about the Overworld to be running around freely. So he either comes back with us, or he dies."

"So you shot him before giving him the option?" Aniya stood up and brought herself nose-to-nose with the assassin. "What, are you crazy?"

Zeta shrugged. "He would just be taking up space. I thought I'd do us all a favor."

"I'm not going back with you," Malcolm said, wincing as he sat up. "I'd rather die."

"Cool." Zeta pushed Aniya out of the way and raised her gun again, but Aniya stepped right back in front of her.

"He lives." Aniya folded her arms and stared the girl down. "Your boss wants me so bad? You let him live, and you let him go. Those are my terms."

Zeta stared back at her for several seconds.

"Fine." With that, the assassin stepped around her, and before Aniya could do anything, Zeta snapped her arm up and fired two shots.

Aniya spun around to see Malcolm crumble to the ground, a hole in each thigh.

"What did you do that for?" she shouted, turning back to the operative as she felt an incredible warmth stir within her.

"You only said not to kill him," Zeta said as she put her gun away. "But I can't have him wandering around, causing trouble. You've seen what happens when he's left to his own devices."

Aniya crouched by Malcolm, examining his wounds and speaking to Zeta with her back turned to the assassin. "He'll die if he doesn't get help. Let me take him with us."

"No-can-do," Zeta said, clucking her tongue. "You heard the man. He'd rather die. He made his choice, so now he gets to stay out here and die on his own time. Now, let's go."

"Go," Malcolm hissed through clenched teeth. "I won't go back there. Let me die alone. I deserve it."

Aniya shook her head. "No, Malcolm. I won't let you die." She grabbed his hand, and instantly, red tendrils shot forth from her hand and thrust themselves toward his.

Malcolm gasped as a red spark formed in his eyes. He looked up at her as glowing tears slid down his cheeks. "I know you didn't mean to hurt Xander. So I forgive you, Aniya. It's what he would have wanted."

With a tearful gasp, Aniya clutched his hand harder as she smiled, and the light around their joined hands grew brighter, spreading over Malcolm and encompassing his body in a crimson web of light.

It seemed that Zeta finally noticed this, because she grabbed Aniya's hair and pulled it backward, jabbing something sharp into her neck.

Black quickly spread across Aniya's vision, and she stumbled backward, Malcolm's hand slipping away. Grabbing at her neck, she yanked out a syringe. She let it fall on to blood-soaked leaves, knowing this was the end.

The last thing she saw was Malcolm crying out in pain, bleeding out onto the forest floor, the bullet still in his chest.

Dying.

Then, Aniya's heart stopped, and she slipped into nothingness.

61

A jolt of electricity shot through Aniya's body, and her eyes flew open.

She was lying on a table, staring up at a giant machine.

"I hear you got to witness the destructive nature of this world firsthand."

At the sound of the Director's calm voice, Aniya tried to push herself to a sitting position but found that she was bound to the table with leather straps.

The Director's handsome, solemn face appeared above her.

"So you can see now how much this world needs you. I hope today's incident will not deter you from your wise decision to selflessly give your life for it."

"Incident?" Aniya fumed. "You mean your assassin shooting Malcolm, who helped you? He's out there right now, just lying there, dying."

"Don't worry." The Director waved a hand. "When he dies, his body will be disposed of respectfully. My men are still cleaning up the areas affected by the solar flare, so his body will be buried before the end of the day."

"That's it? Sorry he's dying, we'll dig a hole? I thought you wanted to *help* the world."

"My sole purpose is to serve the greater good, Annelise. It's a concept you must embrace if you want to change the world. It's why you've chosen to give up your future to preserve the earth."

"I'm not so sure about that anymore."

With a sigh, the Director bowed his head. "Thankfully, my objective does not depend on your consent anymore."

Aniya's jaw dropped open. "I thought you weren't going to force me into anything. You were going to let me choose."

"And choose you did, remember?" The Director gave a soft smile. "I gave you a choice, and you chose the path of nobility. But I'm afraid it's too late to change your mind. No take-backs, as they once said. So, thank you for your very brave choice, dear. It is quite admirable indeed."

The Director turned and typed at a console to his side, and a buzzing noise came from the machine as it powered on. Its massive metal arms opened, waiting for something to latch onto.

"The Underworld," the Director continued as he worked, "has had the privilege of being used for the revitalization of Earth, for the continuation of our species. You should be honored, Annelise, that your destiny transcends simple slavery. You are the catalyst of a new world, a glorious era of plenty made possible only by the energy that lives inside you. You should be thanking me."

Aniya was too stunned to say anything, much less thank the man who held her fate in his hands. She dug deep in an attempt to channel the rage she felt inside, but the light refused to come. Despite the incredible power that she held, she was now completely helpless.

The Director waited a moment longer before waving a hand. "You'll thank me later. At least, everyone else will."

"You're insane," Aniya said, her words coming out as little more than a whisper.

"You don't understand how unlikely that is, Annelise. And I don't have time to explain it to you." The Director frowned. "Well, that's not true. I have all the time in the world. It's you who has run out of time."

A doctor appeared at the side of Aniya's table and freed her from the leather straps, but she remained frozen, staring at the giant machine that waited for her. Her fate now was much different from the one she had faced under the Citadel. That had been a mere glass tank with a few wires hanging from it. This metal prison was something much more menacing.

"A little help, Z?"

Aniya felt herself shoved off the table, crashing to the ground. She looked up at Zeta's smirking face and scowled.

"Easy there, Z. She's our honored guest. We should treat her as such," the Director chided Zeta, then turned to the rest of the room as Aniya stood. "Systems check. All stations report."

From across the room, various men and women in white coats spoke up.

"Extractors ready."

"Distributors ready."

"Relays ready."

On and on they went for several seconds. As Zeta pushed her forward toward the platform, Aniya took the time to mentally prepare herself, trying to focus on the good she would be doing rather than the fact that she wouldn't be around to enjoy its results.

When the room finally fell silent, the Director clapped his hands once and smiled widely. "Good! Ready the subject."

A woman approached Aniya and held out her hands. "Please remove your clothing."

Aniya groaned. "Not this again."

But the woman simply stood, her hands still outstretched. "Fine."

Aniya disrobed and stood naked only for a few seconds before another woman handed her a new piece of clothing, a white bodysuit that would cover her from head to toe.

She looked past the woman at the Director, who she was surprised to see had turned away to preserve what little dignity she had left.

"I actually get to wear something this time?" Aniya asked as she put the suit on.

The Director nodded. "Your body will be on display for millennia to come as the venerable power source of our world. We want to make sure you're presentable."

"So kind of you." Aniya let the straps snap taut against her shoulder as a man approached her.

"Arms up, please." The man guided her closer to the machine, placing her arms in two metal braces, which automatically snapped closed upon sensing her body. The braces stretched Aniya's arms slightly, just enough to be uncomfortable, but she knew her comfort wouldn't be of any concern in a matter of minutes.

The man left the platform, and Aniya jumped slightly as two metal braces approached from behind and snapped around her legs. Almost instantly, she was pulled off the ground and closer to the center of the circular platform.

"Well, Annelise, the time has come." The Director approached the machine as the glass tank began to rise from the floor. "Do you have anything you wish to say to the world? If appropriate, your words will be inscribed on a plaque that will decorate this site for all eternity."

Aniya glared at the smiling man before her. The words spat from her mouth, laden with red sparks. "Long live the Lightbringers."

The Director laughed as the tank settled into place. "I do love irony. It's a good thing sarcasm doesn't translate well to the written word." He turned and walked back to the monitor. "Well, please know that I truly mean this: Thank you for your sacrifice, Annelise. You will never be forgotten."

With that, the Director jabbed at a few keys and stepped away from the machine as water began to flood the tank.

Aniya closed her eyes. It would be her last moments of consciousness, and she didn't want to spend them staring at a room full of liars and murderers.

"Orders, sir?"

She couldn't shut out Zeta's voice, though, and the assassin's voice penetrated the glass barrier.

"You said the boy was still in Level I?" the Director asked.

Aniya's eyes flew open.

Zeta nodded. "Yes, sir."

The Director looked back up at Aniya. A bone-chilling shiver raced over her body as his genuine smile turned into a twisted, wicked grin. "You were right to keep him alive, but now that we have the girl, we no longer have any use for him. Give the go-ahead for his execution. Make sure he dies first."

"No!" Aniya screamed just as a large tube attached itself to her nose and mouth, sealing her skin with tight suction that stole her breath away. The water was rising quickly, now just above her waist.

"Yes, sir." Zeta turned and walked out of the laboratory.

The Director turned back to Aniya and pouted. "My dear, tragedy is a fact of life. You can either let your pain define you, or you can learn from it. Here, allow me to assist further."

He pulled a small device from his pocket and clipped it to his ear. "Squadron leader, this is the Director. Are you in position in Level XVIII?"

Aniya's heart stopped.

"Good. Begin Purge Protocol." A solemn look fell over the Director's face as his steely, cold eyes bore holes in Aniya. "Exterminate the Underworld. No survivors."

Aniya howled in rage as the water rose past her head. White streams of light shot forth from her body as she shook in fury, but the light stopped at the barrier, swirled around in the liquid, and then shot upward into the machine, which whirred loudly in return.

Black began to seep into Aniya's vision as the light faded.

The Director placed a hand on the tank and stroked the glass. "I have done you a great service, dear Annelise. You have learned more in one minute than most will learn in a lifetime. One day, you will thank me. One day, you will know the great good I have done for you today."

Aniya softly sobbed into the tube as she shook her head in painful denial.

A small smile appeared on the Director's face. "I envy you, you know. Emotion is one of humanity's greatest gifts. From the guttural cry of pain to the sensual act of love to the bloodthirsty shout of rage to the purest smile. I don't much care what it is, so long as I can see it and wish I could feel it for myself."

He bowed his head again. "My one regret is robbing you of that for the rest of your life, so I have given you one last moment of raw emotion, one strong enough that you will carry it with you for eternity. Of course, we no longer need the Underworld anyway, so two birds, one stone."

Aniya's eyes flickered as her senses began to shut down. The last thing she saw was the Director backing away from the tank, into the shadows.

He gave a small wave as he whispered, "Good night, Lucifer."

62

Roland sat impatiently at the long table in the Holendast town hall. Corrin sat to his right, and Gareth one seat past that. Across the table was Kendall, sitting in the same place the Chancellor had been just weeks before.

Before Kendall had him killed so he could take over.

"Where's Malcolm?" Corrin demanded, the first one to speak before Kendall could even open his mouth.

"He's safe," Kendall said.

When it was clear that this answer was unacceptable, Kendall continued.

"The Director has him. We needed him to help revive our operative."

Roland clenched his fists. "She's still alive?"

"Yes," Kendall said simply. "Now, please, we have important things to discuss."

"I'm not sure I understand why this discussion is necessary," Gareth said. "It's not like anything is going to change."

Kendall narrowed his eyes, but his frown quickly dissipated as he took a breath. "If nothing changes, you're putting all your friends in danger. I can't allow you to impede our plans any longer. The Web is in disarray. It needs order."

"You've already put us in danger," Corrin said. "You may restore order, but you'll endanger the entire Web by restarting the reactor. I'm sure there's a safer way to supply power, one that doesn't mean the torture of thousands."

"You don't understand. Before humans, the Lightbringers tried everything. It took us hundreds of years to finally resort to using people. Trust me, there is no other way to provide sustainable power."

Gareth shrugged. "Then we live without power. We did it for centuries. We can do it again."

"That's not an option," Kendall said. "We no longer know how to live without power, nor is it safe. To acclimate again would take years, during which the loss of life would be insurmountable."

Roland scoffed. "So in order to prevent people from dying for a few years, you'll torture them for the rest of their lives? That doesn't make any sense."

"It wouldn't be three or four years, but decades," Kendall said. "Without power, there is no way to filter out the radiation that still runs deep within the bowels of the earth. Refuge barely survived the radiation in the caves, and that was very mild exposure since the radiation was filtered out partially from the sectors. But with the Web completely without power, it won't take long for the purified air to run out, leaving us to the crippling radiation that our ancestors got used to. Our bodies are no longer acclimated to the radiation, and exposure to such high levels would be fatal to the vast majority of the population. And for anyone left alive, they would be condemned to a lifetime of pain."

Roland fell silent.

"There has to be a way," Gareth said. "I refuse to believe that this is the only way the Web can survive."

Kendall lowered his voice. "I know it's hard to believe, after everything that's happened, but I really do want the best for Level XVIII. It's why the Director sent me here."

Corrin raised an eyebrow. "He wanted you to destroy the reactor, killing fifty thousand people in the process, only to restart it and put in another fifty thousand? Why not just kill the Chancellor?"

"Aniya," Kendall said. "He wants to use her for . . . something. The whole thing was his plan, start to finish. He must have known what the machine would do to her."

"So he doesn't care about the Web after all?" Roland asked, folding his arms. "It was all a ploy just to use Aniya?"

"He wants Aniya, but of course he cares about the Web," Kendall said. "He's responsible for the entire Underworld. This isn't the first time one of the presidents has caused a problem. Issues have cropped up in the past, and he was always quick to resolve them one way or another. The Director has people he reports to as well, and they would not be happy to know that the Lightbringers were losing control of Level XVIII."

"Then why wait so long to remove the Chancellor?" Corrin asked. "You said the Director was quick to solve these problems, so why delay eighteen years?"

"That, I don't know. I offered to arrange the Chancellor's death when I was first sent here. But by that time, the Director had already decided on a specific course of action that we have been working toward this entire time."

"What I'm hearing is that you have no interest in doing anything the Director does not tell you to do," Roland said. "You're just his puppet, and even if we did find another sustainable source of energy, you would still follow along with whatever he says."

Kendall bowed his head. "I can't question his orders. I won't, and neither would you if you knew him. He's a genius, a master of strategy and forethought. Everything he's predicted has come to pass, without fail, and he has been prepared for every outcome every step of the way. Every time

I think he's been caught off guard, he's proven that he expected it all along. If he says that this is the only way, I believe him."

"You could have just said yes." Roland stood up, kicking his chair away. "I don't know about you guys, but I'm done here. He's obviously not going to change his mind, so we're just wasting time."

"Please, you don't know what you're doing." Kendall stood quickly. "If we wage war, the Web is doomed either way. My victory means the death of thousands today, plus the tens of thousands more that must be used for the reactor later. Your victory means a Web without power, without defense against the radiation, spelling a terrible fate for everyone in Level XVIII. You must see reason. Either a portion of civilization will be offering their lives in sacrifice so that ninety percent of the Web can survive, or everyone dies. The choice is clear."

Corrin leaned across the table and slammed his fist down. "We *will* find a way. That's what you don't understand. Your director has chosen one possible future, but there are countless more. I believe that one of those is a peaceful Web with a safe way of supplying power. I also believe that this future means your death."

Roland folded his arms and nodded firmly. "You had your chance to help us find a better way forward, Kendall. Now you have to—"

It was then that the room froze as the sound of gunfire echoed throughout Holendast.

Corrin turned to Roland. "Did you order the attack already?"

Roland shook his head.

They turned to Kendall, who looked confused.

"They didn't hear from me," he said, frowning.

The door slammed open, and Roland turned to see Corrin running outside, Gareth close behind. Roland followed them out to the entrance of the building, and he stopped short as he was confronted by a terrible sight.

The trainyard, which was elevated in the distance and in full view of the town hall, had erupted into chaos. Kendall's army was dropping like flies, littering the trainyard with a sparkling sea of silver.

Roland turned to Corrin. "Did they start without us?" Without waiting for an answer, he spoke into the radio again. "Did you start without us?"

Corrin shook his head. "I don't know, but it doesn't look good for Kendall. He—"

Then the brown, Refuge army began toppling over, and Corrin fell silent.

"Tami!" Roland let out a pained cry as his heart sank.

The source of the gunfire was invisible, and as Roland's heart raced, he searched the shadows to try to find their enemy.

And then, the shadows moved.

A sea of black fell over the trainyard as brown and silver bodies fell left and right.

The rebels and the Silvers returned fire on the shadows, but barely a dent was made into the attacking force, which mercilessly gunned down everyone in its path.

"What the . . ."

Roland turned. Kendall stood in the doorway, his jaw hanging open and his eyes wide.

"You did this," Roland said, shoving a finger in Kendall's chest. "You're killing all of them!"

But Kendall backed away, his hands up. "My men are dying too. This wasn't me, I swear. This is the Director's doing."

"Roland!" Gareth shouted as he mounted one of the moles that was tied in front of the building. "Come on, we need to help them!"

"There's no helping them," Kendall said, his voice quiet.

"This is the Director's army, a squadron of elite killers. Your friends will all be dead by the time you get there."

"The payload," Corrin said as he mounted in front of Gareth. "Roland, radio them and tell them to deploy the payload. I'll make sure Tamisra is safe."

Then, Corrin kicked the mole, and he and Gareth raced off toward the trainyard.

Roland fumbled for the radio at his side, and he spoke into it hurriedly. "Deploy the package. If you can hear me, deploy the package. Do it now!" Then, he dropped the radio and rushed Kendall, grabbing his collar and shoving him up against the wall.

"Why is the Director doing this?"

A new look was on Kendall's face, and for the first time, Roland saw him completely helpless.

"He doesn't need us anymore." Kendall looked down. "He's tying up loose ends because he finally has what he wants."

"Aniya," Roland said, realizing what must have happened.

"Yes," he whispered. "But I never dreamed he would do *this*. The Underworld has been his responsibility for a long time. I never thought he would destroy it."

Roland's eyes widened. "He's completely destroying the Underworld? Why? What would be left?"

Kendall hesitated.

"There's no more time for secrets, Kendall. We're all dying today, so you might as well tell me what you know."

After a moment, Kendall nodded. "The surface."

"The surface?"

"Earth has been habitable for a long time. The Underworld gives it power. That's the short answer you're looking for."

Roland frowned. "But if he needs the Underworld to power the surface, why would he destroy it?"

"He doesn't need it anymore. Not now that he has Aniya."

"And you're claiming that you had no idea that this was his plan all along? I find that hard to believe."

Kendall gave a half-smile. "He never told me much." He looked around the sector. "And now I can see why."

Roland turned to see the black army move throughout Holendast like tendrils, spreading their massacre to every square inch of the sector. His legs grew weak as muzzle flashes sparked in the distance. His childhood home was being torn apart, his friends slaughtered.

"He knew I would never agree to this."

Roland turned back to Kendall and released him completely. "Is there any other way out of Level XVIII?"

"What difference would it make?" Kendall shook his head. "You'd just be delaying the inevitable."

"We have to try. Please, help us fix this."

Kendall took a deep breath. "The train."

"What about it?"

"There's a spiral tunnel that encircles the entire Underworld, allowing for mass transit between levels. The junction for this level is right here in Holendast. Just inside the train tunnel, there's a track switch that will guide the train up or down the tunnel. It's how the Director's army had to have gotten here."

Roland turned to the trainyard, where the genocide still raged on.

"But it doesn't matter," Kendall said. "You'd have to get through them, and I don't see how you could possibly do that."

"Leave that to me." Roland turned and put his hands on his hips. "Is there anything else you want to share with me before I go fix the mess you made?"

Kendall bowed his head. "Just that I'm sorry. Please believe me. I brought this on us all, and I could never forgive myself."

Roland mounted his mole and readied to leave before

going against his every instinct and turning back toward Kendall. "Do you want to come with us? It's better than staying here and dying."

"No," Kendall said, another small smile gracing his lips. "The captain goes down with his ship."

"What?"

"Never mind."

Before Roland could kick his mole into action, Kendall spoke again.

"If you make it out of here, do me one favor."

Roland looked back at Kendall's steely eyes.

"Kill the Director."

63

Roland raced his mole through the streets of Holendast. He had learned how to ride proficiently, but he still wasn't comfortable moving at anything more than a brisk jog. Now, with the mole running as fast as it could, Roland held on for dear life, positive that he was about to be bucked off at any second.

He managed to avoid any black soldiers, for which he was quite grateful. Though he was moving at an impressive speed, Roland was sure that the Director's army was more than skilled enough to hit a moving target.

Thanks to the mole's breakneck speed, he arrived at the trainyard at the same time as Corrin and Gareth. He tugged the mole to a stop next to a band of maybe three hundred rebels and Silvers that had joined forces and taken shelter on the far end of the trainyard, behind a hill that overlooked the station. As Roland looked around the hill, he saw the black-armored army progress deeper into the station, seemingly unaware of the natives of the Web hiding just a hundred yards away.

"Where do we stand?" Corrin hopped off his mole and approached the joined armies, scanning the men's faces.

"Where's Tamisra?" Roland asked before anyone could answer Corrin.

Lieutenant Haskill stepped away from the huddled soldiers and saluted, still crouched down slightly. "They came out of nowhere, sir. They're tearing us apart." He turned to Roland and bowed his head. "No one's seen Tamisra."

Roland scanned the battlefield, his heart racing. No sign of her.

"It's the Director," Corrin said. "Is this all that's left?"

The lieutenant shook his head. "Our army retreated to the tunnels at the first sign of trouble to protect the children. Most of the Silvers that survived went with them. I ordered this squadron to stay behind to wait for you. Our best estimate is four thousand of our own people still standing."

Roland's face went pale. "That's two thousand. Two thousand people dead."

"Four," a man in silver armor said, stepping forward to stand by Haskill. "We had three thousand ready to defend Holendast, and there are maybe a thousand of us left."

"Just like that," Gareth whispered as his eyes turned moist. "We're being exterminated."

Corrin's face was stern, but his voice was soft. "How many of the black?"

"Too many to fight," the Silver said. "My guess is seven thousand, minimum."

Lieutenant Haskill bowed his head. "It's over, Corrin. The black army is pushing into the caves. They're bottlenecking at the mouth of the tunnel, so our men in the caves are picking away at them slowly, but our last sergeant just radioed and said they won't be able to hold them off for much longer. As soon as they get inside, they'll destroy everything we have left."

"We still have the payload, right?" Roland asked.

The lieutenant nodded and pointed to another mole that

was standing nearby, its gaze transfixed on the flames that raged on in the trainyard.

"Good," Roland said. "We can use it and get out of here."

"And go where?" the Silver asked grimly.

"Kendall told me that if we can just get into the train tunnel, there's a way out of the Web."

"And you believe him?" Corrin asked, an eyebrow raised.

"Do we have any other choice?"

Gareth gave a soft chuckle. "If Roland believes him after everything he's done, that's saying something. As far as I know, this is our only shot."

"It's true," the Silver said. "There's a track that runs throughout the entire Underworld."

"That's all fine and well, but we don't even have control over the payload," the lieutenant said. "Tamisra has the detonator. If she's still alive, she's in the tunnel with the others, and the signal on the detonator has too short of a range to make it out of the caves."

Roland peeked around the mound of dirt again at the entrance to the caves. The black army was crowding the mouth of the tunnel, trying to push their way inside, and he knew it wouldn't be long until they succeeded.

"Whatever we do, we've got to do it fast," he said. "Haskill's right. If we wait any longer, we'll be all that's left, and they'll pick us apart out here."

Gareth groaned. "But what can we do without the detonator?"

"We can detonate it manually," Corrin said.

Lieutenant Haskill shook his head. "That's a one-way trip. No one's coming back from that one."

"I know, but we don't have a choice. I'll do it myself."

"Forget it, Corrin." The lieutenant grabbed Corrin's shoulder. "No one's asking you to commit suicide."

"No one has to ask. If it means that our people survive, then I will gladly volunteer to do it."

"No," Haskill said firmly. "I'll do it."

Corrin smiled. "You and I both know I'm the obvious choice. You always were the better leader, after all. I wouldn't be where I am today without you, Misha."

Before the lieutenant could protest again, Corrin turned and mounted the mole, which was burdened with four large saddlebags.

Almost immediately, he flew off the side of the animal and crashed to the ground, bleeding profusely from a bullet hole in his chest.

Roland spun around to see a band of a dozen soldiers in black armor approach the trainyard from central Holendast. The small army of rebels and Silvers fired on this squadron, and after several seconds, the Director's men were dead.

"Corrin!" Lieutenant Haskill dropped his gun and leaned down by his general's side, placing pressure on the wound. Gareth joined him and examined Corrin's body.

Roland, however, turned and looked around the hill again. Thankfully, the gunfire from the rebels' position had been masked by the sounds of battle by the entrance to the caves, and the large army that amassed on the other side of the trainyard had not noticed. However, they were pushing ever closer into the mouth of the tunnel.

"I can still make it," Corrin said weakly, reaching falteringly at the wound in his chest. "Put me on the mole. I can still do it."

"Can you sit up?" Haskill asked.

Corrin nodded, but as he sat up with the lieutenant's help, he cried out in pain, and blood spat forth from his mouth.

"Whatever we do, we have to do it now," Roland said. "They're getting closer."

Lieutenant Haskill stood up. "I'll do it. These men are my responsibility, and as such, it is my duty to do whatever it takes to get them out of here safely."

"No," Roland said. "They need you to lead them, especially if Corrin's not going to make it. Dying for them might save their lives, but they're lost without you."

"That mantle must be passed on to you and Tamisra, I'm afraid. They believe in you both, and I do too."

The mole behind Roland stirred, and he turned to see Gareth sitting on the animal's back, hunched over for cover.

"Doc, no!" Roland grabbed his arm. "It can't be you. I'm pretty sure we're going to need a medic after this."

Gareth smiled. "I taught you everything I know. It seems my time has come at last, and if this is how I'm going to go after the life I've lived, I think I'm okay with that."

"This is nonsense," the lieutenant said. "We have three hundred men here, all of them willing to give their life to save what is left of the Web. Get off the mole, Doctor. That's an order."

"Sorry, Misha." Gareth's grin grew wider. "You can't boss me around anymore."

Roland shook his head. "I need you, Doc. You're all I've got left."

"No, I'm not. You have Tamisra and all of Refuge now, and when you find Aniya and bring her home, you'll have her too." Gareth gently removed Roland's hand. "You've turned into a fine man, Roland. Know that I'm proud of you, and it has been an honor and privilege to be a father to you in your parents' stead."

Corrin's voice came, weak but stern. "Stop talking. We don't have time for this. I don't care who goes, but someone do it now!"

Lieutenant Haskill stepped forward, pointing a gun at Gareth, but the doctor reached into the saddlebags tied to the mole and pulled out a small device that fit perfectly in his hand, with a short wire running back into the leather packs. Gareth squeezed the device, and as it clicked, the lieutenant froze in his tracks and Roland's heart sank.

"Good call on the dead man's switch, Lieutenant," Gareth said with a smirk.

"Doc . . ." Roland couldn't get out any more as his throat tightened.

Gareth turned to Roland and gave him a nod of respect. "When you find Aniya, tell her I love her."

Roland nodded and forced himself to speak again. "I'll take care of her for you."

"My dear Roland, I don't think she needs you for that anymore."

With that, Gareth kicked the mole viciously, steering it around the hill and into the trainyard as the creature squealed. The doctor let out a shout of rage as he charged into the black squadron, and the army turned its attention to him, firing on the mole and the man who rode atop it.

Then, the ground shook as the trainyard exploded in a massive fireball.

64

Kendall sat on the front steps of the Holendast town hall, watching the battle in the distance. The world he had sworn to protect was burning before his eyes.

From here, he could hear screams and gunfire echo around him, each one sending pangs of guilt through his heart.

He held a gun in his hand, ready to defend himself against the black squadron should they come for him, but Kendall wasn't sure anymore if it would be the worst thing in the world if they killed him.

But the Director's army just swarmed the streets around him, raiding the surrounding houses and businesses but completely ignoring Kendall, even though he sat in full view.

Finally, three men in black armor approached the town hall, and Kendall readied his gun, preparing himself for the worst.

"Kendall Sayan?"

Cautiously, Kendall nodded.

The men relaxed and lowered their weapons to their sides.

"The Director thanks you for your service."

With that, they turned and walked away, leaving Kendall alone on the stairs.

"That's it?" He stood up and threw his arms in the air.

The men showed no signs that they had heard him, and they continued on through Holendast.

"After all I've done for the Underworld, he's going to just destroy it? After all I've done for him, he's going to abandon me here?"

But they were gone.

Kendall dropped his arms and sighed. Roland was right. He was never anything more than a puppet. He slumped down on the steps and buried his face in his hands.

Finally, he looked up, muttering, "You can come out now."

Seconds later, he was joined on the steps by Tamisra.

"How did you know I was here?"

Kendall looked up and gave his best attempt at a smile. "You breathe really loudly."

She grinned and sat down next to him. "Roland says the same thing."

Kendall leaned back on his elbows. "I thought you were supposed to be sneaky. After all those years in the caves, and you're just as loud as the moles."

Tamisra shrugged. "I'm still alive, aren't I?"

"That you are. How long have you been here?"

"Pretty much the whole time. I didn't think Roland would kill you, so I came to make sure someone did."

Kendall nodded. "I thought as much."

They sat silently for a moment, watching the battle from a distance.

Finally, Tamisra spoke again. "You wanted to save the Web, right? And here you are, watching it burn. Tell me, how does it feel to fail so miserably?"

"Not great," Kendall said, repressing something inside that made him want to vomit. "If I had any idea this was going to happen . . ."

They both grew quiet again, and when Tamisra finally broke the silence, her voice was abnormally soft. "You know, I think I understand you now. I don't agree with everything you've done, and I never will, but at least it all makes sense now."

Kendall took a deep breath. "Tamisra, I'm so sorry. I did what I thought I had to. Your father—"

"Stop. I said I understand, but I'm not as forgiving as Roland. You'll forever be the man who tortured me and got my father killed."

"I deserve that," Kendall said, looking down at the steps. "So, are you going to get this over with?"

Tamisra paused for a moment before standing up. "I don't think so. As good as it would feel, it wouldn't change anything. Besides, staying here alone while everyone dies around you is enough of a punishment, I think."

Kendall said nothing.

Suddenly, a giant fireball lit up the sector.

"Strange," Tamisra said, frowning. "That was my job."

"Why am I not surprised?" Kendall gave a wry smile.

"Gotta go." She skipped down the town hall steps, waving behind her, gun in hand. "Have a nice life, Kendall."

Kendall watched her jog back toward the trainyard, and he was alone again.

Alone with the screams, the gunfire, the bombs.

The flames were high enough now that the sky ceiling reflected their orange glow, casting all of Holendast in a hellish hue.

Kendall closed his eyes and blocked out the sounds of death. Maybe this was punishment for his poor performance. Maybe the Director really was just tying up loose ends.

He bowed his head.

It didn't matter. There was nothing left. His assignment was over, but the more Kendall thought about it, the more he realized that there was never any assignment beyond Aniya. She was all that mattered.

All his dreams of a peaceful web were for nothing. Years of hard work down the drain. He had left the beautiful Overworld and traveled to one of the lowest levels possible, obsessed with the idea of fixing a broken world.

But the Director had played him. He had to have known Kendall would never agree on the idea of annihilating the Underworld, but he had arranged everything perfectly so that Kendall jumped at the chance to help him.

A particularly loud scream rang throughout Holendast, and Kendall covered his ears. He had come to rid the Web of pain, but now they all suffered because of him.

He sat on the steps, rocking back and forth, holding his ears closed and shutting his eyes tight.

Hours later, he finally opened his eyes and stood on the steps, gun in hand. The screams were silent now, but they still echoed in Kendall's head. The fire had gone out, but all he saw was red.

He was alone. The last living man in Holendast, surrounded by thousands of dead people he had once sworn to liberate.

He shook his head and spoke to no one in particular.

"Forgive me."

Then, Kendall raised the gun to his chin and pulled the trigger.

65

Aniya sat alone in the void, sobbing.

She had spent what felt like years searching for William, but he was nowhere to be found. In her desperation, she had even looked for the Chancellor, but he was gone as well.

She was truly alone.

Aniya thought that her fate would be more like an eternal slumber, not being able to think or even feel the passage of time. This was so much worse, being banished to her black prison for the rest of her life, fully awake in her own mind, not even able to conjure up an image to keep her company.

Try as she might, she couldn't even use her imagination to paint the void. It refused to even give her a landscape in which to live out her days. She tried to focus on the Hole, Refuge, the Citadel, anything, but her world remained dark.

All she was left with were her thoughts, but they tortured her just as much as the void did. She had inadvertently sentenced the entire Underworld to extinction. If she was indeed helping anyone like the Director had promised, this was too great a price to pay.

And the worst part was that there wasn't a thing she could

have done about it. She never stood a chance against the man who had doomed her to this awful fate since birth.

In some twisted way, she found herself admiring the Director. He had micromanaged her life to the finest detail, ensuring that every move she made would end in the exact same result. She wanted to feel better, knowing that she was completely helpless, that there was nothing she could have done to avoid such tragedy. But as much as she tried to absolve herself of any responsibility, the nagging thought remained that she didn't do enough, that there was indeed some length she could have gone to in order to save everyone.

But none of that mattered now. It was too late. It was all over. She was truly trapped now, and this time there was no Kendall, no Salvador, and no Nicholas to rescue her.

Oh, Nicholas.

Not only would he die now, if he hadn't already, but she had permanently ruined their relationship. She knew that now. He had done something awful, yes, but he had more than atoned for his sins. He had proven to be more than his regrettable action of betraying her. And she had turned him away.

Her sobs continued as she cried into her knees, thinking about what it could have been like if she had just forgiven him.

"Aniya?"

A voice drifted across the void, pricking Aniya's ears as she froze.

She looked up and gasped.

The void was gone, replaced by a giant, panoramic field of vision that wobbled slightly. She was outside, sitting in the dirt arena back in Level I. A man in a gray uniform stood several feet away, backed by a dozen men in silver armor. In the stands, Aniya saw more silver fabric, glinting with shimmering light as her vision slowly focused.

"Aniya, are you there?"

Aniya jumped to her feet, laughing through her tears as she heard Nicholas's voice.

"Yes! Yes, I'm here!"

"Hey, you."

The warmth in his voice was one she had not heard in a long time, and it almost turned her to tears again.

"I don't know how I'm hearing you in my head, but I'm not going to question it. Maybe I'm going crazy."

Aniya held a hand over her mouth as her mind raced. She had so much to tell him that she couldn't decide where to begin.

"Where are you?"

She eventually realized that she hadn't replied in several seconds, so she removed her hand as words blurted out. "I'm on the surface, Nicholas. It's safe up here in the Overworld, kind of. Zeta took me to the Director, who's using me to power the rest of the world. But the Underworld, Nicholas . . . He's destroying the Underworld."

"The whole thing? I'm sorry, Aniya. I was going to take you to him because I thought he could help. I never imagined he would do something like that." Nicholas fell silent for a moment. "Listen, this is going to sound terrible, but even that's not the most pressing matter to me right now. They've sentenced me to death."

Aniya bowed her head. "I know. They said they don't need you anymore."

"I'm just glad I got to talk to you again before I die."

She took a deep breath, trying her hardest to focus on her words over her oldest friend's impending doom. "Nicholas, I'm sorry. I'm sorry for not trusting you, I'm sorry for abandoning you in Refuge, and I'm sorry for hating you. I'm sorry for everything."

"I am too. Please know that. If I could take it all back, I would."

"If you had told me that just yesterday, I would have

argued with you. I would have said that I'd never want you to take it back, no matter how much it hurt. Thanks to what you did, we saved the Web. You and I, we did it. But apparently, it was all for nothing. We were always going to end up here, with you dying and me as good as dead." Aniya bit her lip as tears began to fall again. "I would give anything to go back to the beginning, back to your rooftop, where it was all so simple. And I would say yes this time, Nicholas. I would be with you in a heartbeat. I wasted so much time pushing you away, and I think I regret that the most."

On the massive screen in front of her, back in the Level I arena, the man in the silver suit pulled out a gun and checked the chamber for a round. Behind him, twelve more guns were pulled from their holsters.

Aniya closed her eyes as her heart pounded. "So before it's too late, I have two things to say to you, Nicholas. I forgive you, and . . . and I love you." She broke down in tears and fell back to the ground.

"I love you too, Aniya. I always have. I always will."

Aniya opened her eyes and wiped her tears away, but they kept coming and clouded her vision all over again.

"Don't look."

But she had to. For some reason, she had to.

Aniya gritted her teeth and cleared her sight again just in time to see thirteen guns raise as one and fire.

The bullets flew toward her, one of them directly headed for the pane of glass that stood before Aniya. With a deafening crash, the screen shattered into a million pieces, then crumbled to dust.

And all that was left was the black.

Aniya let out a screeching cry of anguish as the void lit up with an explosive white light.

When she ran out of breath, the light vanished, and Aniya let herself fall into the void, tumbling head over heels, wailing in agony.

It felt like days later that her cries finally died away and she stopped falling, and the last thing that Aniya heard before succumbing to the black was the Shadow.

The phantom spoke to her one final time, its feminine voice purring in her ear.

"I'll stay with you, Lightbringer. I'll be right here with you."

EPILOGUE

Roland quietly rode his mole down the long tunnel at a walking pace. Tamisra rode somewhere behind him, unusually silent. They hadn't spoken since the battle, not since Roland had told her what Gareth had to do, all because she ran off with the detonator. Tamisra had apologized profusely, but Roland couldn't bear to talk to her anymore about it.

And so what was left of Level XVIII followed behind Roland, Lieutenant Haskill, and Corrin, a long train that marched on in silence. The number of rebels and Silvers combined was just over five thousand.

Gareth's sacrifice had eliminated the immediate threat at the trainyard, and Roland and Lieutenant Haskill were quick to assemble the survivors and lead them into the train tunnel. As soon as Tamisra had returned, they set another bomb at the entrance to the tracks, collapsing the mouth of the tunnel and blocking off the black squadron from following them.

The survivors had quickly found the track switch, which neighbored two tunnels that split off from the main path, one going up and one going down with barely perceptible slopes. Lieutenant Haskill had made the executive decision to go down, reasoning that the Director would expect them to go up. Of course, this was just a guess, and even Roland could tell that the lieutenant was not terribly sure about this.

But the immediate danger was gone for now. Of course, Roland knew their peace might not last long. They had no idea what was waiting for them in the next web.

They marched for several days, camping at various points in the tunnel along the way. Each night, Roland was sure that a train would come along and find them. There was enough space for them to be safe from a collision, but surely five thousand people camping out in the tunnel would be noticeable. However, the tunnel remained undisturbed, and the survivors would always wake up a few hours later and proceed on.

As it turned out, the most pressing concern was not being found—it was running out of supplies. No one had packed for such a trek, and Corrin had to ration what little food the survivors had into minuscule portions, hoping to stumble across a mole in the tunnels. But this tunnel was unlike the ones running throughout the Web. Concrete and steel lined the walls, making it nearly impossible for moles to break through and expose another tunnel.

So it was a great relief when they finally emerged from the massive tunnel into a dark trainyard after six days of walking.

But the station appeared abandoned. Train cars lay on their sides, rusted sheet metal hanging loosely from their frames. Piles of aluminum and wood lay scattered throughout, littering the trainyard thoroughly.

"I guess the Director's army beat us here," Tamisra muttered, joining Roland and Lieutenant Haskill at the front. "Where are we?"

Haskill frowned and surveyed the area. "If Kendall was telling the truth, we're in a completely different web now, the one directly beneath our old home. Which would make this Level XIX."

"It doesn't look like an army has been here anytime recently. It looks deserted." Roland dismounted and stepped forward slowly. "Kendall said they've had problems before. Maybe this entire level isn't used anymore."

Tamisra hopped off her mole as well and walked forward slowly into the trainyard. "It would be the perfect hiding place."

Roland pushed down his anger at the sound of her voice and nodded. "That's what I'm thinking."

"It's settled, then." Lieutenant Haskill smiled and turned to the thousands of people gathered in the trainyard. He raised his fist and shouted, "People of Level XVIII and children of Salvador the Scourge, we have found our new home!"

Roland thought that no one would have enough energy to express any enthusiasm at this accomplishment, but he was pleasantly surprised as the people burst into a roaring cheer. Even Corrin, barely alive and strapped to a mole, managed a raspy celebration.

The shouts turned to screams, however, as the tunnel entrance lit up in flames, creating a massive barrier of fire that separated the survivors from the tunnel they had traversed over the last several days. Roland turned around to see that the fire continued in a massive ring around them, revealing a giant metal fence that surrounded the trainyard, trapping them in a large cage that had been invisible in the darkness.

"The Director," Lieutenant Haskill growled as he faced forward. "Ready, men!"

Roland pulled his gun from his side and scanned his surroundings, but all he could see was the flames and the fence. He kicked dirt toward the fire, but it wasn't enough to suffocate the flames.

Then, a figure emerged from the fire and stood directly in front of him.

Roland couldn't tell if it was a man or a woman. Whatever it was, it had no hair, not even any eyebrows. Its stark, white skin gave way only to blood-red eyes. The red robes it wore contrasted strongly against its skin, and they flowed to the ground, leaving the figure's white toes peeking out from under the fabric.

The stranger smiled devilishly, revealing a mouth completely void of teeth, leaving only crimson red gums and a bleeding tongue.

"A feasssst," it hissed, drawing out the word long as its smile widened. The word sounded strange coming from a creature without teeth, and to Roland it only made the word sound more ominous than it already was.

The screams from the rebels grew louder as hundreds more ghastly figures stepped out of the fire, pressing up against the metal cage as they joined in the bone-chilling chant.

"Yes, a feast."

"At last."

Chills ran down Roland's spine as he looked at the ghoulish creatures.

The first figure in front of Roland turned to one on its right. "Bring the Master," it said, its "the" coming out more like "tse."

"Yes," the other one said. "The Master." With that, it disappeared into the flames again.

Roland turned to Lieutenant Haskill, whose mouth was still hanging open as he looked around. Even Tamisra seemed like she had no words. Roland summoned his courage and cleared his throat.

"Who are you?"

The stranger looked in Roland's eyes and said one word that lasted for several seconds.

"Host."

Roland wanted to roll his eyes, but found that he didn't have the nerve. He wasn't quite sure what the thing in front of him would do if he expressed his annoyance.

"And what do you mean by 'feast'?"

The stranger simply smiled.

"Well, you're in danger," Roland said. "Men are coming to destroy this place. They've already kicked us out of our home. We're the only ones left. Let us help you, and we can—"

The stranger laughed, a hoarse noise that spread throughout the pallid figures that surrounded the survivors.

"They wouldn't dare come here," it said when it finally stopped laughing. "Many have come. Many have fallen. We don't need your help."

"What," Haskill finally said, looking around, "you're going to fight them with fire? They have guns. We have guns too, and we still got slaughtered."

The stranger smirked. "Then you are weak."

"Big words from a man hiding behind a metal cage," Tamisra said, approaching the barrier and pressing her face up against the chain mesh, baring her teeth.

Cackling, the figure pulled a forked metal rod from the folds of its robe. It inserted the object into a large device hanging from the cage, and with a twist, part of the cage pulled free, revealing a large door in front of Roland.

The stranger stepped inside the cage and stood face-to-face with Tamisra, folding its arms. "How is this?"

Behind Roland, the survivors grew restless, shuffling and murmuring loudly.

Tamisra stood her ground against the stranger, glaring with wide eyes that reflected the fire that raged around them.

"Master," a voice came from beyond the metal fence.

The Host echoed this word, the noise growing to a din that drowned out all other sound.

With one last smirk, the stranger in front of Tamisra stepped aside as a thin man stepped through the fire and into the cage. Unlike the red robes of the Host, this man was adorned in golden armor, with a long, gray beard that hung low over the chestplate.

The man dropped his mouth open in shock for a moment as he took in the sight before him, but his face slowly twisted into a warm smile as he looked upon his daughter.

Salvador the Scourge laid a hand on Tamisra's shoulder, then pulled her in for a tight embrace. "Hello again, daughter."

TO BE CONTINUED...

THANK YOU

Thank you for reading *The Phoenix Mandate*, the second book in the *Light Thief* saga.

Would you like to be the first to know when the third book is released? How about that free book I mentioned before you started reading? Do you want to read about William's adventures, his escape from the Hub and heroic attempt to destroy the reactor?

Go to jdavidwebb.com/free-book and sign up for the mailing list to be notified of all new releases and special offers, and you'll get a **FREE** copy of *The Saboteur*, a book that expands the *Light Thief* universe. I would like nothing more than the opportunity to get to know you!

I promise not to fill your inbox with spam or share your contact information with anyone, ever.

**Enjoy this book?
You can make a big difference.**

If you enjoyed *The Phoenix Mandate*, the single most helpful thing you can do is leave me a review on Amazon. To explain how grateful I would be for this would take another hundred pages.

Suffice it to say that I can't afford to take out an ad in some big-name newspaper. You probably haven't seen a billboard with my face on it. If you've met me, you're probably grateful for that.

But while big publishing companies are buying out digital signs on Times Square and forcing raunchy books in your face every time you leave the comfort of Gmail, there is something much more powerful that money can't buy. Reviews.

Honest reviews of my books help bring them to the attention of other readers.

So, if you wouldn't mind, take about 30 seconds to leave a dazzling review encouraging others to check out this book! How? Just go to your Amazon order history and click "Write a product review."

Thank you,

David Webb

LIGHTBRINGER

Get it now!

Made in the USA
Monee, IL
06 December 2021